WOMEN OF COURAGE ...
WOMEN OF PASSION ...

PROMISED SUNRISE begins a sweeping saga of the American frontier and the indomitable pioneers who braved the long hazardous journey across the plains in search of their dreams. It is the stirring story of the fiery Branigan family—too proud to go down in defeat after the fall of the South, too strong to allow fate to tear them asunder. Most of all, it is the tender romance of a man and a woman thrown together in adversity, and a love that would triumph over all.

THE EXCITEMENT BETWEEN THEM SPREAD LIKE PRAIRIE FIRE...

Then the night quiet was split as her open palm cracked against his cheek. "Never again, Tucker Branigan," she whispered. "Don't you ever touch me again."

He reached for her, but not in time. In a whirl of skirts, she raced off into the darkness.

Tucker's anger flared. Damn her! Why was *she* angry at *him*? Hadn't he done everything to help her? Hadn't he given her shelter and food and a means of getting to the West? Hadn't he protected her from her brutish uncle when he might just as easily have turned his back on her? Was this the thanks he got for caring for her?

And he did care for her. Too much for his own good. Common sense told him not to let it go any further, to let his anger burn off any lingering feelings for her.

But then he remembered their kiss of moments before. He knew he hadn't imagined her response. She had felt what he felt. She had wanted him as much in her innocence as he wanted her. But he *knew* what it was he wanted from Maggie Harris, and swift kisses in the dark weren't half enough.

"Whatever your secrets are, Maggie," he said softly, staring at the point where she'd disappeared moments before, "I'm going to find out. You're stuck with me for more than a thousand miles yet."

Other LEISURE BOOKS by Robin Lee Hatcher:

PROMISED SUNRISE

ROBIN LEE HATCHER

LEISURE BOOKS   NEW YORK CITY

A LEISURE BOOK®

November 1990

Published by

Dorchester Publishing Co., Inc.
276 Fifth Avenue
New York, NY 10001

To my mother,
Lucille Adams,
who always believed in me, encouraged me,
and stood by me,
who taught me the joy and wonder to be found in books,
and who has always loved others more than self.

To my beautiful daughters,
Michaelyn and Jennifer,
(I'm so proud to be your mother)
for giving me a lifetime of experiences to write about.

And to the heroes in their lives,
Brian Forbes and Wayne Whitt,
for having the good sense
to fall in love with them . . .
May your marriages be blessed with glorious sunrises.

I love you.

Prologue

Twin Willows Plantation, Georgia—March 1867

C*ome along, Mother. There's nothing left that's* ours." Tucker Branigan took hold of his mother's arm and gently guided her out of the house and onto the veranda.

Harlan Simmons rose from a chair near the railing. He removed his hat, revealing thinning brown hair, and offered an abbreviated bow. "Good day, Mrs. Branigan."

"Mr. Simmons." Maureen Branigan stepped away from her son. Her words were deceptively polite; only Tucker recognized the disdain that colored her cultured voice. "I trust you will find everything in order."

"I hadn't expected anything less, ma'am."

"You will need these." She dropped a ring of keys into his hand.

Harlan nodded as a wide grin split his face.

Maureen turned her back to the man before he

could say more. Her green eyes met Tucker's gaze. He saw the unshed tears and the quiver of her chin, but he knew she would never allow herself to cry in front of "that filthy carpetbagger." She would save her tears for later.

Tucker led the way down the steps and out to the small buggy where his sister and aunt awaited them.

"If it were up to me, I'd kill the yellow-bellied—"

"Shannon!" Maureen's warning to her daughter made it clear she would brook no argument.

Shannon Branigan, at twenty the oldest of Tucker's four younger siblings, gave her mother a quick hug before quickly climbing into the buggy and picking up the reins. "Well, I would," she grumbled.

Tucker offered his hand to his elderly great aunt. "You'd better get started for Atlanta, Aunt Eugenia," he said. "It's growing late."

The old woman's faded blue eyes were watery as she glanced up at him. "Shouldn't you come stay with us for a few days, Tucker? Surely a day or two in Atlanta wouldn't make much difference."

"You know we can't."

"Shannon should be going with you." His aunt's voice shook.

He understood. Too old to withstand the arduous journey west, Eugenia Godwin was remaining in Atlanta—remaining in a place no longer her home, no longer the South she had known for so long. Shannon had volunteered to stay in Georgia to care for their father's aunt, and Eugenia felt guilty for still being alive at the age of eighty-nine.

"We love you," Tucker said gently and kissed the papery skin of her cheek.

Eugenia nodded, then allowed him to help her into the buggy beside her niece.

"Shannon." Tucker leaned toward his sister. "We'll write as soon as we reach Boise."

"Don't worry about me, Tuck. Aunt Eugenia and I are going to be fine." Her dark blue eyes looked suspiciously misty as Tucker kissed her good-bye. "The Yankees haven't beaten the Branigans. They just think they have."

Tucker turned away, listening as the creak of leather announced Aunt Eugenia and Shannon's departure. The sound caused him almost physical pain. He felt the breaking apart of his family, piece by piece.

His gaze moved to the lone figure seated on a lanky sorrel gelding. Here was another piece breaking away, and he was helpless to stop it. With a heavy heart, he walked toward his brother. Devlin's handsome young face was filled with bitterness.

Tucker stopped a few feet away. "Are you sure you won't change your mind?"

"No. I'm staying here. I won't be running off with my tail tucked between my legs."

"You're only seventeen, Devlin." He'd said it all before, yet he still hoped he could change the boy's mind.

"There were plenty my age and younger who rode off to fight and die for the South."

Tucker felt his temper rising. "And just what has all that bloodletting brought us? Bitterness. Ruin. Poverty."

"The Yankees brought that."

"We can't blame them for everything."

Tucker spoke without even hearing what he was saying. Besides, the words wouldn't make any difference. He knew it was too late. Too late for

Devlin. Too late for their father. Too late for any of them.

Devlin's coal-black eyes simmered with barely contained fury. "When you see me again, I'll be handing you the deed to Twin Willows."

Tucker's shoulders sagged, weariness taking any remaining fight out of him. He wished they could share the closeness they'd once known, but he'd been gone too many years, fought too many battles.

"Just don't let yourself be so blinded by hate that you can't see how things really are, Devlin. Don't beat yourself to death against a brick wall. And if you finally see you can't win, don't let pride hold you back from joining us in Idaho." He glanced over his shoulder toward his mother and younger brother and sister. "Will you come and say good-bye?"

"I've done it. No point dragging it all out."

Tucker looked back at his brother, then nodded and turned away, walking quickly toward the waiting carriage.

"Will we never come back?" seven-year-old Fiona asked, her voice quavering as tears spilled down her freckled cheeks.

Tucker kissed the auburn curls just above her forehead. "We're going to have us a fine new home out west, Fiona. It's going to be a great adventure. And we'll get you a pony and a kitten once we're settled."

"A kitten? Really, Tuck?"

"I promise." He lifted her up and set her on the leather seat. As he stepped back, he felt a tug on his trouser leg. He glanced down at his nine-year-old brother, Neal.

In contrast to Shannon's anger, Devlin's bitterness, and Fiona's tears, Neal's face was alight with excitement. His coal-black eyes sparkled as he asked, "May I ride up beside Mose? Just for a little while?" His gaze darted from Tucker to their mother, then back again. "Please. Mose won't mind. Do you, Mose?"

Their driver—no longer a slave, yet more than a servant—shook his graying head and grinned as Tucker looked up at him. "I don't mind, sa. He can ride wid me tils I leaves ya in St. Louis."

"Then I guess it's all right," Tucker answered as he ruffled the boy's ebony hair. "Climb on up."

Neal scrambled up the side of the carriage, grinning from ear to ear, oblivious to the wrenching finality of the moment. Tucker wished he were facing it with the same carefree attitude.

Unable to avoid it, he turned once more toward his mother.

Maureen was taking one last look at the red brick manse that had been the Branigan family's home for three generations. Tucker's gaze followed hers.

"We really won't ever see Twin Willows again, will we, son?" Maureen said softly.

"No, Mother. We won't."

"The name isn't right anyway, now that the willows are gone. I remember as clear as yesterday the day they cut them down. It was so very hot. You were with General Lee in Virginia, and your father and Grady were in Atlanta. The Yankees rode in and took everything that wasn't nailed down and destroyed what they couldn't take. They didn't have to cut down the willows. They did it just for spite."

Tucker's arm tightened around her shoulders. He knew it was time to leave bitterness behind, just as he'd told Devlin. But sometimes . . .

"Farrell always said we'd plant new ones some day."

"We will." His throat felt tight. "Just not here."

His mother's gaze drifted from the house toward the family burial plot. "The war changed your father. He was so strong, so full of laughter. I'll always remember Farrell that way." She touched her nose with her handkerchief. "Your father . . . Grady . . . It hurts to leave them behind. You never saw how tall your brother was getting to be. You and Grady . . ." She stopped and swallowed back the tears.

"I know, Mother."

Her shoulders straightened. "Heavens, I'm acting just like Fiona. An adventure will do us all good. You know, son, I've never been farther west than Atlanta. It's time I went to have a look." Maureen's fingers touched the back of his hand and her voice softened to a whisper. "You did everything you could, Tucker. Your father was always so proud of you. You're a fine son."

Tucker's jaw tightened. He might have done all he could, but it hadn't been enough. If he'd been able to do more, perhaps they wouldn't have lost Twin Willows to a Yankee carpetbagger. If he'd been able to do more, their family wouldn't be torn apart, flying in all directions like chaff in the wind. If he'd been able to do more . . .

But his self-flagellation changed nothing. Silently, he took his mother's elbow and helped her into the carriage.

"All right, Mose. Let's go," he said, ready to join his family. That's when he saw her.

Charmaine Pinkham was waiting at the end of

the drive, seated on a small bay mare. Her blond curls were hidden beneath a perky yellow hat, and the matching yellow gown spread over the sidesaddle and horse like rays of summer sunshine. He hadn't seen her since the wedding nearly a year before. She hadn't changed. She was as beautiful as ever.

Why had she come? To rub salt in old wounds? Tucker drew in a deep breath, steeling himself against the emotions he expected to surface.

"Wait here."

Tucker walked along the tree-lined drive, his pace unhurried.

"I couldn't let you go without saying good-bye," Charmaine said softly as he stopped beside her horse.

"I thought we'd said our good-byes months ago. At your wedding."

"Oh, Tucker, why did you have to be so stubborn?" She leaned forward, placing her gloved hand against his chest. "If you'd let Papa—"

"You know why I couldn't work with your father."

"But there wasn't any need for you to lose Twin Willows. If you'd gone to work for Papa last year when he offered, we could have been married and you wouldn't be leaving now. We could have been together. You and I, like we always planned."

She was everything he'd ever thought he wanted in a woman. From the time he was seventeen, when she'd first turned fluttering blue eyes on him and claimed she was helpless to do anything without him, he'd planned to marry Charmaine Pinkham. He'd thought her beautiful and genteel, the epitome of Southern womanhood. He'd loved her. But she'd lied to him. Everything about her had been a lie.

"Does Dennis know you're here, Charmaine?"

She acted as if she hadn't heard him. "We could have been happy, Tucker. You could have come out of the war even richer if you'd been smart like my father and Dennis. You and your pride! What good will it do you in . . . in wherever you're going?"

"Idaho," he said dryly.

"Oh, I don't care where it is." She sniffed as her voice softened. "I only know I'll miss you." She dabbed at her eyes with a white handkerchief.

It surprised him how unmoved he was by her tears. He'd expected to feel again the pain of her deceit, to experience once again the breaking of his heart. But he hadn't enough energy for more pain and heartbreak, not even enough for anger. He felt only a touch of bitterness. That was all.

"I don't think Dennis would like that." There was a hint of sarcasm lacing his words.

She stiffened and pulled her hand from his chest. "At least Dennis is man enough to stay in Georgia and make the best of things."

"It isn't worth staying in Georgia if I have to work with the carpetbaggers and Yankees, taking away the homes of my friends when they've lost everything else already. Even *you* couldn't have made it worth it, Charmaine."

She slapped him across the side of his face with her riding crop. Her blue eyes flashed angrily. "You're a fool, Tucker Branigan. And no woman can ever love a fool." With that, she turned the bay mare and galloped away from Twin Willows.

He watched her retreat, his fingers touching the

stinging flesh on his cheek, and thought perhaps she was right. Perhaps he was a fool.

But at least no woman would ever play him for one again.

PART I

"We forded the river and clomb the high hill,
Never our steeds for a day stood still,
Whether we lay in the cave or the shed,
Our sleep fell soft on the hardest bed;
Whether we couched in our rough capote,
On the rougher plank of our gliding boat,
Or stretched on the sand, or our saddles
   spread
As a pillow beneath the resting head,
   Fresh we woke upon the morrow;
All our thoughts and words had scope,
We had health and we had hope,
   Toil and travel, but no sorrow."

SIEGE OF CORINTH

Chapter One

*D*avid Foster sat astride his big buckskin mare and waited for the wagons to roll out of Independence. It was the twenty-ninth of April, and if all went well, they would reach Portland and the Willamette Valley by October. After ten such trips himself, the wagon master knew that some of the emigrants on his train would never make their final destination. They would be buried somewhere along the Oregon Trail. He hoped the number of deaths would be few.

The first wagon, filled with the wagon master's supplies, rolled passed him. Coop sat on the wagon seat, expertly guiding the mule teams. He lifted a hand and waved to David. Coop had been on the same train when David and his wife, Emily, first went to Oregon to homestead. His parents had died before reaching Fort Laramie, and Emily had, in her own sweet way, adopted Coop, a mute of about fifteen years of age, keeping him on as a handyman to help work the farm. After Emily's death, the young man had just naturally fallen in with David, following him wherever David's restless feet carried him. Although Coop couldn't speak, his presence was comforting, and he was a fair enough cook to keep them from starving.

Next came the Adams wagon. It was easy enough to spot. Children were everywhere. Jake and Dorothy were the parents of eight daughters, ranging in age from five to sixteen. Jake was an enormous man, as quiet as his wife was gregarious. David liked Jake Adams. He was a levelheaded sort, not apt to make quick, careless decisions.

A few wagons down the line were the Bakers. A young couple, hardly more than kids themselves, with two small boys and another baby on the way. Even from here, he could see the excitement on their faces. People filled with hopes and dreams. David nodded to them and returned their smiles, but as soon as they'd moved passed him, the smile disappeared. He hated to see pregnant women on the trail. The journey wore down strong men, let alone a woman close to giving birth. He hoped all would go well for Marshall and Susan Baker and their children.

Behind the Baker wagon came the Branigans. Since their very first meeting, David had taken a special liking to the whole lot of them. Maureen was one of the prettiest women he had ever seen. She was nothing like his Emily, who had always been frail. Maureen Branigan, although every inch a refined lady, was made of steel. Even her coloring was vibrant, with her fiery auburn hair and her sharp green eyes.

Tucker Branigan, tall and handsome with calm,

thoughtful brown eyes, was a natural leader. David had spied that in him right off. Although he was young, perhaps in his mid-twenties, people just seemed to turn to Tucker for advice. Maybe it was because he was a lawyer, but David thought it was more than that. Folks sensed his intelligence, as well as his concern for others. Even though Tucker still clung to some anger from the war and all it had cost him, David had noticed it didn't interfere with his fairness in how he dealt with people. He liked the young fellow and hoped they would become friends.

A few wagons back was the Fulkerson wagon. Ralph Fulkerson, a blacksmith by trade, and his three grown sons were headed for Oregon City to open a smithy shop there. Not a one of them under six feet four inches, with arms as thick as tree stumps, the Fulkersons would make the trip with no trouble—if they could survive their own cooking. David had eaten supper with them one night after they arrived in Independence, and there was a strong possibility, in his opinion, that they might all die of food poisoning.

After them came the Gibsons, then the McCulloughs and more. Thirty-five wagons in all. Thirty-five families with stories all their own. Thirty-five reasons for picking up and leaving home and heading into an unknown future.

David drew a deep breath as he shot up a quick prayer that God would see them through the coming months. Then he turned his buckskin's head and galloped toward the front of the train.

"Let me, Tucker. Let me." Neal's coal black eyes shone with excitement as he stretched out his hands.

"Well . . ." Tucker hesitated.

"I can do it."

Tucker slipped the reins into Neal's small but eager fingers. He didn't suppose it could hurt anything. The wagon train had only been moving for an hour, and the pace was slow.

"You'll have to show me how to do that, too, Tucker," Maureen said as she poked her head out the front of the wagon. "You'll be needed other places on this journey."

"This isn't a job for you, Mother."

"Nonsense. Why do you persist in thinking I haven't a capable bone in my body?"

Tucker grinned. "I never thought any such thing."

"Good." Maureen eased herself onto the wagon seat. "Now, tell Neal and me what to do with so many animals and so much harness."

Even as he showed them how to weave the reins through their fingers, he was thinking how well Maureen was taking everything—much better than he was, if truth be known. She seemed to have forgotten what had driven them from their home, what had torn their family apart, and all that they'd left behind.

No, that wasn't fair. Maureen remembered all that was lost, but she accepted it as God's will. Not Tucker. He knew it wasn't God who had taken his brother and father and home. It was the Northern industrialists who couldn't compete against slave labor. It was the greedy politicians who wanted to line their own pockets with the fruits of others' labor. They had brought about the war, and when it was over, they had sent their scavengers south to pick the Confederates' bones clean.

Tucker had hated to see the war come, but even as

young as was, he'd known there was no way to stop
it. When Georgia chose to secede, he had sided with
her, though he'd known even then there was little
chance they would succeed. He'd been with General Lee in Virginia when the end came, and he'd
returned home hoping they'd seen the worst. But
the carpetbaggers, like a plague of locusts, had been
sent to finish what Sherman's march of destruction
had started.

Tucker hadn't forgotten any of it. He wouldn't
allow himself to forget. He meant to remember for
the rest of his life. He meant to do all in his power
to make sure it never happened again. Not to him.
Not to his loved ones. Not to his country.

And the only way to make sure was to achieve a
position of power. He hoped he would be able to do
so in this new territory of Idaho.

His cousin, Keegan Branigan, had been sent to
Idaho by the Confederacy to try to bring a shipment of gold to the South to pay for much-needed
arms. Wounded during the attempt to steal the gold
shipment, Keegan had been left behind in Idaho.
By the time he was well, the war was over. Keegan
had chosen to stay and had written to Tucker
several times about the opportunities to be found in
the capital city of Boise. Someday, according to
Keegan, Idaho would be a state, just like Oregon.

Tucker wasn't sure when it happened, but
Keegan's dream for a better future in Idaho had
become his own. He meant to have a hand in the
making of this new state, every step of the way. He
was going to make sure there were laws to protect
people. Poor farmers like Jake and Dorothy Adams.
And people who had lived on their land for three
generations, like the Branigans. He was going to
make sure that the Yankee industrialists and their

dishonest, greedy politicians didn't have an opportunity to start another war.

"Tuck?" His mother's gentle voice drew him from his dark thoughts. "Why don't you take Fiona for a ride on Blue Boy? Neal is man enough to handle the wagon."

Tucker glanced down at his young brother. The boy was beaming from ear to ear, his chest about to burst with pride. Looking back up at Maureen, he saw her nod. He supposed she was right. They would all have to learn to pull their weight during the coming months, even little Fiona. This was probably a good time to start. And his mother wasn't completely ignorant of horse-drawn vehicles. She'd done her share of dashing about the county in her well-sprung buggy. But this vehicle was a bit more unwieldy than the lightweight buggy, and the four pair of long-eared mules weren't nearly as attractive as the team of purebred horses that had always pulled the Branigan carriages.

"Go on, Tucker," Maureen said again. "And take your time."

Without further comment, Tucker hopped down to the ground and walked to the back of the wagon. "How about a ride, Fiona?" he called.

His little red-haired sister appeared in an instant, catapulting herself into his waiting arms. Tucker lifted her onto the saddle of his black gelding, Blue Boy, who'd been tethered to the back of the wagon.

"Let's ride up and talk to Mr. Foster, shall we?" he said as he mounted behind her.

Tucker lay on the ground, his arms beneath his head as he looked up at the twinkling stars. He knew he should be sleeping, but no matter how hard he tried, he couldn't. Only one day out and already he could foresee the tedious, uneventful routine of the wagon train—awakened before sunrise by the sentinel on horseback, breakfast eaten and tents struck before seven o'clock, sometimes taking a turn driving the herd of cattle and horses, and finally guiding the wagon into the perfect circle at night. While others in the train were caught up by the excitement of finally being on their way, Tucker felt only dread at the monotony he feared lay before him in the months to come.

At least they were well outfitted. Although the Branigans had come to Independence with little more than their clothes and his boxes of law books, they'd had enough money for four teams of mules, a sturdy wagon, and plenty of provisions. Thanks to Harlan Simmons, they weren't loaded down with lots of family heirlooms as some of the families were, but according to David Foster, most of those heirlooms and other useless items, perhaps even some much-needed items, would be lost before their owners reached Oregon.

And Foster ought to know. Their wagon master, a broad man with a generous shock of gray hair, was leading his tenth train of emigrants west. Tucker had taken a liking to him from the first time they'd met. Foster didn't waste words, but what he said always seemed to have merit.

There were one hundred and twenty-nine people in the Foster train, thirty-five wagons filled with old folks and children, farmers and bankers, the educated and the illiterate, people from different walks of life banding together to forge their way into a new future.

Suddenly it occurred to Tucker that he'd quit pigeonholing everyone as either Confederate or

Yankee. They were the Adamses and the Bakers and the McCulloughs and the Fulkersons. Surprised by this discovery, he also felt a sense of relief. While he still wouldn't forget what had caused the war and while he wouldn't forget what the war had done to him and his family, it was good to quit blaming people simply because they'd lived north or south of the Mason-Dixon line. He would accomplish more with less hate in his heart and more determination in his soul. Despite himself, he smiled.

Less than a week before, Tucker had been wondering what had brought so many strangers to one place to begin their journey west. Now, as he gazed up at the star-studded heavens, he realized how quickly they were becoming a community of friends and neighbors. Thirty-five families, one hundred and twenty-nine people, a town on wheels and horseback.

Perhaps it wouldn't be so monotonous after all.

MAUREEN'S JOURNAL

May 3. We have concluded our fifth day on the trail, but this is the first moment I have found to record my thoughts. Before leaving Independence, Mrs. Adams showed me how to pack our foodstuffs so they will remain fresh. The thick slabs of smoked bacon are packed in the bran barrel and the eggs are with the corn meal (which also keeps them from breaking). No one back in Georgia would believe how we make our butter. The milk from the cow that we don't drink is left in pails and hung in the wagon. By day's end, the jolting wagon has churned it into butter. I didn't believe Mrs. Adams when she told me, but it works!

Sometimes, after the children have gone to sleep and the entire camp is quiet, I admit to my fear of what is ahead. I thought I had grown used to dealing with the unknown each day, but I wasn't prepared for this. Nothing is familiar. Nothing is the same. But I can't let Tucker or the children see how I feel. We share each other's strength and draw courage from it. Except Neal, of course. He fears absolutely nothing. His Grandfather O'Toole would have been pleased with his namesake.

I miss my own father and mother tonight, God bless them. I wish I could lay my head in Mama's lap and she could stroke my hair as she did when I was a little girl. But that was so very long ago.

Chapter Two

Tucker saw the swaybacked animal standing in a copse of trees. He turned Blue Boy toward the river, intent on rounding up the stray and getting it moving with the rest of the herd.

"Poor old guy doesn't look like he'll make it another twenty miles, let alone all the way to Oregon," Tucker muttered as he drew closer to the gaunt-looking horse.

Blue Boy, moving through the dense underbrush, stopped suddenly. The gelding's ears darted forward as he snorted and shook his head.

"What is it, boy?"

Then Tucker saw them, huddled tightly beneath a tree. They were shivering in the cool morning air, their arms wrapped around each other, the little one's face hidden beneath the older one's flowing hair.

Slowly, Tucker dismounted and stepped closer.

She was beautiful, even with a smudge of dirt on the tip of her slightly upturned nose, and he recognized her instantly. He'd seen her outside the mercantile in Independence about a week ago. Her arm had been linked with that of a sour-faced man who was towing her along the sidewalk at a determined pace. "Mr. Jones," she'd called him as they whipped past Tucker. He remembered thinking then that no one so pretty should look as unhappy as she did.

He stared at her now, realizing as he did so that she was even more beautiful than he'd thought at first. She had a compelling face that demanded a man to look and look long; an oval face with high cheekbones, arched brows, alabaster skin, and a heart-shaped, dusky-rose mouth. Her honey-brown hair, abundant and curly, spread across the ground like a thick fur rug before a fireplace. Only one thing marred the perfect picture she presented to him—a yellowish-purple bruise, fading but still evident, along her left jaw.

He wondered if Mr. Jones had hit her, and the thought infuriated him.

It wasn't until he heard her sharp intake of breath that he realized he was staring into wide gray eyes—gray like the color of doves, darker on the outside, then almost silver near the iris.

She sat up, hiding the child behind her, and suddenly, instead of looking into her unusal eyes, he was staring at a long knife. "What do you want?" she demanded.

Something told him she wouldn't hesitate to use the weapon. There was no mistaking the desperation written on her face. Tucker raised his hands and took a step backward. "Not a thing, miss. I saw your horse and thought it was a stray."

Her shoulders relaxed slightly. "He's not." Her eyes remained wary.

"I can see that. May I ask what you're doing out here all alone?"

"We've come to join the wagon train."

Tucker's gaze scanned the area. "We?"

"My sister and me."

"You're alone?"

"Yes, we're alone." She was on her feet now, still holding the knife in her right hand, clutching the little girl's hand with her left. Her chin was lifted high in subconscious defiance, almost daring him to challenge her further. "We're going to talk to the wagon master."

Tucker had a few more questions he would have liked to ask, but he decided to leave those to David. "Get your horse, and I'll take you to him."

She studied him a moment in silence. She wore her distrust like a heavy cloak. Finally, as if succumbing to the inevitable, she let her arm drop to her side, her fingers still gripping the knife handle like the hilt of a sword. She nodded toward him.

"Rachel," she said in a low voice, "gather our things."

While her little sister hurried to roll up their sparse belongings inside the blankets, the older girl saddled the nag of a horse. When all was gathered up, she lifted Rachel onto the saddle and turned toward him once again.

"We're ready."

What had gotten into her? She had actually threatened that man with a knife. Could she have used it? At the time, Maggie had thought so, but the burst of courage seemed to have deserted her now.

Her stomach churned as they approached the tall man with the massive chest and broad shoulders. His face was weathered and lined. His hair was a stony gray. But his light blue eyes seemed friendly enough. She hoped, for their sake, that his heart was as kind.

"David, this young lady would like to speak with you." Her escort glanced in her direction. "This is Mr. Foster, the wagon master."

Maggie swallowed back her fear. "My name is Maggie Harris. My sister and I need to get to Oregon, and we'd like to join your train."

David Foster's eyes flicked over the length of her, then moved to where Rachel sat on the horse behind her. "Where's your wagon?"

"We have no wagon, sir."

"Your folks?"

Maggie never blinked as the lie slipped past her lips. "Our parents are in Oregon."

The wagon master's gaze was unrelenting.

"Maggie . . ." Rachel whispered, her voice quivering.

"It's all right, kitten," Maggie reassured her.

"How'd it happen you're tryin' to get to your folks all on your own?"

"Our parents went to Oregon two years ago. They wanted to get settled before they sent for us. We were to come out with another family—Jack Smith by name—but they changed their mind at the last minute." She didn't know where the words came from. She didn't even know if she was making sense. She only knew she had to convince him to let them go with the train to Oregon. "What else could we do? We have nowhere else to go. We have no other family and our home in Pennsylvania has been sold."

"Wait a minute."

Her heart pounding in her chest, she turned toward the younger man who'd discovered them this morning. Beneath the closely trimmed beard, she perceived a strong jawline and a firm mouth. His eyes were a deep, chocolate brown, and he watched her with a perceptiveness that was unsettling.

"Didn't I see you in town with someone last week? Outside the mercantile. A Mr. Jones, I believe."

He'd seen her with Cyrus, the dour old hotel owner with his graying muttonchop whiskers, bulbous nose, and offensive breath—the man her uncle had chosen to be her husband. She swallowed the bad taste the thought of him left in her mouth and tried to keep her revulsion from showing on her face.

After five years of avoiding abuse at Seth Harris's hands, Maggie had learned to be as quick mentally as she was on her feet. There was no noticeable hesitation before she replied, suitably reluctant, "That was a friend of our uncle. Our uncle died suddenly five days ago. He was the only other family we had left in this world . . . except for our parents. He brought us to Missouri to join the Smiths, but they decided against going to Oregon. He was trying to find other passage for us when he . . . when he died."

"You don't sound like a girl whose beloved uncle has just died."

There was a shrewdness behind the younger man's eyes that warned her to be cautious in what she said. The truth, she thought, might be more to her advantage than a lie.

Maggie's chin tilted up in her habitually defiant pose. "There was no love lost between my uncle and me. But we saw him properly buried with the last of our money." She paused, then added for good measure, "Mr. Jones was not inclined to take us in permanently. We had to leave. Where else could we go?"

David Foster cleared his throat. "We'd better call us a meeting, Tucker. Get the folks together. Girls, you come with me."

Maggie turned around and reached up for Rachel, easing the child to the ground. She knelt beside her and pushed the two blond braids back behind the girl's shoulders. "Remember now," she whispered. "Our parents are alive, Rachel. They must believe that or they won't help us. Do you understand me?"

Rachel nodded.

"Good."

As they followed the wagon master, Maggie glanced over her shoulder. The man Mr. Foster had called Tucker was staring after her. She felt as if he could read her mind and knew she was lying. Quickly, she looked away.

Tucker leaned against the wagon behind him and stared over the heads of the crowd. Maggie Harris stood off to David's left, her back ramrod-straight and her head held high. Small of bone and not more than four inches above five feet, she radiated a strength not often seen in the gentler sex, yet it didn't detract from her beauty any more than the ill-fitting, faded gown she wore did.

But it was her eyes that drew his attention.

Although she was asking for help from strangers, there was no pleading in those dove-gray depths. He had no doubt she was afraid of what the decision might be, yet she revealed none of that to the crowd around her.

While David Foster addressed the people, Tucker's gaze moved to the little sister. The child was terrified, yet she was trying desperately to mimic the brave facade of her sister. There were perhaps ten or twelve years between Maggie and Rachel and their coloring was different, yet there was no mistaking the family resemblance. Rachel might even grow into a greater beauty than Maggie.

Prettier than Maggie? His gaze returned to the elder of the girls. No, he didn't think she could be prettier than Maggie.

What was it about her that affected him so? She was a beauty, true, but he'd spent most of his life surrounded by beautiful women. No, there was something more than just the color of her eyes, the softness of her lips, or the richness of her hair that drew his interest. Something deeper.

Maybe it was her courage. He had to respect her sheer determination when common sense said she couldn't go across the country with little more than an old, broken-down horse, a knife, and a couple of thin blankets. He'd seen grown men back down from better odds than that.

"So, folks, we've got to decide what we're going to do. Miss Harris here says she's certain her parents will be able to pay for their passage once they reach Oregon, but it's a long time between here and there. Someone will have to be responsible for them. You each know what supplies you've got and how far we've got to go. If we decide against it, we'll have to send someone back to Independence with them. We can't be sendin' them back alone. And that'll cost us a day or two of travel." David turned his eyes upon the two girls. "But if we do send them back, there's nowhere for them to go. It's up to you." It was obvious to everyone what the wagon master thought they should do.

Tucker's gaze swept the crowd. He read reluctance on more than one woman's face, no doubt because of the undeniable beauty of the elder sister. Maggie was still young, perhaps eighteen at most, but she was a woman nonetheless. She wasn't exactly going to receive a warm welcome from the wives on the train, nor from the mothers with randy young sons. And it was doubtful anyone would want to take on the added responsibility of caring for them or having two more mouths to feed.

And he couldn't exactly blame them. He suspected Maggie was anything but a pliant young thing who would always do exactly as she was told. He wouldn't want to be responsible for her, no matter how much he admired her pluck.

Above the heads of several others, Jake Adam's gaze met Tucker's. "What do you think, Tuck?"

All eyes turned toward him. He wasn't sure he wanted to help make this decision. He didn't feel unbiased. Something told him this decision would affect his life more than he wanted it to.

He shook his head thoughtfully as he stepped forward. "Well, like David already said, somebody has to take responsibility for them if we let them stay." His gaze moved over the crowd once again. "And they'd have to agree to abide by the rules of the train and pull their own weight, just like everyone else." He looked at the two girls.

Maggie's chin was still held stubbornly high. He saw her fingers tighten around Rachel's hand. Defiant. Determined. Desperate.

"I can't say I care much for turning our backs on them either," Tucker added, even as he did so. "But the decision's up to all of you—and whoever agrees to take them on."

The crowd closed in behind him as Tucker resumed his place beside the wagon. There was a low murmur as folks talked among themselves.

"Tucker." Maureen stepped up beside him. "What's going to happen to those girls if no one helps them?" she asked softly.

It wasn't hard to imagine what might happen to them, homeless and alone.

He looked at his mother, suddenly realizing what she was saying. "You don't mean *you* want to do this?"

"We can make room for them, and we're better supplied than most. It's only two more."

He glanced back at Maggie and Rachel, standing stoically beneath the gazes of so many. Hadn't he enough problems without adding two more? He had his own fatherless family to look out for. They had months of unknown hardship to get through. Surely there was someone else who could volunteer to help them.

But as he looked at Maggie, he finally realized what it was that he could read in her gray eyes. It was a look he'd seen hundreds, perhaps thousands of times in young soldiers headed into another hopeless battle in a war already lost. Yet they'd faced it with courage, even when they were admittedly afraid. If he hadn't made it through the war, it could have been Shannon and Fiona asking strangers for help. His mother was right. The Branigans did have more room than most, and food shouldn't be a problem. He couldn't send them away even if he wanted to. He had to help Maggie Harris. He'd seen enough lost causes in his life.

Tucker nodded. "All right, Mother. If you're willing, we'll give them a hand."

Chapter Three

*M*aggie's heart was racing beneath her ribs. She'd been hopeful after the wagon master finished speaking. It was clear he didn't want to send them back.

But that younger man—the handsome one with the beard and the observant brown eyes, the one who'd seen her in Independence and the same one who'd found them this morning—he didn't seem very eager to have her along. Why was he against her? Did he know she was lying? Could he really see inside her? That's how she felt whenever he looked at her.

Of course, he might dislike her because she'd threatened him with a knife. It had been a foolish thing to do, but she'd been so frightened. She should have apologized, but now it was too late.

She listened to the murmur of voices as the others discussed their fate. There was nothing else she could do but listen. Any moment now she expected to hear someone shout, "Send them away." And could she blame them? What on earth had ever made her believe someone would willingly help two penniless girls travel clear across the vast American wilderness to Oregon, even with the promise of money awaiting them?

"Maggie?"

She was grateful for Rachel's distraction. She knelt beside her sister and placed an arm around her shoulders.

"I'm hungry."

"We'll get something to eat soon, kitten." She hoped she wasn't telling another lie.

"Mr. Foster." A woman clad in a black gown and wearing a black bonnet stepped into the center of the circle. "We're willing to take Maggie and her sister as far as Idaho. From there, I'm sure we can arrange passage on to Oregon for them."

"Good. I'm happy to hear it, Mrs. Branigan. Is that agreeable with the rest of you?" When no one objected, David waved his arm. "All right, then. We've wasted enough time this morning. Let's break camp. We've got miles to cover before dark."

In a matter of seconds, the crowd had dispersed, leaving Maggie and Rachel to face their benefactress alone. Conflicting emotions warred within Maggie's heart. She was touched by the kindness of a stranger, yet suspicious of why the woman would so generously offer them a home. Although Maggie had hoped someone would help them, she really hadn't expected it to happen, especially not this easily.

"Maggie. Rachel. I'm Maureen Branigan."

Maggie squeezed Rachel's fingers within her own as she stood up. "We thank you for your kindness,

Mrs. Branigan. We'll help in every way we can to repay you."

"We can talk of that later. Right now we must hurry. They're already breaking camp, and I'm sure you haven't eaten this morning. We'll have just enough time to put something in your stomachs and introduce you to the rest of the family." Maureen glanced down at Rachel. "I have a daughter about your age. Fiona will be happy to have a new friend traveling with us."

Rachel sidled closer to Maggie, nearly disappearing into the folds of her sister's skirts.

"Rachel's a little shy around strangers," Maggie explained.

It was an understatement, of course. Rachel was terrified of strangers. And how could she be otherwise? She'd scarcely known another soul but Maggie until they'd departed from Philadelphia, and the past few weeks surely hadn't taught her to trust in strangers.

Maureen smiled gently. "No matter. We'll have plenty of time to become friends." She turned and began walking.

It had been a long, long time since Maggie had known kindness. A sudden mistiness clouded her eyes, but she quickly swallowed back the tears as she followed Maureen Branigan. It wouldn't do to become overly fond of this woman nor to put too much faith in the goodness she'd shown them thus far. People could fool a person. Maggie knew that for a fact. Hadn't Uncle Seth appeared kindly when he showed up at their door? Hadn't he informed everyone that he would love his nieces as if they were his own children?

"We just want you and Mr. Branigan to know we don't expect charity," Maggie said gruffly. "We'll carry our own weight and pay for the food we eat by working hard."

"There is no Mr. Branigan. Just me and my three children. My husband died earlier this year."

That news touched a tender spot in Maggie's heart. "I'm sorry. I know what it's like to lose someone you love."

The way Maureen was watching her now caused Maggie to look away quickly. She hadn't meant to say that. She didn't want to tell anybody anything about her past. It was more than just not wanting to be caught in her own web of lies. She knew it was better to keep her distance. She couldn't trust anyone, no matter how kind they'd been to her. Experience had taught her that, and she didn't mean to forget it. She didn't want anything from Mrs. Branigan or anyone else except to be able to travel with them to Oregon. She'd asked for help because it was the only way to get to there.

After that, after they found the Sandersons and could claim their inheritance, she vowed she would never again be dependent upon anyone but herself. Never again would she allow anyone else to control her life.

Never again.

Maggie couldn't believe how quickly everything happened after that. Even as she and Rachel were handed tin plates covered with bacon and pancakes, Maureen was introducing her two young children, Neal and Fiona, then sending them off in different directions.

"My oldest boy is out with the hunters today. You'll meet him tonight at supper."

It was Maureen and Neal who hitched up the mule teams to the wagon, Maureen and Fiona who loaded the last of the cooking utensils and pans into the wagon, Maureen who sat on the wagon seat, whip in hand, and drove the mules into line as the train began its journey while the sun was still young at their backs.

Maureen invited Maggie to share the wagon seat with her, but Maggie declined. Too many hours in close quarters would invite unwanted questions. So she chose to ride her old horse, despite the complaints in her backside from the previous days in the saddle. An exhausted Rachel rode with her.

At noon they stopped by a swiftly flowing stream. Still yoked, the teams were turned loose from the wagons to graze in the lush grass. The midday meal was simple but hardy, and soon they were moving once again. By evening, they'd put another twenty miles between themselves and Independence.

It was amazing to Maggie how precisely the hindmost wagon closed the circle with the leading wagon as dusk turned the sky to lead. As soon as they were stopped, the camp became abuzz with activity, families building fires to cook their evening meals, some of them pitching tents, everyone readying for nightfall.

At the Branigan wagon, Fiona and Neal scurried about doing their mother's bidding. The small lad even unhitched the teams of mules by himself and led them away.

"What can I do to help, Mrs. Branigan?" Maggie asked, her uselessness beginning to make her feel guilty.

"Let Neal take care of your horse. You can help me with supper." Maureen turned toward her daughter. "Fiona, gather some twigs and branches for the fire. Why don't you let Rachel help you?"

Rachel shook her head as she shrank close

against the wagon wheel. Maggie's heart ached. Rachel seemed to be growing more and more fearful by the hour. In a way, she could understand it. While life with Seth Harris had been grim, it had at least been familiar. Then suddenly, the child had been thrown into an unknown world full of strangers. Maggie wished she knew what to do to make things easier for her.

"Go on, Fiona," Maureen said. "I think Rachel will stay and help Maggie and me instead. Can you peel potatoes, Rachel?"

Maggie was once again touched by the kindness and understanding in Maureen's actions. She hoped she would be able to repay the woman someday.

Chapter Four

*T*ucker spent the day hunting but returned to camp with little to show for it. One scrawny hare hung from the horn of his saddle. And he was one of the lucky ones.

The land through which the Foster train was passing undulated in a sea of green, broken by an abundance of streams, woods, and forests; yet it seemed barren of game. Not once had he seen any signs of deer, nor even a prairie hen, though it was spring.

But it did seem to be a happy breeding ground for snakes, frogs, and mosquitoes. Tucker swatted his neck, squashing another of the pesky bugs as he swore silently.

Stopping Blue Boy on a ridge, he looked down on the camp. Cook fires were already blazing, dotting the darkening landscape with splashes of yellow and orange. Someone was playing a mouth harp, the tune rising to drift with the smoke across the broad expanse of plain.

Twin Willows came to his mind. Sometimes, as dusk settled over the plantation, the darkies used to sing a song similar to the tune he heard now. It had been a pleasant sound at the end of the day. He and his father would sit in the drawing room, Farrell smoking his pipe, while a breeze ruffled the lace curtains at the window. They would talk about the business of the plantation and then about Tucker's studies and what it would be like when the day came that they practiced law together.

And there were the evenings when Charmaine and her family came to visit. She and Tucker would sneak off together, strolling through his mother's rose garden, planning for the day they would marry, then stealing a kiss beneath the shadows of the arbor. But Tucker hadn't been enough for Charmaine. The war and the Yankee carpetbaggers had proved that. Charmaine's love had been a lie.

He shook his head. He had no time to dwell on his bitterness over Charmaine's deceit, nor for losing himself in pleasant memories of better days. He'd been just a boy then. Now he was a man with a family to take care of and feed. He held up the rabbit. It wouldn't have gone far with only four of them. Now they were six. How had he ever let his mother finagle him into agreeing to take on those two girls anyway?

Reminding himself that they still had plenty of food in store and there would be better hunting ahead, Tucker rode his horse down the hill toward the livestock. He answered the greetings of several of the men riding herd as he dismounted and pulled the saddle off Blue Boy's back, then hobbled the gelding and turned him loose to graze. His horse

cared for, he headed for his own wagon with quick
strides, hunger beginning to gnaw at his belly.

As he rounded the front of the prairie schooner,
he stopped. Maggie was bending over the Dutch
oven. Her too-short skirt revealed a nice length of
calf and a pair of shoes that were clearly inadequate
for the months ahead. Her curly hair fell forward,
obscuring her face, but Tucker hadn't forgotten how
beautiful Maggie Harris was. He'd thought of her
more than once during the day. Perhaps that's why
he hadn't seen any game. Maybe his thoughts had
been occupied elsewhere.

He paused and watched as she lifted a steaming
pie and placed it on the makeshift table. The sweet
odor drifted toward him. Apple pie. His favorite. If
he was wise, he would concentrate on food rather
than Maggie.

"I'll trade you my share of supper for that pie,
Miss Harris."

With a gasp, Maggie whirled around, her head
falling back to look up at the cause of her alarm. It
was *him* again.

"I'm sorry," he said. "I didn't mean to frighten
you."

"I—I wasn't frightened," she protested, taking
one step back while trying to calm her racing heart.
"You just surprised me, is all."

He held up a pitiful-looking jackrabbit. "It's the
best I could do."

What did he want there anyway? she wondered.
"Thank you," she said, reluctantly holding out her
hand to grasp the animal by its ears. "I'll tell Mrs.
Branigan."

"No. Don't bother Mother. I'll skin it first and we
can throw it into the stew."

A surge of alarm quickened her pulse even more. "Your mother?"

"Mrs. Branigan—remember?" His expression told her she was entirely too dense to converse with further. Without another word, he settled onto a wooden crate and took out his skinning knife.

Of all the men in the world who could have been Maureen Branigan's son, why did it have to be this one? It had been evident from the first moment he'd found them by the river that he didn't want them on this train. He was the one who'd remembered seeing her with Cyrus Jones, something she hadn't counted on. He was the one who, when the others had asked if she and Rachel should be allowed to travel with them, responded with something less than enthusiasm.

Those reasons alone would have been enough to make her uneasy, but there was also the way he looked at her, as if he could see right through her falsehoods. She wasn't particularly troubled by the lies she'd been forced to tell to join this train— except when it came to him. There was something about him, something in his eyes or the cut of his jaw or . . .

She didn't know what it was, but it made her feel uncomfortable, as if his very presence demanded honesty. And now she was actually going to be traveling with him for weeks to come.

A tiny gasp drew Maggie's eyes toward the back of the wagon where Rachel sat peeling potatoes. Her sister's face was pale, her eyes as wide as silver dollars. She knew immediately what was wrong.

"Mr. Branigan? The rabbit. Please don't do that," Maggie said softly, stepping toward him.

He pushed his hat back on his head, revealing shaggy dark hair. "It's a little difficult to eat them this way." Irritation had crept into his voice.

"Please. My sister . . . Please."

He turned to follow the direction of her glance. Rachel had dropped her paring knife into the pan of water and potatoes, and her hands were quivering so hard she was splashing water onto her dress.

"She had a pet rabbit once," Maggie explained in a whisper. "It disappeared. Unc . . . someone told her they ate it for supper."

He carefully placed the jackrabbit out of Rachel's sight, laying the knife beside it on the ground. When he rose, he moved slowly, each motion relaxed and easy. He walked toward Rachel but stopped short of her, turning to lean a shoulder against the side of the wagon.

"My name's Tucker. What's yours?"

There was a tenderness in his voice now that hadn't been there earlier. Maggie saw Rachel's attention drawn to the tall man nearby, saw her struggling with her shyness and fear. Maggie expected her to break into tears at any moment.

"If I were guessing your name, I'd say it must be a pretty one, just like you." He turned his head to one side, leveling his gaze on the young girl. "There was always one name from the Bible I liked best. Let's see. What was it? Ah, yes. Rachel. That's what it was." He smiled. "I think your name must be Rachel."

Disbelief and surprise flittered across Rachel's face. "How did you know that?"

"I told you. Because you're so pretty."

It was the first real smile Maggie had seen Rachel bestow on anyone other than her older sister and she felt drawn toward her sister and Tucker, wanting to be a part of that unfettered moment. But she resisted the urge, instead turning to pick up the dead rabbit, then quickly carrying it out of sight.

By the time she returned, Tucker Branigan was peeling potatoes and spinning a tale about an old hound he'd had as a boy while Rachel listened with a rapt expression on her face. Rather than interrupt him, Maggie settled quietly onto the crate near the fire. She wrapped her arms around her legs, tucked up beneath her skirt, and clasped her hands in front of her shins. For a moment, she listened to the story along with Rachel, enjoying the sound of his Southern drawl and the soft way it lengthened some words and deleted others. But it wasn't long before she was paying more attention to the man than to his voice.

It was probably the first time she'd really taken note of his appearance. He was tall, with wide shoulders and a broad chest. His legs were long, his thighs muscular. His closely trimmed beard was a slightly darker shade of brown than the sandy-colored hair on his head. She hadn't seen many men with beards, but she thought she liked his, perhaps because it did nothing to hide the strength of his jaw or the squareness of his chin. His eyes were a chocolate brown, so dark that the irises were barely distinguishable. Tiny lines around his eyes crinkled when he smiled, which he did often as he talked to Rachel. Watching him, Maggie found herself smiling too.

"Are those potatoes going into the stew or are they just to look at?"

Maggie started at the sound of Maureen's voice, then felt a sudden wave of guilt as she remembered she was supposed to be helping, not sitting idly listening to children's stories.

Tucker set down his knife and picked up the pan. He carried it toward his mother, a teasing grin on his face. "These are the best peeled potatoes you'll ever see. Rachel and I did them." He dropped a kiss on Maureen's cheek, then proceeded to the stew pot and plopped the vegetables one by one into the simmering broth.

"I see you've met my oldest son," Maureen said as she set the wood in her arms near the fire.

"Yes," Tucker answered before Maggie could.

When their eyes met, he grinned, and Maggie felt something strange happening to her heart. It was going to be more dangerous traveling with Tucker Branigan than she'd thought.

MAUREEN'S JOURNAL

*May 4. The prairie swells like the ocean, rolling west
in an endless expanse of green. The trees are in
flower—red clusters of maple blossoms and a profu-
sion of Indian apple. The beauty of the land makes
the journey a little easier, perhaps a little faster.*

*We have two more, a young woman and her sister,
traveling with us now. Maggie and Rachel were on
their way to join their parents in Oregon when
tragedy brought them our way, two people in need.
I'm glad we could help.*

*I think of my own two children left behind in
Georgia, and my heart nearly breaks. Will there be a
helpful and willing stranger nearby should they find
themselves in need? When shall I see them again?
How long must I be separated from Shannon before
she can join us? (And I must hang my head in
shame, for when she joins us it must mean that Aunt
Eugenia has left this life for the next.) What of my
Devlin? He was so angry, so filled with bitterness
when last I saw him. He's a young man now, nearly
as old as Grady when he died, yet he's still a boy.*

*Dear Grady. I shall never visit his grave again.
Gone only three years, but his image dims and I'm
forced to look at his photograph to be certain that he
was as I remember him. Perhaps it's best he could
remain in the Georgia he fought and died for.*

*I see my tears have smeared the ink. I can write no
more tonight.*

Chapter Five

*M*aggie *was surprised to find the sun well up when* she awoke, yet the camp was strangely quiet. Although she'd been with the train only one day, she was certain this inactivity wasn't normal. They had already covered several miles yesterday before this hour. Something had to be wrong.

Dressing quickly beneath the cover of blankets, Maggie was soon out from under the wagon and looking about, leaving Rachel to sleep a while longer.

Lazy ribbons of smoke curled above unused campfires. A few wagons away, two women stood chatting in low voices. Maggie considered walking over to ask them what was going on, then decided against it. If all was peaceful, why draw attention to herself? Instead, she turned and left the circle of wagons. She picked her way across a clear-running brook, stepping on mossy stones and getting the bottoms of her slippers wet in the process. Once on the other side, she dropped her skirt again and began to climb the sloping side of a grassy hill. Upon reaching the top, she turned and stared down upon the wagons.

There looked to be nearly forty wagons in all. During the day they spread out in a long line, but now they were closed into a tight circle. Behind them, grazing on ground the train had covered the previous day, were the livestock—horses, cattle, oxen, and mules. She could see several riders quietly circling the stock, keeping a keen eye out for trouble.

It was from her new vantage point that she saw the gathering of people and heard the sweet strains of a hymn. So that's why the train wasn't moving. It was Sunday.

Her gaze moved from the worshipers toward the broad expanse of blue sky overhead. Several small birds flitted above the treetops, chasing and escaping one another. And suddenly, Maggie felt as free and joyous as the birds looked.

Free! She was free!

For five long years, she had fought against her uncle's harshness, sought to protect Rachel from him, but never had she really thought they could escape Seth Harris. She had built a make–believe world for Rachel, and then hidden in it with her. But now they were free. They were truly on their way to Oregon, a place where their uncle would never think to look nor hope to find them.

Feeling reckless, Maggie plopped down in the grass and removed her shoes and stockings, then plunged her toes into the cool grass. A giggle rose in her throat.

When was the last time she'd done anything like

this? Had she ever been young? Or had she always lived inside the Philadelphia manse, taking care of Rachel in the upper reaches of the house, far away from Seth?

Suddenly a snake slithered across her right foot. With a shriek, Maggie jumped to her feet, stumbling backward, her hand at her throat.

"It's all right." Strong hands clamped around her arms. "It's just a harmless water snake."

Jerking free, she whirled around to face a grinning Tucker.

"Lots of them around." He seemed awfully pleased with that bit of information.

Maggie glanced nervously at the ground.

"Don't worry. They really are harmless." He pushed the hat back on his head, his grin fading slightly. "Quite a sight, isn't it?" he asked, his gaze shifting to the wagons below.

She nodded mutely, wishing he would go away as the silence between them lengthened.

"What sent your parents west, Maggie? The war?"

Maggie folded her arms in front of her. She didn't want to talk about her parents. "Yes," she answered, glad he had supplied her with a plausible reason.

She was afraid more questions would follow, and she hadn't any notion how she would answer them. What if he should ask about her life in Pennsylvania? Although Philadelphia had always been her home, she scarcely remembered anything outside of her own house. She had a faded memory of her father's office at the mill, and there was the restaurant he used to take her to for ices on hot summer days. But what else could she tell him? That she'd spent the past five years locked up in a large brick house? That she knew no one outside of the cook, all the other servants long since gone? That she had no friends?

And what if he asked other questions she couldn't answer? What if she had to make up more lies? The less said, the better. The less said, the less likely she was to be caught in a lie.

She turned her back toward Tucker once again. She knew it was more than just his potential questions that bothered her. She'd realized last night, as she observed the Branigan family over supper, that she was as ill-equipped as Rachel in dealing with strangers. She didn't know how to respond to the good-natured ribbing that went on among the Branigans, nor was she accustomed to the open display of affection that seemed to come so easily to all of them.

"We've a long trip ahead of us," Tucker said, breaking the lengthy silence. "It will be August before we reach Idaho, October before you get to Portland."

"That long?"

"No one bothered to prepare you for what's ahead, did they?"

Maggie shook her head. October. She'd had no idea it would take so very long. But then, how could anyone have warned her? Even she hadn't known she would be taking this journey. If she hadn't seen the wagons camped outside of Independence, she never would have thought of it. And she'd been so desperate . . ..

"That wasn't very fair. You might have decided not to come."

She knew he was watching her with that same intense look. She turned on him, suddenly made angry by his constant scrutiny. "You certainly didn't want us to come, did you, Mr. Branigan? You wish they'd left us behind."

"That's not true. It's just that I—"

"Why did you let your mother say she would take us in?" She stepped toward him, chin thrust up, her fists resting on her hips.

His brows drew together in a frown. There wasn't even a hint of his grin remaining. "Because you were all alone and needed help, and it didn't look to me as if anyone else was going to do it. And you might be just a little grateful that we *did* take you in. Have you thought what would have happened to you if we hadn't?"

She wanted to tell him he could keep his charity, but he was right. She knew exactly what would have happened to her if not for Mrs. Branigan's willingness to help. Even now, Maggie would be married to that old man, Cyrus Jones, and he and Uncle Seth would be sharing the money her father had put away for her.

Tucker was right. She should be grateful. She *was* grateful to Maureen. Certainly no one else had stepped forward to offer aid, even with David Foster's encouragement. Maggie had gotten what she had asked for. She hadn't any right to be angry with Tucker.

Maggie turned away from him again, once more looking down at the peaceful wagons. "I'm sorry, Mr. Branigan. There was no call for me to say those things to you. It's just . . . it's just that I'm a little afraid of what's ahead."

There was a pause before he accepted her apology. "I can understand that," he said at last. "It's a long way from Pennsylvania." Another pause followed before he added, "It's a long way from Georgia."

Hearing the longing in his voice, she couldn't resist turning to look at him. She was suddenly curious about this man. "Why are *you* going west, Mr. Branigan?"

There was another pregnant pause. "My father died."

She read his pain in the hardness of his jaw and the faraway look in his eyes. It was a pain she knew all too well. Unthinking, she lifted her hand to touch his shoulder. "I'm sorry," she whispered.

The look Tucker turned upon her made her feel uncomfortable, as if he somehow sensed she truly understood his loss, as only a child who had lost a parent could. Her discomfort frightened her. She couldn't allow herself to feel sorry for him. She couldn't allow herself to care too much about any of them.

"I'd better see if Rachel needs anything," she said softly, then, grabbing her shoes and stockings, she beat a hasty retreat.

Maureen slipped her dress over her head and fastened the buttons up the front before settling onto a rock and beginning to comb out her damp hair. It had felt wonderful to bathe all over, even if it was just in a foot of icy water instead of a tub with steam filling the room.

The comb slipped from her fingers. Before reaching to pick it up, she gazed at her hands. Blisters and calluses. It was hard to remember a time when her hands had been lily white and downy soft. When Farrell was courting her, he had always kissed the palms of her hands and told her she tasted as sweet as honey. Maureen ran the fingers of her right hand across the roughened palm of her left.

There isn't much left of the girl Farrell Branigan fell in love with, she thought.

Well, there was no point in dwelling on the past. Tomorrow she would be up on the wagon seat again, the muscles in her shoulders screaming in protest as she guided the mules across another fifteen or twenty miles, her calluses growing thicker on her hands and her face being darkened by the sun.

"Farrell wouldn't even know me," she whispered to herself.

The sudden tears were unexpected. She buried her face in her hands and wept silently. She wept for Farrell, the man she'd loved for twenty–five years, the father of her seven children, one stillborn, another killed in war. She was so lonely without him. And she felt guilty, too, for the anger that lingered. Yes, she was angry with him—for giving up, for robbing her of his company, for taking away that special bond they'd shared throughout the years. Why had his pride meant more to him than she?

Maureen dashed away the last of her tears and retrieved the comb. With sharp jerks, she began untangling the mass of auburn hair, but her thoughts remained on Farrell.

She remembered all too clearly the day her husband and son had returned from the North, humiliated and despairing. They had tried everything, but there would be no payment for the cotton crop delivered so long before. She supposed they'd always known it was a desperate hope that the money owed would still be on the company's ledgers. After all, they were the vanquished rebels.

At supper, Farrell had stood at the table and made the announcement. Twin Willows was lost.

After surviving the war, after surviving the death of their second son, Grady, after scraping to feed and provide for their family and servants and trying to rebuild the plantation, the carpetbaggers and the tax man and the Union had won yet again.

But she could forgive their Yankee enemies more easily than she could forgive Farrell for dying as he had—giving up and leaving her to face life all alone.

That day . . . That dark, dark day.

"Ahem."

Maureen started and turned toward the sound.

"Excuse me, Mrs. Branigan."

"Mr. Foster." Her fingers touched the top button of her bodice. She'd thought herself far enough away from the other wagons. Could he have seen her at her bath?

The wagon master cleared his throat again. "I didn't mean to disturb you. I was just taking a walk, sort of clearing my thoughts."

"No, you didn't disturb me." She quickly wrapped her still damp hair into a bun at the nape of her neck and fastened it with hairpins. "I was just about to return to the wagons."

"If you don't mind, I'll walk with you."

"Of course." As she started to rise, he stepped closer and offered her a hand. Self-consciously, she took hold and was pulled quickly to her feet.

They walked in silence for several minutes before David spoke again. "You really shouldn't go so far from the train alone, Mrs. Branigan. You never know what—or *who* might be out there."

"I'm afraid I didn't think of that." She felt herself growing warm as she confessed, "I just wanted to take a bath." She was thankful he didn't turn to glance down at her. It was terrifying to think of a man seeing her unclothed. No man ever had except for Farrell.

It wasn't until they reached the Branigan wagon that David Foster did look at her again. His expression was friendly but detached. He touched the brim of his dusty hat. "Remember what I said about staying close to the wagons, ma'am."

"I will, Mr. Foster."

The wagon master nodded once, then turned and strode away. Maureen stared after him for a moment, her thoughts strangely jumbled.

It wasn't easy to be alone on a wagon train. Maggie couldn't escape to a room and close a door. She had no choice but to spend the day and evening in the company of the Branigans.

Supper was over, the dishes washed and packed away. The clear sky was alight with a full moon and twinkling stars. The fire had burned low, revealing white–glowing coals. Maggie sat on the ground, her back against the wagon wheel, watching as Maureen led her younger children in their evening prayers. Rachel watched, too, from the circle of Maggie's arm.

Maggie didn't know where Tucker was. He'd joined the family for supper but had disappeared as soon as the meal was finished. He'd scarcely looked at her throughout the meal and hadn't spoken to her even once. Maggie wasn't sure why it bothered her, but it did. Hadn't she wanted to be left alone, not to be asked any questions? Still, she couldn't help wondering where he was at this very moment.

"All right. Off to bed, children," Maureen said as she rose from her knees.

Maggie's arm tightened about Rachel's shoul-

ders. "You, too, kitten." She kissed the top of her
sister's head.

"Rachel, would you like to sleep in the wagon
with me tonight?"

Maggie looked up to find Fiona standing before
them, her green eyes watching hopefully as she
awaited an answer. Maggie was certain she would
hear Rachel's quick denial. She expected to feel her
little sister drawing closer for protection. Instead,
Rachel turned to look up at her.

"Would it be all right, Maggie?" she asked softly.

"Well, I . . ."

She felt surprised and strangely betrayed. Rachel
had always turned to her. Only yesterday, she had
been too frightened and shy even to gather twigs for
the fire with Fiona. Now she was asking to spend
the night in the wagon with her. But if Rachel was
working up the courage to make friends, Maggie
couldn't allow herself to discourage it, even if she
did feel deserted and suddenly alone.

"Of course, you can. If it's all right with Mrs.
Branigan."

Maureen grinned as she walked over. "Rachel
doesn't take up much room. She's more than welcome."

It wasn't long before the children were tucked
into bed, and scarcely longer than that before
Maureen had turned in as well. The camp had
grown silent around them. There was little else for
Maggie to do but crawl beneath the wagon and into
her bedroll.

She was still awake when Tucker strolled into
sight. She couldn't see his face, but his form was a
clear silhouette in the light of the moon. She
recognized his shoulders and the way he walked

and . . . There was no mistaking it was Tucker. He paused, still some distance away. Though she couldn't see his face, somehow she knew he was looking her way, staring with those intense brown eyes of his into the shadows beneath the wagon.

There was a strange tingling in her stomach. Maggie rolled over and covered her head with her blankets.

It was a long time before she slept.

Chapter Six

The sentinels on duty fired their rifles, signaling the end of sleep. It was four o'clock.

Startled by the sound, Maggie sat up quickly, cracking her head against the wagon bed. She stifled her cry of pain as she opened her eyes to glance about. It was still as dark as pitch, the moon having long since treked its way across the vast heavens and sunk beneath the western horizon.

"Come along, girls," she heard Maureen saying above her. "It's time to get up. Fiona, tell your brothers to start the fire for me."

The night was over, but Maggie felt anything but rested. When she had finally fallen asleep, it hadn't been a peaceful slumber. She'd been troubled by dreams of her uncle, of running and hiding and being found. And more troubling yet, she'd dreamed of Tucker, watching her, always watching her.

Pushing her tangled mop of curls away from her face, Maggie drew a deep breath, then reached for her dress and slipped into it beneath the cover of blankets. Feet still bare, she crawled out from under the wagon.

The campfire was just coming to life, its weak light flickering across Tucker's face as he knelt beside it, blowing on the sparks. His eyes still had the look of sleep about them; his hair was tousled and fell across his forehead, giving him a surprisingly boyish appearance.

"Good morning, Maggie," he said without looking at her.

"Good morning, Mr. Branigan."

She wasn't certain, but she thought she detected just the hint of a smile near the corner of his mouth. She was wondering what had caused it when Maureen climbed down from the back of the wagon.

"Good morning, Maggie." Without pausing, she walked over to the fire and placed a hand on Tucker's shoulder. "I can do that now, Tucker. Why don't you and Maggie get the mules while I fix breakfast."

He nodded as he rose, dropping a kiss on his mother's cheek as he did so. His gaze shifted toward Maggie, starting at the bare toes peeking from beneath her dress, then moving up until their eyes met. "Better get your shoes on."

She didn't know why his comment made her flush with embarrassment. Perhaps it was because it was the second time in as many days that he'd caught her without shoes. It made her feel childish, and for some reason, that wasn't the way she wanted to feel around Tucker Branigan.

"There's bound to be a snake or two in the grass,

and I don't want you squealing and scaring the livestock." The smile was definitely there.

On the heels of her embarrassment came indignation. He was laughing at her. That's why he was grinning that way.

"I won't be doing any squealing," she snapped, flouncing down on the ground and pulling on her shoes.

Tucker couldn't stop grinning as he led the way toward the livestock, Maggie following close behind. Occasionally, he could hear her grumbling, and he knew he was the subject of most of her muttered comments. He wasn't sure why he was getting so much perverse pleasure from riling her, but he was.

Maggie was a strange mixture of girl and woman. He sensed a stubborn strength within her, yet there was also something strangely fragile about her. He'd thought at first it was merely her undeniable beauty that kept her in his thoughts, but now he wasn't so certain. There was much more to Maggie Harris than her looks that intrigued him.

She wasn't comfortable around the mules, that was clear enough. She had no idea how to handle the stubborn animals as they led them back toward the wagon and began the morning ritual of harnessing them and putting them into the traces. Tucker had to tell her what to do more than once. But she didn't give up or back down. She just pressed her lips tighter together and tried again, her gray eyes narrowing in concentration.

"Never helped your father hitch up a team back on your farm in Pennsylvania?"

Maggie glanced at him over the back of a mule, then dropped her gaze to the harness again. "We didn't have a farm. We lived in town."

He remembered the clumsy way she'd saddled that sorry horse of hers when he'd found them by the river. "Didn't do much riding either, huh?"

"No." She obviously wanted no part in his idle chatter.

What is it you're trying to hide, Maggie Harris? Tucker wondered as he paused to watch her fumbling with the leather straps, holding herself slightly away from the mule whose ears were laid back on its head.

He decided to try a different approach. "I see Rachel and Fiona are becoming friends."

Maggie's gaze followed his. The two young girls were carrying a bucket of water up from the stream. Water was sloshing over the sides, dampening their skirts. They were both laughing.

Tucker looked at Maggie and tried to pinpoint the exact emotion he read there. It was almost bittersweet. Her love for her little sister was clear, yet there was something heartbreaking in her eyes.

"Rachel's never had a friend before," Maggie whispered, as if to herself.

Tucker was just opening his mouth to ask her why that was when he heard a cry of pain. He dropped the harness and dashed around the wagon.

Maureen was seated on the ground, her head bent forward, clasping her right arm against her breast. The black kettle and tripod were overturned beside her. The three youngsters were standing nearby, their eyes wide with alarm.

"Mother! What happened?" He knelt beside her.

"My arm," she managed to say through clenched teeth. "I scalded it."

Gingerly, Tucker took hold of her wrist and drew her arm away from her body. An angry red welt ran the length of it, from the heel of her hand to the inside of her elbow.

"It's my fault, Tucker." Neal stepped forward. His chin was quivering, and he was fighting back tears. "Mother was putting more wood in the fire, and I came running over to help her. My foot kicked the leg and —"

Maureen reached out with her left hand to touch her youngest son's shirt sleeve. "It wasn't your fault, Neal. It was an accident."

"Here, Mrs. Branigan. Stick your arm in the bucket."

Tucker looked up as Maggie knelt on the ground opposite him.

"It'll help ease the pain," she continued, carefully taking Maureen's arm from Tucker's grasp and lowering it into the bucket which Fiona and Rachel had carried up from the stream only moments before. "Don't take it out until the burning stops." Her eyes met Tucker's. "Do you have any gauze? We should wrap it so the air can't get to it."

"Neal, get the medicine kit."

Tucker's brother raced to obey his command, pushing his way through the group of women and men who had hurried over in response to Maureen's cry. By the time Neal returned with the bandages, David had arrived.

"What's happened here?"

It was Maureen who answered, looking up at the wagon master with pain–filled eyes of green. "It's nothing serious, Mr. Foster. I burned my arm, but it will be fine."

"Let me take a look at it."

Maureen lifted her arm from the bucket, wincing as air touched the tender, red flesh. Maggie promptly pushed the arm back under water.

"It's not that bad, really," Maureen protested.

David let his glance sweep over the crowd. "Mrs. Branigan's going to be all right, folks. Best get back to your wagons. We'll be pulling out soon." As the people dispersed, he looked down at Maureen once again. "That's going to be sore for some time, ma'am. You take care of it."

"I will, Mr. Foster."

The wagon master smiled briefly at her, then shifted his eyes toward the children. "Neal, you finish harnessing the team. Fiona, you and Rachel get that tent rolled up and put in the wagon while Tucker and Maggie tend to Mrs. Branigan." With a quick glance back at Maureen, he touched the brim of his hat, then strode away.

"I feel so foolish. All this fuss . . . " Maureen began as she tried to pull her arm from the bucket a second time.

Maggie was having no part in it. "Sit still until I tell you to move, Mrs. Branigan. If you don't, you're going to hurt like the dickens." She looked up at Tucker once again. "She's not going to be able to drive the wagon. You'll have to show me what to do."

Tucker was nearly as surprised as Maureen. He'd seen how nervous Maggie was around the mules, and he knew she had no experience driving a wagon. But then, maybe he wasn't so surprised after all. He'd suspected from the first, as he'd watched her facing the people on the train, that she had grit and gumption.

Still, he protested. "I'll do it until Mother's well."

"You can't drive all the time. You need to hunt. I heard Mr. Foster saying it'll be more than two weeks before we reach Fort Kearny and can restock supplies."

She was right, of course. Tucker was needed away from the wagon a great deal of the time. He knew Neal would volunteer, but although Neal liked to think he could handle the mule teams, the boy wasn't strong enough if there was trouble of any kind. Maggie was the logical solution for the times when Tucker couldn't be with the wagon.

Maggie wasn't looking at him any longer. She had turned her attention back to Maureen. "Let's try and get this wrapped, Mrs. Branigan," she said softly as she drew his mother's arm from the water and began patting it dry with a cloth. "Some folks put butter on a burn, but our cook always said it was better not to. The time I burned my hand helping her with supper, she wrapped it like this and it was well in no time."

Tucker scarcely heard Maggie's words as he watched her carefully wrapping the injured arm with the gauze bandage. His gaze took in not only the angry welt running the length of his mother's forearm but the calluses covering Maureen's once perfect hands.

He felt a sudden surge of guilt. Maybe Devlin had been right. Maybe he *should* have stayed behind in Georgia and fought to get Twin Willows back. Maybe he *had* just given in to the carpetbaggers and thieves. Maybe it *was* his fault his mother was forced to work like a field hand, her hands work–worn and callused.

He got to his feet and walked beyond the circle of wagons. His hands shoved into his pockets, he stared out over the endless plains, feeling suddenly more beaten and tired than he had at Appomattox. It seemed he'd spent most of his life battling unbeatable odds. Where was it he was taking his family, anyway? To an untamed territory called

Idaho where only God knew what awaited them. Might it not have been better to stay where he at least recognized the dangers, where he at least felt equipped to fight the enemy?

"Mr. Branigan?"

He turned his head toward the sound of Maggie's voice. She was standing beside him, her gray eyes staring out over the prairie as his had moments before.

"Your mother will be fine."

"I know."

She looked up at him then. Such large gray eyes. "When your mother was kind enough to take us in, I told her we didn't expect charity. We'd work to pay our way. I meant it. I can handle the team. I'm stronger than I look. You just show me what to do."

"All right, Miss Harris."

Chapter Seven

*T*he muscles in Maggie's neck and shoulders screamed for relief, and the palms of her hands burned despite the gloves Tucker had given her to wear. Through the morning, he'd ridden beside her on the wagon seat, giving her instructions, correcting her when she made mistakes. But after the noon rest, he'd saddled his black gelding and ridden up to the front of the train. He had yet to return.

As nervous as she was handling the mules alone, Maggie was relieved by his absence. She had found it disconcerting to sit next to him for so many hours. At least he hadn't pried her with questions or tried to make small talk. When he wasn't telling her what to do next, he'd seemed to be off in another world somewhere, lost deep in thought. His face had been troubled, clouded.

"Ho! Giddup there," she shouted as the mules started up a short incline.

She found herself leaning slightly to one side, trying to spot Tucker on Blue Boy. She could see some women and children walking alongside the trail and a man with a whip, urging his plodding oxen onward. And she could see dust. Plenty of dust. But she couldn't see Tucker.

She straightened back into her seat, giving herself a mental shake. *Maggie Harris, you quit this. You've got enough troubles without taking on the Branigans' troubles too, whatever they might be.*

But she couldn't help wondering about this family, couldn't help pondering what had brought them west. Tucker had said his father died. But there had to be more to it than that. She might have lived a good portion of her life shut up in a house that was more prison than home, but she wasn't blind—or stupid either. The Branigans were gentry. The clothes they wore, though old and mended, were quality. Tucker's horse was the finest animal on the train, and even she could spot an expensive saddle when she saw one.

She sighed as she stretched her neck to one side, then the other, trying to relieve the ache of tense muscles. She supposed everyone had the right to their secrets. She'd best keep to her own business and let Tucker worry about his.

Tucker rode beside David without speaking, his thoughts miles behind him. He could still see Maggie, her face scrunched up in concentration as she listened to his instructions. She had been nervous but determined.

He wished he understood the girl better. One moment she was as skittish as a newborn colt, the next she was as stubborn as one of their mules. Her clothes were old and of poor quality, yet she spoke about her family having their own cook. There were times when she was shy and uncertain, as if she'd never been around people before. And then, at other times, he thought her eyes looked wise beyond her years, as if she'd seen far more than a girl her age should ever see. She'd been quick to take control when Maureen burned her arm, yet was often tongue–tied in the warmth and peace of a family setting.

Maggie was a puzzle, and he was spending far too much time trying to figure her out.

He'd been glad to turn over the reins to her and ride up to join David. It wasn't that he was needed here more than there. Actually, if there were trouble with the teams, he doubted Maggie would have a prayer of handling them. Still, he had needed some time away from her. He had known it the moment he'd wondered if her lips would taste as sweet as they looked.

"We've been lucky with the weather."

"What?" Tucker turned his head toward David.

"I said we've been lucky with the weather. Spring can be mighty wet along this neck of the woods. Rivers swell up in a hurry. I've been stuck for more 'n two weeks before I could cross, just 'cause of the rain."

Tucker looked up at the clear blue sky.

"Once we get along the Platte, we'll be prayin' for rain." David gave a short chuckle. "Guess there's no keepin' a man happy."

Tucker nodded in agreement.

A few minutes more of silence, and Tucker's thoughts returned to Maggie.

Maggie was too tired that night even to eat supper. Camp was barely set up before she crawled beneath the wagon and fell into a deep sleep.

And there was little difference in the days that
followed. Maureen and the children cooked and
cleaned. Maggie and Tucker took care of the livestock, sometimes with Neal's help, sometimes without. During the day, Maggie drove the mule teams,
becoming a little more proficient each day with the
reins and whip. Tucker made a few offers in those
early days to spell her from the driving chore, but
Maggie refused every one. Finally, he no longer
tried.

Tucker often was out looking for game; he took
his turn with tending the livestock and rounding up
strays. Sometimes he helped David Foster scout out
the trail ahead. There was little or no time for
conversation between Maggie and Tucker other
than a quick good morning. Even while they were
working together hitching the teams to the wagon,
Maggie was too weary to make conversation. And
more often than not, she was asleep before Tucker
returned to camp to eat his evening meal.

Maggie awoke before the sentries could sound the
morning alarm. She lay still for a moment, staring
up at the darkness, wondering if she could even
move. There seemed to be no escaping the
weariness—or the dirt. How she would dearly love
an all–over bath. Perhaps tomorrow, if they were
lucky enough to camp near a clear–flowing stream,
she could find a way to have that bath. Tomorrow
was Sunday, and David Foster being a God–fearing
man, Sundays were always a day of rest. She would
have the whole day to find just the right spot.

She closed her eyes and imagined a steaming hot
tub, filled with perfumed bath soap. Uncle Seth had

been too stingy to supply them with such luxuries, but she remembered well enough all the wonderful perfumes and soaps that had lined her mother's vanity table.

Of course, it wouldn't be like that tomorrow. It would be cold, and the only soap she could probably find would be much harsher than those her mother had used. But she would be skin–deep clean. And she would scrub her clothes too. She worried about how long the already worn clothes would last her. She only had the two dresses. She pictured in her mind a new dress. Something blue and frilly with many petticoats beneath. Something like her mother used to wear.

She remembered the night of that last Christmas ball and how beautiful Elizabeth Harris had looked as she floated down the staircase to take her husband's arm. Maggie had thought there could never be anyone more beautiful than her mother, nor a man more handsome than her father, Jeremy.

Giving herself an angry mental shake, Maggie crawled out from beneath the wagon. It didn't serve her any purpose to go thinking about her parents that way. Elizabeth and Jeremy Harris were dead and buried, and Maggie wouldn't be wearing pretty gowns and looking like her mother nor walking out with handsome men like her father. Her uncle had taken that away from her years before. Her life now, as it had been for the past five years, was survival. All she could look forward to was getting through it as best she could.

She looked up at the heavens, expecting to see stars, but the sky was heavy with clouds.

Perhaps, just perhaps, things would be different for her when she found Marcus Sanderson. *If* she found Marcus Sanderson. If what Seth had said were true, there might be money and security awaiting them. But *only* if she found Marcus Sanderson. Without him, God only knew what the future held in store.

The rain began in midafternoon. It was a mere trickle at first, settling the dust as the Foster train passed along the prairie trail. It felt good as it spattered against Maggie's cheeks, cool and clean. She smiled and stuck out her tongue to catch some rain drops, mimicking Fiona and Rachel who had crawled up beside her on the wagon seat when the rain began.

But before long the wind came up, driving the rain against the wagons like tiny shards of glass. Tucker came galloping out of the darkening storm, shouting to Maggie that they were stopping for the night and for Maureen and Neal to get into the wagon. Another time, Maggie might have been happy for the day to end early, but she knew they weren't in for a night of rest. Not if the storm kept up this way.

They didn't turn the mules loose with the other livestock that night. Instead, they staked them close to the wagon. Maggie and Tucker were both soaked through to the skin by the time they joined the rest of the family inside the cramped quarters of the covered wagon. Maureen gave them each a blanket to wrap up in while they waited for the storm to abate.

When the thunder started, off in the distance, Tucker noticed the change in Maggie's face. He'd been watching her in the dim light of the wagon. Her brown hair, the curls normally so unruly and full, was slicked tightly against her scalp. It made her wide eyes seem even larger than usual. He'd been unconsciously enjoying the look of beaded moisture on her high cheekbones and, for the first time, he became aware of the tiny dimples near the corners of her mouth.

The rolling sound was hardly noticeable at first. It was Maggie who made him aware of its presence. He saw her draw the blanket more closely around her, and he sensed her shivering was due more to the thunder than to the cold. Her gaze went somewhere beyond the tied–down canvas flap.

"Maggie . . ." he said, reaching out to touch her knee.

She jumped at the contact, her eyes turning on him. They were wide with fear, like those of a trapped doe awaiting the first strike of the hounds. He doubted she even saw him.

"It's only thunder."

Rachel moved from Fiona's side and snuggled up against her sister, her short arms wrapping around Maggie's waist. There was nothing childlike in her tone of voice as she said, "She's afraid of the thunder. Our uncle used to—"

"Hush, Rachel." Maggie's eyes focused on Tucker. "I'm all right. Just a little cold is all."

"You need to get out of those wet things," Maureen said firmly. "Girls, help me hang a blanket across here. Then Maggie and Tucker can get into some dry clothes before they catch their death. Neal, you get over there with your brother."

Thunder boomed across the plains, closer this time, rumbling deep as it rolled toward the circled wagons. Maggie's face whitened, her lips pressed firmly together. Her fingers made fists into the fabric of the blanket. Tucker was afraid she was going to faint.

But she didn't.

As the sound faded behind them, she moved to the front of the wagon, digging out her dry clothes while Maureen and the two young girls stretched a blanket across the center of their home on wheels.

MAUREEN'S JOURNAL

May 11. I have been unable to make an entry for several days as I burned my arm, and it has been too painful to write. But my wound is healing quickly, and I shall be completely well soon.

Today we had to stop the wagons due to a storm. The rains fell in great roaring diagonal sheets. The trail turned to mud beneath the wheels. Sharp forks of lightning, like nothing I had ever seen before, lit the sky. The bright flashes of light made the trees look like grotesque skeletons. The lightning was followed by long rolling peals of thunder that shook the earth. When it was over, a cool wind swept across the prairie, carrying with it the most wonderful scent of fresh rain and green grass.

We are wet, as is most everything we possess. I am thankful tomorrow is Sunday and a day of rest.

Chapter Eight

*D*ay dawned, fresh and clean. The sky was clear, the climbing sun bringing warmth. While many of the emigrants, including the Branigans and Rachel, met for the Sunday worship service, Maggie gathered her meager belongings, a bar of soap, a towel to dry with, and a blanket to sit on, then headed for the nearest stream.

Tucker caught up with her before she'd walked fifty yards. "Where do you think you're off to so early in the morning?"

For some reason, she wasn't surprised by his sudden appearance. It was almost as if she'd been expecting him. "That way." She pointed straight ahead. "That's where I'm off to." She smiled, already imagining a long swim in the cool water. Without stopping or looking back at Tucker, she added, "To the stream."

"You shouldn't leave camp without telling some-one." He fell into step beside her.

"Why should I disturb their Sunday worship? It's not that far away. Besides, it's warm and sunny and I intend to wash some things—including myself. And I don't need anyone's help for that."

"Maggie." His fingers closed around her arm, pulling her to a halt and forcing her to look at him. "Haven't you learned anything about the trail? You don't just wander off alone. You heard from Mother what Mr. Foster told her after she pulled the same sort of stunt. It could be dangerous out there."

Maggie's temper flared at his high-handed tone. She glared up at him as she jerked her arm free of his grasp. "I don't care if it is dangerous. I promised myself a bath today, and I'm going to have one."

"Then I'm coming with you."

Was he insane or just simpleminded? Did he think she would allow him to come *bathe* with her?

The determined frown eased from his brow, replaced by a lighter look. "I promise to behave the gentleman." He swept off his slouch hat and exe-cuted an exaggerated bow. "You'll have complete privacy. I'll just post myself close by and keep a look out." His grin was open and friendly.

There was that odd tingly feeling again. The idea of Tucker being close by while she bathed . . .

What was she thinking? "I don't need you," she snapped.

"Need me or not"—his frown returned—"I'm coming. Or you're not going."

She spun away from him and started walking, shouting back over her shoulder, "Who do you think you are to tell me what I can or cannot do?" She lifted her skirt and walked a little faster. Her temper grew hotter with every step she took.

"I think I'm the man in charge until we reach our destination."

She froze in mid-step, whirling around to face him. "You're not my master, Mr. Branigan. Nobody owns me and nobody is going to tell me *what* I can do or *where* I can go."

Tucker's jaw tightened and his brown eyes narrowed. He tapped his leg with his hat. "I'd pity the man who tried to be your master, Maggie Harris, but you needn't worry. I don't want that honor. However, I am responsible for you until we can hand you over to someone else to get you to your parents. And as long as I'm responsible for your safety and well-being, you *will* obey me, like it or not."

What had she done, trusting herself to strangers? She'd sworn no one would ever order her around again, no one would ever control her actions once she'd escaped Seth. Now here she was, beneath the thumb of another dictator.

She was fuming inside, knowing by the look in his eyes that she couldn't win this one. She had two options. Return to the wagons and forget the bath or take him with her. She was tempted to let her temper sway her to the former, but her longing for a bath was too great. Even the odious Mr. Branigan could be tolerated for that cause.

"All right, Mr. Branigan," she said, her voice shaking with anger. Once again, she turned her back on him and stalked off in the direction of the wooded stream. "But if you don't behave, I'll take my knife to your throat while you sleep."

And she meant it, too.

* * *

Tucker wasn't sure how his joking had turned into an argument. When he'd seen Maggie walking away from the camp, he'd wanted only to walk with her, perhaps get to know her a little better. She'd been a real trooper since joining them, never once complaining, though he knew she was tired and must ache from head to toe now that she was driving the mules. Surely, she'd known he wouldn't stoop so low as to spy on a woman in her bath. He'd only wanted to make sure she was safe.

Yet, staring at Maggie's back as she marched toward the copse of trees bordering the swift-flowing stream, swollen by the previous day's rain, he thought it wouldn't be an unpleasant way to spend a quiet morning. He imagined her wild honey-brown hair floating on top of the water, her white breasts barely hidden beneath the surface. What would it be like to feel her pressed against him, her smooth skin touching . . .

Good Lord! He stopped dead in his tracks. *Get hold of yourself, Branigan.*

He couldn't allow himself to daydream about Maggie that way. She was a lady. Maybe she didn't have the same polish as his sister Shannon or his mother or even Charmaine Pinkham, but she was still a lady.

He'd thought himself in love with Charmaine, and he'd never allowed his musings to stray in that direction. When he was away from home during the war, he'd often daydreamed of Charmaine, but he'd always thought of her as sitting sedately by the fire or waltzing with him in the ballroom or riding through the cotton fields at Twin Willows. Never once had he imagined her in her bath.

But Maggie. Maggie in her bath. A beautifully

unclothed Maggie. Fiery and stubborn and willful Maggie. He brought himself up short once again.

Damn! He'd been without a woman too long. The last thing he needed was to get mixed up *that* way with a girl like Maggie.

"I'll wait here," he called after her.

She didn't even acknowledge him.

Tucker sat on a rock and drew a cigarillo from his pocket. As a trail of blue smoke curled skyward, he glanced toward the trees again. She was quite a girl. Scared and shy one moment, determined and feisty the next. He couldn't ever be sure what her reaction would be. She wasn't like any of the other ladies of his acquaintance. But for some unfathomable reason, Tucker wanted to know her better.

While her freshly washed clothing lay across bushes to dry, Maggie dove into the deep, clear water and returned to the surface with a gasp. As cold as the water was, it felt wonderful. It drove all thoughts of anger and Tucker Branigan from her head. She closed her eyes and floated in the current a moment, then swam toward the opposite bank and back again. It had been years since she'd been swimming.

Memories of summers spent by the lake with her parents flooded over her. She and her father had loved to swim. He would take her out in the skiff, and they would dive into the cold water and swim for hours, racing each other to and fro, then returning to shore to bask in the warm sun. Elizabeth would scold her about damaging her complexion, but she never spoiled her daughter's fun by making her hide beneath the shade of the umbrella.

Maggie smiled, allowing the happy thoughts to

flow over her like the rushing stream, then dove underwater, as if to wash them away again.

Finally, she swam toward shore and grabbed the soap. She'd been pleased to find Maureen Branigan had brought along several bars of jasmine-scented soap, and with relish she began to scrub herself from head to toe. She worked up a lather in her thick tresses, then held her breath as she rinsed it away.

Unable to delay it any longer, she reluctantly rose from the water and walked toward shore, her bare feet searching for steady footing between the smooth stones lining the stream bottom. She wrapped herself in the waiting towel, then sat on the blanket amidst the long grass, her legs tucked beneath her, and began to comb the snarls from her hair. The sun felt good on her scalp.

Maggie let the comb fall idle in her hand as she lay back, the warming earth beneath her, the warm sun overhead. She listened to the sound of the rushing water, the chirping of birds in the nearby trees, the slight rustle of the field grass. It all sounded so tranquil. She could almost forget the past few weeks and the hardships that had filled each day. And she wouldn't allow herself to think about the coming weeks filled with more of the same. For now, she wanted only to revel in the sunshine on her face and the glorious feeling of being clean of dust and grime.

Tucker returned to her thoughts suddenly and totally uninvited. She could see the twinkle in his eye, hear the laughter in his voice, as he bowed and promised to be her protector. She'd known even then that Tucker was too much of a gentleman to spy on her from the bushes. She didn't know what

had possessed her to accuse him of such a thing. If
he didn't make her feel so . . . so . . .

"Oooh!"

She sat up, her eyes open, her mood destroyed. In
frustration, she tossed the comb to the ground and
jumped to her feet. She didn't want to think about
Tucker. Every time she did, she became confused.

She turned to see if her clothes were dry yet, then
stopped, the scream rising in her throat.

The Indian's face remained impassive.

The scream turned Tucker's blood cold. He
pulled his revolver from his holster as he raced
toward the stream. Maggie came running out of the
trees, her towel flying open to reveal long, slender
legs. She flew into his arms, then twisted to point
behind her.

"Indians," she gasped.

Even as she spoke, three red men rode toward
them on painted ponies.

Tucker pushed her behind him. "Go on back to
camp," he said quietly. "Don't run, but don't waste
any time either. Find Foster."

"Tucker . . ."

"Go on, Maggie."

Tucker stood his ground, waiting for the Indians
to reach him. Two of them reined in their horses;
the third came closer. His skin was weathered and
heavily wrinkled. His black eyes were tired, his
braided hair as gray as Aunt Eugenia's. Was this the
marauding savage they'd been warned about upon
leaving Independence?

The Indian raised a hand in a sign of peace. "We
come, make trade."

Tucker's glance shifted quickly to the other two.

He saw no rifles, no threat. The three men looked more hungry than warrior-like. He holstered his gun. He was about to speak when he heard the clatter of hooves and turned to see David loping his horse toward him. He breathed a sigh of relief. David had dealt with the Indians before and would be better equipped to handle them than he was.

An hour later, Tucker watched as the three Kanza Indians galloped their ponies away from the wagons, carrying sugar, coffee, and other sundries and leaving behind a promise that the Foster train would have no trouble from their people.

"I doubt they could have caused us much trouble anyway," Tucker said to David as they stood outside the circled wagons. "They were just old men."

"They're hungry mostly. Washington hasn't exactly treated them with fairness. But that doesn't mean they don't know how to fight back. At the very least, they could have stolen a few cows or run off the horses at night." David scratched the stubble on his chin. "Doesn't hurt to deal with 'em this way when you can. But if you're waitin' for Injun trouble, you might still see it before this trip's over. I hear there's somethin' brewin' in West Kansas, and Sioux and Cheyenne country lies ahead of us."

"Believe me. I have no itch to see action with the Indians."

"War does that to most men." He glanced at Tucker, then turned toward the train. "What rank were you, Tuck?"

"Lieutenant Colonel, with General Lee's army in Virginia."

"I was with the Army of the Potomac. Sergeant."

The enemy. David had fought with the enemy. David had *been* the enemy. They might even have fought against each other on the battlefield. Tucker felt a tightening in his gut.

David laid a hand on the younger man's shoulder. "Had my fill of war and hate. It's why I came back to leadin' folks west. Maybe, away from the destruction, we can forgive and forget." The hand slipped from Tucker's shoulder and was offered in friendship.

Tucker stared at David's open palm. It hadn't ever occurred to him that the wagon master had been a soldier in the War Between the States. He'd assumed the man had always lived out West, leading trains even during the war years. He liked David, considered him a friend. Should it matter where he'd been four, five, or six years before? Hadn't Tucker found relief in ceasing to think, "he's a Yank", "he's a Southerner"?

"I can forgive the soldiers," Tucker finally said, taking hold of David's hand with a firm grip, "but I won't ever forget what the swarming scum that came after did. And I mean to see no one can ever do the same to me or mine again."

"Fair enough. Fair enough."

"Tucker!" Neal jumped over a wagon tongue and ran toward him. "Mother says you're to go down to the stream and bring back Maggie's clothes."

"Maggie's . . ." He glanced toward the Branigan wagon. He'd forgotten during all the commotion about Maggie's part in all this. But now that he remembered, he remembered it all. The way she'd run toward him, the towel flying back to reveal her long legs. The way she'd felt in his arms, her shoulders bare, her breasts barely concealed from view.

At the time, he'd been too alarmed by her fearful

cry, and all his senses had been alert to danger. But now he found nothing else worth recalling except Maggie and how she'd looked, how she'd felt, how she'd smelled. That was all there was.

No, there was one more thing he remembered. She hadn't called him Mr. Branigan this time. She'd called him Tucker, and even laced with terror, he'd liked the way his name sounded on her lips.

He felt a sudden surge of desire, strong and urgent.

"Tell Mother I'll get them," he said to Neal, then hurried off toward the beckoning stream.

A dip in that cold water might be just what he needed himself—but not for the sake of a bath!

Blast her hide, anyway.

Maggie sat inside the wagon, still wrapped in the blanket. She didn't know if she'd ever been more frightened than when she found herself staring into those black, expressionless eyes. Yet it wasn't her fear she kept remembering. Nor was it the Indian's silent threat that caused her pulse to race. It was the memory of Tucker's arms around her, his brown eyes filled with concern, the protective way he'd pushed her behind him, putting himself in harm's way to save her.

She leaned forward, looking out the back of the wagon, wondering when he was going to return with her clothing. She'd washed both of her dresses, thinking they would have time to dry before she donned one of them again. And she'd washed more than just her dresses. Her face warmed, thinking of Tucker gathering her intimate undergarments and returning them to her.

"Why doesn't he get back?" she mumbled to herself.

At least then she could get out of this stuffy wagon. But she couldn't very well traipse around all day in this blanket. Didn't he know she was almost a prisoner until he brought back her clothes?

"You waiting for these?" a voice said from the opposite end of the wagon.

Maggie turned quickly, nearly falling over the clutter that filled the Branigan wagon. Her hands tightened on the blanket, holding it closer around her, unknowingly revealing more of her figure than she concealed.

"You had quite a scare. Guess David was right about it being dangerous to wander off alone."

"They didn't mean me any harm." She reached for the clothing, snatching the articles from his hand.

"You didn't know that."

She wasn't in the mood for an "I told you so" from Tucker. Besides, she didn't like the way his gaze was lingering on her—or perhaps she liked it too much. "Well, I *wasn't* harmed, so it's better forgotten. Now, if you'd leave me alone so I can get dressed . . ." She let her voice drift off while she leveled a speaking glance his way.

That cocky grin flashed again. "Your pardon, ma'am."

The flap fell shut, leaving her in semidarkness.

"You won't trust him, Maggie Harris," she whispered aloud. "You won't *ever* trust him, no matter what he does. You can't trust anybody ever again. Don't you forget that."

She pulled on her drawers and gave the draw-string a hearty tug.

"You'll take care of yourself and Rachel, just like you planned." She squeezed her eyes shut, as if to give emphasis to her words, repeating one more time, "Just like you always planned."

MAUREEN'S JOURNAL

May 12. We had a terrible fright today. Three Indians—Kanza Indians, Mr. Foster called them—chanced upon Maggie while she was bathing in the stream. It seems they only came to barter for food, but it still causes me to wonder about the tales I've heard of the savages' atrocities upon white women. These were old, tired men, yet I know there are younger men of their tribe out there somewhere. Our wagon train seemed large when we left Independence. Now it seems terribly small and the men too few. I know I shall be more careful about wandering away from camp in the future.

I am reminded of the Yankees' attack on Twin Willows in '64, and the sense of helplessness as men ransack and destroy even the smallest mementos, items of no monetary worth but filled with memories. The fear that they mean to do you bodily harm, and you are without power to stop them. It all came flooding back with Maggie's terrifying scream.

This wilderness seems unfriendly and I friendless. I shall not sleep tonight.

Chapter Nine

*The luxuriant grass of the Kansas prairies in mid-*May spread before the Foster wagon train like a rolling green sea. Wild flowers bloomed amid the grass like colorful banners, proclaiming the beauty of this untamed land to all who came near. The spring climate was mild, the plains bucolic.

By their third week on the trail, the emigrants had become more proficient at handling their live-stock and wagons. The routine was a part of them now. Though the days were long and filled with hard work, their moods were light. By evening, the wagons circled and their camps made, they still had the energy for games and dancing.

Night had fallen. The May evening was balmy, friendly. The sky was dotted with a thousand tiny lights. Beyond the wagon at her back, Maggie could hear the fiddle playing, the hands clapping as couples danced and sang. It was a merry sound.

Sometimes she was tempted to join the others. She felt lonely, yet stubbornly kept herself at arm's length from everyone on the train, reminding herself again and again that she couldn't trust anyone but herself to take care of Rachel, to insure the security of their future.

But her determination didn't lessen her loneliness, a feeling exacerbated by Rachel's defection.

Her shy little sister had become fast friends with Fiona. She slept every night in the wagon now, and as much as Maggie sometimes wanted to deny her the request, she couldn't allow herself to force Rachel to sleep on the hard, lumpy ground when she could share a bed with Fiona.

But worse than the friendship with Fiona—in Maggie's opinion—was Rachel's affection for Tucker. It had begun that first night when he'd told her the story about his dog to distract her thoughts from the dead rabbit. Each day, she'd grown a little more at ease with him, until last night, Maggie had actually seen her climb into Tucker's lap and ask him to tell her another story about his hound.

Was she destined to be all alone in this world?

"Why don't you join us, Maggie?"

Tucker's softly spoken words, coming in the wake of her own silent question, brought a started gasp to her lips. She turned her head to find him leaning against the end of the wagon, hidden in shadows, only his outline and the red glow of his thin cigar letting her know he was really there.

"I'm fine where I am," she replied. Even she could hear the lie in her words.

The cigarillo dropped to the earth and was ground under the heel of his boot. He stepped toward her. "You know, the Branigans aren't really such a bad lot."

"I know." She looked back up at the night sky.

He came closer. "Come on. You might make some friends if you let yourself. Everyone on the train would like to get to know you. I know Mother would enjoy your company." He was silent a moment. "I would too. Come with me."

She shook her head. She wanted him to go away, yet knew she would feel worse if he did. There was a funny thudding in her chest that she'd never felt before.

"Maggie . . ."

She refused to look at him, her thoughts a mass of confusion.

"Dance with me, Maggie Harris."

She hugged herself with her arms, suddenly chilled, her pulse quickening even more. "I—I can't. I don't know how to dance. I never learned."

He reached out and took hold of her hand, pulling her to her feet. "It's easy," he whispered somewhere near her ear. "I'll show you."

Don't do this. Don't do this. Don't do this.

He was right. It was easy. His hand in the small of her back guided her effortlessly in slow, easy circles. Her tiny, callused hand had disappeared within his much larger, more callused one. There was a strange buzzing in her head. She could barely hear the music now.

Maggie had never been held in a man's arms like this. She was aware of his scent. He'd washed in the stream. She could tell because it wasn't the smell of sweat and dust. It was . . . it was Tucker.

Her nostrils flared slightly. Her head felt light, and she was scarcely aware that he'd drawn her closer to him.

When she was little, she had stolen down from her room, drawn by the melodic strains of an orchestra playing. With her face pressed between the rails of the banister, she'd sat still for hours, watching the dancers twirling around the ballroom, entranced by the beautiful women in their elegant clothes and sparkling jewels, women held so correctly by their dashing partners. She had always wondered what it must be like to be one of them.

Had those women felt as she did now?

Her heart was racing even though the dance was slow and graceful. Tucker held her close within the circle of his arms, yet not so close as to be improper. Or was it? She sensed the heat emanating from his body, seemed aware of the muscular strength of his chest and arms and even his thighs. If she should look up, surely his beard would brush her cheek. Even now she could feel his breath in her hair.

And there was his hand on her back. . . . It seemed so very intimate to have it there, pressing, guiding. She wished the hand would press harder, drawing her against him. And then she was appalled by such a thought. Whatever was wrong with her?

Suddenly, he stopped dancing, although the music played on. Questioning, she lifted her face so she could look up at him, her mouth opening to speak. She was silenced by his descending lips.

Heat spread through her, searing but lazy, like red lava flowing from a volcano. She couldn't move. Couldn't think. She could only feel as his mouth covered hers. Could only feel as his tongue played across her lips. Could only feel . . .

Tucker still held her head between his hands as he drew back. She didn't move. She didn't seem to be breathing. He stared at her, unable to see her face in the darkness, yet knowing exactly how she must look. Like she'd been kissed for the first time.

Why had he done it? What was it about her that made her so desirable, so unforgettable?

It was more than her beauty. There was an innocence about her, as if she'd spent her life closed off from everything else in this world. And, despite her strength, her stubborness, her determination, he sensed fear was very much a part of Maggie. He wanted to drive that fear out of her. He wanted to make her feel safe and secure. He wanted . . .

What did he want from her? To find relief for the building fire within him? No, that wouldn't be fair to Maggie. He couldn't use her lightly. But he hadn't anything else to offer her. He'd learned his lesson with Charmaine. He wasn't about to make a fool of himself again with a woman. Besides, he was virtually penniless, bound for who knew what in a scarcely settled territory, armed only with dreams for a better future but no guarantees he would find it. He had a mother and two small siblings to look after. Tucker had nothing left to offer Maggie Harris.

Tucker dropped his hands. "I'm sorry, Maggie. I shouldn't have done that."

He turned and walked into the night shadows.

Maggie stood still for what seemed an eternity, letting the foreign sensations sweep over her again and again. Then, at last, she realized what he'd said.

I'm sorry, Maggie. I shouldn't have done that.
Shouldn't have done that . . .
Shouldn't have done that . . .

Tears stabbing her eyes, she crawled beneath the wagon, feeling more alone than ever, and wept.

MAUREEN'S JOURNAL

May 15. *It is the middle of night and I write by candlelight. I can hear the lowing of the cattle that follow the train by day, a gentle sound against the darkness, yet I cannot return to sleep.*

I dreamed of Farrell. I dreamed he was here with me, inside this oakwood wagon with its hickory bows and unsightly canvas top. He asked me about our carriage and matched pair of chestnut geldings. He wondered why they weren't here. I did not know what to tell him. He was always so proud of the Twin Willows stables, yet he had forgotten that what the Confederates didn't buy were later stolen—by both armies.

And then he said he had always loved me and asked me to say good-bye to the children, before he turned and walked away into the mist. I called after him. I said good-bye. It was so strange and seemed so very real. Yet I was not afraid.

But I do feel a deep yearning to see those things which are lost forever to me. Twin Willows, where I went as a young and foolish bride, where my children were born and raised. I would love to sit in the shade and smell the magnolias in bloom while I pour tea for Mrs. Rochard and Mrs. Howe and Aunt Eugenia. My mother's china. Shannon's first doll. Grady.

Chapter Ten

It was late afternoon when the train approached the Big Blue, a tributary of the Kansas River. Tucker sat on his black gelding, waiting while David's eyes surveyed the river.

He'd spent the day riding point with the wagon master, and he'd done it for one reason only. He wanted to avoid Maggie. Every time he thought of her, he was reminded of the way she'd felt in his arms as they'd danced the night before. He could almost smell the fragrance of her hair, taste the sweetness of her lips.

Branigan . . . , he warned himself silently, cutting off that particular train of thought.

". . . should be able to ford it."

Tucker realized David was speaking. "What?"

"I said, looks like we'll be able to ford it." David looked toward Tucker with a puzzled expression, then glanced up at the sky. "It'll be another hour 'fore the wagons get here. Soon as they do, we'll start 'em across."

Tucker surveyed the green oasis before them. "Why not stay on this side of the river tonight? Looks like a good place to rest to me. We've made camp in worse."

David chuckled. "You're right about it being the perfect place to stop. This is Alcove Springs. Wait'll you drink the water. You've never tasted anything so good." The wagon master's smile vanished. "But our luck's held just about as long as it's going to. It's going to rain tonight, and we'd better be on the other side when it does or we could be stuck here a long time."

Tucker glanced up at the sky. Only a pale blue expanse met his gaze, not even a whiff of clouds on the horizon. Rain?

Reading his thoughts, David said, "I can feel it in my bones, son. Trust me."

Tucker nodded. He knew it must be important or David wouldn't push the day into evening. He suspected there would be some grumbling, though, when people saw they weren't going to make camp in this idyllic little spot on the trail.

By the time the Branigan wagon reached the bank of the Big Blue and was ready for crossing, black clouds were rolling across the sky, ominously heavy with rain. The wind had risen, whipping words away as men shouted at mules and oxen.

After tying Blue Boy to the rear of the wagon, Tucker climbed up beside Maggie on the wagon seat. He didn't speak to her. He hadn't spoken to her all day. Maggie kept her eyes averted as Tucker took up the reins, aware of his quick glance inside the wagon at his mother and the children before he said, "Hold on, everyone."

She gripped the side of the seat. Was it Tucker's closeness that frazzled her nerves or the darkening storm clouds overhead? Would they get all the wagons across before the rain came? The clouds had already made it nearly as dark as night. Would they be able to see? She peered across the river, her fingers tightening their hold as the wagon jerked into motion.

No, it wasn't Tucker who was making her feel this way. This was more than just nervousness. She was afraid. There were lots of emotions Tucker stirred in her, but true fear wasn't one of them. It couldn't be the river crossing either. They'd crossed rivers and streams before this. She'd even driven the teams across one or two herself this past week. Still, as the wagon rocked from side to side, the wind whipping at the canvas cover behind her, she had a terrible sense of doom.

It became reality midway across the river. But it wasn't the Branigan wagon disaster struck. Maggie heard the sound, like a tree splitting before it topples to earth; then the Baker wagon in front of them tipped sideways into the water.

"Tucker!" She grabbed hold of his arm. "The children!"

She could see the two Baker boys bobbing in the current as the river swept them away while their mother clung to the side of the wagon. Mr. Baker was nowhere to be seen. Without hesitation or forethought, Maggie jumped into the river and swam after them. Wind-whipped waves washed over her, hiding the young boys from her sight. Her skirts, heavy with water, dragged at her ankles; the sturdy shoes Maureen had given her threatened to pull her under. She gasped and choked as the choppy water smote her face.

Where were they?

She caught a glimpse of blond hair off to her left and pulled herself in that direction. "Hang on!" she called, but it was useless. Nothing could be heard above the roar of the wind and river.

Just as she neared him, the boy was swallowed in another wave. Panicky, Maggie groped beneath the surface.

No! No!

Her fingers touched something. His shirt. The collar of his shirt. With every ounce of her waning strength, she pulled upward. He fought against her, his arms flailing. She almost lost him, but held tight as she sank with him into the darkness of the river. Together, they returned to the surface, and from somewhere deep within, she found the needed forces to help her pull the drowning boy to the edge of the river.

She pushed him onto the muddy bank, then dragged herself up beside him. She lay face down, drawing ragged breaths into her aching lungs and coughing up the river she'd swallowed moments before. Finally, her head clearing, she pushed herself onto her hands and knees and crawled over to the youngster. He was whimpering in fear, but he was alive.

"Miss Harris!" The voice was muffled, but she heard it all the same. "Maggie!"

She lifted her head. "Over here, Mr. Foster. We're over here."

The wagon master's big buckskin burst through the underbrush. David jumped down and hurried over to them. "Wills," he said as he picked up the boy.

Wills began to cry in full volume. David held him close against his burly chest. "What about Timmy?"

Maggie stared at him blankly, not understanding.

"What about his brother?"

Maggie shook her head. "I lost sight of him."

A pained expression passed across his weathered face before he said, "Come on. I'll get you back to the wagons." He pulled her to her feet. "It was a brave thing you did," he added.

She didn't feel brave. Just tired.

With a hand under her elbow, David helped her into the saddle, then passed Wills Baker into her arms. The four-year-old lad snuggled close against her as she wrapped her arms around him. She tried not to think about Timmy.

Tucker reached out to stop Maggie, but he was too late. She was swept away in the current, never hearing him call her name.

A moment later, a gust of wind shook the Branigan wagon. It rocked, then righted itself. The canvas top blew free from one corner and flapped noisily overhead.

Behind him, Fiona and Rachel were crying in fear. He glanced back to see Maureen, her own face registering horror as she held the two girls against her. Neal stood close by, his hand on their mother's shoulder, offering what boyish courage he could.

"Neal! Hold that canvas down!"

Tucker raised the whip and cracked it over the mule teams. He had to get his wagon out of the river. He had to get the rest of the family to safety before—before he could search for Maggie.

They skirted the Baker wagon as several men fought to right it against the river's current. He saw Mrs. Baker being carried to shore by a man on horseback. But he couldn't see Maggie.

God, don't let her drown, he prayed silently.

The moment the wagon wheels rolled up the bank, Tucker jumped to the ground and started running downriver, hardly aware that it had started to rain. He came upon them all of a sudden, Maggie and the boy astride David's enormous mount.

He stopped and stared at her in the growing gloom. Her hair was plastered against her scalp. Her dress was torn and muddy, clinging to her like a second skin.

She looked like a drowned rat.

She looked beautiful.

He moved slowly forward, reaching up to take Wills from her arms, then passing the boy to David. Turning once again toward Maggie, he took hold of her waist and lifted her to the ground. He was only vaguely aware of David riding on, leaving them alone.

"That was a crazy thing to do." He pushed her straggling hair back from her face.

She didn't answer, only looked up at him with wide gray eyes.

"Don't you ever do anything so foolish again." His hand slipped to the nape of her neck.

Rainwater streamed down her face. Such a pale face, her skin almost iridescent.

"Do you understand me, Maggie?" he said, so softly he could barely hear himself.

She just kept staring up at him with those blasted big eyes of hers, pools of gray he could almost drown in.

"Maggie . . ."

"I hear you, Tucker."

Heaven help him. He *was* drowning in her eyes.

The rain streamed down her face and into her eyes. She blinked to clear them, wanting to see him clearly, needing to understand the play of emotions she saw there. She ached for him to draw her closer. Ached for his mouth to touch hers once again.

What was happening to her?

She shivered as gooseflesh rose on her arms.

"You're cold. We'd better get you back to the wagons."

Not yet, her heart protested.

"Come on." His hand took hold of her elbow as he turned her around.

Was it rain or tears that blinded her? She stumbled as she took a step and suddenly found herself cradled in his arms. She pressed her face against his chest as her hands clasped behind his neck. She wished the wagons were farther away.

Chapter Eleven

It was still raining when they buried Marshall Baker in the morning. Despite an intense search downriver, Timmy's body had not been found.

Susan Baker, a girl not much older than Maggie, turned away from the grave, Wills's hand held tightly within hers. Her face was drawn. Dark rings smudged the hollows beneath her eyes. Her gait was awkward as she walked away from the grave; she looked as if she could deliver her third child at any time.

Stopping before Maggie, she said, "I want to thank you for savin' my Wills."

Maggie swallowed the lump in her throat, unable to speak.

"He's all I've got left. Him and . . ." Susan's free hand rested on her swollen abdomen. "God bless you," she whispered and then moved on.

Maureen's arm tightened around Maggie's shoulders. "It's time to leave."

"What's going to happen to her?" Maggie asked, her voice flat, lifeless.

"She's going on with us. Her brother and family are in Oregon."

"But how will she manage without her husband?" Maggie looked at the woman at her side. "She can't handle those oxen and a little boy and a baby."

"The people on this train will help her. Just as you did when you jumped in to save Wills."

Maggie wished she could believe her. She wanted to believe folks would help just for the sake of goodness, but it hadn't been her experience to see that sort of thing happen. Sure, she had gone after Wills, but she hadn't had time to think about what she was doing. She'd just jumped in. What would these people have to gain by helping Susan and Wills reach Oregon? Maggie had promised the Branigans money, but Susan didn't have anything except what was in her wagon.

Maureen tugged on her arm once again. "Come along, dear. Mr. Foster is about ready to pull out."

With one last glance at the grave, a simple wooden cross and some wildflowers adorning the mound of dirt, Maggie turned and walked toward the Branigan wagon.

Tucker was already on the wagon seat. "I'll drive," he said when she saw him. "You deserve a rest. Climb in back and sleep if you can. We probably won't get very far today anyway with all this rain."

Maggie nodded and went to the back of the wagon.

I really am tired, she thought as she pulled herself up. *Maybe I will sleep.*

She certainly hadn't slept much during the night. Her groundcloth had soon held more water than it kept out, but the problem hadn't been the wet bedding nor the chilled air. It wasn't even the Baker tragedy that had kept her awake. It had been thoughts of Tucker that held sleep at bay. Thoughts of Tucker and her own traitorous reactions to him. As if she didn't know he could only mean trouble.

Maggie closed her eyes and pulled a semi-dry blanket over her shoulders. Maureen and Neal sat up front with Tucker, while Fiona and Rachel snuggled into a cramped corner of the wagon. Everyone would ride today because of the weather.

It wasn't long before the train began to break its circle, stretching out into a long line as it headed northwest toward the Nebraska–Kansas border. Maggie tried to convince her tired body that the jerk and roll of the wagon was as restful as a porch swing, that soon it would rock her to sleep. Her body wasn't fooled.

Barely two weeks. Just two weeks she and Rachel had been with these people. Two weeks and her life seemed only to have become more complicated. She'd been so naive to think she would just join a wagon train and hurry on her way to Oregon, as if she were hopping a passenger train from Philadelphia to New York. But worse than the dust and sweat, the hardships and dangers, she was beginning to care about them. She was beginning to care for Maureen and Fiona and Neal and David Foster and Susan Baker and Wills and . . . And Tucker.

She was beginning to care too much for Tucker by far.

*   *   *

The rain continued that day and on through the night. In the morning, as the heavens wept upon the soggy, saddened train, David made the decision not to move out. They would stay encamped and await a break in the storm.

Tucker used the day to go in search of fresh game for the family. Wearing his rubber coat, water running off the brim of his hat like rain through a gutter, he scoured the surrounding countryside. Luck was with him. He shot a young buck that would feed the Branigans for the better part of a week if it was cut and cooked properly. He also bagged two rabbits which he intended to give to the widow Baker. He would have to be careful that Rachel didn't see them.

He grinned to himself. The little blonde had certainly changed since he'd first seen her. She had been frightened of her own shadow back then, hiding always within the folds of Maggie's skirts. Now she bounded about the camp with Fiona, both of them laughing and shouting, as if they'd grown up together. And it didn't hurt his ego any that she'd taken such a shine to him.

He wished his feelings for Maggie were as simple.

Tucker halted Blue Boy, then removed his hat, shaking off the water as he looked up at the clearing skies. He ran his fingers through his hair, then thoughtfully fingered his beard.

There wasn't much point in denying it. He wanted Maggie. Not just her body, which any red-blooded man would lust after, but all of her. He wanted to know her inside out. He wanted to find out about her girlhood and her home and her family. He wanted to make her laugh, and he wanted to kiss the sweetness of her mouth. He wanted to lie with her in the grass and watch the clouds float by overhead, and then he wanted to make love to her, blending her cries of ecstasy with his own. God help him, sometimes he even imagined her holding a child—*his* child!

"I must be insane," he muttered as he slammed his rain-sodden slouch hat back on his head.

Didn't he have enough problems to face without adding a love affair? And what made him think he could ever love her? He didn't even *know* her. He'd known Charmaine for the better part of his life, and look how she had fooled him. But Maggie was so different from Charmaine. There wasn't any artifice about Maggie. He would stake his life on that. He'd bet she didn't even know how beautiful she was.

He clucked his tongue at Blue Boy. "Let's go, fella."

It was time to get back to camp.

Maggie sat near the wagon, mending the tear in her dress. Fiona and Rachel were mixing batter and getting more flour on themselves than in the large bowl they held between them. Hearing their laughter, Maggie let her needle still as she glanced up from her sewing.

Her heart tightened as she looked at Rachel's glowing face. She'd never seen Rachel like this, never so happy and carefree. She should have been glad for the change in her sister. And she *was* glad for her. It was herself she was feeling sorry for. She felt unneeded, unloved. And that wasn't fair either. Rachel loved her.

Maureen turned from the campfire. "Children, we'll never have cake for supper if you don't pay attention to what you're doing."

"Yes, Mother," Fiona answered, stifling her giggles.

Maureen shook her head. Then her eyes met Maggie's. Wiping her hands on her apron, she walked over to the wagon. "I guess I can't blame them. They've been cooped up for so long."

Maggie nodded.

Tucker's mother settled onto the bench beside Maggie, her glance dropping to the fabric in Maggie's lap. "What beautiful stitches. Did your mother teach you to sew like that?"

"Mama?" Maggie had a vision of her mother, so beautiful and gay, the society butterfly. "No, Mama couldn't sew a stitch. My nanny taught me."

"Your nanny? But I thought—"

Realizing what she'd said, Maggie quickly added, "That was a long time ago. The servants were all let go when Rachel was just a baby."

"The war," Maureen said softly. "It took our home and servants too."

Maggie had hoped that would be what Maureen Branigan would assume. She hadn't ever meant to reveal that the Harrises had been wealthy at one time. She'd tried so hard not to say anything about her family at all.

"Twin Willows was the name of our plantation. We grew cotton. Lots and lots of cotton. Farrell, my husband, was a lawyer, and a good one too. Honorable and honest and fair." Her expression was wistful. "Tucker's so much like him. They always planned to practice law together one day."

"Tucker wanted to be a lawyer?"

Now her expression was one of pride. "Oh, he is one, my dear. And a very good one too."

"I didn't know," Maggie whispered, realizing

how little she did know about Tucker and his
family. She hoped Maureen would continue, but
just then, Wills Baker appeared.

His wan little face turned up toward Maggie and
he stared at her for a long time. Then, unexpectedly, he crawled into Maggie's lap and snuggled
against her breast. Her arms wrapped around him,
smoothing his hair, as her gaze met Maureen's.

"Wills," she said gently, "where's your mother?"

Wordlessly and without moving his head, he
pointed toward his wagon.

"She'll be wondering where you are. You mustn't
frighten her this way. Let's go back." Maggie
started to rise, the child still in her arms.

Maureen stopped her. "Maggie, wait. Leave
Wills here with me."

She hesitated, then understood. "You stay with
Mrs. Branigan, Wills, and I'll tell your mother that
you're with us." She handed the boy to Maureen.

Maggie heard the weeping before she reached the
Baker wagon. Not that it was loud. No, it was
muffled and obviously restrained. For some reason,
that made the sound all the more wrenching.

"Mrs. Baker?" She moved aside the rear flap,
staring into the gloomy interior. "Susan?"

She heard a sniff, then, "Yes."

Without waiting for an invitation, she climbed
into the wagon. Susan was lying on her bed, her face
turned toward the canvas covering.

"Susan . . ." Maggie knelt on the floor of the
wagon and touched the woman's shoulder. "Wills
is worried about you."

"Wills?" She struggled to sit upright. "Where is
he? I thought he was here."

"It's all right. Mrs. Branigan is with him."

Susan Baker managed at last to straighten, turning on the thick mattress until her back was propped against the side of the wagon. "I can't seem to stop cryin'," she said over a choked sob.

"You needn't apologize."

"I keep hearin' that awful snap when the wheel broke and seein' my Marshall's head hittin' the side of the wagon and my babies floatin' away."

Maggie looked down at her hands, nodding wordlessly.

"I'm so scared. I know I shouldn't be actin' this way. Everyone's been so kind to us, offerin' to help, bringin' us food. But I don't know what's to become of us."

"Aren't you going to your brother's in Oregon?"

Susan nodded as she dabbed at her swollen eyes with a handkerchief. "George'll take us in, but he ain't going to like it any."

"I'm sure you're mistaken." Maggie wasn't sure at all, of course, but it seemed the right thing to say.

The young widow looked at her for a long time before asking, "How old are you, Maggie?"

"I'll be eighteen soon."

"I was already expectin' Timmy when I was your age. He would have been three in the fall." Her eyes took on a faraway look. "Marshall an' me was married when I was sixteen and he was nearin' nineteen. Not even five years ago yet, but it seems a long time now. He come callin' and told me I was the one and the next thing I knew, we was standin' before the preacher. He was a good man, but times were hard for us." Tears came again, streaming down her cheeks unchecked. "I don't know how to take care of us. I don't know how."

Maggie grasped Susan by the shoulders and gave

her a little shake. "You listen to me, Susan Baker. You'll do just fine. You can take care of Wills and the baby and get by. It's not going to be easy, but you can do it. I know because I've had to get by myself. A person can do whatever they need to do. Whatever they have to do." She sat back on her heels. "But lying in your bed and crying all day isn't going to help anybody. Now, you get up and wash your face and comb your hair and come get little Wills. I know you miss your husband and Timmy, but your boy Wills is still alive and *he* needs you now."

Susan stared at her, her face registering surprise. Finally, she nodded.

"That's better. When you're ready, just come on over. You and Wills can eat with us tonight, if you want. I'm sure Mrs. Branigan won't mind."

Susan didn't feel comfortable around a woman like Maureen Branigan. Maureen was a real lady. Everything she did or said, the way she moved, even the gentle lift of an eyebrow or the motion of a hand bespoke her station in life.

Susan felt ignorant and plain beside her. She didn't know how to read or write, hadn't ever had any schooling. All she'd ever done was work beside her mama in their farmhouse when she was a child and then work in her own house after she married Marshall. Marshall had been all she'd ever wanted. Marshall and her younguns.

She held Wills on her lap—what there was of it—and kissed his blond head as tears burned her eyes. She felt the baby's movements inside her bloated abdomen and placed a hand there, as if to assure herself that the feeling was real.

Maureen sat next to her, a cup of coffee in her hand. She stared thoughtfully into the fire, allowing the silence to stretch between them.

"That was a right nice supper, Mrs. Branigan," Susan said, her head ducked down, embarrassed by the sound of her voice but unable to bear the quiet any longer.

"Thank you, my dear. We're glad you joined us."

Wills slipped away from his mother and walked over to Maggie, who had resumed her mending. Without a word, he pushed her arms aside and climbed up into her lap, laying his head on her chest. Maggie dropped the sewing and closed her arms around him, her gray eyes bemused at the child's sudden action.

"Wills—" Susan began.

Maureen leaned forward and took hold of Susan's hand. She shook her head. "Don't scold. Let him find comfort where he can."

But it hurt to have him seeking it elsewhere. Susan was grateful for what Maggie had done. Wills could have died along with his little brother and his papa. He *would* have died if not for Maggie. Still, Susan's arms felt empty without him.

Maureen slid her camp stool closer and wrapped an arm around Susan's shoulders. "I lost my husband last winter, and one of my sons nearly three years ago. We all, my children and I, had to find comfort in our own ways. It takes time to heal, Susan. Give yourself time. And Wills too."

Suddenly, the differences between them didn't seem so vast. Maureen was a widow with children. Susan was a widow with children. They each understood the other's heartache.

Susan blinked back the tears that had formed

again, swallowing the lump in her throat. "You've been right kind, ma'am," she whispered.

"That's what friends are for, Susan. To help each other when times get hard."

Susan hadn't ever had a woman friend before. Now it appeared she had two in Maureen and Maggie.

Chapter Twelve

*D*avid Foster paused at the corner of the wagon and surveyed the family scene before him. The entire Branigan clan was gathered around the campfire, joined by the Harris girls, the Widow Baker, and little Wills. Maggie was holding the lad on her lap while Rachel and Fiona tried to entice a smile from him. Neal was helping his older brother repair some harness, while Maureen and Susan finished packing away the supper dishes.

He couldn't help noting once again what a fine figure of a woman Maureen Branigan was. She didn't look to be much more than a girl herself; it was hard to believe she was old enough to have a son Tucker's age. It had been a long time since David had looked at a woman and had thoughts of hearth and home. Not since his Emily died in childbirth more than two decades ago. Not until he'd met Maureen.

She was a grand lady, too. Always so soft-spoken. Never a word of complaint over the material things she'd left behind or the loved ones she'd lost. A son and husband dead. A daughter selflessly staying behind to care for an aging aunt. Another son refusing to leave Georgia, determined not to let the war end until he'd fought one more battle and won. And yet no complaint. She was a special woman, Maureen Branigan.

And it wasn't just the quiet strength he recognized. David knew she had a generous heart, as well. Taking in the two Harris girls, and now offering help to the widow—as if she didn't have enough family of her own to care for.

David removed his beat-up hat and ran a hand over his gray hair, smoothing it back from his forehead. Then he walked toward them.

"Evenin', folks," he said as he stepped into the firelight.

Maureen greeted him with a friendly smile. "Good evening, Mr. Foster."

"Heard Tucker brought in a fine deer today."

"Yes, we had fried venison for supper tonight. Would you care for some? I could—"

"No, thank you, ma'am. I've had my supper. I just came by to see how Mrs. Baker is doing."

"I'm much better, thank you, Mr. Foster," Susan answered, her face still swollen from crying.

Tucker motioned toward a stool. "Sit down, David. Have a cup of coffee with us."

Maureen was already filling a cup with some of the dark brew by the time he'd settled onto the stool. As she passed it to him, their fingers touched, and he had the urge to take hold of her hand and keep it captive within his. Wisely, he resisted.

"I talked to one of the Fulkerson boys today, Mrs. Baker. The middle one. Paul. He said he's willin' to drive your wagon to Oregon for you. His brothers and pa can handle their teams."

"I don't know how I can ever repay him," Susan said softly, her eyes glittering with quick tears.

"I don't imagine he'll want more than your thanks."

His Emily hadn't been much older than this girl when she died, all alone in their cabin in Oregon while he was out felling trees. His daughter, his only child, had died with her. If there'd been folks around to care for her, maybe . . .

He shook off the dismal memories. Hardship was a part of life in the wilderness. Every train he had led west had its tragedies. Sometimes he wondered why he did it. His place in Oregon hadn't brought him much happiness. It had cost him his wife and child. Yet, there was something about that new land, something about the hope it offered, that just kept drawing him back.

David pulled his thoughts to the present once again as Maggie rose, Wills asleep in her arms.

"I'd better put him to bed."

Tucker was on his feet in a snap. "I'll go with you. Here, let me carry him," he said, taking the boy from Maggie.

Susan bade good-night to the remaining people around the fire, then followed Tucker and Maggie. A few minutes more and Neal had crawled into the tent and the two girls had disappeared into the wagon.

David traced the brim of his hat with his fingers, then, reluctantly, put the hat back on his head and got to his feet. "Guess I'd better check on the rest of the camp. Thanks for the coffee, Mrs. Branigan."

Maureen offered a smile. "You're welcome any-time, Mr. Foster."

Dad blast it, he felt like a schoolboy.

"Night, ma'am."

He walked away.

Maggie could have let Tucker carry Wills to the Baker wagon on his own. She wasn't needed to tuck the lad into bed. His mother was there to do that. Yet, somehow she found herself walking by his side, followed by Susan. It wasn't long before mother and child were inside their wagon, their good-nights said and the flaps pulled closed.

Tucker set the pace—a slow, leisurely one—for their walk back toward their own wagon. But Maggie's heart didn't feel slow or leisurely. It felt as if she were climbing a hill or running a foot race. She wondered if Tucker could hear its thundering in her chest.

Searching for anything to fill the silence, she asked, "Will we move on tomorrow?"

"Tomorrow's Sunday," he replied without look-ing at her. "I imagine we'll stay right here and let things dry out a bit."

"Oh." She nodded. "Of course."

They'd reached their wagon.

"Look's like everyone's gone to bed," Tucker said, glancing around the darkened campsite.

"Yes. Well. It's late."

"Sky's clear. Lots of stars."

She looked up. "Yes, they're pretty."

"Maggie." He placed a hand on her arm, holding her there. "Tell me about you. Tell me about your family."

Her skin felt hot where his fingers touched, and the heat seemed to spread right up into her cheeks. "My family?" Her throat felt thick. It was hard to speak. "There's not much to tell."

"There must be something."

If he ever found out . . . if he ever knew she'd been lying all this time . . . what would happen to her then? "No," she answered hastily. "There's nothing to tell. Only that I miss my parents. Good night, Tucker." She scurried into her bed beneath the wagon before he could stop her again.

Maggie heard him sigh, then listened to his footsteps as they moved away. She pulled her blankets up beneath her chin, thinking, *What a coward you are, Maggie Harris.*

But how could she tell him about her uncle or her parents without taking the chance of revealing too much? What did she know of the things he knew? Her memories of happiness and a life filled with people and laughter were too far in the past. She'd been held captive too long in a dark, empty house with only herself and Rachel for company.

Seth had done this to her. How she hated him! How she hated him for taking away any shred of a normal life from his two nieces. All because of his greed. He could have been kind to them. They could have been a family if he'd wanted them to be.

Giving the blankets an angry jerk, she covered her head and tried to find solace in sleep. Instead she found memories . . .

The early spring storm had raged down from the north, leaving ice on the Philadelphia streets. Returning late from a party, the carriage skidded as it turned a corner, throwing the driver from his perch before it rolled down the embankment, killing the two passengers instantly.

For twelve-year-old Maggie, the following nightmarish days would be forever burned upon her memory. The people streaming through the Harris mansion, words of condolence on their lips, tears in their eyes as they spoke of poor Maggie and baby Rachel, growing up with no parents. The quiet way the servants moved around the house, speaking in hushed voices and sniffling. The black curtains at the windows and mourning wreath on the door.

And then Seth Harris had appeared. Seth, Jeremy's mysterious older brother, the one Elizabeth refused to let him speak of in front of the children. Maggie would be older and wiser before she learned that his timely arrival had been coincidental, that he had merely been hiding from conscription in those early months of the war. At the time, she thought he was there to love and care for them.

It didn't take her long to learn not to expect affection from him—nor even simple kindness.

Tucker felt the strange silence, as if the prairie were holding its breath. Beside him, Neal snored and mumbled in his sleep. Quietly, Tucker threw off the covers of his bedroll and left the tent. A quick glance at the sky revealed the return of clouds, but it didn't feel or smell like rain. The hair on his arms seemed to be standing on end. He rubbed them vigorously, then slipped on his shirt before sitting on a bench and pulling on his boots.

The livestock were restless. He could hear them milling about, the cows mooing, the occasional nicker of a horse. He heard one of the watch singing, trying to calm them. He wondered if he should join them.

The first flash of lightning and the explosion of thunder that rode on its tail caused Tucker to reach for his gun, so like was it to the sound of the opening cannonade of a battle. There was scarcely time for the tick of a clock before the heavens lit once more, incessant, violent. The earth beneath his feet trembled as the thunder roared.

Tucker turned, ready to race toward the corralled animals, but was stopped by the terrified scream that came from beneath the Branigan wagon. The sound nearly stopped his heart.

"Maggie!" he called to her above the din, but when she didn't reply, he crawled under the wagon bed.

The lightning bathed her in bursts of white light. She was huddled in a tight ball, her hands over her head, covering her ears, her elbows hugged around her face.

"Maggie. Maggie, it's all right. It's only thunder." He tried to pull her arms away from her head.

She swung at him. "No! No!"

He captured her hands and held them within one of his. She looked at him with unseeing eyes, trying desperately to pull free of him.

"Don't shut it! Don't shut the door! Please don't! Please!"

Not knowing what else to do, he trapped her arms at her side as he pulled her close against him, squeezing her in a tight embrace. "Maggie, it's me. Tucker. It's all right."

Another flash of lightning crackled from earth to heavens, and the resounding boom that followed elicited another shriek from Maggie. But this time, she burrowed into him instead of pulling away, as if seeking a place of safety.

Perhaps he should have been with the other men, trying to keep the livestock from stampeding away, but nothing could have drawn Tucker from this place. He'd never seen such fear, not even on the faces of men dying on the battlefield.

"Shhh, Maggie. It's all right," he repeated. "It's only a storm."

"Don't let him lock me in. Please don't let him."

"I won't, honey."

She quivered in his embrace, wincing with every crash above them. He stroked her hair and whispered nonsensical words of comfort, not even knowing if she could hear or understand him, not even hearing the words himself.

For nearly two hours, the storm raged, without releasing a drop of rain. Only the racing wind, the blinding lightning, and the deafening thunder. Finally, mercifully, the clouds rolled on, the thunder fading in the distance.

He knew she wasn't sleeping, though she hadn't moved at all throughout the storm, except for the shivering that accompanied each crack of thunder.

"Maggie, look. It's sunrise. The storm is over."

She shook her head against his shirt.

"I promise. The sun is up." Taking her face between his hands, he gently pushed her away. "Look, Maggie. It's a glorious sunrise."

And it was. The rising sun had stained the lingering clouds a spectrum of reds and oranges and yellows. Sunrise. Just as he'd promised.

She looked. For a long time, she stared at the sky. Then, ever so slowly, she turned her gaze upon

Tucker, lying there beside her. Her gray eyes no longer held fear. They were filled with wonder instead.

Chapter Thirteen

Maggie *wasn't really certain what had changed* between them, yet she knew something had. Suddenly, she wasn't afraid to care about Tucker. She wasn't worried about what tomorrow would bring. She was ready to believe that whatever came would be good.

Neither Blue Boy nor Maggie's swaybacked horse had strayed far from the wagon train's camp, but most of the livestock had scattered in all directions during the storm. When Tucker set out with the others to round up the cattle and horses, he invited Maggie to go with him. Unwilling to lose the way his presence made her feel, even for a few hours, she agreed. She knew she would be miserable later, her bottom sore and her legs chafed, but she didn't care. If Tucker wanted her with him, she wanted to be there.

To Maggie, the day was as beautiful as the sunrise

had promised. The sky spread from horizon to horizon in a stark blue canopy. Wildflowers bobbed and sparkled beneath the clinging moisture. Even the ground smelled good.

Tucker didn't talk much as they searched the countryside. He didn't need to. Maggie was content to just ride beside him and look at his profile, his slouch hat pulled low over his forehead. She thought about the way his eyes twinkled when he was holding back laughter. She thought about the way his mouth turned up slowly at the corners before his smile was complete. She thought about how broad his shoulders were, and the way the muscles in his arms flexed when he lifted something heavy. She considered the size of his hands, yet knew them to be gentle when he wanted them to be. She thought about his beard and how it had felt against her skin when he kissed her, and then she wondered what he would look like without it. Would he be as handsome as she found him now? Perhaps more handsome? Would his skin feel as smooth as his lips on hers?

He looked over at her, discovering her studying him. She felt herself blush as he grinned at her knowingly, as if he knew exactly what she'd been thinking.

"How about a rest?" he asked. "My legs could use a stretch."

Maggie wasn't even sure her legs would hold her, but she nodded her agreement. Tucker dismounted, then stepped over beside her horse and helped her to the ground. Her legs were, indeed, shaky. Was it because of the unaccustomed horseback ride or was it Tucker's hands on her waist?

He didn't let go immediately. He looked down at her, his chocolate brown eyes thoughtful. She felt that wonderfully awful thudding in her chest again.

Was this what it felt like to fall in love?

"Let's walk." He took hold of her hand and led her through the long prairie grass, the horses following behind.

The air was filled with the fragrance of wildflowers in bloom and that special just-after-the-rain scent that made everything seem so clean and new. Maggie felt clean and new too.

"Why are you so afraid of the thunder?" Tucker asked the question without looking at her.

Her voice caught in her throat. She didn't want to bring up bad memories, bad thoughts. She wanted to just enjoy being with Tucker. Why did he have to start prying into her past?

But if there was a chance she loved him, couldn't she trust him with the truth?

Trust. When was the last time she had trusted anyone?

He stopped, looking down at her once again. "Tell me, Maggie."

She hated to remember. . . ."

He had been with them only a few days. He'd gone out for a while, and when he returned, he'd been in a foul mood. Maggie'd been just a child—lonely, afraid, missing her parents. She'd badly needed comforting and innocently sought it from her uncle. The moment he saw her, he'd started screaming at her, calling her a thief and her father all sorts of vile names. When she began to cry, he'd grabbed her by the collar of her dress and tossed her into a closet, turning the key in the lock and laughing when she'd begged him to let her out. Then the storm had come, shaking the house to its foundation with every burst of thunder. He'd found her fear perversely funny,

*and ever after, when a storm threatened, he would
seek her out to lock in the closet again.*

She wished she could tell Tucker. She wanted to
tell him everything. But still she couldn't. She was
too ashamed, as if her uncle's brutal nature was her
own fault. No, she couldn't tell him about anything
from her past. Not yet.

"Nothing really. Something happened when I
was a girl, and every time I hear thunder, it reminds
me of it."

His hand touched her cheek. "You begged me not
to let him lock you in. Who? Lock you in where?"

"Please, Tucker. Don't ask." She tried to smile.
"Let's talk of something else."

"All right. But you're going to have to tell me
some time. You know that, don't you?" There was
an assumption of a future together in his words.

She knew there couldn't be, mustn't be, but she
couldn't voice the words. Her mouth felt dry, her
palms moist. Despite herself, she nodded.

Without another word, he guided her to the side
of her horse and lifted her onto the saddle again.
With an easy hop, he was mounted, turning Blue
Boy toward the train, the stray cattle they'd gathered in their search driven before them.

Despite Maggie's reluctance to talk about herself,
Tucker's mood was light. It felt right to be with her.
Now that he'd quit fighting it, he knew he was going
to fall in love with Maggie. Not today or tomorrow,
but it would happen. When the time was right, he
would ask her to marry him. They would build a
home together in Boise. She would be at his side as
he established his law practice and sought to bring
justice to the West. Perhaps she would be the wife

of the territorial governor someday, or maybe a state senator. The future stretched before him, filled with promise.

He saw the crowd of people gathered in the center of the circled wagons as they dismounted. "What's going on?" he asked Jake Adams, who was standing off by himself.

"Got us some company." He glanced at Maggie. "Says he's kin of yours, Miss Harris."

Tucker turned his head. Maggie was white as a sheet.

"Where's Rachel?" she whispered.

Jake answered, "With David." He jerked his head toward the gathering.

"Maggie—" Tucker began, but she was already hurrying away, pushing her way through the onlookers. Tucker followed close on her heels.

He recognized the man instantly. Nothing on God's green earth would ever make him forget Seth Harris. The man was holding onto a cowering Rachel with a none-too-gentle grip.

"I'll teach the two of you—" Seth stopped as Maggie broke into the center of the circle. "So, you've decided to show yourself."

"Let go of Rachel," Maggie demanded, her voice surprisingly strong.

"I've come to take you back to Independence, girl, and I'll have none of your sass."

"We won't go."

Seth gave Rachel a shove and grabbed for Maggie, catching her by the forearm. His fingers bit cruelly into her skin, and before anyone knew what was coming, he'd raised his hand and struck her a telling blow across the cheek.

"You'll do as I say," he ground out, his face blotted with growing rage.

Seth's arm swung up to hit her again, but Tucker jumped in to stop him, deflecting the blow meant for Maggie with his own arm.

"That's enough, Harris," Tucker growled in warning.

Seth eyed him with cruel eyes. "Well . . ." Recognition showed on his face. "So, it's you again, Reb. I thought I'd seen the last of you when I threw you and that broken old man of yours out of my office."

"Release Maggie." Tucker's voice was deathly quiet.

At last, he did so. As soon as she was free, Maggie stumbled over to Rachel. Kneeling beside her, she hugged the little girl, their cheeks pressed together as they stared at their uncle.

"I've told these folks, and now I'm tellin' you, Reb. These are my nieces and they've run away. Stole money off me, too. I'm their rightful guardian. You can't keep them from me."

There was a sick feeling in the pit of his stomach as Tucker turned his gaze upon Maggie. "What's your father's name?"

She looked at him, her face white, her eyes wide and frightened.

"What is your father's name?" he repeated.

"Jeremy Harris," she whispered.

"Jeremy Harris is dead!" Seth exclaimed. "Him and that worthless woman he made his wife. More'n five years ago now. I've been saddled with the brats ever since. You'd think it was enough for him to leave me with a dyin' business, wouldn't you, without doin' this to me."

Tucker ignored Seth, brushing past the man as he moved to stand in front of Maggie. "I want to talk with you."

Maggie stood up, lifting her chin and meeting his

gaze straight on. "I won't go with him," she said stubbornly.

He took her by the elbow and hustled her through the crowd, not stopping until they were beyond the circle of wagons. "You lied to us, Maggie. Why?"

"What difference does it make? You never wanted us on this train anyway. You left it up to the others whether or not they'd let us come. If it hadn't been for your mother, we would have been taken back to Independence."

Tucker wasn't going to let her change the subject. "Why did you lie to us?" he asked again.

Defiance sparked in eyes of gray. "Would you have let us come with you if you'd known we had family? You know you wouldn't have. I lied because we have to get to Oregon."

"Why?"

"Because my uncle is lying. I think our true guardian is in Oregon. My father wouldn't have left us to his brother. You've seen how he treats Rachel." She touched her cheek but didn't mention her own treatment. "Would you leave your daughter to—to a man like him?" There was a tiny catch in her voice. "My father loved us. He wouldn't have left us to his brother. And I don't mean for Rachel to live with him any longer, no matter what I have to do."

"And just who is this *true* guardian?"

"He's an attorney. His name is Marcus Sanderson. He drew up my father's will before he went to Oregon."

He wanted to believe her, but there was a simmering bitterness in his chest. Of all the people in the world who could have been her uncle, it had to be this man.

And she'd lied to him. She'd lied to him about

her uncle and her parents. What else might she be lying about? Lying was the one thing he hadn't expected from Maggie. He'd thought she was different, special. He'd thought . . .

But she was right about Seth. He was a brute, and he obviously didn't care for his nieces. And there was something else nagging at Tucker. Why was Seth so anxious to take them back if he only felt saddled with them?

"Stay here," he said, his tone stern. "I'm going to talk with your uncle."

Maureen stepped over to David's side. "What are you going to do, Mr. Foster?" she asked in a whisper, her gaze still fastened on Seth. The man was tall and looked as if he might have been extremely strong at one time, although now he had more of a tendency toward fat. His chin was darkened by several day's growth of beard, and his black eyes looked glassy, as if he'd been on a drinking binge the night before.

"I'm not sure, Mrs. Branigan. He *is* their uncle. Even Maggie hasn't denied that."

"There must be something we can do. We can't just let him take them."

David gave her an understanding glance. "Let's see what Tucker has in mind. He's the attorney. If we have to, we'll call a council meeting."

As if on cue, Tucker appeared once again, stopping outside the circle of emigrants. "Harris, let's talk."

Maureen recognized that look in Tucker's eyes. She'd seen it through the years in Farrell's. Steely determination to see justice done. A passionate desire to seek out the truth. But there was something more here. Tucker was personally involved.

She should have seen it coming. Why hadn't she?

Seth grunted his assent and shouldered his way through the people around him, following Tucker off to a secluded corner of the camp.

"Don't worry, Mrs. Branigan," David's voice said near her ear. "I don't think Seth has a chance against Tucker."

"Harris, Maggie tells me her father left their guardianship to another man. A Mr. Sanderson."

The burly man's eyes bulged. "That's a lie. Her father was my brother. He left everything to me. His business *and* his daughters. It's my duty to see them taken care of until they get married so someone else can have the sorry job."

"She says Mr. Sanderson drew up her father's will and will be able to clear up this matter when they reach Oregon."

"Those girls belong to me. They're mine to do with as I please, and I don't think lettin' 'em go to Oregon is going to please me. You've got no right . . ."

The muscles in Tucker's neck and shoulders tensed. He fought the desire to dispense with reasonable conversation and just hit the man. "It should be easy enough to prove what your brother's wishes in the matter were. Do you have a copy of the will with you?"

"Do you think I run around with his will in my pocket?"

Tucker couldn't resist the tiny smile. "No. Of course not. Then I guess we'll just have to wait until we can talk to Mr. Sanderson."

"You thievin' Reb. You can't blackmail me into payin' you for that cotton by holdin' my nieces."

"It never occurred to me, Harris."

"The hell it didn't!" Seth stepped forward, going almost nose to nose with Tucker. Tucker could smell whiskey on his breath. "You cross me and I'll have you up before a judge for kidnappin' before—"

"I think that would prove most interesting, Mr. Harris. As a lawyer, I always enjoy a good case in court."

Seth took a step in the opposite direction, his eyes narrowing. "You're a damn lawyer, like that father of yours?"

"I like to think I'm a very good lawyer." His voice was frigid. "And so was my father."

"Reb . . ." Seth's fingers touched the gun tucked in his belt.

"I wouldn't do that if I were you," Tucker warned.

Seth's gaze shifted across the camp to the gathering of emigrants, all of them watching him, then back to Tucker. "All right, Mr. Fancy Lawyer. What is it you think you're going to do with my nieces?"

"Maggie and Rachel will continue on with the train in my custody. I will assume full responsibility for their welfare."

"I just bet you will." Seth snorted. "And just how much of Maggie's *welfare* do you mean to sample? Or have you sampled some already?"

Tucker took a threatening step forward, feeling murder in every bone of his body. "I'm going to forget you said that, but don't ever make the mistake of saying it again."

Seth swallowed hard as he nodded.

"My mother and I will take Maggie and Rachel with us to Boise, the capital of the territory, where we'll be making our home. I'll send inquiries to Mr. Sanderson. If your version of the story is correct, you'll have legal grounds to take your nieces back with you. If not—" his voice was stone cold—"you can be sure I'll do everything in my power to see you get what you deserve."

"And what am I supposed to do in the meantime?" Seth whined.

"I don't care as long as you're not doing it on this train."

"So I'm to meet you in Idaho?"

"If you think you'll get them back."

Seth clenched his teeth. "I'll get them back. You can be sure of it, Reb." He turned away, then looked back. "I want to talk to Maggie before I go. I got that much of a right."

Chapter Fourteen

Maggie was leaning on the wagon wheel when she heard the footsteps. She straightened and turned, a terrible sinking feeling dropping her heart a notch when she saw her uncle walking her way. Tucker was beside him. She stared at Tucker's face, trying to read what was written there. It was closed to her.

Well, then if it was up to her, it wouldn't be the first time. She had brought them this far. If they were to be thrown off the train, back into the clutches of Seth Harris, then she would find some other way to escape him. But she wasn't going back with him to Independence. She wasn't going to marry Cyrus Jones and help Seth get his hands on the money her father had left in trust for her. And she'd meant what she said to Tucker earlier. She wasn't going to let Rachel live with the horror she'd known since she was an infant. Maggie would lie, cheat, and maybe even kill if she had to, but she wasn't going to let that happen to Rachel anymore.

Maggie drew herself up to her full height, throwing back her shoulders and lifting her chin. With eyes as cold as steel, she met her uncle's gaze.

"Your uncle is going to be leaving you with us, Maggie," Tucker said as the two men stopped.

His words caught her totally by surprise, and she knew the shock must have registered on her face. He was leaving them? Just like that? She couldn't believe it. Seth had come all this way to bring them back, and now he was giving up so easily. Why? Her eyes narrowed. What was he up to?

"Before he leaves, he wanted to speak with you alone. I'll be just the other side of the wagon." With that, Tucker turned and left.

"I've always figured you for trouble, Maggie, but I never thought you'd turn out to be a thief. Stealin' from your own kin."

The irony of his opening words almost made her laugh aloud. She the thief? She'd taken a few dollars from his money clip—just enough to buy a few blankets, a bit of food, and that old broken-down horse—and she was branded a thief. She stared at him, not even trying to disguise the hate she felt toward him.

"Do you know how much trouble I've gone through to find you?"

Maggie felt a strange surge of power and couldn't help smiling a little. "Whatever it was, it wasn't enough."

"You've a tart tongue, Maggie Harris, but it won't do you any good with me. You think you've gotten too smart for your uncle, don't you?"

She couldn't stop her sharp retort. "I must be. We're staying and you're leaving. You'll never get your hands on the money Papa left us. Mr. Sanderson will see to that."

"So." His thick eyebrows, like fuzzy caterpillars, jumped up onto his forehead. "You know about the trust, do you?"

"I know you've driven Harris Mills to the brink of ruin. I know you've tried to break the trust and couldn't. I know that's why you dragged us to Independence, so you could marry me off to Mr. Jones and try to get the money that way. I know you lied to me all these years about Papa's will."

"So you spend your time listening at keyholes, do you? Well, you're not as smart as you think, Maggie. You didn't hear everything. Sanderson can't help you. He's dead and the mill's nearly bankrupt and the money's gone from the trust. That bastard brother of mine ruined me."

She wanted to hit him. She wanted to scream. She'd lived in fear of him for a long time, but she wasn't going to be afraid of him anymore. "My father didn't ruin you. You did that yourself."

"What do you know about it? If it wasn't for him, the mill would have been left to me from the very start. I could have made a fortune before the war."

"Papa had a fortune and you lost it all." She tossed her head defiantly. "You can't do anything right."

He took a quick step toward her. "I know how to make you keep quiet, girl, and don't you forget it."

"Go on," she said, thrusting her head forward and turning her cheek. "Hit me. But Tucker will stop you before you can do it again."

Seth clenched and unclenched his hands, then moved back from her. The sly smile returned to his mouth. "No, I'll just bide my time, Maggie. Your fancy lawyer—Tucker, is it?—wants to take you to

Idaho. Why do you think that is? I'll tell you why. Because he hates the sight of me. Because I wasn't willin' to pander to the rebs the way your father used to. You ask him about it if you've got the nerve. He wants to keep you here to get even with me. You wait and see. He means to ask you to marry him. He told me so. He thinks he can get his hands on the mill and get even with me that way. I didn't tell him it wouldn't do him any good."

"That's not true. Tucker isn't like that."

"You think not? You think he's any different than me? Than most men?"

Silence was her only answer.

Seth chuckled softly as he turned away. "I think I'll just come to Boise some time to see for myself. You be a good girl now, Maggie, and do as he says. You just mind him. That's what he'll want in a wife."

Maggie watched his retreating back as an icy numbness spread through her.

She didn't *want* to believe him. She tried *not* to believe him.

But what if what he said was true? What if Tucker was only helping her now to get even with Seth? She knew her uncle had many enemies. Was Tucker one of them? Would she be a means of revenge?

Worse yet, now everyone knew she'd lied about parents in Oregon and the payment for getting them there. If Seth had told her the truth, if Sanderson were really dead, there would never be any money.

Then what would become of them?

Tucker leaned against the tree at his back, his eyes closed against the torrent of memories . . .

He'd gone with his father to Philadelphia to talk

with the owner of Harris Mills. "Jeremy's a fair and honest man, for all that he's a Yankee," Farrell had said. "We've sold him cotton for years. Once we talk to him, he'll pay us for the bales we shipped to them. He couldn't pay us after the war began, but now . . ."

But Jeremy was dead, and in his chair had sat his brother Seth. He'd said he had problems of his own, too many to worry about what was happening to a bunch of stinkin' rebs. Spoils of war, Seth had called the cotton Twin Willows shipped to Harris Mills just prior to the start of the war.

"But the cotton was worth well over a thousand dollars," Farrell had protested. "We only want three hundred." Only three hundred dollars to save Twin Willows.

Seth had laughed, then ordered them out.

A few days after their return to Georgia, Farrell Branigan had kissed his wife, then walked to the barn, placed a rope around his neck, and hanged himself. All because of Seth Harris.

And Maggie was his niece.

Maggie waited until she saw her uncle riding away before she reentered the camp. The people had already dispersed to their wagons and Sunday activities, leaving only the Branigans, David Foster, and Rachel to wait for her return.

Rachel broke free of Maureen's hand as soon as she spied Maggie and ran toward her. Instead of the quaking, fearful child she'd left only minutes before, her sister was smiling. "Isn't it wonderful, Maggie? He's gone. Tucker sent him away."

Sent him away? Or had Seth merely left so Tucker could inflict a different kind of punishment on her?

Maggie looked over the top of Rachel's head, her

gaze meeting Tucker's. The warmth they had shared
earlier today was gone. They were back to being
strangers. No, it was worse than being strangers.
She had begun to care for him, just started to
believe she might learn to trust him, and now he
was lost to her. She hurt as she hadn't allowed
herself to hurt in a long, long time.

"Yes," she whispered. "It's wonderful."

"We won't ever have to live with him again, will
we?"

"No, kitten. We won't."

And come hell or high water, they weren't going
to live with any other man, either.

Brooding in the darkness, a cigarillo held between
his fingers, Tucker watched Maggie from outside
the circle of light. She hadn't spoken with anyone
except Rachel since Seth rode out of the camp.
Even when Maureen had tried to draw her into
conversation at supper, she had only nodded or
shaken her head.

What bothered him more? That she was Seth's
niece or that she'd lied to him? He wasn't sure
himself.

But, damn it, she *had* lied to him. Truth meant
everything to Tucker. His life was based on sifting
out the truth and making it stand for something.
Why hadn't she just told them they were running
away from their uncle?

Because, he admitted reluctantly, *we would have
sent them back to him, just like she thought we
would.*

He had no legal grounds to interfere with Harris's
right to his nieces, unless Maggie's story of Mr.
Sanderson was true. And even she had admitted

that she only *thought* her father had left their guardianship to this man in Oregon. If Seth Harris hadn't struck Maggie in front of him . . .

His jaw clenched, remembering how close he'd come to murdering the man with his bare hands when that happened.

Maggie rose from the stool. Firelight danced in the golden highlights of her hair and formed a soft white outline around her perfectly formed figure.

What's the truth, Maggie? What's happened to you? Why do you want to go to Oregon? Why are you afraid of the thunder? And why did you lie to me?

He wanted to crush the feelings he had for her the way he did his cigarillo beneath his boot heel. But he couldn't. They were as strong as ever. He still wanted to protect her, to cherish her, to hold her, to make love to her.

More than anything, he wanted to make love to her. He wanted to make love to the niece of the man who'd driven his father to suicide. The idea was abhorent to him, yet it couldn't be denied.

He turned and walked outside the camp, not able to look at her any longer. Time would take care of these feelings. He knew it would. He'd been surprised at how easily he'd gotten over Charmaine. It would be the same with Maggie.

Except Maggie would be living with his family for several months to come—maybe longer if he couldn't locate Marcus Sanderson. How was he to deal with Maggie and his treacherous feelings in the meantime?

Scarcely aware of her own movements, Maggie poured herself another cup of the strong coffee, then settled back on the camp stool. She stared into the fire, her thoughts drifting back in time.

Cook had warned her years ago. Maggie had been thirteen, fourteen at most, the day she'd sat in the kitchen, listening to the woman talk as she prepared Seth's supper.

"Men are devils, Maggie dear, and you'd be wise not to forget it. You marry them, and suddenly they own you."

"Mama was happy."

"Of course she was happy. She didn't have the sense to know any better. She had this house and servants and fancy clothes. But mark my words, none of it was ever really hers." Cook pushed graying brown hair back from her face with floury fingers. "A woman's owned by her father 'til the day she weds, then she's owned by her husband 'til the day she dies."

Mama not happy? Maggie found it hard to believe. Her memories of her mother were of sunshine and laughter, and she'd always thought she would grow up and marry and be just like her.

"I remember the day my pa brought Danny home from the docks," Cook continued. "Oooh, he was a handsome one, with a glib tongue and a smile that melted ice. Before I knew it, my pa and Danny had decided we would marry. And since I fancied myself in love with him, I thought I was happy. Little did I know."

"What happened?" Maggie asked as she snitched an apple slice from the table.

"I became his little workhorse, that's what happened. It wasn't enough for me to keep his home for him. He sent me out to work for others so's he could spend his time drinkin'. I tried to go home to my pa, but he threw me back, quick as you please."

"Your papa must have been like Uncle Seth."

Cook shuddered. "All men are like your uncle in their souls, girl. All men are. It's just some manage to hide it longer."

Not Papa. Her father had been the most kind, most loving person, always bringing her gifts.

"So, you think your papa was different, do you?" Cook asked, seeming to read her mind. "Well, if he thought so much of you, why is it you're livin' in this house with no more rights than I've got? Did he leave this house to you? No, it fell to that scoundrel of a brother of his. Just like my pa's house went to my Danny and not to me. Sold it, he did, and pocketed the money before he took off to sea."

"But it was your house."

"Not when you're married. The instant the preacher calls you Mrs., nothin' is yours again. Not ever again." Cook shook her head. "You hear me, girl."

"But if you love him and he loves you . . ."

Cook laughed harshly. "Love is for fairy tales and fools. Don't ever trust yourself to no man, Maggie."

The phrase repeated itself in Maggie's head as her thoughts returned to the present. *Don't ever trust yourself to no man.*

Her gaze moved toward the wagon beyond the firelight. She'd seen Tucker standing there some time ago, his cigarillo glowing red in the dark. Was he still there?

Don't ever trust yourself to no man.

Cook was right.

Maggie had told herself not to trust anyone when she joined the train, but she'd allowed herself to start caring for these people. It was her own fault. Perhaps Maureen meant her no harm. Perhaps she could be Susan's friend. But Tucker . . .

Don't ever trust yourself to no man.

No, she couldn't trust Tucker. Cook was right. He was no different from any other man. Love didn't make any difference.

Love was for fairy tales and fools.

MAUREEN'S JOURNAL

May 19. Our train has been touched by tragedy this past week. Three days ago, Marshall Baker and his small son Timmy drowned in the Big Blue River. Poor Mrs. Baker is expecting her third child before long and has another boy to raise as well.

We were not yet over the shock of the accident when we were intruded upon by a man claiming to be Maggie and Rachel's uncle. To our surprise, we learned that Maggie's father was the late Jeremy Harris—of Harris Mills, Philadelphia. (What dark memories that company's name brings with it!) Tucker has chosen for the two orphan girls to continue on with us rather than sending them back with their uncle, a truly odious man.

Nature and mankind conspire against us, and we either become stronger and better because of it or we weaken and die. God grant me strength.

Chapter Fifteen

In the days that followed, Maggie used every opportunity to avoid seeing or speaking to Tucker, and he seemed more than willing to be avoided, taking himself from camp before light and not returning until most people had retired to their beds. Even though he was giving her the solitude she thought she desired, his absence only made her feel worse than before, and her mood turned snappish.

The wagon train followed the trail into Nebraska. Slowly, they left behind the gentle rolling of the Kansas prairie with its trees and streams and colorful wildflowers. The grass-covered plains before them were barren of trees and seemed a foreign land to the emigrants from the forested East.

When David had spoken of the Platte River being flat, muddy, and shallow, Maggie hadn't dreamed how exact his words could be. About two miles wide at the point where the trail first joined the river, the flowing silt known as the Platte was knee-deep at most. She heard the men saying that quicksand dotted the river bottom, and in places the steady flow of the river surged surprisingly strong. Maggie was relieved to learn they wouldn't be fording the river any time soon. It was an experience she would rather put off as long as possible.

Just over four weeks after departing from Independence, the Foster train rolled into Fort Kearny, near the river's south bank. The fort comprised two corner blockhouses, powder and guard houses, a lookout, barracks, and officers' quarters. In addition, there was a post store and the homes of a few settlers. This tiny outpost of civilization drew homesteaders and trappers from hundreds of miles around, and it represented something familiar to the emigrants, making the unknown future less threatening for a time. They stayed for two days.

Supplies were quickly replenished. Wagons were mended. Livestock were reshod. The women embarked on a frenzy of washing and baking during the day, and during the evening hours, the men imbibed liberally of the liquor offered by the friendly merchants of the fort's post store.

It was their last night at Fort Kearny. Tomorrow they would hit the trail once more, traveling farther into the strange, unfriendly interior of North America. As the campfires burned low, Maureen went to sit with Susan Baker, who was feeling poorly, while Maggie saw the children tucked into their beds, the two girls in the wagon and Neal in the tent.

The Branigan campsite silent at last, Maggie sat

down beside the fire and held out her hands before her. They were so rough now she could scarcely do any mending without snagging the fabric. At least her callused hands no longer blistered as badly. Maureen had insisted she could resume driving the teams of mules now that her burn was healing, but Maggie refused to give up the duty. Driving the wagon was something Maggie could do to repay Maureen for all her kindnesses, and it also kept her busy from morning to dusk, leaving her tired enough at night to fall into dreamless sleep—if she was lucky.

With a sigh, Maggie reached forward and poured herself a cup of coffee, then sipped it slowly as she wondered how long they were going to continue this way. Even here at Fort Kearny, she hadn't seen Tucker more than a few minutes a day. She was angry with herself for even noticing his absence. A man—any man—would only bring more trouble into her life. She'd been wrong even to start trusting Tucker. Yet, she couldn't deny how much she missed sitting across from him at supper, how she missed the way his dark eyes followed her about the camp, how she missed his arms around her and his . . .

"Good evening, Maggie."

She started, spilling coffee into the dust at her feet, as Tucker strode into the dying light of the fire.

"Where's Mother? In bed already?"

"No." Her pulse was erratic. She wished he would sit down so she didn't have to bend her head back so far. "Susan wasn't feeling well so Mrs. Branigan went to sit with her."

Tucker removed his hat as he sat on a stool across from her. "Any coffee left?"

Maggie nodded, then poured him some. Their fingers touched briefly as he took the cup from her hand. Maggie felt a small jolt at the contact and wondered if he'd felt it too. Then she pulled back and settled onto her own stool once again.

Surreptitiously, she studied him as he drank his coffee. The red glow of the coals cast strange shadows across the patrician angles of his face.

He's had his hair cut, she noted.

He was wearing the shirt Maureen had been working so hard to finish. He looked different than when they'd first met, she realized. Leaner. Stronger. And more handsome than ever.

She looked away, irritated with herself and her train of thought.

"Maggie, we need to talk."

Their gazes collided above the hot coals. She'd been wanting, yet dreading this moment.

"I'm not sure what your uncle told you about the plans we made."

The plans *they* had made. *She*, of course, had no say in the matter. Her temper began to rise. "He didn't tell me much. Why don't you explain them to me?"

"I've assumed responsibility for you and Rachel until we can locate Marcus Sanderson and verify the contents of your father's will. Your uncle has agreed you can stay with us in Boise until we find Mr. Sanderson."

"I see."

"If we can't find him, of course, we'll have no legal grounds to keep your uncle from taking you back east with him. But I'll do all I can to see that that doesn't happen."

"How very kind of you, Mr. Branigan. I'm sure

you'll do just as you say." Her blood was boiling in her veins. She wanted to ask why he hadn't just sent them back. She wanted to tell him the mills were worthless and he'd gain no riches from marrying her. And she wanted to say no man would ever rule or manipulate or bully her again. But instead of saying any of these things, she rose slowly and turned away. "Good night."

"Maggie—wait."

She glanced over her shoulder. Tucker was standing now. She could feel the intensity of the gaze he leveled upon her, despite not being able to see his eyes.

"There's a lot you haven't told me. Maybe I could do more to help if you did. Why don't you talk to me, tell me the truth?"

Her restraint snapped. "The truth!" She whirled around. "*You* want the truth?" She stepped toward him, leaning over the fire. "Here's truth for you. Not you or anybody else is going to stop me from getting to Oregon. You can make all the plans and agreements you want with my uncle, but we're not staying with you in Idaho—under any circumstances. I don't need your help or your say so to find Mr. Sanderson. And even if he can't help us, even if I'm wrong about Papa's will, even if Sanderson's dead, nothing in heaven or on earth will ever make me take Rachel back to live with Seth Harris. I'll die first."

The gray of her eyes had turned to molten lead. They sparked with fury as she fearlessly faced him. She was even more beautiful in her anger. In that moment, he didn't care that she'd lied to him and the others to get on the train or that she was Seth's niece. He didn't care about anything but Maggie. He scarcely heard and did not understand her angry retort.

He stepped around the fire and grabbed her arms, pulling her tight against him, smothering her protests with a kiss as hot as the glowing coals of the cook fire. There was no tenderness in the way his mouth plundered hers, the fingers of his right hand twining through her hair, forcing her head back, while his left hand held her ever closer to him. He could feel the hammering of her heart beneath her firm breasts.

At first she struggled against him, but suddenly she stilled. And then the kiss became hers as well. She melted against him, her arms clinging around his neck. The fire he'd seen in her eyes was now in her lips, burning him, searing his heart as the heated blood pulsed through his veins. A desire such as he'd never known exploded inside him.

If he didn't stop now, he wouldn't be able to.

Tucker's hands returned to her arms. Firmly, he set her back from him. He could hear her rapid breathing, matching the pace of his own. Her eyes resembled gathering storm clouds, dark and mysterious and threatening.

He was confused about a lot of things when it came to Maggie and the way he felt about her, but he wasn't confused about the desire she stirred in him. He wanted her more than he'd ever wanted a woman, and the wanting only worsened every time he was near her. It didn't help matters any when he lost control and kissed her as he just had.

He wished there was some simple explanation for his feelings for her. He'd sworn no woman would ever again make a fool of him, but Maggie was doing a pretty fair job of it now. She had him talking to himself and taking long walks. She'd lied to him, and even that he found forgivable. If he could just get her to talk to him as he'd asked, to tell him everything . . ..

The night quiet was split as her open palm cracked against his cheek. "Never again, Tucker Branigan," she whispered. "Don't you ever touch me again."

He reached for her, but not in time. In a whirl of skirts, she raced off into the darkness.

Tucker's anger flared. Damn her! Why was *she* angry at *him*? Hadn't he done everything to help her? Hadn't he given her shelter and food and a means of getting to the West? Hadn't he protected her from her brutish uncle when he might just as easily have turned his back to her? Was this the thanks he got for caring for her?

And he did care for her. Too much for his own good. Common sense told him not to let it go any further, to let his anger burn off any lingering feelings for her.

But then he remembered their kiss of moments before. He knew he hadn't imagined her response. She had felt what he felt. She had wanted him as much in her innocence as he had wanted her. But he *knew* what it was he wanted from Maggie Harris, and swift kisses in the dark weren't half enough.

"Whatever your secrets are, Maggie," he said softly, staring at the point where she'd disappeared moments before, "I'm going to find out. You're stuck with me for more than a thousand miles yet."

He turned and picked up his coffee cup, took a

sip, then tossed the remaining liquid into the fire, sending up a shower of sparks. No, not even a thousand miles would be enough for the two of them.

Chapter Sixteen

Maureen Branigan couldn't have been more surprised if a chorus of angels had suddenly appeared on the horizon one morning to herald the news than she was to have the realization come to her in the dead of night.

She was lying on her bed in the wagon, staring up at the canvas cover. The night was hot, and sleep refused to come. She'd been thinking of Twin Willows, of Farrell and Grady, and of Shannon and Devlin. Then she thought of David, and her eyes widened as her hands folded above her chest.

David Foster was, after a fashion, courting her.

And the next thought was just as surprising.

She was enjoying it.

She thought about it often in the following days as she trudged beside the wagons, the train following the trail along the Platte River.

In the distance, to the north and south of the

Platte, sandstone cliffs rose sharply, becoming more jagged and higher still the farther west they traveled. The only trees to be seen anywhere grew on the river's sandy islands. It was a strange, seemingly unfriendly land, and the wildlife that roamed the prairies was equally strange—antelope, buffalo, coyote, black bear, and the ever-present prairie dog.

At night, men, women, and children gathered the dried buffalo dung that littered the ground, digging fire pits to create the draft needed to bring the chips to a blaze. Cooking methods changed. Those few with sheet-iron stoves found they were virtually useless now. Baking became a challenge of improvisation, but the women on the Foster train showed tremendous fortitude and imagination.

The journey progressed with little to break the monotony. Once there was an Indian sighting, and two days later, some Indians approached to trade buffalo meat for tobacco and clothing. The McCullough wagon's axle broke and had to be repaired, and the Adams wagon lost a wheel. The men rode out to hunt and could be seen from miles away across the flat terrain. They brought back all forms of meat for the women to try to make palatable, a nearly impossible task if one was cooking prairie dog.

And whenever Maureen saw David, she felt again the wonderful sense of discovery, felt again the surprise that something so special could happen to her at her age.

She was falling in love.

Maureen straightened, bending backward to stretch her aching muscles, then wiped the beads of perspiration from her forehead. She glanced toward the west. The sun was hovering on the horizon, disinclined to relinquish its reign. The sky had faded from azure to ash, but still the heat lingered, rising up from the earth as if from the bottom of an oven. She felt wilted and weary, but there was still much to be done before she could call it a day. Strips of antelope meat had been baked and were now suspended over the fire to smoke and dry into jerky. Cornmeal cakes were frying in a greased pan.

Standing at the back of the wagon, Maureen, her brief rest over, returned to her task of rolling pastry for the crust of a dried apple pie. Maggie and Neal were tending to the livestock while the inseparable Rachel and Fiona had gone with some other members of the train in search of more fuel for the fire. Tucker, if Maureen had guessed right, was probably somewhere nearby, watching Maggie.

She shook her head thoughtfully. She wished she knew what was going on between those two. You could almost touch the tension in the air whenever they were near each other. She was certain she was right about Tucker's feelings for Maggie. He was falling in love with her—if he hadn't done so already. But Maggie . . . Something about Maggie had changed since her uncle's appearance back near the Big Blue. The door that had opened slightly, allowing people to get to know her, had slammed closed again. Maggie kept to herself, saying little, stubbornly doing more than her share of the chores every day. Something was driving Maggie as hard as she was driving the mules.

"Late supper, Mrs. Branigan?"

"What?" Pulled from her deep thoughts, Maureen turned to look at David as he sauntered into camp. "Oh, yes. I'm afraid so, Mr. Foster." She quickly tucked the stray strands of auburn hair that had slipped from her hair pins back behind her ears, unknowingly leaving traces of flour on her cheeks.

He removed his hat and wiped his brow with a large handkerchief. "Whew. Mighty hot for June."

Maureen agreed with a nod.

"At least the river's low. We'll be crossing the south fork tomorrow. Ought to be at Ash Hollow in 'bout three days."

"Ash Hollow. Is that a town?"

David grinned. "Not hardly a town, ma'am. But it's a nice relief once we get there. Shade trees and plenty of fresh water."

A bath, was the first thought to run through Maureen's head at the words "fresh water."

David leaned toward the fire and sniffed. "Smells mighty good."

She felt slightly flustered. "Where are my manners? Have you had your supper, Mr. Foster?"

"Matter of fact, I haven't. Coop's been a mite under the weather, and my own cookin' isn't very invitin'."

"Won't you join us?"

"Well, I . . ."

"Please, Mr. Foster. You're more than welcome."

His grin broadened. "On one condition, ma'am. That you call me David. I think we've traveled together long enough for that to be proper."

"I think it would be most proper. And my name's Maureen, not ma'am."

His voice was deep and sure. "I know . . . Maureen." Then, as if he too felt the sudden wave of shyness she was experiencing, he cleared his throat. "Guess I'll go wash up." He touched the brim of his hat after settling it over his thick gray hair. "I'll be back shortly."

Maureen felt almost giddy, as if she were seventeen again.

She turned her back toward the side of the wagon and leaned against it. Was it wrong to want to feel like that again, the way she had when she— Maureen Briana O'Toole of Sugar Hill Plantation —was falling in love with Farrell Branigan of Twin Willows?

Farrell. How very handsome he'd looked, riding up to her home astride that tall white stallion of his. A young lawyer with dreams for the future. Their future.

And most of them had come true. Tucker had arrived before they'd been married a year, looking so much like Farrell that she couldn't help but think him the most beautiful child ever born. Farrell's practice had grown as quickly as their family. He'd been involved in Georgia politics and had become a respected man among his peers. They'd been happy. Always happy.

Until the war. The war had taken away more than their plantation and their son, Grady. It had robbed them of the unique closeness they'd shared through the years. It had robbed them of each other. Long before Farrell strung the rope and slipped the noose over his neck, ending his life on this earth and, according to the Church, damning his soul in the next, the man she'd known and lived with had been taken from her. His body had been there, but the spirit of the Farrell she'd loved had already died.

Was it wrong for her to want to know happiness again?

The smell of burning food permeated her wandering mind. "Good heavens," she muttered, dashing away the tears that had sprung to her eyes. "I haven't time for such silliness." She hurried toward the frying pan to salvage what she could of the cornmeal cakes.

Still, she hoped she would have time to wash and change before David came for supper.

Tucker hadn't seen his mother wear anything but black or gray since his father's death. Even before that, her gowns had been the somber shades of mourning. There'd been so many deaths in the family, both the Branigans and the O'Tooles, during the war, and when it was over, there was little enough money for food, let alone clothes. She had just kept wearing the gray and black gowns that had served her through the war, mending and repairing them and making them stretch.

But when he walked into camp that night, Tucker found Maureen wearing a green gown the color of grass in the deep of summer, a green only slightly lighter than her eyes. True, the dress was faded and patched, but on her, it looked beautiful.

When their gazes met, he saw the slight flush of her cheeks, and he thought it better not to mention the sudden change lest her face flame with embarrassment. A moment later, when David Foster strode into their camp wearing a clean shirt, his hair slicked back, Tucker suddenly realized what the change was all about.

His mother and David Foster?

"Please sit down, David," Maureen said softly. "Tucker's just arrived and everyone's waiting to eat." She looked toward her son again. "Tucker? Please join us. The children are hungry and it's growing late."

For a change, it wasn't Maggie who drew his attention throughout the meal. It was his mother. She looked like a young girl, not a woman of forty-one and mother of six. Her smile was frequent, especially when David addressed her, and he heard her crystal-clear laughter more that evening than he had in recent memory.

His mother and David.

And why not? True, David wasn't a Catholic, but he was a God-fearing man. Although the priest back in Georgia wouldn't have agreed with his liberal thinking, Tucker thought it more important that a couple share the same love than the same religion. He wondered if his mother had even thought of it. Maybe marriage wasn't something to be considered between the two. Maybe she was only flattered by his interest.

Tucker dispensed with that notion. Maureen Branigan was no flirt. She was a lady and was as true to herself as she was to others. No, if she were to fall in love, it would be for a union of the heart, for eternity.

His gaze shifted to David across the fire from him. A big bear of a man, he was as different from Tucker's father as a man could be. Farrell had been a handsome man, tall and slender, with aquiline features and hair and eyes the color of rich, dark chocolate. Educated at Harvard. A scholar and a gentleman. Raised in privilege and wealth. David Foster, on the other hand, had spent his life working just to survive. He was more attuned to nature than to the manipulations of men in a courtroom or in government. He operated by common sense and instinct rather than what he might have learned in books.

Yet there were probably more similarities between the two men Tucker was mentally comparing than he at first thought. They were men of good heart and fair play, strong men who knew how to be tender.

He glanced at his mother once again. If David could make his mother look like this, if he could make her laugh and treat her with kindness and dignity, then Tucker couldn't want more. Maureen had been tested enough. She'd lost enough. She deserved to be happy.

Supper finished, Maggie excused herself to go sit with Susan Baker while the children cleared away the supper dishes and Maureen poured the men more coffee. Having settled his mother's situation in his mind, Tucker's attention was drawn to the matter of Maggie.

What was he going to do about Maggie? It was a question that plagued him daily.

Several times, Tucker had thought his anger forgotten, but Maggie's hadn't cooled a bit. He felt it whenever they chanced to be near each other—which wasn't often if Maggie could help it. When their gazes met, he could see her temper simmering in the swirling gray of her eyes. He could read it in the stiffness of her back. And then his own anger would return, magnified each time by the injustice of it all. Ungrateful wench! Didn't she know what he'd done for her? Didn't she understand that he *wanted* to help her? What had she to be angry about? So he'd kissed her. Was that some unforgivable crime? Did she think she was the only woman on earth he might want to kiss? She wasn't *that* desirable. He'd nearly forgotten their kisses already. And he wasn't the one who'd lied to her. He'd always been open and honest with Maggie. So why . . .

"Listen, Tuck." David leaned forward, resting his

elbows on his knees as he sipped his hot coffee.

Tucker looked at the man across from him and couldn't help wondering if David had read the flash of sudden anger in his face.

Blast Maggie anyway! She'd done it to him again. Relentlessly, he shoved her from his thoughts.

"We've come a long way, but things are just going to get tougher from here. The next three days are going to be only a taste of what's to come. We've got the Rockies ahead of us and the Blues and the Cascades after that. Time's gettin' precious. We'll start travelin' on Sundays when we can. We'll allow for service on Sunday mornin', but then we'll have to move on."

"I think folks will understand."

"Oh, I know they will. But not havin' that day of rest is going to shorten people's tempers, wear them thin. Summer heat's here already and not likely to let up much 'til we get to the Rockies. And even there the days'll be plenty hot enough. You're a level-headed fellow, and I'll be countin' on you to help me where you can. Folks look up to you, a lawyer and all."

Tucker watched the frown crease David's weathered face and began to understand what the wagon master was saying. The train was barely more than a quarter of the way to Oregon. What time and fatigue didn't do to the emigrants, the weather and the country would.

"I'll do whatever I can, David."

"I know you will." David nodded, then rose, his gaze moving to Maureen once again. "It was a fine supper. Thanks much, Maureen."

"You're always welcome, David. Tell Coop we're thinking of him and hope he'll join us next time."

His mother's gaze followed David as he left their camp. Then, with a dreamy smile, she walked toward the wagon. "Good night, Tucker."

Well, at least he could take comfort in knowing his mother was happy. It might be the only comfort he had in the days to come.

Chapter Seventeen

The south fork of the Platte was a mile wide at the point David chose to cross. The train was lucky enough to have caught it at low water, but it still wouldn't be an easy fording.

Wagons were raised with blocks of wood and the goods stored inside were offered some protection by tacking buffalo hides to the wagon boxes. Eight yoke of oxen or teams of mules were needed to pull the heavily laden wagons to the other shore. Time and again, the men of the Foster train forded the river, taking over a wagon, then returning with extra animals to attach to the next in line.

Maggie watched as the Baker wagon started across, Paul Fulkerson guiding the ponderous oxen. She could see Susan huddled in the back, her arms wrapped tightly around Wills. She understood the young widow's fear; she knew Susan must be reliving the nightmare of the crossing that had cost her husband and son.

"Are you sure you want to do this?" Maureen asked from her place at Maggie's side. "Tucker said to call him . . ."

"I'm sure. Mr. Foster needs Tucker's help with everyone. I can drive the teams."

Despite her assurances, there was a niggling apprehension in the pit of Maggie's stomach. She'd driven the teams across rivers before, but none so vast as this.

Jake Adams stepped back from the lead team. "All right, Miss Harris," he shouted at her. "You're all hitched up and ready to go."

Maggie drew a deep breath, then glanced over her shoulder at the children. "Sit down and hold on," she warned them. She braced her feet against the footboard as she slipped the reins through her fingers, holding the leather in a death grip. Then, with a shout and a flick of the reins, they moved forward.

They plunged into the South Platte, veering to the right on a diagonal course, going with the current. Despite the propping up with wooden blocks and stakes, the water rushed through the wagon bottom, soaking the children and some of their supplies. Mud sucked at the mules' hooves and the wagon wheels. Men on horseback rode on either side of the wagon, shouting at the straining animals, egging them onward.

Maggie's arms felt as if they would break before they were even halfway across. Time and again, the lunging mules nearly pulled the reins from her hands, jerking her about the wagon seat like a rag doll. The muscles in her back and neck burned.

She spied Tucker near the lead mule. She felt a sudden relief, knowing he was nearby, but it was quickly forgotten as they dropped suddenly into deeper water. A sense of helplessness washed over her as cold as the river water; she was certain they were about to be swept away. Then, just as suddenly as they'd dropped, the wheels rolled up onto higher ground once again.

She glanced at Maureen and saw the strain, mirroring her own, written on the woman's face. Shouting over the sound of the river, Maggie asked, "How are the children?"

With a quick glance over her shoulder, Maureen assured them both that Neal and the girls were fine. Drenched, but fine.

Taking a deep breath, Maggie slapped the reins against the rumps of the nearest mules. Safety and the river's edge still seemed far away. There would be no rest until they reached it.

It took three-quarters of an hour for the Branigan wagon to reach the opposite shore, and the better part of a day for the entire train to cross the South Platte. Except for a few boxes that floated free from the Fulkerson wagon, there were no tragedies to mar this river crossing as there had been on the Big Blue.

They camped for the night just beyond the bank of the South Platte.

The quarter moon rocked on its back in the star-dotted heavens. The ripples of the flowing river reflected the moonglow, turning the murky water into a glittering stream of light. Maggie sat on a rock, staring at the pretty display. The river looked so harmless, so benign. It was difficult to believe the hardship wrought just to cross it.

It was almost as if she were the only person left in the world, so alone, so quiet was the night. The sounds of the wagon camp had faded as people dropped into weary sleep. She was weary as well, yet for some reason, she had sought the solitude of the night rather than her bed.

Pulling her ankles up against her thighs, she hugged her legs and rested her chin on her knees. Every muscle in her body ached as never before. Was it going to get even worse than this? From what she'd overheard David saying, it would, indeed.

How far had she come from Philadelphia by now? A thousand miles? Two thousand miles? Who would have dreamed she would find herself in the midst of this vast wilderness? Surely not her mother or father.

A poignant smile tilted the corners of her mouth as her eyes closed. Her parents wouldn't even know her. The little girl with tight ringlets in her hair, clad in frilly dresses over thick petticoats, had been another person completely. That child had had nothing more on her mind than the new doll she wanted for her birthday or being allowed to stay up to see the guests arrive in all their finery for a house party.

Her mother, had she lived, would have seen that Maggie attended a fine finishing school, perhaps even given her a trip abroad after her coming out. Her father would have scared off unsuitable young men with a dark glower, though she had never been afraid of him. She had always seen through him to his soft heart. And when at last she fell in love with the proper man, her parents would have given her a beautiful wedding and seen her settled into a comfortable house of her own. Her life would have been one of tranquility and joy, one without want. Her parents would have seen to that.

Would that husband have loved her in return? she wondered now. Would she have blindly trusted in him and would he have proved worthy of that trust? How would her life really have turned out if her parents had lived?

Maggie sighed as her gaze returned to the river. She would be eighteen this summer, and she'd left childhood behind forever the night her parents died. It did her no good to look back.

But it was even more difficult to look into the future. There was nothing familiar about any of it. There was nothing certain about it. *If* she got to Oregon . . . *if* she could find Marcus Sanderson . . . *if* he'd drawn up the will and *if* her father had left her money and *if* she could get it and . . .

If . . . if . . . if . . .

Pushing her recalcitrant curls back from her face, she sighed deeply, a sound echoing the futility she felt. It was as pointless to wonder what would happen once she reached Oregon as it was to imagine what might have been if Jeremy and Elizabeth Harris hadn't been killed in that carriage accident. She would do better to get some sleep and worry about just getting through the next day.

She shoved herself off the rock and turned back toward camp, her way dimly lit by the last quarter moon.

She saw the glow of his thin cigar before she saw his silhouette. She wasn't surprised. Even though the few words they'd exchanged over the past week had been heated ones, she often had the feeling he was somewhere close by, looking out for her.

Maggie meant to walk by him without speaking, meant to pretend she hadn't seen him, but he didn't let her do so.

"You did a fine job crossing the river today."

"Thank you," she replied, hesitating briefly, then moving on.

"It's hard to believe you never handled a team of mules until a month ago. You looked like you'd been doing it all your life."

She paused again, giving a half-laugh, her musings by the river returning. "I'm sure my parents would have preferred people thought otherwise."

He stepped closer, his voice low. "What would they have wanted for you, Maggie? Tell me about them."

It was so tempting to talk about them, to pour out all the memories, all the hurts, all the joys, all the shattered dreams. She'd kept it bottled up for so very long, and Tucker sounded so—

"No," she said abruptly. "I don't want to talk about them."

She tried to summon up the anger that had served her so well this past week. But at the moment, there didn't seem to be any anger left. Feeling vulnerable without it, she hurried back to the wagon.

Tucker watched her retreat, but made no move to follow. He finished his smoke as he stood staring at the river. The night was hot and humid, making his shirt cling to his back in damp folds.

He remembered another hot night when he'd stood beside a river, wondering what the next day would bring. . . .

They made camp long after dark. His men were too tired to talk and, instead, sat staring into the campfires. Their faces were smudged with gun powder. Their uniforms were tattered, a mockery of the finery they'd worn when they rode off to join the

Confederacy three years before. There were holes in the bottoms of their boots, at least in the boots of those lucky enough to have them.

Tucker knew it was over. The war had been over for the Confederacy ever since Gettysburg. It was just that they refused to admit it. They would go on fighting until there wasn't an able-bodied man left in the South. Which would probably suit the Yankees just fine.

He turned and looked at his men. They were so young. Boys, some of them. Some probably no older than Devlin, though they would lie about their ages if asked. And tomorrow he would watch a lot of them die in a battle against impossible odds. He was tired of the fighting and bleeding and dying.

Lord, he was tired.

He wondered what was happening at home. How were his mother and father, brothers and sisters? He hadn't had a letter in weeks. Were they alive? Were they well?

He longed for the peace of home. . . .

Tucker flicked the butt of the cigarillo into the river. He wondered why he had thought of that night. Perhaps because his future seemed no more certain now than it had then.

MAUREEN'S JOURNAL

June 8. *We forded the Platte River today. Platte, I am told, means "flat and shallow," and that certainly describes both the river and the land it passes through. The silt makes the river too thick to drink, too filthy to bathe in, and barren of fish. Some have said the river is a mile wide and an inch deep. I dare say it was deeper than that where we crossed, however. Once again all our belongings are wet.*

Mr. Foster took supper with us again. He has the most wonderful laugh.

Chapter Eighteen

The dust rose up from the rolling wheels and the trampling hooves of the animals. It covered everything. It was in everything. The emigrants tasted it in their food, drank it in their water and coffee, walked with it in their clothes, slept with it in their beds.

Overhead, a hot, relentless sun followed them west as they trudged up the steep tilt of earth rising from the flat river valley to the high tableland above. It took them a day and a half to traverse the twenty-two waterless miles, and when they reached the end of the plateau, they found a steep, sudden drop to the valley of the North Platte awaiting them.

Blue Boy's tail slapped lazily at flies as Tucker stared down the forty-five-degree grade. He swore beneath his breath. "How do we get down there?" he asked David.

"We'll chain the wheels to the wagon boxes, tie ropes to the back, and skid 'em down. Everyone walks down. No passengers."

Tucker looked behind them at the approaching train. "Do we wait 'til morning?"

David squinted as he looked up at the sky, then took off his hat and sopped up the sweat on his brow with his sleeve. "No. We're running low on water. I doubt we could hold the livestock here, even for a night. We'll have to do it now."

Tucker knew he was right. The Branigans' water barrels were nearly dry, and the livestock hadn't had anything to drink since leaving the Platte. 'I'll tell my family." He turned his black gelding's head and set off at a canter.

He'd be glad when this day was over. He was worried about his mother and Maggie and even the children. The fatigue never left their eyes, even after a night's sleep, although he'd yet to hear a one of them complain. But they all needed the rest that had been promised to them when they reached Ash Hollow.

He reined in beside the wagon. Maureen had finally managed to force Maggie from the wagon seat to rest her arms and stretch her legs. Maggie and Rachel were walking along the opposite side of the wagon while Fiona napped in the back and Neal handled the mules under the watchful eye of his mother.

"There's fresh water and shade trees at the bottom of the hill, but it's not going to be an easy task getting there," he told Maureen.

He saw the light in her eyes. It seemed forever since they'd tasted fresh water, free of the dust and dirt of the trail, and it seemed even longer since they'd had any shade from the blistering sun.

He felt the familiar sting of guilt. Had he done right to bring his mother and siblings west, putting them through this hell and torture to start over again with next to nothing? Could he have done better for them in Georgia? If he'd gone to work for Charmaine's father . . . He stopped himself in mid-thought. He could never have done that. He couldn't have thrown in with the carpetbaggers for all the money in the world, and Maureen wouldn't have wanted him to, no matter what the rewards.

"Pull up close to the bluff," he told his mother. "I'll take over from there."

Maggie stood at the top of the plateau, staring down the sharp drop of land. She wondered how they would ever manage to reach the bottom in one piece. She heard David Foster shouting instructions as the first wagon began its slow descent, men and beasts straining against the ropes as they fought to keep the heavy load from slipping away on its skid to the bottom.

It was the fifth wagon in line that demonstrated what could happen if the ropes broke free. There was a shout of warning, then it tumbled down the hill like a child's toy, showering splinters as it went, breaking apart and leaving behind all the precious cargo it had held moments before.

Maggie heard Mrs. Gibson's wail and saw her being comforted by other women. *It must be her wagon*, Maggie thought. She didn't know the woman well, but her heart went out to her anyway. What would the Gibsons do now? How would they go on? What would happen to their belongings? Had they come so far only to fail now?

"What happened?" Maureen asked as she rushed

up to Maggie, her gaze turned upon the circle of women where the crying continued.

"They lost a wagon."

"Who?"

"The Gibsons."

Maureen's glance moved to the scene below. "Holy Mother of God," she whispered. Then, looking once more at Maggie, she said, "We've got more troubles. Susan's in labor. She can't walk down that hill and she certainly can't stay in the wagon while they lower it."

"What will she do?"

A flash of amusement sparked in Maureen's eyes. "She'll have a baby." The smile faded. "I'm going to stay with her. They'll have to come after us tomorrow." She put a hand on Maggie's shoulder. "Will you stay and help me? I'll need someone. I could ask one of the other women, but—"

"I'll stay, Mrs. Branigan."

"Good. Now, you'd better let David know what's going on. And tell Tucker. I'm going back to Susan."

The wagon was cramped and stuffy. The lantern hanging overhead was turned low, casting a dim light over the inhabitants. Maureen bent over the young woman, placing a damp cloth on her forehead, then took hold of her hand. "I don't think it will be long now, Susan," she said softly.

But when she looked at Maggie across from her, she couldn't disguise her concern. It was already the wee hours of the morning, and still the child hadn't arrived. Maureen had had some long labors of her own, but there was something different about this. Susan was weakening. Her water had broken long before. Too long. It was going to be a dry birth. And if the child didn't come soon, they might lose them both.

And Maggie . . . The girl was nearly scared to death. She was trying not to let Maureen see her fear. She was trying to be as brave about this as she tried to be about everything else she encountered. But for once, her courage was noticeably failing.

Maureen moistened a cloth and stroked Susan's hot forehead with it. She prayed for a breeze to whisper through the wagon to cool them all.

Susan groaned as she gripped the cloth ties Maureen had rigged at the front of the wagon. Her eyes were pressed tightly closed, her teeth clenched. Her face turned red. The contraction lasted at least a minute as her body fought to expel the life it had nurtured for nine months.

I'm going to faint, Maggie thought as she watched. *How can she go on like this?*

To Maggie, it seemed an eternity since the labor began.

As if Maureen had read her mind, she whispered, "Why don't you step outside for some fresh air, dear? I'll call if I need you."

Maggie nodded, then climbed down from the back of the wagon. Hot and sticky, she longed to be with the others in their camp below, longed to take advantage of the cool streams. She longed to be anywhere but here, watching Susan suffer. Hour after hour, Susan had strained to bring the reluctant child into this world, moaning as each pain wracked her exhausted body. If the baby didn't come soon . . .

She glanced toward the bluff, not surprised to find horse and rider, bathed in the pale moonlight, standing near its rim. She'd known he wouldn't leave them there, all alone in the night. She moved toward him, instinctively seeking comfort in his presence.

"Not yet?" he asked before she reached him.

"No."

"Do you need anything?"

"Just for the baby to come."

Tucker dismounted. Maggie looked up into his face and wished it weren't hidden in shadows. She needed to see him clearly, needed to see the encouragement in his eyes.

"I'm afraid she's going to . . ." Maggie choked back the words before she could utter them.

His arms wrapped around her, gentle but strong, and he drew her against his chest. His hand stroked her hair as he rested his chin on the top of her head. He didn't speak. He didn't need to. Maggie closed her eyes and allowed herself a moment to lean upon someone else, letting the tension and anxiety drain out of her, leaving her as limp as a rag doll, arms dangling at her sides.

Slowly, she became aware of the beat of his heart against her ear. She could feel the heat of his skin through his shirt. She felt the urge to lift her hand to feel the sinew and muscles of his arms and shoulders, but felt frozen in place, daring not to move lest she break the fragile spell.

His lips brushed lightly over her hair, sending shivers racing down her arms. Her pulse quickened.

Tucker . . .

Maureen's cry split the night. "Maggie, come quick!"

Maggie was wrenched back to her senses. She shoved herself away from Tucker and, holding her skirts high, ran back to the wagon. She scrambled inside to the accompaniment of Susan's groans.

"It's coming, Maggie. Hand me those clean blankets." She motioned with her head. "All right, Susan dear. Push. Scream if you want. No one can hear you."

It all seemed to happen quickly after that.

She saw a dark thatch of hair, then the baby's head. With the next push came first one shoulder, then the other, the baby rotating while Maureen supported its head. With a groan that started low and grew louder, Susan found the strength to push one more time, and suddenly, the infant was in Maureen's arms. Even as Susan's final cry filled the interior of the covered wagon, her daughter was lifted high by Maureen and swatted. The thin, objecting wail sounded almost joyful.

Maggie, who knew next to nothing of the acts of marriage or procreation, was awed and fascinated. She hadn't time to be embarrassed by the other woman's exposure. It seemed natural, beautiful, and she felt blessed to have been a part of it.

She knelt near Susan's head. "It's a girl."

The new mother struggled to raise up from the bed. "Is she all right?" she asked weakly.

Maureen looked up. "She's a beauty, my dear. And healthy. Listen to her."

The umbilical cord was tied and severed. Maureen handed the infant to Maggie, instructing her on the bathing and diapering while she cared for the mother. Susan was washed, the soiled sheets disposed of, her torn flesh soothed with a poultice. Even as Maggie cared for the baby, she watched Maureen, admiring the woman's tender ministrations.

Finally, the baby, bathed and wrapped in a soft blanket, was laid in her mother's arms. Susan touched the child's cheek, her smile as old as the ages.

Life was renewing itself.

For now, the hardships of the trail were forgotten as the three women gazed upon the newborn babe, their hearts warmed, their spirits united.

MAUREEN'S JOURNAL

June 11. *Susan Baker's daughter arrived in the wee hours of the morning. It was a difficult birth, but mother and child are doing well. The birthing brought back memories of my own confinements. What joyous times those were! I find myself both happy for Susan and sad for myself. There is a part of me which mourns, knowing I shall never hold a baby of my own again. I am ashamed. God blessed me with six wonderful children, and three of them are with me right now.*

I wonder if all is well for Shannon and Aunt Eugenia. Atlanta is not the city it was before the war. Are they safe? Would they have been better off with us, despite Aunt Eugenia's poor health?

And Devlin. What of my boy?

Ash Hollow is a beautiful oasis in the midst of a harsh land. I wish we could stay at least a week, but always we must prepare to press on.

I'll not complain. We are in good health.

Chapter Nineteen

Clear streams flowed into a translucent pond in the center of a verdant meadow. Wild roses scented the air of the wooded glen called Ash Hollow. The tall hercules-club trees rose nearly thirty feet above them, spreading spiny-leaved limbs in a canopy of green to shade the trail-weary emigrants. Children ran and gamboled like woodland fairies. Everyone, with the exception of the wagonless Gibsons, seemed light of heart.

Throwing off the mantle of adulthood, Maggie frolicked with Rachel and Fiona, wading in the creeks and chasing tadpoles, playing tag with them in the meadow and a game of hide-and-seek amongst the trees and wagons.

Tucker returned early in the afternoon, his game bag filled from a successful day of hunting. Tonight he would grease the wheels and mend a small tear in the canvas cover of the wagon. For now, he wanted only to watch Maggie at play.

She was so beautiful it almost hurt to look at her. Even with her feet bare and her skirts hiked up higher than was proper for a young woman her age, she was nothing short of perfection. Her cheeks were bright with color. Her brown hair was spun through with gold. The bodice of her dress hugged her high, firm breasts and revealed the smallness of her waist.

He felt the familiar tug of wanting and forced his thoughts in other directions.

He grinned as Maggie raced across the meadow, chased by a gaggle of girls and boys. It looked as if nearly every child on the train was now involved. He wished he could take off his shoes and join them. Lord, it had been a lifetime ago since he was that young and carefree. He was almost envious of her.

Tucker remembered the way she'd felt in his arms last night, small and helpless. She'd needed him then. He wished he could get her to talk to him, to tell him about her parents and her uncle and what had brought her to Independence and driven her to follow after the train on that bag of bones she called a horse. It was easy enough to understand why she wanted to escape Seth Harris, but why hadn't she appealed to other members of her family or to friends in Philadelphia? Why go all the way to Oregon? Surely there had been someone she could have turned to. There was so much he needed to know if he was to help her when they got to Idaho. She would have to talk to him then, but he hoped she wouldn't wait that long.

Maureen's hand fell upon his arm. "She's a

special young woman, isn't she?"

He nodded, not sure he wanted his mother to know what he was thinking and feeling.

"Maggie tries not to let anyone get close, but she's really a very loving, selfless person. Look at all she's done to help Susan Baker, taking care of Wills and cooking supper for them. And she's invaluable to me, driving the wagon day in and day out, helping with the cooking and mending—and so good with the children."

"It doesn't bother you that she's Seth Harris's niece? If it weren't for him and Harris Mills, maybe—"

"None of us can change the family we're born into, Tucker. We can only change ourselves."

Tucker couldn't argue with the truth in what she said.

Maureen watched the children as she spoke. "Rachel told me she can't remember her parents. They died when she was a baby. Maggie raised her. If it weren't for her sister, Maggie could have escaped that tyrant of an uncle years ago. And if Harris Mills was so successful, why is she dressed the way she is? Why is she so unspoiled and unpampered? Makes you wonder what-all she's had to go through, doesn't it?"

"I'd like to know," Tucker answered, "but she won't talk to me. She resents my interference."

"I think she's afraid of caring too much. Be patient, Tuck. If it's meant to be, you'll both know it."

Tucker, wearing a wry smile, looked at his mother. "Does it show?"

"Remember, son. You're very much like your father. I almost always knew what he felt."

He chuckled in wordless agreement, then kissed her forehead and turned back toward the wagon. He still had work to do before the day got any later.

Maggie waited until dark, then returned to the pond. She'd taken a quick spit-bath that morning, but she'd promised herself a leisurely swim before they left this idyllic spot.

The night air was warm, contrasting sharply with the icy coolness of the water. Clad in chemise and drawers, Maggie slipped beneath the surface of the pond and swam the length, sinking down until the water closed over her head. She swished her hair back and forth, enjoying the tugging on her scalp. Finally, after soaping her body and hair and rinsing clean, she returned once again to the shore where she wrapped herself in a blanket and sat on a rock.

The night was deathly quiet. Not so much as a breeze disturbed the tall ash trees. The moon had already completed its arc, leaving only the stars to dot the black sky. They glittered down through the leafy branches which formed a canopy over the crystal pool.

Maggie knew it wouldn't be long before the sentries announced the hour of their departure from Ash Hollow. She wished they didn't have to leave this place. It was the first real peace she'd known in a long time.

She heard the baby's cry and turned her head toward the wagons. Susan's baby seemed always to be hungry. So much appetite for one so small. Annabelle Maggie Maureen Baker—a big name for such a tiny person. Little Annie was named for her paternal grandmother first, but also for the two women who had helped bring her into the world. It gave Maggie a twinge of pleasure every time she thought of it.

The crying stopped suddenly, and Maggie knew the baby was nestled at her mother's breast, warm and safe. Maggie hoped little Annie's world would always be warm and safe, but, she knew, even as she wished it, that it wouldn't be so. Even if they weren't out in the middle of the wilderness with many hundreds of miles of trail between them and Oregon still to be traveled, life was never always warm and safe.

Her own peace shattered by such dismal thoughts, Maggie picked up her clothes from the bushes where she'd laid them and started back for the Branigan wagon. She might get an hour of sleep or so if she went to bed right now.

She was almost to her wagon when she saw Tucker leave his tent. She stopped, unconsciously holding her breath. Without a moment's hesitation, he walked toward Susan Baker's wagon.

"Mrs. Baker," he whispered. "Susan."

It wasn't until it stopped that Maggie realized she'd heard the muffled sobbing.

"Susan, are you all right?"

The crying resumed.

"Are you decent? I'm coming in." He hoisted himself over the tailgate of the wagon.

In a moment, the lantern sprang to life, casting the silhouettes of Tucker and Susan onto the canvas cover. Maggie moved closer without realizing she did so.

"Look at them," Susan said in a tear-thickened voice. "My two babies. How am I going to care for them?"

"You've done all right so far."

"Oh, Tucker, you don't understand. I can't. I just can't."

The crying resumed. The male silhouette reached out and drew the female form against him, cradling her head against his chest as she sobbed softly.

Maggie felt an ugly feeling inside, as if she wanted to barge into that wagon and shove Susan right out onto the ground.

"I *do* understand. I've felt just what you feel." Tucker's voice was barely discernible. "There have been times I've sworn I couldn't do what I knew had to be done. It looks bad now, Susan, but you'll do fine."

Maggie stepped up close to the Baker wagon.

"Night's the worst," he continued. "You feel small and helpless. But morning always comes, and somehow you make it through another day. That's the best way, Susan. Just make it through one day at a time. And don't look back. The looking back can kill you if you let it."

Maggie heard something in his voice that made her heart ache.

Susan sniffed. "Thanks, Tucker. You've been more'n kind to me. You and your mother and Maggie. You've all helped me as if you were my own kin. More'n my own kin, likely."

"We're glad we could help. Now you keep that pretty chin up. You're going to be fine. You'll see."

The wagon creaked as Tucker rose inside. Maggie held up the blanket and hurried away, afraid she'd be caught eavesdropping. She crawled beneath the Branigan wagon and forced her breathing to be calm. She knew she wasn't going to get any sleep now. She kept seeing Tucker holding Susan. She kept hearing the pain in his voice when he'd said,

"And don't look back. The looking back can kill you if you let it."

She was angry with Tucker. She felt sorry for Tucker.

Neither emotion helped her to sleep.

It was a night for lying awake, for being lost in retrospection, for wondering about the future.

David rolled onto his back and stared up at the stars. He'd been thinking about the Gibsons. What items they'd managed to salvage after the accident had been stored in several other wagons. The people of the train had been generous in offering a place for Doug and Rose to take their meals, promising Rose a place to ride when she was tired. Once they reached Fort Laramie, Doug would be able to buy a new wagon. But he wondered if the young couple themselves could be salvaged. Rose hadn't quit harping at Doug since it happened. She was either telling him she wanted to go home or crying about all they'd lost.

He thought of the Connolly family—two wagons full of them. Rex Connolly and his wife and daughter rode in one, Rex's elderly parents in the other. Old Mrs. Connolly had been frail at the outset of the journey, and as much as he hoped and prayed otherwise, he didn't think there was much chance of her surviving to see Oregon.

And finally, as was common for him these days, he thought of Maureen. He reminded himself again what an old fool he was becoming. What on earth did he think he had to offer a woman like Maureen Branigan? And she still had two younguns to bring up. What made him think he could be a father to anyone? Closest he'd ever come had been with

Coop, and Coop wasn't that many years younger than David.

But wouldn't it be grand to make a life with her? Wouldn't he love to hold her in his arms as they drifted off to sleep? Wouldn't he like to wake up in the morning to see her pretty face on the pillow next to him?

God Almighty, he wanted Maureen for his wife more than he'd ever wanted anything in his life. If he had the nerve, he'd ask the Almighty Himself to give her to him, but he didn't figure he was worthy enough to ask for something so wonderful, so special as Maureen Branigan.

For nearly five days, they followed the sandy banks of the North Platte. The uphill grade was slight but constant. The June nights grew chilled with the rising altitude. In the distance, the emigrants could see the Laramie Mountains, their peaks whitened with snow even in June. Beyond them, they were told, lay the Rockies.

As plodding day followed plodding day, Maggie found herself growing restless. She had too much time to think. Too much time to think about Tucker. That was the real problem. Tucker. He no longer avoided her as he once had. Nor did he pay any particular attention to her. In fact, all his spare time seemed to be spent seeing to the needs of a certain young widow just one wagon away.

What was he up to, anyway? Susan Baker certainly didn't have any money to marry into. If he wasn't careful, he was going to waste the better part of a thousand miles. Didn't he know he was supposed to be winning her over before they reached Idaho? He certainly wasn't cut out to be a conniving Lothario.

She didn't stop to think how irrational her irritation with Tucker was.

And she was mistaken about Tucker's lack of attention. Maggie would have been surprised to know just how often Tucker was looking at her across the campfire, watching for her as he returned to the train from a hunting foray, listening to her as she told stories to the children. She would never have guessed how often he lay awake in his tent, hoping to hear her mumble or sigh in her sleep, just so he would feel close to her.

Between Ash Hollow and the Laramie Mountains, the earth had spewed up several strange formations of rock and sand as landmarks for the emigrants. For days they could see them, rising oddly toward the sky. Court House Rock came first, a many-tiered heap of volcanic ash and clay, rising four hundred feet into the air. Several of the young men tried to scale it, carving their names midway up its side.

One hundred feet taller and fourteen miles to the west rose Chimney Rock, likened by some to a church steeple or a lightning rod. For countless years, perhaps centuries, wind and weather had worked to erode the stone shaft, changing its conformation until perhaps one day, far into the future, it would disappear from the earth forever.

Twenty miles beyond Chimney Rock, the train reached the towers and gulches known as Scott's Bluff, and two days later, on the last day of June 1867, they rolled into Fort Laramie.

Chapter Twenty

*T*ucker *stepped into the Post Trader's Store. Sta-*
ples lined the shelves—flour, sugar, coffee, beans,
lard, salt. Floor space was filled with barrels, tables,
and heavy tools. There was a cabinet at the back of
the room lined with whiskey bottles and another
with guns and rifles for sale.

The store proprietor greeted him with a smile.
And well he should. The Branigans, like most of the
people on the train, had depleted more than a third
of their supplies getting this far. They would need
to restock before tackling the Rockies to the west.

"Welcome to Fort Laramie. What can I do for
you?" the man behind the store counter asked.

"I have a list of supplies I need." He passed the
list, written in his mother's neat hand, to the
proprietor.

The man glanced at the notepaper. "Won't take

but a minute. You like a drink while you wait?"

Tucker shook his head. "It's a little early for me."

"My name's Burt. I take it you're with the wagon train that pulled in last night." He didn't wait for confirmation as he began pulling items off the shelf behind him. "Where you hailin' from?"

"Georgia."

"Georgia, huh? Is that right? I'm from Iowa myself, but me and the Mrs. have been here for more'n six years now."

The door to the store opened again. Tucker glanced behind him. Several men and women from the train entered the store, their eyes sweeping hungrily over the array of items available.

"Well, I better quit jawin' and get the rest of your supplies together. Place is fillin' up. You're lucky. You're one of the first trains through this season. Still lots to choose from. You look around. See if there's anythin' else you've got a hankerin' for."

Tucker nodded and turned away. He said hello to Paul Fulkerson and his father. Just behind them stood Louise Adams, pert and freckled at thirteen; she blushed bright red when he smiled at her. Seeing her daughter's face, Dorothy Adams laughed aloud, her eyes twinkling with a mother's understanding of a daughter's first crush, then gave Tucker a cheerful good-morning.

Tucker wandered idly among the display tables. He doubted there was anything else he might need that wasn't on the list. Maureen had made a thorough inventory of the items they needed most, and they hadn't any extra money for frivolities. They would be minding every last cent of their meager funds until Tucker set up practice in Boise.

But then his eyes discovered the pretty gray-and-white striped dress. Gray, the color of Maggie's eyes. He picked it up, holding it out in front of him. He'd never bought a woman's dress before, but it looked like it would fit her. Wouldn't she look pretty in it? Or truer yet, wouldn't it look pretty on Maggie? And, if truth be known, he was sick of her two faded, thread-bare, one-size-too-small dresses. Maureen had offered several times to cut down one of her dresses for Maggie to use, but Maggie always refused.

Hang the cost! He wanted to see Maggie in something pretty.

Before he could change his mind, he carried the gown to the counter. "I'll take this, too," he said.

Burt nodded and grinned. "Yes, sir. Lucky woman, your wife. This'll look right pretty on her. My Iris—that's my wife—she made this herself. Does some sewing for the officers' wives, she does. She likes to keep one or two in the store here, just in case someone else is in need of a ready-made. Course, I carry fabric, too, if your wife's lookin' to make herself some more duds."

Tucker didn't bother to correct the man's impression. What was the point? Chances were, Burt wouldn't give him a chance to get a word in edgewise anyway. "No, that will be all."

Monday, July 1, 1867, Fort Laramie

My dear Aunt Eugenia and dearest Shannon,

We have arrived safe and well at this army post. Mr. Foster, our wagon master, has been kind enough to show me maps from his emigrant's guidebook, but I'm still not certain what territory we are in at present. There have been many changes made in recent years which leave me a little confused. But I do know we grow closer every day to Idaho Territory and our new home.

We have traveled through some of the most amazing countryside. Strange formations erupt from the earth with names like Chimney Rock and Court House Rock. And peculiar animals such as the great bison and a small sort of deer called an antelope. Fiona and Neal continue to be excited by each new experience. Even I confess to feeling a sense of wonder at times.

I heard in camp last night that gold has been discovered along the Sweetwater River, and since we will be traveling in that direction, I will not be surprised if some of our fellow travelers leave the train at some point. I feel sorry for their families. I'm sure it would be much more sensible for them to continue to Oregon and build their new lives there. Thank heaven that Tucker is a sensible man. I need not fear he will be struck by the sickness they call gold fever.

We have had two orphan girls traveling with us ever since Independence. Shannon, I think you would take to Maggie, and I hope you will get to meet her soon. She is a year older than Devlin. Her sister, Rachel, has become Fiona's constant companion. They will be staying with us in Boise while we try to locate their guardian. I won't try to tell you more by letter but will wait until we see each other in person.

I hope this letter finds you feeling better, Aunt Eugenia. I am glad you made the decision to remain in Georgia, even though I miss you

more than I can say. We have some elderly
people traveling with us on this wagon train,
but I fear they are not doing well. It comforts
me to know that you are in your own home,
safe from the travails we face daily.

   My darling Shannon, I hope you have written us in care of your cousin Keegan. I long for
news of my children who are not with me now.
Are you well and happy? Have you heard from
Devlin? Is he well?

   I close this letter with a prayer that we shall
be reunited soon.

Your niece and mother,
Maureen Branigan

His arms laden high with bundles, Tucker stepped out of the post store. He'd brought Maggie's
horse with him to use as a pack animal. It stood
waiting at the hitching post, head down and eyes
half closed. He moved to its side and began filling
pouches with the various packages of food staples
and supplies.

"Tuck Branigan?"

Tucker froze in place. It sounded like . . . No, it
couldn't be . . . He turned around slowly.

Wearing a blue uniform, Harry Jessup leaned
against a support post. He was taller than Tucker
remembered. He looked older too. But why
shouldn't he? It had been six years since they'd
bade each other an angry farewell.

"By heavens, it is you." Harry straightened. His
blue eyes peered at Tucker, waiting.

Old feelings of betrayal rose quickly in Tucker's
chest. "It's been a long time, Harry."

"A long time," the soldier repeated, his voice
heavy.

They'd been friends when they were boys. They'd been schooled together by the tutor at Twin Willows and later at the academy. They'd roomed with each other at the university. They'd played more tricks on their brothers and sisters and gotten into more trouble than all their siblings put together. Was this all they were going to find to say to each other now?

"How are my parents?" Harry asked at last. His face was browned by the relentless western sun. Deep lines creased his forehead and the corners of his eyes. A scar ran the length of his face, from left temple to jaw.

Tucker squinted up at the sun, then looked back at Harry. "Fine. They've hung onto The Grove. Doing better than most folks."

"And Peter?"

"He's bitter. But what can you expect? He lost an arm and a wife in the war."

"And a brother," Harry added. "When I tried to see him, he told me I was dead."

That's just how I felt about you, Harry.

Tucker had thought he was finished with these feelings of bitterness. He'd thought these past two months on the trail had wrung from him the last of his anger. He had thought he'd risen above the differences that had divided the nation and thrown them into war. But Harry . . . Harry in his Union blues . . . Could he forgive Harry?

Harry Jessup stepped down from the porch. "What are you doing here, Tuck?"

Tucker's belly went rigid with trapped emotions. "The carpetbaggers got Twin Willows. I'm taking the family to Idaho. Keegan's been there since '64 and tells us there's lots of room for struggling young attorneys."

"Sorry to hear about Twin Willows. But with Farrell at the helm, you'll have the best law office in the west."

"My father's dead." His voice sounded flat, emotionless.

Harry rubbed a hand across his eyes, trying—but failing—to hide the pain that filled them. "My God, Tuck. I'm sorry. I didn't know. No one writes . . ."

It dawned on Tucker that he was looking at one of the loneliest men he'd ever seen. He'd believed in something and taken a stand. He'd fought for the Federals to keep the union together, but in doing so, he'd lost everything—his parents, his brother, his friends, his home.

"Well, I won't keep you any longer," Harry said as he stepped back onto the boardwalk in front of the post store. "It was good to see you, Tuck."

It was good to see you, too, Harry. Real good. I'm glad you made it through the war alive. I'm glad you didn't lose an eye or an arm or a leg. I wish . . . I wish . . .

He turned toward the packs and pulled the straps closed.

"Tuck?"

He looked behind him once again.

"I'm finished with the army. I was planning to head west. Oregon. California. I wanted to join this train."

"That right?"

"If you don't want me to, I won't. I'll wait for the next one."

Tucker shrugged his shoulders in feigned nonchalance. "It's a free country. If David Foster says there's room, then that's up to the two of you."

"Thanks, Tuck."
It's all right, old friend.

Maggie held little Annie in her arms, rocking and cooing, while Susan tended to Wills's skinned knee.

"I've told you not to go with those boys, Wills," his mother scolded. "They're too big and too fast for the likes of you. And they run off too far. I want you to stay close where I can keep an eye on you. Hear?"

"Yes, Mama."

"All right now. You play right here in camp. Understood?"

Wills nodded, then scampered away.

Susan sat down with a sigh. For a brief moment, her hands lay idle in her lap as she stared after her towheaded son. Watching her, Maggie noted the dark circles under Susan's eyes and the gaunt look of her cheekbones. She had such a sad, lost look about her, like a waif begging on street corners.

Was Susan pretty? Maggie supposed so. Or at least, she would be if she weren't so thin and tired looking. Was it the sadness that drew Tucker to her? Maggie wished she understood Susan's appeal, but then, she couldn't even understand why it bothered her that Tucker was doing so much for the young widow. Maggie liked Susan, and she adored the two children. Why shouldn't Tucker help her? She certainly needed all the help she could get.

"Mr. Foster says we're just about a third of the way to Oregon," Maggie said to break the silence.

"Only a third." Weariness lingered in each word. "All this way and only a third."

"Do you ever think of turning back?"

Susan shook her head. "There's nothin' back
there for me. Marshall an' me didn't have much
before. It can't be much worse in Oregon, and
Marshall always said it would be better."

"Do you . . ." Maggie glanced down at the baby.
"Do you ever think of marrying again?" She looked
quickly back at Susan, almost afraid of what she
would see in the girl's face.

Susan's eyes took on a faraway look. "I loved my
Marshall more'n I ever thought a woman could love
a man. He was good to me, an' I've seen a lot of
husbands that ain't. I suppose someday I'll take me
another. My brother's not gonna want to raise these
two younguns of mine. But it'll be a long time 'fore
I'm ready to be another man's wife. A long, long
time."

Strange how a person could feel both sad and
overjoyed at the same time. But that was just how
Maggie felt. She got up, passed Annie into her
mother's arms, then sat beside Susan and hugged
her, sharing the widow's heartbreak while at the
same time, relief spread through her, knowing
Susan had no interest in marrying again soon.

Tucker rode up to the wagon on Blue Boy,
Maggie's horse following behind. He dismounted
and looped the reins around the wagon wheel.

"Were you able to get everything?" Maureen
asked as she approached.

Tucker nodded. "They had plenty of supplies on
their shelves. The man said we're one of the first
trains through this season." He began unloading
the saddle bags.

"David came by while you were gone. Doug
Gibson bought himself a new wagon."

"I thought for certain they would be turning

back," Tucker said, continuing to unpack. "Rose Gibson hasn't quit crying since Ash Hollow. There isn't anyone who doesn't know how she feels about going to Oregon. Only so much of that a man can take."

"She lost her mother's china when their wagon crashed down that mountain." Maureen's voice was filled with gentle understanding.

Tucker turned around, his hands settling on Maureen's shoulders. "You lost a lot more than that, and look at you. You never complain. You never cry. You take care of all of us and help out with Susan and her children too." His eyes thanked her for making it easier for him.

"Hard to believe I was ever the spoiled Maureen O'Toole, is that what you're saying?" Maureen tossed a coquettish grin up at him, dispelling the seriousness of the conversation. She mimicked her own father's thick Irish brogue as she said, "Well, you should know by now that there's no stopping an O'Toole or a Branigan."

Tucker took the hint. Maureen didn't want to be praised for doing what had to be done. Yet he loved her for it. It would have broken him, just as it appeared to be breaking Doug Gibson, if Maureen constantly cried and mourned the loss of family and Twin Willows.

He turned back to the packhorse. His hand touched another package, this one soft and light. The dress. Maggie. She was a lot like Maureen. She never complained. She was a survivor. Vulnerable, yet tough as rawhide. She would stand with a man and fight right along beside him. And she'd probably do her share of fighting the man himself.

"Mother . . ." He took the package from the bag and handed it to Maureen. "I saw this. Thought it might make a nice dress for Maggie." He shrugged, feeling suddenly uncomfortable. "See that she gets it, will you?"

Maureen's eyes were shrewd. "Of course, Tucker."

He picked up the reins and started to lead the horses away, then stopped and looked back over his shoulder. "I saw Harry Jessup at the fort. He's thinking of joining the train."

Before Maureen could respond, he walked on.

Chapter Twenty-one

*M*aggie *stepped down from Susan's wagon and* turned toward her own. She could see Maureen busily sorting through foodstuffs and other supplies and knew Tucker had returned from the fort. A quick glance located him. He was leading Blue Boy and her own gelding back toward the rest of the livestock. It was strange the way she felt sometimes when she looked at him.

No, not sometimes. Always.

You're a dunderhead, Maggie Harris. He's a lying, no-good scoundrel, and you'll be wise to remember it. With that reminder to herself, she nodded for emphasis and hurried on.

Maureen looked up. "How is Susan today?"

"Tired. Much more so than she'll admit."

"All women are tired when they have a newborn. But out here on the trail . . . I don't know how she's done it with no husband to help her. I know I couldn't make it without Tucker." A trace of a smile brightened her face as she turned toward the supplies sitting on the tailgate of the wagon. "Tucker picked up our supplies and brought this back." She handed a package to Maggie. "He thought you might like it."

Maggie stared at Maureen, questioning with her eyes.

"I don't know what it is, dear. Open it up so we can see."

She sat down on the bench beside the wagon; her fingers broke the string tying the package. Pushing the paper back, she revealed Tucker's gift. It was a dress.

She ran her rough hands over the shiny fabric of the gray and white gown. Her throat felt dry and scratchy.

"Why did he buy it for me?" she whispered to herself.

Maureen answered, "Because he likes you and wanted you to have something nice."

Maggie glanced up, but her vision was blurred by sudden tears. She quickly returned her gaze to the dress. It had been a long time since she'd had a brand-new dress. Since she'd developed a woman's figure, she'd been cutting down her mother's old clothes to wear, and most of them had been left behind in Philadelphia. All she had now was the dress she wore and the one extra she'd been able to fit into the makeshift satchel they'd brought from Independence. And she'd thought that would be all she would have until she reached Oregon.

Why had he done it? Why had he bought it for her?

Because he had to. He can't go on ignoring you forever if he plans to marry you.

But the dress was so pretty. He shouldn't have had to spend the money, not when money was so short.

But he thinks he'll get his money back when you're his wife.

Still . . .

"Try it on, Maggie," Maureen prompted.

She shouldn't, of course. She should give it right back to Tucker and tell him she didn't want anything from him. She was working hard to pay her way to Oregon, driving the wagon and helping Maureen. But she couldn't pay him back for the dress. She should . . .

"Get in the wagon and try it on. You can wear it to the camp dance tonight if it doesn't need altering."

Perhaps it wouldn't hurt just to try it on. Then she could give it back to Tucker and tell him to return it. She could make it clear that she wanted no gifts from him of any kind. But it couldn't matter to just put it on for a moment, just to see if it fit. It was so very pretty.

She climbed up into the wagon before she could change her mind.

David was helping Paul Fulkerson and his father, Ralph, repair their wagon axle when the blond stranger approached.

"Excuse me. Are you Mr. Foster?"

David wiped off the grease from his hands with a rag as he looked at the young man. "I am."

"I'm Harry Jessup." He held out his hand toward David. "I'd like to join up with your train."

David took hold of Harry's hand. He had a firm grip. "You from around these parts?"

"I've been assigned to the fort here for nearly two years. I've mustered out of the army now and I'm headed for Oregon."

"Got a family?"

"No, sir. It would be just me and my horse. I'd provide my own supplies but would need a place to store them. I'm willing to work anywhere you need me. I can scout for you, and I'm a good hand with a gun if you need one. I'm not asking for pay. I just want to travel with the train."

David squinted as he looked the young man over. Mid-twenties would be his guess. Tall and good-looking and with a pair of piercing blue eyes that never wavered. Experience with hard times was chiseled into the handsome face. It didn't escape his notice that the man's accent was Southern, although he'd avoided saying where he was from. But unless his instincts were wrong, David believed he was looking at an honest man.

"You can store your things in my wagon." He pointed toward it. "That one yonder."

"Thanks. I'll be back in a couple of hours."

David nodded and returned his attentions to the Fulkersons' axle.

"Maggie, please hurry," Fiona said as she watched Maggie weaving Rachel's golden hair into two long braids. "The music's already started."

"Hurry, Maggie," Rachel added, fidgeting and trying to turn her head to see what was happening.

Exasperated, Maggie rushed to finish. "All right," she said. "You're done."

Maureen picked up her shawl. "Are you coming,

Maggie?" she asked as Fiona and Rachel each grabbed one of her hands.

"In a little while. I think I'll just sit here and enjoy the quiet."

The two girls tugged on Maureen's arms. Laughing, Maureen gave in and was pulled off toward the dance at the far end of the camp.

Maggie watched them go, a faint smile tilting the corners of her mouth. Rachel looked as if she'd grown at least two inches since they left Philadelphia. Her cheeks were rosy, and her eyes had a special sparkle in them. She laughed and played with the other children. Completely forgotten was the shyness that had kept her huddled against Maggie when they first arrived. If their journey west brought them nothing else, the changes in Rachel had already made it worthwhile in Maggie's estimation.

Maggie rose from the stool and crossed to the end of the wagon. The new dress was hanging from the bow just inside. She'd planned to tell Tucker to take it back, but as usual, she'd seen very little of him that day.

How did he manage it? she wondered. How could he always be around when she *didn't* want him and always absent when she *did*?

She stepped up into the wagon, her fingers stretching out to touch the dress. Even here, away from the campfire, the high sheen of the fabric seemed to glow with a light of its own. It was a simple dress with a plain, unadorned bodice. The neckline was scooped, the short sleeves puffed. She'd seen her mother in gowns that cost her father a small fortune, yet somehow—unreasonable though she knew it to be—this dress was the prettiest one she'd ever seen.

Would it hurt so much to try it on just one last time?

Tucker watched as Maggie let herself down from the wagon, so careful not to snag the new dress. It fit her perfectly.

She set a small mirror on the side of the wagon and brushed her thick curls back from her face, fastening her hair with combs. She leaned closer to the mirror, touching her cheeks with her fingertips, then shook her head as if in despair of what she saw there.

"You look very pretty, Miss Harris," he said as he stepped forward into view.

She whirled around to face him. Her wide eyes revealed her surprise at finding him there. "I—I thought you were at the dance."

"I was waiting for you."

She had such an open face. He wondered how she'd ever been able to carry off the lie about her parents as long as she had. He could see her embarrassment at being caught staring at her own reflection, then he read confusion when he told her he was waiting for her. The confusion was replaced by anger and distrust. "You don't have to wait for me. I can find my way there on my own."

"I wanted to wait," he replied as he stepped closer, his voice soft and persuasive.

There went that little jut with her chin. Stubborn as the day was long. That was Maggie Harris.

She turned her back toward him and pretended to fuss with her hair. "Well, *I'm* not ready yet. You go on without me."

"Maggie . . ." He sought the right words. "Don't

you think we can call a truce? I'm not sure what I did to make you angry, but I'd like to make amends. I'd like us to be friends." He longed to reach out and pull her into his embrace. Truth was, he wanted to be *more* than friends, but he knew now wasn't the time to tell her so. "I know I was angry when your uncle came and I found out you'd lied to us. But I told you later that I understood, and if you're right about Mr. Sanderson, I can make sure your uncle can't take you or Rachel back with him. I'll do anything I can. I promise."

She faced him again. Her eyes were narrow with suspicion. Her chin was still held high. "Why did you buy me this dress?"

Because I couldn't help myself. Because I knew it would look lovely on you, and it does. Because it was the same color as your eyes. Because . . .

But he knew he couldn't tell her any of those reasons, so he settled for, "Because I knew you needed one."

"I'll pay you back as—as soon as I can."

She was so damned proud. So determined not to trust or depend on anyone. So resolved to do it all herself. Why did she have to be that way? The dress was a gift. Couldn't she just accept it and say thanks?

"I don't want you to pay me back," he replied, keeping his irritation in check.

"You may not want me to, but I will. I promise. I don't want your charity." Up went that blasted chin another notch.

He wasn't sure what he wanted to do more, throttle her or kiss her. But if he stayed where he was, he was going to do one or the other any moment now. Maybe both.

"Do what you like," he grumbled and stomped off in the direction of the fort.

She was trembling all over. For a terrifying moment, she'd thought he was going to kiss her. And what was worse, she'd realized she wanted him to.

What was wrong with her? She'd had to remind herself several times that he was lying to her, that he cared nothing for her, that he only wanted to use her to get even with her uncle for some reason, and that he thought her an heiress to Harris Mills. Greedy, just like Uncle Seth!

So why didn't she hate him as she did Seth Harris? Why, when he stood so close to her, did her knees want to buckle and her breathing come short and shallow?

With a sigh, she leaned back against the wagon. Jarred by her action, the mirror tumbled to the ground. She bent to pick it up, then paused to look at her reflection.

Why? she asked the girl she saw there. *Why can't you think straight when he's around*?

She hated this feeling of confusion.

It should all be so simple. She'd joined this train for one reason only. To reach Oregon. She'd promised herself she wouldn't become involved. But somehow, she *had* become involved. She'd doctored Maureen's arm and driven the mules and played with the children and helped bring Susan's baby into the world. She'd watched these people struggling across barren, waterless plains; ford high rivers; slide wagons down steep hillsides; sweat beneath a relentless sun and shiver beneath sheets of rain. And she'd gone through it too, struggling and fording and sliding and sweating and shivering right along with them. She had become a part of them.

How had she allowed it to happen?

Maggie set the mirror on the tailgate of the wagon. It wasn't the others that had her confused, she confessed to herself. It was only Tucker. She had a right to be angry with him. So why did she have to fight so hard to remain angry?

She heard laughter and clapping and sounds of fun mingled with music drifting across the camp. Until she'd joined this train, Maggie hadn't ever danced before. It was Tucker who gave her her first dance. Tucker who gave her her first kiss. Tucker who . . .

Maggie stiffened her back and lifted her chin. She might be inexperienced when it came to men, she told herself, but she wasn't stupid. She was a quick learner. If she could learn to drive a prairie schooner and handle the mule teams, she could certainly learn how to handle Tucker Branigan.

With that resolve made, she headed for the dance.

Chapter Twenty-two

Harry Jessup stood beside the wagon master as he was introduced to some of the men on the train. A large campfire blazed off to his right, while a man with a fiddle tuned his instrument off to Harry's left. As the sun settled beyond the horizon, more families approached for an evening of fun and celebration. Tomorrow it would be back to the realities of the trail.

"Here's someone I'd like you to meet," David said, drawing Harry away from Jake Adams and Ralph Fulkerson.

Harry turned his head just as Maureen stopped before them.

"Harry Jessup, this is Mrs. Branigan. Maureen, Harry has joined up with us."

Harry felt his stomach tighten, as if expecting a blow. "Hello, Mrs. Branigan."

"Harry . . ." Her voice was warm and familiar.

Her hands rose to his shoulders and drew him down so she could kiss his cheek. "It's so good to see you again. Tucker told me he'd seen you at the fort."

Harry scarcely heard the wagon master's surprised question. "You two know each other?"

Maureen's eyes never left Harry's. "Our families have been friends for many years, David. Harry here is just like one of my own sons."

Something relaxed inside of Harry, and he smiled at Maureen. He would never forget the sense of peace her words provided, a peace he hadn't known in many long years.

"Well, that's fine," David said. "Just fine." Then, after a brief pause, he drew Maureen away from Harry, saying, "I think it's time for our dance, Mrs. Branigan."

Harry watched as Maureen was swept away to a lively tune. He wished he'd had time to tell her he was sorry about Farrell and to ask after the rest of the family. He looked around for some familiar faces. Finally, he spied a young boy with coal-black eyes and hair standing near a table spread with cakes and pies and cider. There was no mistaking the look of a Branigan about him. He sauntered toward the boy.

"Devlin?"

The boy looked at him. He shook his head. "I'm Neal Branigan. Do you know my brother?"

Of course. Devlin had been about this boy's age when Harry left Georgia in '61. He wouldn't be a boy anymore. He would be a man. And Neal . . . He'd been just a toddler of three last time Harry saw him.

Harry nodded. "I'm Harry Jessup. Tucker and I were friends when we were youngsters." *Before the war*, he might have added. *We were friends before the war*. "I've seen your mother. Where's the rest of the family?"

"That's Fiona over there." Neal pointed toward two small girls dancing together on the fringe of the dancers. "I haven't seen Tucker tonight."

Harry waited, but when Neal didn't continue, he had an odd feeling the news wasn't good. "What about the others?"

"You mean Shannon and Devlin? They didn't come with us. Shannon stayed with Great Aunt Eugenia in Atlanta. We don't know where Devlin is. He just refused to leave."

Would the tearing apart of families never end? Harry wondered. He felt the knot returning to his stomach. "And Grady?" he asked softly, somehow already knowing the answer.

"Grady's dead. He was killed in the siege of Atlanta." Neal spoke matter-of-factly, and Harry realized the boy would only vaguely remember the brother who'd marched off to die for the Confederacy at such a young age.

The siege of Atlanta. Just like Grady, Harry had been there. Only he'd been with the Federals, bombing and blasting the city he'd known and loved. Could he have fired the shot that killed Grady Branigan?

Neal pointed at Harry's scar. "Did you get that in the war?"

He touched the side of his face. "Yes." He'd spent weeks in the hospital after that battle, not for the saber cut on his face, although an inch over and he would have lost his eye, but from the gunshot wound to his side. He'd been lucky. He'd watched more than one man die an agonizing death on the field after being gut-shot.

"Wow! Look at Maggie!" Neal exclaimed.

Drawn back from his ugly memories, Harry followed Neal's gaze. The girl was standing just on the other side of the food table. She was a slight thing with the narrowest waist he'd seen in years. Her thick, curly hair, turned golden in the firelight, was pulled back from her face and fell halfway down her back. She had a pretty face, but even from this distance, it was her wide, round eyes that elevated her to the realm of a real beauty. In her striped gown, so obviously new, she looked more ready for a picnic in a park filled with green trees and shiny black buggies than for a dance amidst the tumbleweeds, sagebrush, and canvas-covered wagons.

"Who is she?" he asked Neal.

"That's Maggie. She's traveling with us."

He searched his memory for a child who might have grown into this woman while he was away. "Is she a relative of yours?"

"Maggie? No. It's just her and her sister." Neal peered up at Harry. A look of disgust came over his face. "Come on. I'll introduce you. You can tell me how you got your scar some other time."

Maggie's hands ran over the skirt of her new gown, then she clasped them behind her back. Her gaze moved slowly around the circle of people, trying to locate Tucker. She told herself it was just so she could avoid him.

"Maggie . . ."

She turned her head to watch Neal and a tall, blond stranger approach.

"This is Harry. He wanted to meet you." With that, the boy turned toward the table laden with goodies, snatched up a couple of pieces of cake, and darted off toward the other children.

His face was rugged and scarred, yet he was without a doubt handsome. His blond hair was shaggy against the collar of his red shirt. His eyes were a piercing blue, their bright color a little disconcerting, especially when he was standing so close to her.

He bowed briefly at the waist. "Harry Jessup. My pleasure, Miss . . ." He waited, his brows lifted in question.

"Harris," she supplied for him.

"My pleasure, Miss Harris." He didn't quite smile, and his gaze never wavered.

There was the look of a hungry man about him. She thought it might have been frightening in someone else, but for some reason, Harry didn't frighten her. There was something in him that struck a cord with Maggie. He seemed . . . alone. And Maggie knew what it was like to be alone. Besides, he seemed somehow familiar. Perhaps it was something in his voice; she had the feeling she'd heard it somewhere before.

"Are you—are you from the fort, Mr. Jessup?" Maggie asked to break the silence.

"I was. I joined the train today."

"Is your family with you?"

He trained his eyes on the dancers. "I haven't a family anymore."

So, she'd been right about him. He was alone.

"I'm sorry," Maggie said softly. "I know what that's like."

They fell silent after that.

Harry's gaze moved over the emigrants. Many of them were families with small children, but there were several young men in their late teens and early twenties. It surprised him that no one had approached Maggie to ask for a dance. Perhaps it was because he was standing beside her.

He glanced once more at Maggie. "Would you care to dance, Miss Harris?"

Maggie shook her head. "I don't dance."

"I'd be happy to—"

"No, thank you, Mr. Jessup," she said firmly. "I really don't care to dance." She sounded almost angry.

"How about some cider then?"

Maggie turned to look up at him. The stubborn set of her mouth relaxed into a smile. "I'm sorry. I didn't mean to snap at you. I would like some cider, thank you."

Harry crossed to the other end of the table and picked up two cups of cider, then turned back toward Maggie. She wasn't alone now. Maureen and David had finished their last dance and were standing in front of Maggie. Harry remembered then that Maggie was traveling with the Branigans, and he wondered how that had come about.

"Harry," Maureen said as he handed Maggie her cup of cider, "I see you've met our Maggie."

"Neal introduced us," he answered.

"She and her sister are traveling with us to Boise."

Maggie's words were abrupt. "Rachel and I are on our way to *Oregon*."

Harry caught the concerned look in Maureen's eyes, then was surprised to see the comforting arm David Foster spread across her back. A moment later, David and Maureen joined the dancers as the music started up again.

"We *are* going to Oregon, Mr. Jessup," Maggie said softly, "and nobody's going to stop us."

But her words didn't really sink in. Harry had

closed his eyes a moment as he rubbed his fingers across his forehead. He'd been glad to find the Branigans aboard this wagon train, glad to know someone familiar would be near him for a change.

Yet they weren't the same. Farrell and Grady Branigan were dead. Shannon and Devlin had remained in Georgia, dividing the family. Neal and Fiona weren't little babies any longer. Maureen Branigan was dancing in the arms of a man not her husband—and she was enjoying it. She was laughing and smiling, and there was that unique glow in her eyes that a woman had when she was in love.

He opened his eyes again, acceptance sweeping over him. How could he have expected them not to be touched by the war? Of course, their lives had changed. And being the Branigans, they had surged forward, accepting what fate brought them and making a better life from it.

Suddenly, he realized Maggie had said something to him. "I'm sorry, Miss Harris. What was it you said about Oregon?"

She glanced at him, then answered, "Nothing, Mr. Jessup."

Tucker remained in the shadows some distance from the blazing campfire. It wasn't enough that he had to deal with Maggie's stubborn and irrational moods. Now he had Harry Jessup to contend with as well. And there they stood, side by side, as if they'd known it would make it all the more difficult for Tucker.

Harry was out of his Union blues now. He didn't look much different from any of the other men. He was wearing a red shirt and denim trousers. His head was bare. Even from across the camp, the scar along the side of his face was visible.

Since leaving Twin Willows, Tucker had slowly come to terms with the war. It had taken him years to reach this point, but he'd been relieved when he quit categorizing people as Yanks and Rebels, them and us. The war had been brought on by politicians and greed, but it had been fought by plain folk who chose sides mostly according to where they'd been born and raised.

But not Harry. It hadn't mattered that his home, family, and friends were in Georgia and, therefore, part of the new Confederacy. He had argued for months against their right to secede from the Union, and when war came, he had sadly ridden north, estranged from all he loved by his principles.

If anything had haunted Tucker through those dark years, it had been the memory of Harry and the angry way they had parted from each other. No brothers had ever been closer than they were at one time. Seeing him now, reading the hurt and pain in his eyes, Tucker wondered if they could find the way to mend the bridge between them.

Tucker's gaze and thoughts shifted from Harry to Maggie. He was struck again by her beauty. If she just weren't so infuriating. . . .

Maybe it was just as well that she was, he thought as he glanced around the gathering. Several young men were obviously enjoying looking at her, but none of them approached to ask her to dance. From nearly her first day on the train, Maggie had managed to make it clear that she wanted to be left alone. Except for the Branigans, Susan Baker, and David Foster, she had succeeded in keeping herself aloof. Most folks wouldn't know what a tender heart she had.

But Tucker knew. True, she could be tough and determined, unreasonable and aggravating, but she was also, by turns, shy, frightened, and uncertain, as well as loving and giving. Others wouldn't know because she held them all at arm's length. But Tucker knew. Tucker had held her in his arms, felt her heart beating against his chest. Tucker had kissed her, tasting her sweetness.

Somehow, Tucker meant to break through to the real Maggie Harris. And he meant to begin right now.

With quick, yard-eating strides, Tucker crossed the ground that separated them. He cast Harry only the briefest of glances before he took hold of Maggie by the wrist.

"This is our dance, Maggie."

Startled eyes stared up at him, but she made no protest as he pulled her close. To the sweet strains of a waltz, they moved across the prairie dance floor, the ballroom ceiling a black sky lighted by a full moon and a million twinkling stars.

So that's how it was. Tucker and Maggie.

Harry wondered what had happened to Charmaine, but he wasn't sorry Tucker hadn't married her. He never had thought she was right for his best friend. Tucker needed someone with a little more fire for life. Charmaine's only interest was herself.

He watched Tucker and Maggie dancing. Her gray eyes were locked on Tucker with a look of wonder and surprise. Tucker's look was darker, as intense as Harry had ever seen him.

Maggie's right for him, he thought—and began to smile.

Harry had liked Maggie right off tonight. His first thoughts had been about how attractive she was; beyond that, he'd felt he had found a kindred spirit in her. He hadn't had time to sort out exactly what it was that made him feel that way. Maybe, if it hadn't been for Tucker, he would have wanted more from Maggie than friendship, but now he knew friendship would be the best thing for them.

Maggie and Tucker.

Harry's smile grew. He felt a little less lonely tonight.

The music seemed to end abruptly. While they danced, she'd scarcely been aware of the movement of her feet or of other people around them. Even now, she felt as if they were all alone in the world.

"You can trust me, Maggie," Tucker whispered near her ear. "I'm your friend. Remember that."

He let the words linger between them a moment, then he turned and walked away, leaving her once again in a state of confusion and chaotic emotions.

MAUREEN'S JOURNAL

July 1. *God sees and takes pity.*

Today, one that I loved was restored to me. Harry Jessup of The Grove has been serving his army at Fort Laramie and now is heading west with our wagon train. And I am not the only one blessed by his return. I see his sorrow, share his pain. In a face so young, his eyes are old. They have seen too much. I have lost a son and a husband to death. He has lost his entire family, yet they are still alive. Perhaps I can fill a small portion of that void.

It will be good for Tucker to have Harry with us. They were always together, from boyhood through law school. Only the war divided them. Perhaps, in their peace, we can put the rest behind us as well.

Chapter Twenty-Three

Maggie tossed restlessly in her bed. Every time she closed her eyes, she could see Tucker, waltzing her beneath the stars. She imagined she could feel his hand on her back, her skin warm beneath his touch. She saw the way her right hand had disappeared inside his much larger left hand. She could hear again his whispered words, "You can trust me, Maggie."

"Damn you, Tucker Branigan!" she cursed softly, tossing aside her blankets. She was never going to get any sleep this way.

She crawled out from beneath the wagon and looked up at the sky. The moon had finished its trek across the heavens, and in the east, the stars were already beginning to fade. It wouldn't be long before the sentries sounded the morning alarm.

Shivering in the cool summer night, she pulled

out a blanket and wrapped it around her shoulders, then set off for a walk to the river's edge. As she neared the Gibson wagon, she could hear their restrained voices. They were trying to talk in whispers, but anger increased the volume.

"I won't go on! I don't care if you did buy this new wagon. I'm not going one step further."

"Rose, there's nothing for us back there. We've no home. I've no job. In Oregon we can have our own farm. It's been my dream ever since I first read about it. Rose, be reasonable."

"Reasonable!" Rose laughed sharply. "Why should I be reasonable? You haven't been. Dragging me out into this God-forsaken country. I could have died if I'd been in that wagon when it fell down that mountain."

"But you *weren't* in the wagon. Nobody was left in their wagons." Defeat laced Doug's words. "We're almost half way there."

"You're going to take me back, do you hear me? You're going to take me back tomorrow. Tomorrow!" The crying resumed.

Maggie shook her head. *Poor Doug.* She moved on silently.

Away from the wagons now, she could see the darker outline of the fort. It didn't have the traditional stockade surrounding it as Fort Kearny had. The buildings—officers' quarters, barracks, bakery, post store, guardhouse, hospital and more—formed a rectangle around the large parade grounds, and it was these individual shapes she could see as night began to fade.

"Stop right there," a voice warned.

Maggie gasped as she froze in place. She heard the footsteps behind her.

"Turn around. Real slow like."

She hugged the blanket close about her as she obeyed.

"Miss Harris?" She saw the man holster his revolver. "What are you doing out here in the dark?" He stepped up to her.

Maggie let out a deep breath as she recognized him. "Mr. Jessup, you frightened me within an inch of my life."

"Good. Maybe it'll teach you not to go wandering around like this. Don't you have any sense?"

"You're not the only one who doesn't think so," she muttered, thinking how much he sounded like Tucker. Miserable man.

He laughed. "Come on. I'll walk you back."

She started to object, then decided against it. As much as she hated to admit it, she knew he was right. David had strict rules about such things. He'd made it plenty clear that the women especially weren't to walk about alone after dark. Out on the prairie, it could be Indians who were the danger. Close to the fort, it could be the soldiers.

Harry matched his pace to hers as they turned toward the wagon camp. "What takes you to Oregon, Miss Harris?" he asked.

"My father," she replied, her words abrupt in hopes he would ask no more.

"Your father? But I thought you were traveling with the Branigans."

She finally understood what was so familiar about him. It *was* his voice; she *had* heard it before. He sounded like Tucker. The voice of the Southern gentleman. It wasn't quite as deep as Tucker's, didn't have that special timbre that was so distinctly his, but the similarity was there all the same.

"I'm afraid I'm a bit confused, Miss Harris."

She *was* being a little unfair. Harry Jessup hadn't

done anything to deserve her rudeness. "My father is dead, Mr. Jessup. I'm going to Oregon to settle his estate. His attorney is there."

"Clear to Oregon? You couldn't settle it back home?"

"No."

"Where is home to you, Miss Harris?"

She should have listened to her instincts and kept quiet. He was asking too many questions, bringing up too many memories. "It *was* Philadelphia, but no more. Rachel and I plan to stay in Portland once we get things straightened out."

"Have you known the Branigans long?"

Long enough so Tucker thinks he can run my life for me. "No, we just met outside Independence. My sister and I were traveling alone, but we had no money for a wagon. Once we reach Oregon, I'll be able to repay them for their kindness to us."

He glanced at her. "I doubt Tucker wants any repayment from you."

"I don't need Mr. Branigan's charity, Mr. Jessup. Like it or not, he'll be repaid."

The sentries fired the morning signal just as they reached the Branigan wagon.

Maggie opened her mouth, prepared to thank Harry for walking her back, when Tucker stepped out of his tent. He stared at the two of them, standing so close together. She knew how it must look, Maggie wrapped in her blanket, her hair tousled after her restless night.

The air seemed to crackle with tension.

"You remember to stay close to the wagons from now on," Harry said to her, then he walked on.

Maggie was only vaguely aware of the sounds of morning all around her as the emigrants prepared for the coming day. She felt heat rising in her cheeks as Tucker continued to watch her. Then, ducking her head, she scurried toward the wagon so she could get dressed.

As soon as he could get away from his morning chores, Tucker headed toward David's wagon. He tried not to think of how angry he'd felt when he saw Harry and Maggie together this morning. It wasn't any of his business if she was interested in Harry. He had no claim on her. He'd told himself time and again that there was no room for her in his life, that he had enough problems of his own without adding hers.

But he also knew it was too late for that. He cared for Maggie. He never thought about his future any more without thinking of Maggie there with him.

David was deep in conversation with a man Tucker hadn't seen before. When David saw him, he waved him closer.

"Tuck, this is Walt Weatherspoon. He wants to join up with us."

Tucker looked at the man. He was a short, wiry man in his late thirties, with a black mustache and wire-rimmed spectacles.

"Mr. Weatherspoon had to stop at Fort Laramie last year when his father fell ill. It was too late to join another train by the time his father died, so they wintered here at the fort."

"The missus an' I've been waitin' for a train bound for Oregon. We would've struck out on our own this spring, but the injuns have been trouble-some along the trail, I hear. We thought it best to travel with others."

Walt Weatherspoon didn't quite look Tucker in the eye as he spoke. Perhaps that was why Tucker had a feeling of instant dislike for the man. But it certainly wasn't a good enough reason to deny him the safety of the train. Glancing at David, he gave a slight shrug and a nod.

David cleared his throat. "You're welcome to join us, Mr. Weatherspoon. You'll have to pull your turn driving the herd of livestock we've got with us, and we expect everyone to pitch in and help when one of the wagons is in trouble. And your wife will have to drive your team when you're out huntin' game or occupied elsewhere. Can she do that?"

"She does what I tell her," Walt replied tersely.

"Fine. You can take your place at the back of the train then," David said. "We'll be pulling out in half an hour."

Walt put his hat back over his thinning black hair. "I'll be ready."

David and Tucker stood side by side as they watched the man walk away.

"I'm not sure I care for Mr. Weatherspoon," David said softly. "I just can't quite put my finger on why."

While Tucker silently agreed, he'd come to see David about other matters. "Is Jessup around?" he asked.

"No, he's left already. I sent him out to scout the water holes ahead of us. There's plenty of bad water between here and the Sweetwater River. Most of the springs are bitter, some are poisonous. I want to make sure we bed down where the animals aren't going to get sick." David gave him a sharp look. "Somethin' important you need to talk to him about?"

"No. Nothing important."

"Your mother tells me he's an old friend of yours. Must be quite a surprise runnin' into him clean out this way."

"Yes, quite a surprise," Tucker answered as his gaze turned west.

He could barely see Harry's dust as he galloped his horse along the trail. Their talk would have to wait. But they definitely were going to talk.

When the train pulled out, Doug Gibson turned his wagon from the line and watched as the other wagons passed him by. For him, the dream of a better future in Oregon had died.

As the Branigans drew up beside the Gibson wagon, Maggie raised her hand and waved at Doug. Though she'd never spoken with him, she felt a little like crying.

Maureen, seated beside Maggie this morning, shook her head sadly. "Rose is making a mistake. When you take away a man's dream, you take away a part of the man."

Maggie gave Maureen's comment some thought, then agreed with a nod.

The road beyond the fort began the ascent toward the Rockies in earnest. The land around them was mostly barren, dotted with sagebrush and greasewood. Ahead of them, the mountain range rose majestically, seemingly benign and covered with green meadows, and deceptively near.

The trail rose steadily upward, trying the patience of men and sapping the strength of their beasts of burden. The air was filled with the snapping of whips and shouted curses as mules and oxen strained beneath the weight of the wagons. Those items that had seemed too precious to leave behind when they left Independence became less so with each passing mile. Where cursing the animals failed, lightening their load succeeded. The side of the trail became littered with objects. The

Fulkersons' anvil was the first thing to go. The McCullough piano was next, followed by Dorothy Adams's much coveted sheet-iron stove.

It all seemed very sad to Maggie, and her mood was extremely blue by the time they made camp that night.

Tucker found Harry just beyond the circle of wagons, rubbing down his horse. He knew Harry was aware of his presence, though he didn't acknowledge him in any way. Tucker drew one of his cigarillos from his breast pocket and lit it, then leaned against the wagon at his back, one knee crooked, his boot heel resting on a spoke.

Harry finished the rub-down, then hobbled the lanky bay and turned toward Tucker, patting the mare's rump as he did so. He picked up the bridle and carried it over to the saddle which lay on the ground not far from Tucker.

Silence stretched between them as Harry leaned against the front wheel of the same wagon, his pose nearly identical to Tucker's. Tucker wordlessly offered one of his cigars. Harry accepted and struck a match. The two men quietly smoked as they stared into the gathering darkness.

It was Harry who spoke first. "You came to tell me to stay away from Maggie?"

"Something like that."

"What happened to Charmaine?"

"She married her cousin, Dennis Pinkham."

Harry nodded thoughtfully, his eyes on the cloudless sky. "Pinkhams always did like to keep it in the family."

"Yes, I guess they did."

"Charmaine wasn't ever right for you anyway."

Tucker didn't reply, though it suddenly dawned

on him that Harry was probably right.

"Don't know anything about Maggie Harris, of course, but my guess is she'd be good for you. There's just something about her. Maybe it's in her eyes. Or maybe it's that stubborn streak of hers."

Now Tucker looked at Harry. He'd expected some sort of objection, at the very least, not Harry telling him Maggie was just exactly who he needed. And it rankled him just a bit to know Harry had already found Maggie's stubborn streak.

Harry turned to meet his gaze. "I mean to be her friend." He stated it simply, firmly. It was a fact, plain and clear. "And yours too if you'll let me."

Tucker felt something give inside him.

"Neither of us was wrong for fighting for what we believed in, Tuck. But we will be wrong if we let the war go on long after Lee's surrender." He held out his hand.

For the first time, Tucker felt as if everything hadn't been lost in the war after all. He took hold of Harry Jessup's hand.

MAUREEN'S JOURNAL

July 2. We left Fort Laramie this morning, and I had the terrible feeling that I would never see civilization again, that I would spend the rest of my life traveling with this cumbersome wagon, eating dust and baking beneath the hot sun. Moving and moving and moving.

And still so far to go.

Chapter Twenty-four

Walt Weatherspoon planted himself in front of David. "You can't expect my family to always travel at the rear. It ain't fair. My children are already coughin' from the dust and gettin' sick from it."

"Mr. Weatherspoon, you'll be moved toward the front when it's your turn. You've only been with us one day. Now get ready to pull out. You're already holdin' us up."

"I can see folks don't have much say in the runnin' of this train," Walt grumbled as he turned away.

David felt his temper rising. Weatherspoon didn't know how lucky he was that David hadn't thrown him off the train then and there. He already didn't like the fellow. Trying to tell David how to run things wasn't going to improve the relationship.

David mounted up, turning his big buckskin

west. He touched his hat and greeted folks as he
rode slowly along the edge of the camp. As was his
usual practice, he stopped beside the Branigan
wagon.

"Mornin', Maureen."

Her smile was like the sunrise—glorious. "Good
morning, David."

"Gonna be another hot one."

"I believe you're right."

Dang, if he wouldn't like to get down from his
horse and give her a kiss. No woman ought to look
that pretty in the morning without having some
man kissing her to start her day right.

"Well, I'd best get these wagons movin'."

She smiled again, and he rode off feeling as if
she'd just given him a present.

Maggie walked alone some distance from the
wagon. Tucker was taking a turn with the mules
today, giving Maggie a much needed rest—if one
could call walking fifteen miles in a day a rest.

She'd had another restless night, tossing and
turning, her thoughts always on Tucker.

You can trust me, Maggie.

She stopped on a swell of land and glanced down
at the train. She thought back over the past months
since she'd first met him. When had he done her
any harm?

She remembered her terrible fear the night of the
lightning storm and the way he'd held and comforted her. She remembered the times he'd kissed
her. She remembered the times they had danced.

She also remembered the infuriating way he'd
told her she couldn't go bathe in the creek unless he
came along. How she hated to be told what to do!
But he'd been right that time. If he hadn't been

close by, what might those savages not have done?
She shivered as she turned and began walking
again.

If she were to be fair, she had to admit it was
Tucker who'd sent Seth away when he came for
them. Only, *why* had he done it? Was it to get even
with Seth as he'd told her? She found Seth's story
harder to believe with each passing day. Perhaps it
was listening to Maureen tell about Twin Willows
and Tucker's boyhood and his dedication to the
law. Perhaps it was hearing about his gallantry
during the war. Perhaps it was knowing how hard
he'd fought to keep home and family together, and
when all was lost, his determination to start anew
some place else.

Again she stopped. Again she looked down at the
wagon. Tucker's familiar gray slouch hat was pulled
low on his forehead so she could see little of his
face. His shirt was dark with sweat. A layer of dust
covered his trousers. His forearms and hands had
been bronzed by the sun. Large, strong hands,
expertly guiding the sure-footed mules up the hillside.

Harry Jessup cantered down the line of wagons,
pulling his bay to a halt at the Branigan wagon. He
and Tucker exchanged a few words. She saw Harry
smile and touch his hat brim before moving on
toward the back of the train.

Harry was a nice fellow. He'd treated her with
respect from the first time they'd met. Why didn't
she find herself thinking about the way he smiled or
the way he walked or the way he sat a horse or the
way he smelled when he pulled her close and kissed
her or . . .

You're an imbecile, Maggie Harris.

She kicked at a rock and felt a sharp, well-deserved pain shoot up her leg from her big toe.

She'd thought herself falling in love with Tucker once. But surely she'd convinced herself of the folly of that. She didn't love him. She wasn't going to ever fall in love. Not if it meant turning over control of her life to a man.

Fairy tales and fools, she reminded herself.

But what if the trust fund was truly gone? Maybe being with Tucker . . . No, she would rather be poor and destitute. She could sew a fine stitch. Even Maureen had told her she'd never seen better. If Maggie had to, she would open a dress shop in Portland and support herself and Rachel that way.

And what if Seth lied to me about Tucker just wanting the mill? Or what if the trust fund isn't gone? She stopped again, her eyes widening.

Of course the trust fund wasn't gone. Seth had lied to her plenty in the past. He most surely had lied about this as well. Her father would have provided for his daughters no matter what. In fact, Jeremy had done it so well that Seth hadn't been able to steal the money from them for all those years. That's why Seth had followed after them.

If only she hadn't been so young when her parents died. If only she'd been smart enough to go see the banker years ago. If only she'd tried to find out about the will. If only someone had just once questioned Seth Harris's authority. If only Marcus Sanderson hadn't moved to Oregon. If only she'd known enough to seek out an attorney. If only . . .

Tucker's an attorney.

She turned her head to look at him once again.

You can trust me, Maggie.

Could she trust him?

Why do you hate my uncle? What did he do to you

that would make you try to use me? Would you try to use me?

Heaven help her. She was so confused.

Tucker returned to the wagon after caring for the mules and checking on Blue Boy and Maggie's horse. The two women were preparing supper. Maggie's dress was damp with perspiration and clung to her soft curves, revealing her high, round breasts and her narrow waist even more than usual. She'd swept her long curls up from her neck, pinning the rebellious tresses in a knot at the back of her head. Long, damp wisps curled around her nape, and he had a strong urge to brush them aside and kiss the skin of her neck.

"Good news," he said loudly as he walked into camp, forcing his thoughts in another direction. "Harry tells me there's a hot springs near the river. Good place for a private bath if you ladies are interested."

Maureen and Maggie looked at him as if he'd just offered them manna from heaven.

He raised a hand before either of them could speak. "After supper, I'll take you there and keep watch so nobody bothers you."

It seemed to Tucker that the meal was prepared and eaten in record time that night. Before dusk had even settled, he and Harry were leading the way to the hot springs.

Tucker settled his back against a river boulder while Harry sat on a tree stump. For a time, they were silent, listening to the muffled sounds of the women and children.

Harry was drawing in the dirt with a twig and didn't look up when he spoke. "Neal told me about

Grady. It must have been hard on your mother."

"It was hard on all of us." Tucker envisioned his younger brother. Maureen said Grady had become a man while Tucker was away, but he could only imagine him as the boy of fifteen whom he'd left behind.

"Remember the time we caught him kissing Carol Anne behind the spring house at The Grove? I didn't think he'd ever forgive us for the ribbing we gave him in front of his friends."

Tucker grinned. "Could you blame him? Carol Anne wasn't exactly the sweet maid of the county, nor much to look at either."

"No, but she sure could teach a fellow a few of the facts of life."

"Harry—not you too?"

Harry laughed and shrugged.

Tucker stared at him for a few moments, then said, "We had a lot of good times together, didn't we?"

"We sure did, Tuck. We sure did."

Another period of silence stretched between them, but it was a comfortable one, shared between friends.

"Why didn't you stay in Georgia?" Harry asked softly. "Atlanta's being rebuilt. There'll be lots of room for men like you."

"We probably would have if Father hadn't . . ." He swallowed. He wasn't sure he'd ever said the words aloud. "Father killed himself, Harry. He'd tried everything to get the money for the taxes on Twin Willows, and when he'd failed for the last time, he took his own life."

Harry stared at him, pain etched in his face.

"After that, there didn't seem to be many reasons to stay but plenty of reasons to go. Keegan had been writing, saying that Idaho was the place for us, and I decided he was right. So we pulled up stakes and here we are."

"I'm sorry about Farrell. Real sorry, Tuck. He was—he was like another father to me."

Tucker nodded, then sought to change the subject. "I just hope Keegan got my letter that we were coming. He lives in a mining town called Idaho City. I've asked him to try to arrange for a place for us to stay while I start my practice in Boise. Some place inexpensive. There's not going to be much money for staying in a hotel or rooming house for long."

"You're not going to be happy staying in town, anyway," Harry commented. "You're going to want a place to spread out, a place to grow things. You're a planter, Tuck. It's in your blood."

Tucker gave a dry laugh. "I don't think they raise cotton in Idaho."

"No, but they grow other things. You need to think about homesteading some land, my friend."

"What about you, Harry? What are you going to do?"

"I'm not sure. But if Keegan's so set on Idaho, maybe it would be a good place for me too." As he spoke, Harry rose from the stump. "Well, I'd better check in with David and see what he needs from me tomorrow. Night, Tuck."

"Night."

For a long time after Harry walked away, Tucker's thoughts drifted into the past, remembering so many good times the two friends had shared as boys. But slowly, the sounds of laughter and splashing intruded on his musings, bringing him back to the present.

Maggie's laughter—that's what he heard above

the others. Hers was like tiny bells jingling in the
breeze.

How had she done it? How had she become so
important to him? She'd fought him nearly every
step of the way. She'd made it clear she wanted no
part of him. Yet, every time he imagined his new
life in Boise, he pictured coming home from the
office each night to Maggie.

She wasn't like any girl or woman he'd ever
known. She wasn't coy or flirtatious, nor was she
worldly-wise. She was just Maggie.

"Tucker?"

He hadn't heard her approach. She was wearing a
clean dress and carrying the clothes she'd washed in
the stream. Her wet hair clung to her back, dampening her bodice. It looked dark brown now, rather
than the honey-gold color he knew it to be.

Unexpectedly, she reached out and touched his
arm. Her gray eyes observed him with a look he'd
never seen there before. "Thank you for bringing us
here," she said softly.

"Glad to."

And then Rachel and Fiona spilled out of the
private bathing spot, followed by Maureen. Maggie
turned from him and hurried with the others back
to their wagon, leaving Tucker to ponder her words.

Maggie's and Tucker's moments together were
brief in the coming days, and their attempts at
conversation were cautious, as if each were testing
the new waters of peace that had sprung up between
them. Days were long, and each mile gained came
hard as the Foster train climbed ever higher into the
Rockies.

Tucker spent more time in his own campsite in
the evenings, and it wasn't long before Harry was as

regular a part of the family gathering as David and Susan had become. The women usually busied themselves with sewing or cooking. The men used these hours to grease the wheels and axles or mend harness and canvas. There was seldom any truly idle time to be found.

Maggie was surprised when she realized that she now knew every family on the train by name. She had discovered people weren't trying to pry into her past. If she was open and friendly with them, they were friendly right back.

And better yet, suddenly it seemed that Rachel was hers again. For so long, she'd felt she had lost that special bond between them, that Rachel had deserted her in favor of Fiona and even Tucker. But now when she saw Rachel with Tucker, instead of jealousy and betrayal, she felt something warm blooming deep inside, as if happiness were a real possibility and not just a pipe dream.

MAUREEN'S JOURNAL

July 4. *What a gala day! The members of the wagon train celebrated the Fourth of July with great fanfare. Although for some of us, it is still difficult to participate in the Union's birthday celebration with a full heart, we are agreed that it is better to move forward than look back.*

The ladies of the train prepared a fine banquet from our food supplies and the wild game the men brought back from the hunt. A number of wagon beds were taken apart to form long tables. Mr. Foster gave a fine oration, and Mr. Adams read the Declaration of Independence. Then everyone gathered around the tables which were beautified with evergreens and wildflowers.

Our refreshments surely proclaimed the fine culinary skills of the ladies of the train. We supped on roast rabbit and antelope, sage hen stew, and antelope pot pie. There were boiled Irish potatoes from Illinois and Mrs. Adams' delicious pickles, and the Fulkerson men made the finest Boston baked beans I have ever tasted. Maggie made two of her dried apple pies, which were joined on the tables by fruit and jelly cakes, two peach pies, and a smooth custard made by old Mrs. Connolly. We washed it all down with tea and coffee and chocolate, and all the good cold mountain water we could drink. Certainly no one left the tables hungry.

The day ended with three cheers for the ladies who had worked so hard to prepare the feast. I shall certainly never forget this Fourth of July.

Chapter Twenty-five

*T*he *Foster train reached Independence Rock on* the eighth of July and made camp near the banks of the Sweetwater River. While Tucker, Neal, and the two younger girls climbed up the landmark to chisel the Branigan and Harris names into the side of the famous mountain, Maureen made a pot pie of sage hen and rabbit with a rich gravy for supper. Maggie, using some of the precious eggs purchased at Fort Laramie, made a pound cake for dessert. Reaching Independence Rock seemed a good reason to celebrate.

David sauntered into camp before Tucker and the children had returned. Maureen saw immediately the sadness in his eyes. "What is it, David? What's wrong?"

"Old Mrs. Connolly. I don't think she's going to make it through the night." With a heavy sigh, he sat down near the fire. "A man leads these people to

Oregon, he sees a lot of 'em die, but it never gets any easier. We've been lucky this time, losing only Marshall Baker and his boy up to now." He raked his fingers through his shaggy gray hair. "The old and the young. It's hardest on them."

Maureen set aside the ladle she'd been using to stir the gravy and went to sit beside him. She placed her hand on top of his where it rested on his knee. "Mrs. Connolly hasn't been well since we started."

"I know. I cautioned her husband against making this trip. He's not so spry himself, but they were determined to go with their children and grandchildren."

Maureen started to rise. "I should go see if I can be of some help."

"There's plenty with her now," David said, pulling her back down beside him. "Mind if we just sit here a spell?"

Maureen shook her head and offered him a smile. With her free hand, she reached up and brushed some hair away from his forehead. He looked so terribly tired. And why shouldn't he? He worked harder than all the rest. He took his responsibility for the people on this train to heart. Their problems were his problems.

"You and Coop will take supper with us, won't you?" she asked softly. "Maggie's made a cake."

He sniffed the air and, finally, smiled. "Appears I'd be a fool not to accept."

"Good." As she rose, she kissed his cheek, surprising herself nearly as much as she surprised David. Feeling the heat rushing to her cheeks, she turned and scurried back to her supper preparations.

"We'll be back for supper, Maureen," David said behind her.

She nodded. She couldn't bring herself to look at him. How could she have been so bold? In all these weeks, he'd never once tried to kiss her, although she'd been certain many times that he was about to. She hadn't even known she was going to do it now. It just happened.

And then she heard it. She turned, her eyes wide as she watched him walk away, a new spring in his step. He was whistling.

Halfway down the rock, Fiona sat down. "Tucker, I'm tired."

"Come on. Going down's the easy part."

She shook her head. "I can't."

Several yards farther down the mountain, Neal stopped and looked back. "Don't be such a baby, Fiona."

"That's enough," Tucker warned his brother as he leaned over to take Fiona's hand. "Here. I'll help you."

Fiona looked up at him. Her eyes looked glassy, and when he closed his fingers around her small hand, he found her skin hot to the touch. He placed his other hand on her forehead. She was burning up.

"Neal, run on ahead. Tell Mother that Fiona's sick and to get her bed ready. Hurry."

He scooped Fiona up in his arms. "Don't worry, princess. I'll have you back in camp in no time."

"She's going to be all right, isn't she?" Rachel asked, her sweet face pinched with worry.

"She'll be fine," Tucker replied. But the feel of her hot skin through his shirt quickened his steps.

Maureen was awaiting him anxiously when he arrived at the wagon. "Tucker, what's wrong?" She held out her arms for Fiona.

Tucker shook his head as he carried his sister toward the wagon. "She's got a fever. It's probably nothing. Too much excitement and heat while we were climbing the rock, is all."

Maureen followed him into the wagon. Her hand caressed Fiona's forehead. "How do you feel, sweetheart?"

"Just tired," her daughter answered. "And my eyes hurt."

"Tucker, have Maggie bring me some water and a rag."

He nodded, then glanced at Fiona. She looked small and helpless, and Tucker felt a tiny stab of fear as he climbed down from the wagon.

It wasn't necessary for him to ask Maggie to get the water. Anticipating the need, she'd brought cool water from the river. Their eyes met for just a moment. His anxiety was mirrored in her eyes.

"She'll be fine," he said again, uncertain if it was to allay her fears or his own.

Maggie offered a gentle smile. "Of course she will." Then she disappeared into the wagon.

It didn't take long for the news of illness to spread. Mrs. Connolly. Now Fiona Branigan. People stood in groups, whispering among themselves. Could the illnesses be related? Could someone they loved be next? Perhaps even themselves?

"What's she got?" Walt Weatherspoon demanded as he approached the Branigan wagon, followed by several other men and women.

It was David who answered. "We're not sure, but we've no call yet to be worried. Probably just a cold."

Walt glanced quickly at the people with him. "I'm not sure we want to take that chance." There were some general murmurs of agreement. "We think they ought to leave the train."

"Now just a minute . . ."

"I've seen how it is with you and the widow." Walt was warming to his role now. "But that's no excuse to endanger the rest of us. Some of us has got younguns of our own to worry about. You think I want 'em takin' sick and dyin' out here just 'cause you've got a fancy for the Widow Branigan?"

David's face grew dark. His voice when he spoke was low. "I don't need the likes of you tellin' me what's right for the people on this train. I made a pledge to these folks that I'd get them safely to Oregon. That's every last one of them, not just the ones that whine and complain like you, Weatherspoon. Now when I think there's reason to ask the Branigans to fall back, I'll do it."

"What if it's cholera?" someone asked.

Tucker could feel the welling up of fear at the word.

"I've seen cholera," David said, his voice louder this time so it would carry across the camp. "And the Branigan girl doesn't have it. Now go on back to your wagons and have your supper. We'll let you know when there's anything to be known."

The grumbling was a little louder, but the people dispersed.

"I don't like it," David said as he turned toward Tucker. "If they start turning against each other, there'll be more trouble than we can handle. If she's not better by morning, I'll have to ask you to fall out of line and travel back from the rest of us."

"You'd better do it now, David."

The two men turned toward Maureen at the sound of her voice. She was standing in the back of the wagon, one hand gripping the canvas as if to hold herself steady. Her face looked pale and pinched.

"It could be just a cold . . . but I think it's measles. Or scarlet fever."

Rachel was running a fever by morning. The following day, the Adams wagon dropped back from the train to travel with the Branigans. Beth Anne, the youngest of Jake and Dorothy's children, was the first to start complaining of a sore throat and fever. Louise was next, then Dorothy herself was laid low.

Tucker drove the wagon while Maggie and Maureen attended the girls. Once Dorothy became ill, Maureen rode in the Adams wagon and cared for both the woman and her children.

Maggie swept the strands of damp hair up from her neck. It was so hot inside the wagon today. She longed to roll up the sides of the canvas, but the light was too painful for the girls' weakened eyes. She arched her back, trying to find relief from the constant ache she felt. Her dress, damp with sweat, clung to her uncomfortably, rubbing her breasts and the skin beneath her arms. She looked forward to the coming of evening, even though on the heels of evening's cool breeze came the shivering cold of night.

She glanced back at her patients. Both Fiona and Rachel had been coughing this morning, and the fever was still present. Their small faces were covered with a purplish-red rash. She'd bathed them earlier and tried to coax them to drink some broth, but neither had any appetite. At least for now they slept.

The flap at the front of the wagon moved aside.

"Why don't you join me, Maggie?" Tucker whispered.

She glanced first at Rachel, then at Fiona, and finally nodded. Her legs felt unsteady as she stood and stepped toward the front of the wagon. Tucker took her hand and helped her onto the wagon seat. She couldn't help the deep sigh that escaped her.

"You could use a rest. Why don't we stop and you can stretch your legs for a while."

She shook her head. "We shouldn't fall any farther back from the train. I can make it until evening." She leaned out to the side and looked back behind them. Jake saw her and waved, indicating they were all right. Straightening, she said, "I'm more worried about your mother."

"She's been through measles before. She had six of us, after all."

"I know, but she had servants to help her then. I should never have let her go to the Adamses. She should be with Fiona. I'll go with them tomorrow."

"Why don't you quit worrying about it for now? Here. We're on a pretty easy stretch." He put an arm around her shoulders and drew her close to him. "You close your eyes and try to get some sleep. I'll listen for the girls."

Maggie stared up at him. The look in his eyes made her feel peculiar inside. Strange but good. His arm around her felt secure. His body was solid and strong. It seemed right to do as he said.

She smiled at him, closed her eyes, and slept.

MAUREEN'S JOURNAL

July 11. *Fiona and Rachel are sick with measles. We are traveling back from the rest of the train in hopes of preventing an epidemic. Normally, I would not be frightened by this illness since I have nursed my older children through it without mishap, but the rigors of the trail make everything seem worse. I pray for a quick recovery, not only for us but for the Adams family, which has also been stricken with the disease.*

We are camped in a valley of the Sweetwater Mountains. The grass is rich and lush; the animals shall not go hungry. The water is good and cold, and we can drink it to our hearts' content. So often the springs we've found since leaving Fort Laramie are filled with bitter water. Sometimes, we gave the mules coffee when they refused to drink the water. The coffee beans can disguise the taste—sometimes.

Chapter Twenty-six

Seventy-seven miles beyond Independence Rock, the emigrants reached a place called South Pass. Seven thousand feet above sea level at the crest of the trail, they were now on the Continental Divide. At this point, about a foot beneath the sod, they found a bed of ice. They chipped away at it, placing big chunks into their water casks.

The ice was an especially welcome relief for those feverish with measles. Fiona and Rachel were over the worst now, as was Louise Adams, but Beth Anne had died suddenly two days before. Dorothy Adams was so stricken by grief that Maureen feared she wouldn't recover from the illness herself. Old Mrs. Connolly, though not a victim of the measles outbreak, had surprised them all. She was still with them, fooling death one day at a time. No other families had yet shown signs of illness, and most were breathing a sigh of relief at having escaped an epidemic.

The nights at this altitude were like the dead of winter. Maggie pulled a blanket tighter around her shoulders with one hand while she stirred a stew with the other. Every so often, she would feel a sudden wave of cold sweep through her, and she would shiver so hard her teeth rattled. The smoke from the cook fire seemed especially strong tonight. Her eyes just wouldn't stop watering.

And she was tired. So very tired. What she wouldn't give for one uninterrupted night of sleep.

"Evening, Maggie."

She straightened and turned around as Harry Jessup rode into camp. "Hello, Harry."

"Tuck around?"

"He and Mr. Adams are hobbling the mules, I think." She motioned with her head in the direction Tucker had gone moments before.

Harry dismounted. "How are the girls?"

"Much better today."

He stepped closer. "You look tired, Maggie. Why don't you sit and let me take care of supper."

"I'm all right," she said with a shake of her head.

He took hold of her hand and removed the ladle, giving her a little shove toward the stool. "You do as I say." He glanced toward the Adams wagon. "How's Mrs. Branigan holding up?"

"She amazes me," Maggie confessed. "She tends to Mrs. Adams all day, and then sits with the girls most of the night. I don't know how she does it." She leaned her back against the wagon wheel, closing her eyes for a moment. "Should you be here, Harry?"

"I had the measles when I was a boy. Tucker and I shared them with Shannon and Grady. You can't get them more than once. But you know that."

"No, I didn't. I don't know much about illnesses like Maureen does."

Harry's eyes were sharp as they looked at her. "You've never had the measles?"

She shook her head as she closed her eyes. "No. Like I said, Rachel and I weren't ever sick much. And we didn't go out often so I guess we just weren't exposed to it." She heard Harry walking around the camp and forced herself to look at him. "Was there something you needed, Harry? Nothing's wrong, is there?"

"No," he answered quickly. "No, I just wanted to see Tucker." He looked at her for a moment, then said, "We found out how Fiona got sick. Weatherspoon's youngest had the measles at the fort. He knew she was sick when he joined up with us."

"Mr. Weatherspoon? But he—"

"Is the one who wanted your wagon off the train," Harry finished for her. "I thought David was going to kill him when he found out. But we won't be having any more trouble from him. He's left the train. Struck out on his own for Fort Bridger. It's a good thing he left before Tucker heard about it. Good riddance, I say."

Maggie sighed. "I guess it doesn't matter now how the children got sick. Just as long as they get well."

Harry looked as if he might argue with her, then simply shrugged his shoulders. "I suppose so. By the way, I brought something for you. For all of you."

She waited, arching her eyebrows in silent question.

"I bagged an antelope today."

Maggie offered a tired smile. "Fresh meat. Maybe the girls will have a little more appetite when they hear that. We—" Another shiver gripped her, causing her to stop in mid-sentence.

"Maggie?" Harry stepped over to her, dropping to one knee beside her. Worried blue eyes looked into hers. "What is it?"

"I'm just cold. It's so hot during the day and so cold at night."

"Here." Harry shucked out of his coat. "Put this around your shoulders."

"The blanket's enough," she protested. "You need your coat." Then she shivered again.

Tentatively, Harry reached up to touch her forehead. "Good lord, Maggie. You're as hot as a skillet."

They heard footsteps and turned together as Tucker walked into camp. His gaze went first to Harry, then to Maggie.

Harry stood up quickly. "Tuck, Maggie's sick."

In an instant, he was beside her, his cool hand on her forehead.

"I've just taken a little chill," Maggie insisted, but her voice was weak. She couldn't be sick. She had too many people who depended on her. She had supper to fix, not just for themselves, but for the Adamses too. Maureen already had too much to do, and the two men were busy trying to keep their wagons in view of the train. No, she just simply couldn't get sick. "I'm all right, I tell you."

Tucker didn't seem to hear her. He lifted her into his arms, just as he had Fiona the previous week, and headed for the back of the wagon.

Tucker placed the damp cloth on Maggie's forehead just as the wagon hit another rut, jarring the passengers. Maggie moaned but didn't open her eyes.

"Careful, Harry," he called out gruffly, knowing even as he said it that there was little Harry could do to keep from hitting the rocks and ruts of the trail.

A small hand tugged at his shirtsleeve. He glanced over at Rachel. The child's worried blue eyes were large in her thin face, but her spots were fading, and there was a new look of health about her. In another day or two, he'd probably have a hard time believing she'd ever been sick.

With a gentle hand, he touched Rachel's cheek. "She's going to be fine," he assured her.

She has to be fine.

He wished his mother were there, but she was still riding in the cramped quarters of the Adams wagon. Although Louise was quickly recovering, three more of the children were ill now, and Dorothy's health declined with each passing day. It wasn't the measles that was killing her, Maureen had told him. It was losing her baby, her Beth Anne, and having to leave her in that small grave at the side of the trail. Maureen had tried to tell Dorothy she had seven other daughters who needed her, but the woman seemed beyond hearing or caring.

Maggie began to cough. She rolled onto her side, gasping for breath, then turned onto her back once more. Complications in the lungs. That was the true danger of the measles, Maureen had said. And now, every time Maggie coughed, Tucker grew more anxious.

Dark circles rimmed her eyes. The purplish-red rash had appeared two days before and had spread from her face to her arms and legs. Her fever continued, bringing chills with it. Tucker would cover her with extra blankets, and then, before long, she was tossing them off and mumbling about the heat.

"May we sit beside Mr. Jessup for a while?" Fiona asked.

He nodded without taking his eyes off Maggie. "Just don't tire yourselves."

"We won't."

Tucker tugged on the blanket, drawing it up to Maggie's chin. Then he allowed his fingers to stroke the side of her face. "Get well, Maggie," he whispered. "Get well."

He felt so damned helpless. Tucker detested the feeling. Even as a boy, he'd usually found himself in positions of control. He was a natural leader. Other boys had always looked to him to decide what sort of mischief they would get into. He'd been younger than many of his schoolmates as he'd waltzed through courses beyond his years, but even so, he'd been more often a leader than a follower.

When the war came, he'd found himself an officer, commanding some men twice his age and more. He'd led them into battles. He'd watched many of them fall. He'd sat beside men and boys who'd become his friends and watched the life flow out of them in a stream of red, hating himself for not being able to stop it.

The helplessness. How he hated it!

Tucker dipped the rag into a basin of water and used it once more to cool Maggie's fevered brow. He smiled sadly as he looked at her. He'd always been helpless with Maggie, too, he thought. And he hadn't ever been able to figure her out either.

Yet it didn't matter. He loved her anyway.

Yes, he loved her. There was no point in fighting

the words any longer. He'd tried to tell himself he would get over her just as he had Charmaine, but the feelings he had for Maggie went deeper than anything he'd ever felt before. It didn't make sense. She wasn't elegant or especially refined. She didn't have a case full of beautiful clothes, nor did she fuss over her hair for hours. He'd never heard her complain about driving the mules or helping with the cooking or mending or any of the other dozen chores she performed daily. She was sometimes shy and often as stubborn as one of the mules. He doubted she knew how to play the piano or the harp, and she was definitely no horsewoman.

No, Maggie wasn't anything like the girl he'd always thought he would marry. Maggie was different. Maggie had grit and courage and determination. And he loved her.

She opened her eyes suddenly, but he wondered if she were really awake. Her beautiful gray eyes were dull and fevered.

"Why do you have a beard?" she asked in a husky whisper.

"Wha—" It was such a strange, unexpected question, he almost laughed. "I guess I don't know, Maggie. Why do you ask?"

"I just wonder what you'd look like without it." Her eyes drifted closed. "I think I'd like your face. I'll bet your chin is square."

She started coughing again, this time rolling onto her side and staying there. Tucker straightened the blanket she'd thrown off as she rolled over, then allowed his hand to remain on her shoulder.

She wouldn't believe him if he told her he loved her. Maggie didn't trust him. He wasn't even sure if she trusted Maureen, despite how close they'd become these past months. No, he would have to wait awhile. He would have to give her time to learn to trust him.

One thing he knew for certain. She wasn't going on to Oregon. She was going to stay in Boise—as his bride.

He raised a hand and thoughtfully rubbed his beard. His smile returned. What would he look like without a beard? What a strange question for her to ask.

"Get well, Maggie," he whispered as he leaned toward her, "and I'll let you see what I look like without it. And if you like it, I'll never grow one again." He brushed his lips against her temple. "I love you, Maggie."

MAUREEN'S JOURNAL

July 16. Beth Anne Adams died. Mrs. Adams is failing. Now Maggie is sick too.
Where will it end?

Chapter Twenty-seven

She can't go on," Tucker said as he sat on the stool, facing his mother and David. "She needs rest and quiet. She's sicker than any of the others have been."

David shook his head. "I can't stop the train, Tuck."

"I know. That's why I'm going to stay here with her. When she's able to ride, we'll catch up with the train."

"Tucker!" Maureen exclaimed.

He raised a hand. "Don't say it, Mother. My mind's made up. Harry can help you with the wagon, and Neal's been working like a man all along. Fiona and Rachel are almost completely well now, and the Adams wagon should be able to join the train before long. At least the older children are well enough to help with the young ones and their mother so you can take care of your own."

"But it's just not right, son. You and Maggie alone out here . . ." Her green eyes were filled with doubt.

He knew what she was saying and he didn't care. People could talk all they wanted about the two of them left alone for days, maybe weeks, in this country. Gossip was the least of his worries. But if she died, he would never forgive himself. He wasn't going to subject her to one more day in that jouncing wagon.

"There's no other way," he said. "The children need you. Besides, we couldn't stay back with the wagon. We'd never catch up with the train. Once Maggie's well enough, the horses will be able to cover the same ground in a third, maybe even a quarter of the time."

David placed his hand over Maureen's. "Tucker's right."

Maureen nodded in resignation. "If it's what must be done."

"We'll be all right, Mother." He offered a smile. "I promise."

She smiled gently in return. "I know, son," she whispered, her eyes caressing him with a mother's gaze.

David slapped his hat against his shin a few times, his expression thoughtful. "Tomorrow we take the Sublette Cutoff. There's more water on the route to Fort Bridger. Better trail. More forage for the animals. But we lose a full week that way. The first fifty miles of the cutoff's a rough stretch. No water, barren, grassless. We'll push hard across it to reach water at the Green River. Two days if nothing goes wrong. The trail's pretty easy to follow. You won't lose us."

Tucker nodded as he listened, knowing that tomorrow the wagons would move out of sight and it would be up to him to see that they rejoined the train safely.

"'nother few days, the cutoff joins with the main trail up from Fort Bridger. We turn northwest then. It'll take us about a week to reach Soda Springs. You should be back with us by then."

"Don't worry," Tucker said firmly. "We'll be there."

Maggie opened her eyes slowly. It was a moment before she realized she was staring at a clear blue sky overhead, a moment more before she knew she was lying on the open ground. It was morning. She could tell by the way things smelled. A warm wind gusted, sending a flurry of dust into her face. She turned away from it, coughing as she sat up to look around.

She felt the blood drain from her head. She was alone! The wagons were gone! There was a moment of heart-stopping panic before common sense asserted itself. She couldn't be entirely alone. She was lying on a bed made of dried grass and blankets. A cook fire, the ashes cooling, was only a few feet away; a skillet and coffee pot sat nearby. Two saddles lay in the shade of a scrub pine.

She rubbed her fingertips against her forehead, trying to get her bearings. She remembered she'd been sick. Fevers and chills. Measles. Just like Rachel and Fiona and the Adams children. She'd been put to bed in the wagon. After that . . . She shook her head. Everything after that seemed a blur.

No, not everything. Tucker had been there. She could see him bending over her, giving her sips of water, placing a cool cloth on her forehead. Tucker. Always Tucker.

She raised a hand to the top of her head, encountering a tangled mass of curls. It would take hours of tugging to get her hair in order again. She wondered if her comb was nearby.

Maggie heard his footsteps only moments before Tucker stepped into view. His eyes looked tired, his face care-worn. He seemed different somehow, even more handsome than usual, if that were possible.

"Maggie." He said her name softly, simply. It flowed over her like warm honey. A tender smile stole across his mouth, vanquishing the look of fatigue she'd seen there just seconds before.

Her heart did a little skip. "Tucker." Her voice came out cracked and broken.

His smile broadened.

It was then she knew why he looked different. "You shaved off your beard."

Tucker approached her, hunkering down beside her bedroll. His grin had a boyish appeal to it now. "I had a bit of extra time while you slept. Besides, it was hot. Seemed like the thing to do."

His jaw was square, just as she'd thought it was, and there was a dimple near the left corner of his mouth. Even shaved, there was a shadow of the beard just below the skin's surface. She remembered how surprised she'd been when he kissed her and the beard didn't scratch. What would it be like for him to kiss her now?

Her eyes widened, and she looked quickly away before he could read her mind. "Where is everyone?" she asked in a hoarse whisper.

"The train moved on a couple of days ago. We'll

catch up with them as soon as you're able to ride."

"We're here alone?" Instantly she was aware of her scanty attire. She was wearing only a chemise and muslin drawers beneath the light blanket covering her. She looked at him again. "Have you been taking care of me all this time?"

He nodded, and something in his eyes made her wonder if he'd seen her in less than what she wore now.

"I've been terribly sick?"

"I was afraid I was going to lose you a time or two. But I just kept telling you you had to get better. And you did."

Better? Was he so sure? It seemed that her heart was acting terribly funny, and her breathing wasn't at all steady.

"I'll fix you something to eat. Your fever broke yesterday, and you've been sleeping like a log ever since." He rose and stepped away from her, speaking as he neared the campfire. "How about some bacon and fried potatoes? Mother left us what she could. There's a loaf of bread too."

Bacon and potatoes and bread. Her mouth instantly began to water. Yes, she was hungry. Starving, in fact. "May I help?"

He glanced back over his shoulder at her. "No. You sit right there. I'm a fair cook when I have to be." He began stirring up the fire.

Maggie touched her tangled hair again, wondering suddenly how she must look. She had no idea how long she'd been sick, but she knew it must have been quite some time. She hated for him to see her this way.

"Is there somewhere I can wash up?" she asked hopefully, her hunger completely forgotten.

"Matter of fact, there's a stream right down in that draw."

Maggie started to rise, but fell back with a thud, her legs behaving like wet noodles. She tried again with the same results. Tears of frustration sprang to her eyes.

Tucker must have heard her. He turned around. From the way his eyes looked at her, she knew if she'd been able to stand before, her knees would have turned to jelly beneath that gaze. She didn't understand. She'd never been the recipient of such a look. It almost frightened her with its intensity, yet it wasn't an angry look. It was more like . . . like . . .

"Here." His word broke the spell that had surrounded her. "I'll carry you down to the stream. But you give a shout when you're ready to come back. Don't try to walk up. Promise?"

She nodded. There was a lump in her throat which prohibited a verbal reply.

Tucker gathered a few things together—a bar of soap, a blanket from his bedroll, and Maggie's satchel—then walked over and lifted her effortlessly from the ground. Without a word, he carried her down the slope into the narrow draw.

The clear mountain stream gurgled and splashed over a layer of smooth stones. The grass beneath the trees, pines and aspens mixed in together with the indefinable scrub, was green instead of the sundried shade she'd grown so used to. There was even an impudent wildflower flaunting its purple hue near the base of a quaking aspen.

Tucker set her gently near the edge of the stream. "Remember to call me when you're ready," he reminded as he handed her the satchel.

"I will." She didn't look at him as she clutched the bag to the front of her chemise.

When he had disappeared over the ridge once again, Maggie opened the bag. Her two older dresses were inside, along with a change of undergarments and a pair of stockings. Beneath them she found a couple of hair ribbons and her comb.

Glancing once more toward their camp to make sure Tucker was nowhere in sight, Maggie crawled behind a nearby tree and relieved herself before shucking out of her clothes to begin her bath.

The water was icy cold, in sharp contrast with the increasing heat of late morning. Without the strength to stand, it wasn't easy to wash, but somehow, Maggie managed it. She splashed water on one leg, lathered and rinsed, then moved to the other leg. In like fashion, she slowly cleansed away the accumulated sweat and dust of the previous days. Finally, she lay on the blanket and leaned her head toward the stream. The cold nearly took her breath away, but she was determined to wash her hair before combing out the snarls.

Maggie knelt on Tucker's blanket while she dried off as best she could with the small towel, then struggled into her clean undergarments and dress. Her strength on the wane, she sat on the blanket and began the arduous task of combing the thick mass of tangled curls. It seemed an impossible chore. She could scarcely find the energy to lift her arm, let alone pull and struggle with the knotted tresses.

"Maggie? May I come down?"

"Yes," she answered, her frustration clear in the lone word.

Tucker was down the hill in no time. "Feel better?"

"No." Dark depression hung over her like a cloud.

"What is it?" He knelt beside her.

"How will I ever be able to ride a horse? I don't even have enough strength to comb my hair." Tears returned and she sniffed them back with an unladylike sound.

Tucker had the gall to laugh softly.

She shot him a look meant to shame him into silence.

"I'm sorry," he apologized. "But you're worrying too soon. We've got plenty of time for you to get your strength back before you have to ride a horse. As for your hair . . ." He took the comb from her hand. "I can do that."

He moved behind her, and soon she felt the tug from the comb on her scalp. She closed her eyes, bracing herself with her hands, her arms slightly behind her.

There was a sudden flash of memory, of her nanny brushing her hair at bedtime before her parents came to kiss her good-night. Elizabeth had always smelled of lilacs and Jeremy of pipe tobacco. No one had combed her hair in years, and it felt so good. So very good.

It was peaceful for a while, soothing. Then things began to change. She became aware of the heat of his body near her back, a heat that seemed to sear her skin through the bodice of her gown. His hand was almost caressing as it stroked the comb through her damp hair, tugging gently as it worked out the tangles and snarls. She imagined his hand caressing the rest of her as gently. The sounds of the gurgling brook and the rustling aspen in the summer breeze faded into the background until all she could hear was her own heartbeat, thudding in her ears.

What was wrong with her?

She turned her head until she could look into Tucker's brown eyes. His hand stilled in midair.

"Tucker . . ."

His gaze flicked to the collar of her dress, then drew back to meet her eyes. He leaned closer. Everything about him seemed to take on a darker, harder edge.

"I'd better take you back," he said, his whispered words sounding harsh. "You've already done too much for your first time up."

Maggie felt the sting of disappointment, yet didn't know why. The last of her energy drained from her, and she allowed herself to go limp in his arms as he carried her back to her bedroll. Once there, she fell into a troubled, exhausted sleep.

MAUREEN'S JOURNAL

July 25. It has been nearly a week since we left Tucker and Maggie behind. I think about them constantly. Has she recovered? Are they even now following our trail? Are they in danger from Indians or wild animals? Tucker has been my strength and courage for so long, although he may not know it. What would I do without him?

We crossed the Bear River Mountains today. Thick clouds of dust—almost always a part of our journey—surrounded the wagons as we descended into the valley, making it difficult to see what lay below. We are now most assuredly in Idaho Territory. There have been several arguments among the men about it. It seems the boundary has changed several times. This land has been part of Washington Territory and Oregon Territory and now it is Idaho.

Whatever its name, it seems we are nearly to our destination. I pray so.

Chapter Twenty-Eight

Tucker filled the canteens from the stream. One more day of rest for Maggie and then they would be able to begin their journey. For someone who'd seemed so close to death, she was rebounding with amazing speed.

He was almost sorry the time had come for them to leave this place. There was plenty of game available in the area and ample fresh water. The weather had been mild. The past few days with her, watching her strength returning, seeing the color come back to her cheeks, had only made him love her more.

But they had to leave. Not just so they could catch up with the train, but because if they didn't, he wouldn't be able to keep his promise to himself to give Maggie time to fall in love with him. He wasn't sure what she felt for him now, although he thought the anger and disdain she'd once expressed was forgotten. Eight weeks and hundreds of miles had helped, but she was still confused about her feelings for him. He knew it. He could see it in her eyes when she looked at him.

Tucker wasn't confused. He loved her and he wanted her.

His fingers tightened around the canteen. *Lord,* how he wanted her!

Sometimes he didn't think he'd be able to control himself. Like that first morning after the fever broke, when they'd been right here beside this stream. When she'd turned to look at him and whispered his name, he'd been tempted to lay her back on that blanket and make love to her then and there, even if she was still too weak. That same fire of desire was simmering inside him yet.

He straightened and glanced up the hillside. The delicious odor of frying venison wafted down to him. She was cooking their lunch. He'd tried to make her let him continue the cooking duties, but she'd insisted she could do it.

He grinned. Yes, she was getting well. Her stubborn streak had returned.

Tucker climbed up the side of the draw, pausing at the top when their camp came into view. Maggie was standing over the cook fire. Her honey-brown hair, as abundant and unruly as ever, was tied at the nape with a ribbon, then fell in a mass of curls over one shoulder. Her faded brown dress clung to her high breasts, molded to the firm curves.

When he was caring for her, when he'd thought she might be dying, he hadn't given any thought to the perfection of her body. But now it was different. Now he could think of little else.

She turned, as if sensing he was there. Her smile was tentative. "Are you hungry? The steaks are almost ready."

He was hungry, all right, but not for food. He nodded and started toward her.

Maggie stabbed a piece of meat with a knife, then dropped it onto a tin plate which she held out to Tucker.

"We'll be leaving here in the morning," he said as he settled onto a felled tree. "I think you're well enough. We'll try and make twenty miles tomorrow if you can handle it. After that, we'll need to move a little faster. As fast as you can take. With luck, we'll be able to catch up with the train in less than a week."

"I'll do whatever's necessary. I can handle it."

He met her gaze. "Yes, I believe you can." He thought she could probably handle anything she set her mind to.

Maggie lay on her bedroll, pretending to be asleep while she surreptitiously looked at Tucker across the blazing campfire. The light flickered across his face, making him look both appealing and sinister at the same time. That strange feeling in the pit of her stomach intensified.

She wished they didn't have to leave tomorrow. Something—*different* had happened in the past few days. She wasn't sure what it was, but she didn't feel it was complete quite yet. It was as if they were leaving with something still unfinished.

She closed her eyes. It wasn't as if they'd talked a lot or shared anything of great importance. She wished they had. She wished she'd had the courage to ask the questions that rolled around inside her head. She wished she knew who and what Tucker really was. Was he the man who'd stayed behind to care for her so tenderly? Or was he the man who would go to any length to get his hands on her inheritance?

Memories of Tucker drifted through her thoughts. Tucker with Rachel and Fiona. Tucker with Maureen. Tucker with Harry. Tucker bringing in a fresh kill. Tucker straining to lever the wagon out of a rut. Tucker rubbing down Blue Boy. Tucker with his beard. Tucker clean-shaven. Tucker watching her as he was now.

She realized with a start that she'd opened her eyes to find him staring at her. Her mouth felt dry. Her heart beat erratically in her chest.

"I thought you were sleeping," he said.

Maggie sat up, her gaze locked with his. "No." She knew it was growing cold as the night deepened, but she felt strangely flushed.

"You should be. It'll be a hard day tomorrow."

"I'm not sleepy. Maybe I'll walk down to the creek."

Tucker glanced at the dark sky overhead. A quarter moon spread a soft light over the earth. "I'll come with you."

"No," she said quickly. "I . . . I need to be alone." She felt her face grow warm. It wasn't for the reason it sounded, but she let him think so. She needed a moment away from him, a little time to bring her racing heart under control.

"All right," he answered. "But be careful going down that hill."

She got to her feet. "I will." Ducking her head, she hurried past him.

She made her way carefully down into the draw, slipping a little on unsteady legs, walking as quickly as the faint moonlight allowed. She dropped to her knees on the bank of the stream and dipped her fingers into the cold water, scooping up palms-full to splash against her hot cheeks.

Was she getting sick again? She couldn't shake this strange feeling. Hot and cold at the same time. Almost dizzy, but different somehow. Her stomach was turning cartwheels.

Once again she splashed water on her face, then sat back on her haunches and stared out into the darkness.

Tucker waited what seemed a very long time. The fire burned lower. The moon traipsed across the cloudless sky. Finally, he could wait no longer. He got to his feet and went in search of Maggie. He found her kneeling by the stream.

"Maggie, what's wrong?"

She didn't jump at the sound of his voice, didn't look surprised as she turned her head toward him. She made no reply, just looked at him in silence.

"Maggie?" He stepped closer.

Gracefully, she rose from the ground. Her face looked pale, her damp cheeks sparkling in the moonlight. She was unbelievably, undeniably beautiful. She needed no jewels, no fancy gowns. She was perfection personified.

He couldn't stop himself. He was drawn to her as irresistibly as a child to a peppermint stick. His arms went around her, and he drew her close. She raised her face to him and accepted his lips against hers without protest.

All the tenderness, all the concern he'd felt these past ten days was represented in his kiss. He wanted to cherish her, love her, care for her for the rest of his life.

Maggie. His Maggie.

One of her hands drifted up his back, lacing her fingers through the shaggy hair at his collar. Her other hand rose to his cheek where her fingertips lightly brushed the skin.

Her touch lit a fire in his veins.

His dark facial hair *was* more scratchy than his full beard had been. That thought flitted through her mind as he drew her closer. But as his mouth became more demanding, it drove all conscious thought away.

His hands cradled her face as he nibbled on her lower lip, then traced hungry kisses down her neck before returning once more to her mouth. Maggie moaned deep in the back of her throat as a new wave of emotions washed over her, leaving her weak in the knees. Her skin tingled.

"Maggie, look at me."

It was nearly impossible to open her eyes. She no longer seemed to have control over her own body. It strained toward Tucker of its own volition, seeking something she didn't understand.

"Look at me."

She forced open eyelids made heavy with passion.

His fingers gripped her arms as he held her back from him. "Maggie?"

He seemed to be asking her a question, and her only answer was to sway toward him once again. She wanted to be close to him. She *had* to be close to him.

"Maggie—" Her name came from deep in his chest and was torn from his lips.

His arm scooped beneath her knees as he lifted her against him. He carried her quickly, silently up from the creek and into their campsite.

Hot embers were all that remained of their fire, embers that mirrored the heat searing the secret-most part of her. As Tucker set her feet on the ground, she felt her whole body quiver in expectation. She looked up to meet his gaze. His umber eyes were afire with a light of their own. They burned into her soul, holding her forever captive in their hypnotic depths.

His hands traveled leisurely down from her shoulders, slowly stroking the length of her arms. His fingers closed around her wrists, lifting her palms to his lips. He kissed one hand and then the other and then the first again. When he freed her wrists, it seemed the most natural thing in the world to lift her hands to his shoulders, if only to seek balance.

But there was no balance to be found. Her world was rocking in an exhilarating, terrifying, mesmerizing storm of emotions.

Tucker's fingers moved along the front of her bodice, freeing each tiny button from its hole. As he pushed the fabric open, his hands brushed her chemise-covered breasts. She sucked air into her lungs as the flesh grew taut.

He pushed her dress from her shoulders. It slid over her heated flesh to fall in a circle of fabric around her feet.

Maggie closed her eyes. She felt like a tree buffeted by a strong wind, bending to his will, knowing she would break if she resisted. She was vaguely aware of Tucker lifting her arms so the chemise could be drawn over her head. She felt the cool air of night only in comparison with the warmth of Tucker's fingers as they caressed slowly down from her shoulders until each hand cupped a breast.

Never! Never had she felt anything like this. There was an ache—a wonderful ache—deep inside her, crying for him to stop, begging him to go on.

And he did.

His tongue lathed her nipple, causing another moan to rise up from some deep well within. Her fingers tightened on his shoulders as her head dipped backward. Her hair swayed against the bare flesh of her back. Tucker's mouth worked upward, sending jolts of tingles over the surface of her skin.

"Tucker . . ." she whispered hoarsely.

He kissed her throat, then returned to her lips. She opened to the probe of his tongue and reveled in the taste of him. And as he kissed her, his hands roamed over her, delighting all the undiscovered places of pleasure. Her head spun. Her knees weakened . . .

And suddenly they were lying naked beneath the stars and a sliver of silver moon. Only nature was a witness to the explosion of wanting, to her reaching out and drawing him to her. Only the night knew of the joy they gave and received. Only the wilderness heard their cries of ecstasy.

And only Tucker saw the look of love written on her face as he held her in his arms and, still entwined, they drifted into an exhausted sleep.

Chapter Twenty-Nine

"*Maggie.*"

She stirred at the whisper of her name near her ear. She moaned in protest at the interruption of her dreams, then snuggled closer to the warmth nearby.

"Wake up, sweetheart."

Reluctantly, she opened her eyes.

It wasn't a dream. She was lying naked in Tucker's arms. It had happened. Every glorious moment of it had been real.

"We need to talk."

Talk? No, she only wanted to feel.

He kissed her temple, allowing his lips to linger lightly, the morning breeze whispering against their flesh.

She brought her hand up from her side and played with the hair on his chest. Her foot slid along his leg from ankle to knee, then back again. She kissed his throat just above his collarbone. He tasted salty. She felt his muscles tense and, for the first time, had a glimmer of understanding of the power she wielded.

"Maggie . . ." Restraint made his voice sound hoarse as he drew slightly away from her. "I mean it. We need to talk."

With a sigh of resignation, she let her head fall back onto the blanket and closed her eyes. "All right."

"I didn't mean for—for last night to happen, Maggie. I meant for us to wait."

Her eyes opened slowly. "To wait?" Why, for any reason under heaven, would they have wanted to wait to share what they had shared?

"Until we could find a priest or a minister."

"A priest?" She scarcely knew she parroted him. She was too consumed by the pleasure of just looking at him.

"But to be honest," he whispered, "I'm not sorry it happened. Now there's no reason for us to wait to be married. You can't turn me down now." He grinned seductively, then drew her close against him. "We'll be married just as soon as we reach Idaho. Later, I know the family would like it if you took instruction from the church, but I'll understand if you don't."

She heard little of what he said. She only knew that wild, warm feelings swept through her at his touch. He was going to make love to her again. And then, she hoped, again.

"You won't have to worry about Mr. Sanderson. You won't have to meet him or talk to him. I'll take care of everything. And you won't have to face your uncle again either or worry about wills or guardians. I'll take care of you and Rachel. You won't want for anything. I promise. I'll build you a fine house and you'll have plenty of everything you might want."

The warm feelings cooled to solid ice as his words began to break through the physical sensations his touch aroused, finally making sense to her dazed mind. He was talking of marriage and big houses and fine clothes. He was talking of taking care of her. But just how was he going to pay for all those luxuries? With profits from Harris Mills perhaps?

She drew her head back from him, looking up to meet his gaze. No, she didn't want to believe it. Uncle Seth had to have been lying.

But that wasn't the worst of it, she realized. Tucker was talking as if she had no choice in the matter. He was trying to take over her life, to tell her what she could and could not do. What was it he said? *You can't turn me down now*?

"But I *must* go to Oregon," she insisted.

"Nonsense." He sounded like he was talking to Rachel. "You'll be my wife. You'll have no reason to go."

"I *want* to go."

"Why? Just to meet the man who *might* have been your guardian? You won't need a guardian once we're married. You'll be my wife."

"Who *says* I'll be your wife?" She shoved away from him, sitting up and covering her bare breasts with the blanket.

"Of course you're going to be my wife." His voice rose in anger to match her own.

"I'm not ready to marry you or any other man, Tucker Branigan."

"But last night—"

She jumped to her feet and began struggling into her clothes, not an easy task when she was trying to hide her nakedness behind the blanket. "Last night was a mistake, just like you said. It shouldn't have happened. Did you think if you bedded me it would give you the right to control what I do? I'm no slave, Mr. Branigan. You can't *own* me like you did your darkies." She fumbled with the buttons on her dress. "Last night was a mistake, all right, but that doesn't mean I'm going to make another one by marrying you. And you're not going to tell me what to do or where I can go. I *am* going to Oregon and I *am* going to find Marcus Sanderson and you're *not* going to stop me."

Tucker stood before her, now wearing his trousers, his chest still bare. "I told your uncle you would stay with me in Boise until this matter is settled."

Cook's warning echoed in her head. *Don't ever trust yourself to no man.* Cook was right.

"I don't care what you told my uncle. I'll do what I please." She tossed the blanket at him, then turned and picked up the saddle and bridle. "Isn't it time to break camp?"

Maggie rode ahead of him. Her back was ramrod straight. Her head never turned left or right. Anger seemed to emanate from every pore.

Aggravating woman!

He couldn't remember ever being so furious with anyone in his life. To accuse him of trying to make a slave of her! What did she take him for? It was an insult that cut deep. Yes, they'd owned slaves, and he couldn't say he'd been proud of the practice. Farrell had freed many of his slaves through the years and tried hard to change the order of things. Tucker would have followed that practice if it had been left to him to do so.

Slave, indeed!

But that wasn't really the point. Why had she gotten so riled at him? All he'd done was propose marriage. Tried to make an honest woman of her, for heaven sake. She should have been grateful to him, not furious.

What woman didn't want to be loved and cherished and taken care of? Was it so terrible that he was an honorable man, prepared to do the right thing by her? Good Lord, she could even now be carrying the beginnings of his child within her. Had she no common sense at all?

Not one moment of peace!

He'd not known one moment of peace since he met that blasted female. So why didn't he let her go to the devil if that's what she wanted? Why should he give her another thought?

Because he loved her.

Hell's bells and damnation!

He'd sworn he would never let a woman make a fool of him again. Well, *she* hadn't made a fool of him. He'd proven he was quite capable of doing it all by himself. He didn't need her help.

He pulled back on Blue Boy's reins, stopping the horse abruptly. He stared after Maggie and, slowly, the anger left him. For some odd reason he felt like smiling.

So she thought she didn't need him? So she thought she would just ride out of his life once they reached Boise? Well, the little minx had another thing coming. He'd found her. He loved her. And he wasn't about to let her go. She might not know it yet, but she was going to find out.

Maggie Harris, meet your match, he thought as he nudged Blue Boy forward once again.

* * *

Maggie was exhausted. Her body ached from head to toe, but there wasn't anything in this world or the next that would have possessed her to admit it to Tucker. She had refused to speak to him all day, nodding tersely when she was forced to acknowledge something he'd said.

It wasn't just physical fatigue that caused her weariness. Her heart was heavy, too. No. That wasn't right. Her heart *would* have been heavy if she'd still had one. But it felt to Maggie as if her heart had been ripped violently from her chest and discarded.

Anger had left her miles ago. She was forced to pretend it remained when he spoke to her, but what she really felt now was a deep sense of loss.

And she was tortured by memories of last night. Each time she thought of it, her nipples grew firm beneath her chemise and her loins burned in a way that was both pleasure and pain.

Tucker cantered up beside her. "We'll make camp here for the night."

She nodded and stopped the bay mare, glancing around. The tableland they were crossing was barren of trees and water, although there was evidence of dried-up alkali lakes. The hot July sun had beaten down mercilessly on them all day as they crossed the gravelly rifts and ravines. Only a few miles back, they'd come upon the bloated carcass of a milk cow, obviously lost from the Foster train. It wasn't the first to die along this stretch. The way was littered with the bleached bones of animals that had died before.

"Make your bed and lie down. I'll take care of the horses and fix us something to eat."

She bristled at his command. Even though it was exactly what she wanted to do, she still resisted following his orders. She wanted to defy him even when what he said made sense.

But when she slipped down from the saddle, her legs crumpled beneath her. She didn't have the strength left to stand, let alone argue.

Tucker was beside her instantly. "Maggie, are you—"

"I'm fine," she snapped, shrugging off his hand on her arm. She forced herself up on wobbly legs. "I just tripped."

He backed away, hands raised.

She had the distinct feeling she amused him. Maybe she wasn't too tired to be angry after all. She turned her back toward him and carried her bedroll a few feet away, then spread it quickly and collapsed upon it.

Tucker freed the canteen from the saddle and brought it to her. "Here. Take a drink. A long one. We should be at the river David told me about by tomorrow." He didn't wait to see if she followed his instruction this time. He turned away and began unsaddling the animals.

The water was warm, but at least it was wet. She let it trickle down her parched throat. Still holding the canteen in two hands, she watched Tucker rub down Harry's mare and give it a drink from water poured into his hat.

She would rest a moment, she decided, and then she would fix their supper. She wasn't going to be beholden to Tucker Branigan.

Moments later, she was sound asleep.

They found Dorothy Adams's grave early the next morning. Her name had been carved into a rough stone and set upon the packed dirt. Her resting place had been driven over by the wagons so her body couldn't be dug up later by coyotes or wolves. It somehow made the end seem all the more stark and painful—to be buried out in this wasteland in a grave pounded down by the hooves of oxen and the wheels of the cumbersome wagons.

"Seven daughters without a mother," Maggie said as she stared sadly down at the woman's resting place. "It doesn't seem fair."

"Life is rarely fair."

She glanced at Tucker. His face, bronzed by the sun, revealed his sorrow. For a moment, they shared a feeling other than anger.

"Jake's going to feel mighty lost without her." He set his hat back onto his head.

Maggie nodded as they turned their horses down the trail.

Another grave awaited them at the Green River, this one belonging to old Mrs. Connolly. At last the expected had happened, but it didn't lessen the sadness in Maggie's heart. Or the wondering how many more would be buried along the trail before the journey's end.

Chapter Thirty

Maureen stepped outside the circle of wagons and stared back along the stretch of trail they had covered the previous day. The blood-red light of a rising sun splashed across the aspen and pines of the mountainous terrain, giving everything an other-worldly look.

"They'll catch up with us soon," David said as he joined her, instinctively knowing the train of her thoughts.

"It's been ten days since we left them. Do you think Maggie could have . . ." She couldn't bring herself to say the words.

"She's a survivor, that girl. I'd bet my last dollar she's still alive."

Maureen sighed. "I think it would kill Tucker if she didn't live. He loves her, you know."

"I know." David's arm slipped around her shoulder, and she laid her head against him. "Just as I love you."

She'd known it, of course, but David had never said the words aloud. She had wondered if he were the type never to speak of it. She'd wondered if she would have to be satisfied with only knowing it in her heart. And so now, hearing it, her heart swelled with joy.

"Maureen, I'm not a young man and I haven't much to offer. I'm rough and uneducated and I don't have any knowledge of the kind of life you've had before. I can only imagine. You're a lady. A real lady. And an old trail hand like me . . . Well, I'm no match for a fine gentleman like Farrell Branigan was. I don't suppose I've even got a right to be sayin' such things to you." He cleared his throat and fell silent.

Maureen lifted her head and pulled back from him so she could look up into his face. He really was a giant of a man. His face was lined, proof of a hard life etched deeply into his forehead. But there was goodness there too, in the curve of his mouth, in the sparkle in his light blue eyes. She smiled softly at the hesitancy of his speech.

"David Foster, are you trying to propose to me?" she asked.

Was it the rising sun or was he actually blushing?

"I haven't settled any place long since my Emily died. Always had that yen to move on. Restless like, I guess. You understand?"

She understood more than he knew. "Yes," she answered simply.

"Not sure how I'd be at livin' a normal life. Might be a terrible embarrassment to a woman such as you. I don't speak as proper as I should, and I don't have fancy manners."

"David . . ."

"And I'm not even sure what I'd do for a livin' once I left the trail. Always planned to farm that land of mine in Oregon, but never did after—after Emily and the baby died. Don't know that I'd be much of a success at it, anyway. Besides, being a farmer's wife isn't much to offer any woman."

Maureen laid her hand on his forearm. "David, look at me."

He did.

"You're an intelligent, caring man. You could do anything you put your mind to. If you want to be a farmer, you'd be a good one. I know. I was the wife of a planter." Her voice softened. "And a planter is just a farmer, after all."

There was a new note of hope in his voice. "Don't reckon I'd need to have that farm in Oregon. I kinda liked Boise last time I was through there. Lots of different opportunities for a man like me, I suppose." He offered a half smile. "Probably be a good place to raise children."

"Mr. Foster," she said with a smile, "*are* you proposing?"

"Damn right, I am." He *was* blushing. "Sorry, Maureen. Didn't mean to cuss. I don't usually, but—"

She raised on tiptoe and planted a kiss on his mouth, silencing him. "You talk too much, Mr. Foster," she said as she drew back. "And the answer is yes." Then she kissed him again.

Thunder clouds rolled before the strong winds, cloaking the sun in a black shroud. Blue Boy crow-hopped and tossed his head. The bay mare rolled her eyes, flashing whites in the corners.

"We'd better take cover," Tucker yelled above the

wind. He pointed toward a ravine. "In there."

Maggie nodded and turned the skittish mare in the direction he'd indicated. Tucker followed after her.

With the hills rising on both sides of them, the gusting storm seemed not quite so threatening. Once in the draw, they dismounted and led the horses farther into the narrowing passage, stopping beneath a copse of quaking aspens.

The thunder crashed with a vengeance upon the heels of the flash of white light. Maggie let loose a strangled scream as she backed up against a tree. The mare reared up, pulling the reins free from Maggie's hands. Tucker had to dive forward to catch the bay before she bolted away.

As soon as he had the horses calmed and staked in the narrow ravine, Tucker returned his attention to Maggie. She was standing where he'd left her, her hands pressed tightly over her ears, her eyes squeezed shut.

He tried to embrace her, but she pushed him away.

"Leave me alone," she yelled above the storm.

"I only want to help."

"I don't want your help, and I don't need it."

Another clap of thunder silenced her, and even in the dim light of the storm, he could tell she had lost all the color from her face. She needed his help, all right, but he knew Maggie well enough by now to recognize when her guard was up. She would die before she let him help her. He backed away.

He squatted on his heels and watched from a few yards away. It had been hard enough to see her suffering when he'd held her through that first thunderstorm back in Kansas. It was harder now because he loved her. Her fear had something to do with Seth Harris. He had caught that much from Rachel before Maggie silenced her sister. But he'd never been able to get Maggie to tell him more.

Come to think of it, Maggie never talked about herself or her childhood, never revealed anything of her past. She'd only confessed to the death of her parents because she'd been trapped into it.

What had happened to her? What had Seth done?

He felt certain that the key to winning Maggie's love and trust lay in his ability to learn about her past, to breaking through that infernal barrier she'd so carefully erected around her heart.

The storm roared on, whipping the trees into a frenzy and blowing dirt and pebbles into dust clouds. Tucker pulled his hat low to protect his face. There was nothing they could do now but wait it out.

Rain fell in a torrent, nearly drowning the two travelers as they huddled beneath the trees, blankets spread over their heads. Maggie's nerves were still frayed from the thunderstorm, but she couldn't say she liked the rain much better.

Tucker had done as she demanded. He hadn't tried to hold her or speak to her again. For some reason, his compliance with her demands didn't make her feel any better. In fact, she found herself wishing he *would* hold her. She found herself remembering their night of lovemaking and wishing . . .

She clenched her teeth and pulled the blanket down further over her face. It didn't serve any purpose to think about it. It was over and done. She *didn't* want his lovemaking. So help her, she didn't.

When he'd held her, when he'd kissed and caressed her, she had believed with her heart that he loved her. But he didn't. He'd only made love to her to trap her into marriage. He'd said so himself. *You can't turn me down now.*

And even if she didn't know his real reason for wanting to marry her, she wouldn't have agreed, she told herself. Tucker Branigan was overbearing. An ogre of the first degree. Telling her what she could do and where she could go. She'd had her fill of that nonsense in her short life. She wasn't going to have it anymore.

Uncle Seth lied to you before. He could have lied about Tucker.

Where did that traitorous thought come from? This time Seth hadn't lied. She knew it was true.

When did you ever give him a chance?

Maggie covered her ears, just as she had during the thunderstorm. She didn't want to hear those thoughts in her head.

He was good to you long before Uncle Seth showed up.

She lifted the blanket slightly and peered out through the rain at Tucker.

Would it be so awful to let yourself fall in love with him?

That was a pointless question, she realized, for she *did* love him. And it *was* awful. Cook was right once again.

Maggie let the blanket fall back over her face.

MAUREEN'S JOURNAL

July 30. *We made camp early today due to violent rains. Everything is drenched. What chance is there for a mere canvas cover brushed with linseed oil? The mules, poor dumb beasts of burden, stand with their backs to the wind, their heads hanging down. They have served us well these past months.*

No sign of Tucker and Maggie.

David Foster has proposed marriage, and I have accepted.

Chapter Thirty-One

Harry borrowed one of David's horses and went looking for Tucker and Maggie. He found them less than a half day's ride behind the train. One look, and he knew what had happened between them. They were both in love and hating each other for it.

"You look like a drowned rat," he said to Maggie, grinning all the while.

"Thank you," she replied dryly. "I needed a compliment."

Harry shrugged. "I'm out of practice with the ladies." His expression sobered. "It's good to see you're all right. Mrs. Branigan's been frantic about both of you."

"We would have caught up sooner if the weather hadn't turned sour," Tucker said as he pulled up beside Harry.

"It's got the train mired down up ahead." Harry

looked once more at Maggie. "You've taken fine care of Bay Lady, I see."

"Bay Lady . . ." Maggie patted the animal's wet neck. "I wondered if she had a name. Thank you for leaving her for me. My horse never would have been able to catch up with the train."

"She's a good horse. Saved my life more than once," Harry acknowledged.

His eyes met Tucker's, and he knew they were both remembering the same spring day in Georgia. At Twin Willows, Farrell's favorite brood mare had delivered a fine black colt which was promptly named Blue Boy for the blue sheen in his coat. At The Grove, Harry had christened his newly arrived filly Bay Lady. The two foals shared the same Twin Willows sire and were trained side by side by the best friends who would later ride their horses into separate sides of a bloody war.

But it was the joy of the two young men—two boys, actually—that Harry remembered now. How proud they had been of those foals and how fitting that they'd arrived the same day. He'd thought they would always be as inseparable as they'd been that spring.

"We saw the graves along the trail," Tucker said, ending the reminiscing. "Anyone else sick?"

"No. The Adams wagon and yours are traveling with the train now. Fiona and Rachel are as energetic as ever, but Jake's taking his wife's death pretty hard. Your mother's doing all she can to lessen the blow, helping with the cooking and such." Harry smiled secretly to himself. "Quite a lady, your mother."

Harry was itching to tell Tucker about Maureen and David, but he managed to keep himself from it.

No matter how much a member of the family the Branigans had made him, it still wasn't up to him to reveal that news. Besides, it wasn't his place to tell, since he'd found out by accident.

Tucker pushed his hat back on his forehead. He glanced up at the cloudy sky. "At least we avoided an epidemic. It could have been a whole lot worse."

Harry's thoughts had been elsewhere, and it took him a moment to realize what Tucker was saying. Then he nodded in agreement. "We were lucky, I guess. Not that it makes it any easier on Adams."

They fell silent and quickened their pace, all of them wanting to reach the wagon camp before nightfall—or the next rain storm.

As badly as Maggie had wanted to rejoin the train so she could avoid Tucker, she knew the moment the wagons came into sight that she would rather have had him to herself for just a little longer. Even when they hadn't spoken—or when they'd only spoken words of anger—he had been hers alone.

The moment they rode into the circle of wagons, they were surrounded by people.

Maureen hugged Tucker tightly, then did the same with Maggie. "We were so worried," she said. "How are you, my dear?"

"I'm fine. Just a little tired."

Rachel threw her arms around her sister then, interrupting any further questions. Fiona's enthusiasm matched Rachel's. They bombarded her with news of their own recovery, embellishing more than a little, Maggie guessed.

Susan and her children were there, too, welcoming them back with kisses from Susan and Wills and mewling noises from Annie.

David clasped his big hands over one of Maggie's and winked at her. "Glad to have you back, Maggie."

"Thank you, Mr. Foster." She felt suddenly shy, surrounded by so many loving, caring people. It was overwhelming.

She turned, and her eyes met Tucker's. He, too, seemed to be looking at her with love and caring. It was almost more than she could bear.

"I think I'd like to lie down," she whispered to Maureen.

Maggie was led away from all the well-wishers and ushered into the wagon. Maureen pulled a clean, white nightgown from her trunk. "Here. Let's get you into this and into bed."

"I can't wear your things, Mrs. Branigan. I—"

"Hush. I want you to have it. Now, don't argue. Just put it on."

Tears spilled over before she could arrest them. "You've always been so kind to me. I don't know why."

"But Maggie dear," Maureen said as she put an arm around Maggie and drew the younger girl's head onto her shoulder. "Don't you know we've all come to love you?"

Maggie shook her head, unable to speak over the large lump in her throat.

"Well, we do." Tucker's mother pushed Maggie's wet hair away from her face and placed a gentle kiss on her forehead. "Now, you get out of those wet things and into bed. I'll bring you some supper before you fall asleep."

"Thank you," Maggie managed to croak.

The moment Maureen had climbed out of the

wagon, Maggie sat on the edge of the bed and did some serious crying.

Maureen observed her son across the fire from her. She wondered what had caused him to shave his beard. Maggie, perhaps?

Like Harry, she had guessed what had happened between her son and Maggie Harris. Her upbringing told her she should be horrified that Tucker had taken advantage of a girl like Maggie. It also told her a *true* lady would never have allowed it to happen.

But her heart told her that these two young people were destined for each other. It was clear to her that Tucker was very much in love. She wasn't as sure, however, of Maggie. That girl was a bundle of confusion, and so full of heartache. She wished she had answers for them.

David strolled into the light of the campfire. "Evenin'," he said, grinning all the while at Maureen.

It was time to tell Tucker and the two younger children about their plans for marriage. Maureen promptly forgot Tucker's romantic problems as a flurry of butterflies took flight in her stomach.

Maureen rose from her camp stool. "Fiona. Neal. Come join us a moment," she called to the children. "You, too, Rachel, if you'd like."

Tucker's gaze moved between his mother and David, and Maureen thought he'd probably already guessed what was going on.

David stepped up next to Maureen and casually placed an arm around her shoulders.

"Children . . ."

David interrupted her. "Let me." He turned his eyes upon the three Branigan siblings. "Guess the only way to put this is plain and simple. I've asked your mother to do me the honor of being my wife, and she's given me loads of pleasure by sayin' yes. We hope you'll be happy for us. I know I can't expect to take the place of your pa, but I hope you'll let me go on bein' your friend."

Maureen held her breath as she waited for a response from her children. Neal and Fiona both seemed to be waiting to see what Tucker's reaction would be.

Tucker stood and placed his right hand on Neal's shoulder, his left hand on Fiona's. There was just the hint of a smile on his lips as he said, "I can't think of another man I'd like to see as part of our family. I know you'll be good to our mother. That's all I could ask for."

As soon as the words were spoken, Neal and Fiona darted forward to throw themselves into the big man's arms. Maureen observed them for a moment, a bittersweet feeling in her heart. The children were young. In a few years, they wouldn't remember Farrell. David would become their father.

She loved David with all her heart. She knew he would make her happy. But she felt sorry for all that Farrell had chosen to give up—not the least of which was the love of his two youngest children.

Maggie awakened to the sway and jolt of the wagon. She couldn't believe she had slept so soundly that she hadn't heard the commotion caused by the breaking of camp. She dressed as quickly as was possible in the tight, cluttered quarters of the moving wagon, then pushed aside the front flap to find Maureen on the wagon seat.

"Good morning, Maggie."

She mumbled a greeting in return as she looked about. Mountains rose on both sides of them. The sky was scattered with high clouds, and the trail before them was muddy from the previous day's downpour.

"I put back a plate of food for you since you missed breakfast," Maureen continued. "It's beneath the stool there."

"I'm not hungry."

"You'd better eat, dear. You still look peaked."

Not wanting to disappoint Maureen, Maggie obeyed, eating quickly before clambering through the opening to join Maureen on the wagon seat.

Maureen slapped the reins against the backs of the mules. "Get up there!" she shouted at them. Looking at Maggie, she added, "We've already had two wagons get stuck this morning. Tucker and Harry are back trying to help one of them now."

Maggie leaned out to the side and glanced behind them. The wagons were spread out along the trail that curved around a sloping foothill. She saw no sign of a mired wagon. Straightening, her eyes swept forward. "Where's Rachel?" she asked.

"The girls are riding in the front wagon with Coop. Neal has taken your horse and is scouting ahead with David. He says we're less than a month from Boise now. Think of that, Maggie. We're almost there."

"*You're* almost there. It's still a long way to Oregon."

"Maggie . . ."

She clenched her hands in her lap.

"Tucker told me how determined you are to go on to Oregon. But we want you to stay with us."

"I can't. I have to find Mr. Sanderson. It's important."

"But we can send word to him for you. Tucker's a lawyer. He can take care of any details that might be necessary."

"Mrs. Branigan—"

"We love you, Maggie. We want you and Rachel to make your home with us." Maureen smiled then. "David and I are to be married. We would like you to be with us at the wedding. Would you stand up for me?" She reached over and squeezed Maggie's fist. "Please. And later, if you decide you don't want to stay in Boise and we've found your Mr. Sanderson, we'll help you get to Oregon. Please say you'll stay."

Maggie didn't know how to argue against her gentle plea. If it were Tucker demanding that she remain, Maggie's reply would have been automatic. But how could she resist Maureen's loving request?

It struck her suddenly what Maureen had said. "Married?" she said as she looked at the older woman beside her. Maureen's face fairly glowed with love. Maggie didn't think she'd ever seen anyone lovelier than Maureen Branigan in that moment.

"Yes. He asked me yesterday. We're going to wed two weeks after we arrive. He's going to make his home in Boise so our family can stay together, although I would have gone with him to Oregon if it was what he wanted."

"But what about the train?"

"He'll find a replacement to take the rest of the people on. If he can't, he'll have to take them to Oregon and return as soon as he's able. We don't want to postpone the wedding, but—well, I'm sure we'll find someone. I have every intention of being Mrs. David Foster come September."

Maggie shook her head slowly. She'd counted on

convincing David Foster to take her and Rachel the rest of the way to Oregon. She could have slept just as easily beneath his wagon as the Branigans', and she could have helped Coop with the cooking and driving and anything else to pay their way. But now David was staying in Boise. He and Maureen were going to be married. Things had a way of changing so fast.

"Please stay, Maggie," Maureen said again.

Maggie looked into Maureen's emerald-green eyes and knew that the woman meant every word she said. She loved Maggie and Rachel. She truly wanted them to remain, to be a part of her family.

She thought of Tucker. She thought of his mouth moving hungrily against hers, of his hands caressing her body, of his . . . How could she live so close to him? It was impossible. She was in love with him. If he chose to, he could take her willing, traitorous body at any time, and he would know it, too. If she stayed, he would trick her into marriage. He would twist her thinking until she didn't know what she wanted to do, until she didn't know truth from wishful thinking. She knew he would. And then she would lose her hard-won freedom.

"I'll stay," she said softly, "but only until after the wedding. Then I must go to Oregon."

"All right," Maureen accepted. "But I hope you'll change your mind about leaving."

Maggie shook her head, still picturing Tucker. She didn't dare change her mind. The extra two weeks might already prove too dangerous.

Chapter Thirty-Two

Exhausted by the muddy trail, the emigrants stopped early and made camp. Maggie, feeling the need of some solitude, told Maureen where she was going, then slipped away to bathe and wash her hair. She took along the gray-and-white dress Tucker had bought for her at Fort Laramie. She didn't consciously realize how much she wanted to look pretty for him when he caught up with the train with the last of the straggling wagons.

She bathed in the cool spring water, then dressed quickly. Sitting on the blanket she'd brought with her, she combed and plaited her hair while her thoughts roamed. Her mood was contemplative as she reflected on the vast changes in her life. Three months ago she wouldn't have believed this could happen. She had been offered what she'd wanted most and thought she could never have. A loving family. If only it weren't so complicated by her feelings for Tucker.

He appeared as if conjured up by her thoughts of him. "Maggie, we need to talk."

He'd said the exact same words to her the morning after they made love. She felt a shiver run through her as she rose to her feet.

He leaned against a boulder and lit one of his thin cigars. "Mother told me she's convinced you to stay in Boise until after she and David are married."

"Yes."

"What about us, Maggie?"

She didn't know that she'd ever felt such pain. "There isn't any *us*."

"There could be if you'd let it happen. I've offered you marriage, a home. What more do you want from me?"

"You wouldn't understand, Tucker." *I don't even understand myself*, she thought as she looked at him.

He took a step toward her. "Help me to understand."

Maggie backed away. If he touched her, she would be lost.

A resigned look passed across his handsome face. He leaned once more against the rock at his back.

How did she tell him she loved him but it still wasn't enough? How did she explain how important it was to be in control of her own life? It was an obsession. To never again be told where she could go and what she could do. To choose her own life, her own destiny. Even to make her own mistakes.

She looked at him, and suddenly all doubt was gone about his motives for wanting to marry her. She knew with a certainty that he had no thoughts of revenge toward Seth when he was with her, no designs on Harris Mills should it ever be hers. She believed, even though he'd never spoken the words, that he loved her.

And still it wasn't enough.

"When my parents died," she began, suddenly feeling free to tell him things she never had before, "everything changed."

"How did it happen, Maggie?"

"They were in a carriage accident. I was twelve and Rachel was just a baby. We didn't think we had any other family in the world until Uncle Seth showed up. I thought then that he'd come to take care of us." There was a bitter tinge in her voice as she added, "But he only cared about money, and he wasn't any good at making or keeping it. It wasn't long before the mills were in trouble."

Maggie picked up the blanket from the ground and folded it as she spoke.

"Uncle Seth cut us off from all outsiders. I think now that he always wanted to be accepted by the people who were my parents' friends, but he knew he wouldn't be. My mother had always called him a lost soul. I guess he spent his life wandering around, trying lots of things but never succeeding at any of them. Uncle Seth resented everyone and everything, but most of all, he resented Papa's inheriting the mill instead of him. So he hated us most of all." She drew a deep breath.

"Didn't anyone think to check on you?" Tucker sounded skeptical. "Your father was an industrial giant. Harris Mills was known throughout the South. Someone must have wondered about Jeremy Harris's children. He was an extremely wealthy man."

"I suppose I never wondered why no one came. I never thought about being rich. To me, the mill was just the place where Papa worked. He would take me to his office sometimes and then out for ice cream. I don't suppose I ever gave much thought to all the things we had. I just took them for granted."

The look on Tucker's face said he understood that too. He probably had taken the luxuries of his plantation home for granted before the war had stripped them from him.

"Uncle Seth told us our father left us penniless. That we were a burden to him. He never let us leave the house, not once in all those years. He fired all the servants except for Cook. I took care of Rachel and did what I could to run the house."

"But you were only a child yourself," Tucker said gently.

"You grow up fast when you have to." She fell silent as tears threatened and was relieved when Tucker didn't push for her to continue. Another deep breath helped. "I overheard my uncle talking to one of the men from the mill, who'd come to the house to see him. After he left, Uncle Seth was angry. So very angry. I suppose that was when he realized he was about to lose the mill, maybe the house too. Then, shortly after that, Uncle Seth took us to Independence. I didn't know why until we got there."

"Why, Maggie? You never told us the real reason."

"He'd arranged for me to marry an old friend of his. You see, my father had left money in a trust, a trust that my uncle wasn't able to break. I guess the money becomes mine upon marriage, and he planned to split it with Mr. Jones after the wedding." She met his gaze. Her chin came up. "He always told me my own father hadn't loved me enough to see I was taken care of if he died. Now he was going to sell me to Mr. Jones for the money that was rightfully mine."

Tucker dropped his cigarillo and ground it into the soft, moist earth beneath his heel. "Cyrus Jones? The man you were with in Independence? But he . . ."

Maggie pictured her "intended" in her mind. A portly man in his forties with graying muttonchop whiskers and a red, bulbous nose. He'd always had the stub of a fat cigar stuck in the corner of his mouth. But it was the gleam in his eyes as they ran over her that had made her tremble with revulsion.

She shuddered even now at the memory. "I couldn't let him do that to me," she whispered, "so we ran away. I'd seen the wagons camped outside of town, and I was sure Uncle Seth wouldn't think to follow us here. I guess I wasn't careful enough when I bought the horse. I must have said where we were going." Maggie picked up the rest of her things, and as she straightened, their eyes met.

"What about Marcus Sanderson?" Tucker's voice was gently probing. "What does he have to do with all this?"

His eyes were such a dark, rich brown. Like the chocolate bonbons her mother had sometimes brought her when she was little. She felt as if he could see straight into her soul, as if those wonderful eyes of his could search out all the secrets, all the pain and loneliness she still hadn't revealed.

She turned her back to him and stared at the forested hillside. "I didn't lie about him, Tucker. I heard my uncle telling Mr. Jones about the will he'd

drawn up, about the trust. I remembered Mr.
Sanderson from before the war. He and his family
were good friends. I use to play with his daughter.
They went to Oregon because they were sure the
war was coming. Papa told me later that Mr.
Sanderson was a pacifist and couldn't condone the
war, so he went west." She lifted her chin and set
her shoulders. "Uncle Seth said the money was
gone from the trust and the mills were bankrupt.
Maybe they are, but I don't think the trust is gone.
Papa managed to protect it all these years, and
Uncle Seth means to get that money any way he
can. He'll be back for us if that's the only way. I've
got to find Mr. Sanderson."

"Maggie . . ."

Reluctantly, she turned to face him once again.

"Let me help you, Maggie. I'm an attorney. I can
make sure your uncle can't hurt you anymore. Stay
with us in Boise."

"I've got to find Mr. Sanderson, Tucker."

"Will you give me a few weeks to try to find him
for you? We can send word by stage, perhaps even
hire someone to go to Oregon. Let me do what I
can. Just give me a few weeks."

Why didn't she just give it up and marry him as
he wanted? What did she have to prove? Tucker
loved her. He must love her. Why wasn't that
enough?

No matter what the reason, it wasn't enough.
Marriage was so final. It would take away all the
control she had over her own life. She would belong
to someone else again. "You promise you won't try
to stop me if I decide to leave?"

"I promise." Tucker pushed off from the rock and
started to walk away. Suddenly, he stopped and

looked back at her. "You look beautiful tonight, Maggie. I love you, you know."

I know, Tucker, she thought silently as her gaze dropped from his. *I love you, too.*

He'd promised to help her, yet he didn't know how. Tucker knew there was still much she was keeping from him. He'd seen the pain written on her face. He didn't know what Seth Harris had done to her in those years he'd kept her locked up, but he knew that if he ever saw the man again, he would want to kill him for it.

He walked along the narrow track back to the wagons, his mood shifting from anger to sorrow. He'd told Maggie he loved her. There had been a time, not all that long ago, when he'd sworn he would never say those words to a woman again. But with Maggie . . . with Maggie, it was worth the risk. His love for her revealed the feelings he'd had for Charmaine to be a shallow mockery of the emotion.

He had secretly hoped, he now realized, that by confessing what he felt for her, she would say she loved him too. But she hadn't. She was afraid to. He'd seen it in her eyes.

The anger returned, sharper this time. His hands curled into fists. If Seth Harris were there right now . . .

Tucker stopped suddenly. Seth had said he would come to Idaho for his nieces. For all Tucker knew, the man was there right now awaiting them. A man alone or by stage could cross the country in a fraction of the time it took families moving all their possessions. If Tucker were to help Maggie, he had to know for a fact what was in Jeremy Harris's will. He had to know the truth about the trust. He had to find Marcus Sanderson. Maggie's uncle was a desperate man. He might do anything to get his hands on that money. Seth wasn't above skulduggery.

Tucker was going to have to be more careful from now on. He was going to have to keep a watch on both Maggie and Rachel. He couldn't take a chance on anything happening to them.

The livestock grazed peacefully in the valley between the mountains. In the wagon camp, someone was strumming a guitar and singing softly. The music was carried to them on a gentle evening breeze, the same breeze that had carried the clouds from the sky, leaving a thousand twinkling stars and a growing moon to light the earth.

As they rode guard on the herd, Harry listened gravely to Tucker's request. "That's not much to go on, Tuck."

"I know, but will you do it?"

"Just a name. You don't even know if Sanderson's still in Portland. A lot can happen in six, seven years. He might be dead. He might have returned east after the war."

Tucker removed his slouch hat and brushed it against his leg. "I know that, too. But I don't have anything else and I don't have much time. I'd go myself but . . ."

"It's all right, Tuck," Harry said, leaning sideways in his saddle to lay a hand on his friend's arm. "I understand. I'm glad to do it for you. I'll leave at first light."

"Send word to Keegan in Idaho City if you can. Let him know we're almost there."

"I'll do it."

"And Harry . . ."

He looked at Tucker.

"Thanks."

Harry shrugged and grinned. "No thanks needed. Just be sure I'm invited to the wedding. Yours and Maggie's, I mean."

MAUREEN'S JOURNAL

July 31. It is interesting how love seems to find a man and a woman no matter where they are. We have lived with dust and rain and bad water and poor hunting. We have nearly worn through the bottoms of our shoes and our faces and hands are as brown as the Indians'. We should be too tired for matters of the heart, yet it isn't so.

Not only have I found a good man to love, but Tucker is in love as well. It is not easy for a mother to see her first-born prepare to pledge himself to another woman. But Maggie will make him a good wife. Perhaps, if times had been different, if the war had never come, Tucker might have been happy with Charmaine. Yet I confess I will give him to Maggie with a freer heart, without reservation. She will bring him joy—once she admits to loving him in return.

Chapter Thirty-three

The Foster train rested for a day near Fort Hall, then continued the journey along the winding Snake River. Day after day, they crossed the sagebrush-covered land as the hot August sun blazed down on them. Any threat of rain had disappeared with the last cloudburst near the Bear Mountain descent. Sometimes it seemed they were being punished for their complaints about the muddy trail, causing more than one person to wonder if it might never rain again.

Purple mountain ranges shot skyward to the north and south of them as they followed the river's boulder-strewn south rim. It was easy to imagine the thick pine trees and long for the cool air that must linger near high mountain lakes. But on the plains, there were no trees. Just sagebrush and snakes and jackrabbits.

Even getting water for cooking and drinking was an arduous chore, for it meant descending the precipitous sides of the deep river gorge, followed by an even more difficult climb back up. Large game grew more difficult to find, and the hunters roamed across the high desert land, far from the train, to bring back fresh meat to feed themselves and their families.

Maggie insisted she would drive the wagon again. There was no reason for her to walk beside the wagon while Maureen drove the teams. Maggie was young and strong. Her health was completely restored. Besides, idleness gave her too much time to brood on things she couldn't change.

At least she had plenty of time alone. Tucker, who had become David's second-in-command even more than before, was often needed elsewhere. When not helping David, he was usually hunting for food for the Branigans and Susan Baker's small family.

Maggie felt keenly Harry's absence. She had been disappointed that he hadn't said good-bye to any of them. Although she hadn't known him long, she had thought him her friend, and it seemed strange for him to leave so abruptly, without a word to anyone but Tucker.

The train had traveled better than twenty miles that day and made camp as the sun rested on the western horizon. The desert was tinged with a pink light, making it appear almost gay.

As Maggie walked back to the wagon after caring for the mules, Susan stopped her.

"Maggie, can you stay with Annie for a moment?" she asked. "She's inside sleeping and I don't want to leave her alone. She's been so fussy for days, and I've been worried about her. Please sit with her. I must talk to Mr. Foster." She didn't wait for a reply. "Thanks." She hurried away, pulling little Wills along beside her.

"Of course, I'll sit with her," Maggie said to the empty air, an eyebrow raised. Then she smiled as her fatigue slipped away. She always enjoyed a chance to be with little Annie. She turned and climbed into the Baker wagon.

The baby slept peacefully in the dim light of the covered wagon. The canvas flaps at the front and back were tied open, allowing a warm breeze to move through the close quarters. Maggie knelt on the bed of the wagon and leaned against the small wooden cradle.

It was hard to believe Annie was nearly two months old already. And so pretty, too. A light furring of blond hair covered her perfectly shaped head, and when she was awake, she had the brightest blue eyes Maggie had ever seen. Rachel had looked a little like Annie when she was a baby— blond-haired and blue-eyed and cute as a porcelain doll.

Maggie had raised Rachel, but what would it be like to have a baby of her own? A baby to love and nurse at her breast. She closed her eyes. It would be a boy with dark brown hair and eyes of rich chocolate.

She opened her eyes quickly, surprised at how complete and full-blown the image had been in her mind. She even knew what his name would be. Kevin. She stopped that train of thought just short of adding the baby's last name.

Annie stirred, and Maggie felt free to pick her up from the cradle. The baby was soft and warm in her arms. Her tiny mouth opened as she nudged Maggie's breast.

"Sorry, angel. Your mama's not here."

As if she understood, Annie's suckling motion stopped, and she fell back to sleep.

Maggie was nearly dozing herself when Rachel popped into view at the back of the wagon.

"Hi, Maggie. Susan's in our camp. Mrs. Branigan invited her for supper again. She says to bring Annie. Come on."

Rachel's face looked slightly flushed and her eyes had an odd light in them. As she climbed out of the wagon, Maggie considered placing a hand on the girl's forehead to see if she had a fever, but Rachel was dancing around her, as if it were impossible for her to stand still. She was just about to order her sister to quiet down when there was a shout that stopped her in her tracks.

"Surprise!"

"Happy birthday, Maggie!"

There they stood—the Branigans and the Bakers and the Adamses and Mr. Foster and Coop—all of them around a table holding a large cake.

Rachel was giggling almost hysterically. "I told them. Mrs. Branigan asked me if I knew when your birthday was a long time ago, and I remembered and she kept track so we could surprise you. Coop helped us bake the cake at Mr. Foster's wagon so you wouldn't know about it."

Still holding Annie in one arm, Maggie knelt down beside her excited younger sister. "I'd forgotten today was my birthday. Thanks for remembering, kitten."

Rachel planted a wet kiss on Maggie's cheek. "Come on. See what else we've got for you."

Susan stepped forward to take Annie from her arms, and as she did so, she gave Maggie a hug. There were tears in Susan's eyes. Maggie felt a little like crying herself. She hadn't had a birthday party in years.

There were presents—handkerchiefs embroidered with her initials and a knitted scarf and an apron and even a pair of satin slippers. The slippers were from Maureen. They were a silvery gray.

"I thought they might match the dress Tucker gave you. I'm sorry they're not new, but I think they'll fit as well as those old shoes you're wearing now."

Maggie glanced at her feet. When Maggie's shoes, almost worthless for the journey cross country, had worn through, Maureen had given her the sturdy pair she now wore. They'd been a necessity. But these silver slippers . . .

"They're beautiful," was all Maggie could think to say.

"I wore them to my very first ball. I've saved them ever since."

"Oh, I can't take . . ."

"Of course, you can, my dear. They were meant to be worn by someone young and lovely like you." Maureen placed a kiss on Maggie's cheek.

Suddenly her hand was captured in a much larger one and she was being drawn away from the celebrants. She followed Tucker without protest as he led her from the clustered wagons and into the darkness of the night.

When he stopped, he turned to face her, placing his hands on her shoulders. "I'm sorry I've no gift for you now, Maggie."

"It doesn't matter. The party . . ."

"I know what I want to give to you, and when we

reach Boise, I'll find it. Until then, this will have to do."

He pulled her slowly toward him, his hands slipping from her shoulders and down to her back. His mouth descended toward hers, and there was nothing she could do—nothing she *wanted* to do— except allow her head to fall back so she could receive his kiss. His lips moved over hers with agonizing gentleness, stirring a hunger in her soul.

Maggie swayed away from him, and then toward him, her body melding against his, her hands moving up to circle his neck, her fingers twining through the silky hair at his nape. His arms tightened. She sensed the wanting in him and knew her own wanting was just as strong.

If only . . .

Reluctantly, she drew her hands back to his chest and pushed him away. "I can't, Tucker," she said in a voice husky with emotion. "I don't intend to stay with you."

She was back in his arms so quickly she had no time to protest. He kissed her again—thoroughly, completely, lovingly kissed her. When he set her away from him, he said, "I can wait. And I don't mean to give up." Then he took her by the hand and led her back to her party.

Tucker stood back, watching and listening. Maggie had that special carefree look about her again, the same one he'd witnessed at Ash Hollow. She was beautiful anytime but especially so now with that big smile on her delightful mouth. He reveled in her laughter. If he had a goal in life at all, it was to hear that laughter often.

More than ever, he was anxious to reach Boise, eager to begin building a law practice so he could support a wife and children. Children with Maggie.

He grinned at the picture he conjured up in his head.

"What are you smiling about?" Maureen asked as she stepped up beside him.

"Oh, nothing in particular. Just thinking how glad I am we decided to come to Idaho." He placed an arm over his mother's shoulders and drew her close.

"Mmmm. It's surprising how finding someone to love can make the things we left behind seem less important."

He squeezed her upper arm with his fingers. "The Branigans are a lucky bunch, aren't they?"

"They are, indeed."

Maggie lay beneath the wagon, her birthday presents piled nearby. Even in the darkness, it was nice to be able to reach out and feel them, to know that they were real, that people cared enough for her that they would spend so many precious hours to make her a gift or, like Maureen, they would give her something that was special to them.

But none of them seemed as real to her as Tucker's kiss. Even now she could feel it. She lifted a hand to her mouth. Her fingers moved slowly over her lips, certain they must be swollen, must still be warm from his touch.

When, she wondered, would she stop this constant thinking about him? When would the moment come that he wasn't in her thoughts throughout each day, throughout each night? Would she go through the rest of her life wanting him as she did now?

She rolled onto her side and curled into a tight ball.

I can wait, he'd said. *And I don't mean to give up.*

"Oh, Tucker," she whispered, "please give up. Please don't wait for me. I can't be what you want me to be. I can't do what you want me to do. I can't let a man take all that I have, all that I am. Not even if you're the man. I just can't."

She closed her eyes, squeezing them tight. Sleep. She had to get some sleep.

But instead, she saw herself in Tucker's arms, that slow, tender smile of his lighting his beautiful brown eyes as he gazed down at her. And between them, cradled in her own arms, was a baby with matching eyes of brown.

She cried then. She cried for the things she'd once had that had been lost. And she cried for the things that could never be.

Maggie cried long into the night.

MAUREEN'S JOURNAL

August 8. David tells me one route of the trail follows this Snake River for three hundred miles for those who choose not to cross it and turn toward Boise City. Three hundred miles, climbing up and down that canyon wall to get water. It is terrifying in places, so steep and ragged. I cannot imagine knowingly choosing such a course. But perhaps I do not know what lies ahead of us once we cross it. Could it be even worse?

David also tells me we are about three weeks from Boise. Three weeks. Perhaps there will be a letter from Shannon awaiting me, God willing.

Chapter Thirty-four

Dust rose from beneath the wheels and hooves and lingered in the still air. The emigrants coughed and squinted their eyes as they pressed forward. Those further back in the train suffered the most, the dirt cloud growing thicker with each passing wagon.

Maggie glanced off to the side from her perch on the wagon seat. Fiona and Rachel were walking on either side of Wills Baker, each of them holding one of his hands. She could hear their laughter as they teased the little boy. Even after more than three months of this, the children still acted as if the journey west were a grand adventure and not the hard work, danger, and drudgery the adults found it to be. Maggie wished she had a little of their fortitude.

She slapped the reins lightly against the mules' backsides. "Get along," she said, out of habit rather than necessity.

Less than two weeks to Boise. That's what David had told them last night. It seemed almost impossible to believe they were so close to the end.

No. Not *they*. She and Rachel would be continuing on in a few weeks, but at least they could enjoy the rest while it lasted. And the chances were good they would be able to travel by stage rather than in the cumbersome, slow-moving wagons of an emigrant train.

She saw Tucker galloping toward the wagon. He slowed Blue Boy and flashed Maggie a grin, then disappeared behind her. She thought he'd gone on until she heard a thump and felt the wagon rock. She peered through the wagon and found him tying Blue Boy to the back.

"Thought you might like a breather from this," he said as he stepped over the clutter of the wagon to reach the front. With an easy motion, he was on the seat beside her and taking the reins from her hands.

"We'll be stopping for our noon meal soon, won't we? I can wait until then."

"Fine. Then we can just enjoy one another's company." He smiled at her, and she could see the unspoken words in his eyes. *And I don't mean to give up.*

He certainly seemed to have meant exactly what he'd said. In the days since her surprise birthday party, Tucker hadn't given her any real peace. He was always there. Always smiling at her, touching her in small, gentle ways, kissing her when they chanced to be alone. He never pushed. He never tried to make love to her, yet there was something hot burning just beneath the surface, and both of them were aware of it.

"Maybe I *will* walk," Maggie said softly as she

prepared to scramble down the side of the slow moving wagon.

"Mother's still riding with Coop. You can take Blue Boy if you'd like to go up front out of the dust."

"No thanks." She might have had to ride Bay Lady all those days to catch up with the train, but she'd had no choice about it. She had no intention of pressing her luck now. Blue Boy was far more horse than she felt capable of handling.

Holding her skirts out of the way, Maggie hopped down. She took a quick step away from the wagon, pausing to let it move by her before she set off through the aromatic, silvered-green sagebrush. She angled off to the side, drawing in a deep breath of dust-free air.

Her gaze swept across the arid plain of the Snake River basin. To the north, jagged mountains that resembled the blade of a saw pierced the wide expanse of blue sky. Although she longed for a cool breeze and the shade of trees, she was thankful the trail hadn't taken them through those mountains. They looked impenetrable.

The child's scream lanced her daydreams like a shard of broken glass. She was running before she even knew where it had come from, instinct carrying her toward the cliffs of the river gorge.

"Maggie! Maggie!"

She saw Rachel as she ran through the tall brush. Her sister was waving her arms and stumbling over the rocky terrain.

"What is it? What happened?" Maggie cried as she grasped Rachel's shoulders.

"Wills. It's Wills. He fell over the side."

Maggie didn't wait for the girl to say anything else. "Get Tucker."

Her heart pounding in her ears, she raced on toward the canyon rim. Fiona was standing close to the edge, looking down.

"Get back, Fiona!" Maggie shouted as she drew closer.

Fiona turned. Her small face was white as a sheet and streaked with tears. "We were playing tag, and he ran away from us. He fell. Maggie, he fell over the side before we could catch him."

Maggie paused long enough to hug the child. "It's all right. It's not your fault. Go for help, Fiona. Run. *Run!*"

Lying on her stomach, Maggie edged forward until she could see down into the gorge. She felt a swirling dizziness sweep over her, and her fingers dug into the dirt. Far below, the river wove its way through the steep and narrow canyon. Even the rays of the midday sun didn't touch the water at this point. Maggie felt sick to her stomach. No one could survive such a fall. Even if Wills had avoided the jutting, rocky slopes of the canyon walls, he would drown before they could hope to find him.

And then she heard the whimpering sounds.

"Wills?"

She pushed herself out a little farther, fear clutching her throat.

He was there, hugging a narrow ledge at least twenty feet below her. She could see blood on his forehead and his arms.

"Hold still, Wills. Don't move. Do you hear me, Wills?"

"Mama . . . I want Mama."

"She's coming, honey. Just lie still. We're coming to get you."

Maggie heard the shouts and sounds of running feet behind her. *Be Tucker. Please be Tucker.*

And then he was on the ground beside her. "Dear God," he whispered. He turned his head to look at Maggie. "If he moves—"

Maggie swallowed the bile that rose in her throat.

"You've got to keep him calm, Maggie. Talk to him. Can you do that?"

"I'll try."

He squeezed her upper arm, then slid back from the rim.

"Neal, get Blue Boy. Paul, I'm going to need some rope. Long and sturdy."

Maggie shut out the rest of his firm commands, turning her attention to the small boy whose life hung so precariously on the edge of the canyon. "Wills, your mama's coming now. But you have to promise to be very still and wait for us."

"My . . . my arm hurts."

"I know. I can see that it does. But we'll have it fixed in no time."

Wills shifted as he looked up at her, sending a cascade of pebbles crashing down into the canyon. The sound frightened him and he jerked closer to the rocky wall.

Maggie caught her breath as she watched the movements playing out. "Wills, stay still," she ordered. She drew a deep breath, then proceeded more calmly. "If you promise not to move again, Mrs. Branigan says she'll bake you a cake just like the one we had for my birthday. Remember, Wills? Remember how good it was?"

"Uh-huh."

Susan's frantic voice reached Maggie's ears. "My baby! It's my baby."

She turned her head to look behind her. "Susan," she said in a low voice, feigning a calm she didn't feel. "You mustn't let him see that you're afraid."

Maggie feared Susan wouldn't hear or understand her, but somehow, her words got through the
mother's terror. Susan nodded as she walked the
last few steps to the rim. She lay on her stomach
and inched her way forward, just as Maggie had
done.

Hurry, Tucker. Please hurry.

His feet slid along the side of the precipice,
holding his body away from the rock wall of the
gorge as he was lowered toward the ledge. The rope
bit into his armpits.

"Hold still, Wills," Tucker called to the small
boy. "I'm almost there."

"Mama . . ." Wills whimpered.

"I'm going to take you to your mama."

He came even with the ledge and worked his way
over to it. There was scarcely room for his feet. He
leaned into the canyon wall, then squatted down
beside the boy. He checked the bloody wounds on
his forehead and arms, relieved to find they were
superficial.

"Can you stand up?"

Wills shook his head.

"I need you to hold onto my back while they pull
us up, son."

"I can't. I'm afraid and my arm hurts." He began
to cry again. "I can't."

Tucker touched the boy's arm. "Sure you can."

"I can't!" Wills jerked away, moving precariously
close to the edge.

Tucker was certain the boy was right. He was too
afraid and he was shaking too hard. If he pressed
him further, the next move Wills made might
topple him over the edge. And there was no way
Tucker could hold on to him while they went up the

wall if Wills was struggling. Quickly, he made his decision.

"All right. I'm going to tie the rope around you and let them pull you up first. You won't have to do a thing. The rope will hold you. You just lie still."

Tucker swallowed nervously as he worked at the knot in the rope. The ledge felt as if it were swaying beneath his feet, and he was afraid if he looked off to the side, he would tumble from the narrow perch.

Steady, he reminded himself.

With careful movements, he slipped the rope beneath Wills's back and under his arms. He knotted it securely, then helped the boy stand.

"Now, Wills, you're going to have to help them get you up. Are you listening?"

Wills nodded, staring at Tucker with wide, frightened eyes.

"When they start pulling, you just walk up the wall like you were walking on the ground. That way you won't get skinned up." He squeezed the boy's thin arms. "Okay?"

Wills sniffed, then nodded once again.

"Good." Cautiously, Tucker stood, his back against the canyon wall. "He's ready, David" he shouted. "Okay, Wills. Your mother's waiting for you at the top. It's going to be all right."

The rope grew taut, then began to lift the boy off the ledge. Tucker helped him get his feet under him and watched as he moved up the canyon wall. Sweat trickled down Tucker's forehead and into his eyes, but he didn't try to wipe it away.

Damn, how he hated heights! But it hadn't occurred to him to suggest that someone else go after Wills.

The ledge seemed to be growing smaller beneath

his feet. He hoped they would get the rope down to him soon.

Sheer terror gripped Maggie the moment she saw what he'd done. Tucker had left himself below on the ledge while they pulled Wills to safety. It was such a narrow ledge and he was such a big man.

"Hang on, Tucker," she whispered. "Hang on."

She had the strangest feeling in her breast, as if she were standing on that ledge beside him, as if she could see the sway of the canyon wall and hear the roar of the river below.

"Don't look down," she said softly.

Wills came over the edge of the rim and was quickly clasped into Susan's waiting arms. Maggie wanted to snap at them to get the rope off the boy and throw it down to Tucker. Her nerves felt as if they were exploding. It seemed to take the men forever to do her silent bidding.

"Here comes the rope, Tuck," David shouted as he tossed the thick cord over the side.

The rope swayed back and forth, then snagged on a rock out of Tucker's reach. David tugged on it until he pulled it loose. He hiked it up the canyon a few feet, then gave it another toss.

Each little movement burned itself into Maggie's memory. She saw the rope swing toward Tucker. She saw him reach out to grab it. She saw the ledge crumble beneath his foot and break away. She saw the fragments of stone bounce and roll and fall toward the craggy floor below. She saw Tucker sway wildly, grasping for anything to stop his fall. And then she saw him sliding away, his fingers digging into the canyon wall.

He stopped with a thud on a second, slightly wider ledge another good thirty feet below.

Maggie's heart seemed to stop the same moment he did. She thought for sure she was screaming, yet all around her was deathly quiet.

"Tucker!" David shouted.

"I'm all right," came the reply.

But Maggie knew he wasn't all right. She could hear it in his voice. He was hurt. And it was bad.

Chapter Thirty-five

His right ankle felt as if hot spikes had been thrust through it, hot spikes that were being slowly twisted. Tucker tried to push himself up on his elbows so he could survey the damage, but his left arm collapsed beneath him, unable to support his weight. His shirt was torn and blood flowed from the wound like a mountain stream. His head pounded to the beat of a hundred devil drummers.

"I'm coming down," David called to him.

"No, don't," Tucker returned. "There's no room."

Besides, he thought, two men would be too much weight, and he didn't want to take the chance of someone else falling. There might not be another ledge below this one to break a fall. The next person might not stop until he hit the river bottom.

"Let down the rope," he shouted.

It came snaking its way down the rock wall. He

could only hope there was enough length to reach him. It seemed to take a long, long time, but finally, he was able to lift his right arm and take hold of the thick hemp rope.

He wasn't sure how he managed to get it around him. His left arm was almost useless. He didn't think it was broken, but it was badly sprained, the skin and muscles torn by the jagged rocks as he'd slid down the cliff, and he was losing a dangerous amount of blood. The loss was quickly sapping his strength.

After what seemed an eternity, he was able to tie a secure knot. At least, he hoped it was secure.

As he looked up toward the rim, the faces, and the blue sky beyond, he felt a wave of dizziness sweep over him. *Hold on*, he told himself. *You've got to stay alert until you get out of here.*

"David! You're going to have to drag me up. I'm not going to be much help."

"We'll try to go easy on you. Ready?"

"I'm ready."

The first jerk of the rope sent a jolt of pain from his shoulder straight through his body to his legs. He tried to pull on the rope to release some of the pressure beneath his arms, but it was no use. What reserves he'd had left drained from him like the blood from his arm.

Hanging like a rag doll, he slid up the side of the gorge.

Maggie held her breath, unable to move or look away. He was so limp. Was he conscious? Was he even alive?

Why didn't they hurry? Why didn't they get him out of there? If the rope should slip or break . . .

"Maggie, get back." Maureen's voice was firm.

Her fingers tugged at Maggie's bodice.

"He's hurt."

"I know, but it won't help to have you falling too."

Maggie allowed herself to be pulled back from the edge of the precipice, but only a few inches. She had to see him. She had to be there the moment he reached the top. In the back of her mind, she recognized that Maureen was as worried as she, but she had no strength left to comfort or reassure anyone else. All she could think about was Tucker.

Dear God in heaven, she prayed. *Let him be all right. Don't let him die. I'll do anything. Just don't take his life.*

It seemed an eternity before his dark hair came into view, and it was agony waiting for him to be pulled to safety. As soon as he was, Maggie was at his side.

"Tucker . . ." She brushed his shaggy hair back from his forehead.

He opened his eyes. "Wills?"

"He's fine. He's back at the wagon with Susan."

"Good." He groaned and closed his eyes again.

"Where do you hurt most, boy?" David asked as he squatted at Tucker's other side.

His reply came slowly through clenched teeth. "My ankle's broken, I think. And I've ripped up my arm pretty good."

David pulled back the torn fabric of Tucker's shirt sleeve. Tucker sucked in a whistling breath and squeezed his eyes more tightly closed. David looked at Maggie and shook his head. The wagon master took off his shirt and tied it around the arm above the open wound.

"Owww," Tucker groaned as David's examination moved to his right ankle. "That's the spot."

"It's broke, all right." David stood up. "Let's get him to his wagon."

As they placed him on a cot, Tucker took hold of Maggie's hand. He held on, keeping her close as the men carried him on the stretcher back to the train. They set him down on the ground next to the Branigan wagon.

"Coop, bring me a bottle of my best," David said to his friend.

The mute darted quickly off in the direction of the lead wagon.

"This is gonna hurt plenty, Tuck." David looked behind him at Maureen. "I'll need scissors and bandages and something to use for splints for his ankle. Needles and thread, too."

Maggie listened with only half-awareness. She was staring down at Tucker. There was a paleness beneath the sun-bronzed skin of his face. Occasionally he grimaced, as if with another stab of pain.

"Can you hear me, Tucker?" David asked, leaning low.

"Yes, I can hear."

"You've lost a lot of blood. I've got it stopped for now, but your arm needs stitchin'. I'm not much of a seamstress, but I'll do the best I can."

Tucker opened his eyes. "Maggie's good with a needle."

"Me?" Her eyes flew wide. "But I can't—I couldn't—"

"I trust you, Maggie," he whispered.

Coop returned with a bottle of whiskey and handed it to the wagon master.

"Take a few swigs of this," David said as he slipped a hand behind Tucker's neck and lifted him from the pallet. "You're going to need it."

Tucker obeyed, then sank back to the ground with a sigh.

"Hold on," David warned. His gaze once more met Maggie's, then he poured whiskey on the open wound in Tucker's arm.

Tucker's hand squeezed Maggie's so hard she thought her fingers would break. His jaw flinched, but he never made another sound.

"Take another drink or two," David suggested.

Maggie slipped her free hand beneath Tucker's neck. "I'll help him," she said softly. "Here, Tucker. Drink this. Mr. Foster says it will help ease the pain."

Glazed eyes opened to stare up at her. "You're all I need to ease the pain," he whispered. His grin was forced.

"Please drink it." She tried to sound firm, but her voice broke.

"Worried about me?" He flinched again. Pain was etched in every angle and plane of his face.

"You know I am. Now be quiet and drink this."

He took a swallow, then another, never taking his eyes from her. When he spoke, his voice sounded even more hoarse than before. "Worried enough to tell me you love me?" he asked so only she could hear.

How could he joke with her at a time like this? He was hurt and in pain. He could have died down on the ledge. He might never fully recover. And here he was asking her such foolish questions. If she weren't so worried and frightened, she would have given him an unladylike punch right then and there.

"Do you, Maggie?"

There was no resisting the pleading in his eyes. He wanted to hear the words. He *needed* to hear the words. Was it too much to ask?

She leaned down, placing her lips near his ear. "Yes, Tucker. I love you." She straightened, her voice louder this time. "Now drink this before I hit you over the head with it."

David smothered a chuckle. "Better do it, boy."

But Tucker wasn't laughing. His eyes were still locked intently upon Maggie. He pulled her down to him, his voice barely audible. "Do you love me enough to marry me?"

"I love you. Now drink."

It was clear he had no strength left to argue with her. He took another long swallow before collapsing back onto the cot beneath him. His eyelids drooped closed. His breathing, ragged and shallow, slowed.

"We'd better work quickly," David said to Maggie. "I'll take care of his ankle. You and Maureen sew up that arm. He's gonna be in a heck of a lotta pain when he wakes up."

David's words were an understatement.

Tucker resisted the return to consciousness. Pain sliced at him from all directions. His head whirled and spun; he felt sick to his stomach. He groaned and sought refuge in the black hole from which he'd just ascended.

"Tucker . . ."

Her gentle voice called to him. It seemed to echo from the end of a long corridor, urging him onward. It was an irresistible call, and despite the pain, he hurried toward it.

"Tucker . . ."

He opened his eyes. Her hair fell over her shoulders in that familiar state of disarray. He had always like it this way best. Her rebellious tresses always managed to pull free from the ribbons or plaiting anyway. He liked her hair curling near her temples and over her shoulders, so full and free. Her eyes seemed a darker shade of gray today. Perhaps it was the lack of light in the wagon. Wide and wise and full of love. Her mouth was a delightful shade of pink. Her lips would be sweet if he could kiss her now, as sweet as strawberries in cream.

She was frowning as she looked at him. "Tucker, can you hear me?"

"Are you an angel from heaven?" he asked in a weak voice.

A shadow of doubt crossed her pretty features, as if she thought his mind had gone, and then she smiled. "Hardly," was her wry reply.

He found enough energy to chuckle. *Hardly*, he repeated silently to himself.

"How do you feel?"

"Like somebody beat me against a rock wall."

"They did." Her smile broadened. It was like a ray of sunshine captured miraculously in a glass jar. It brightened the whole interior of the wagon.

Finally, Tucker tore his gaze from Maggie and bent his head back so he could see out the front of the wagon. "We're not moving."

"David thought it best if you were allowed to rest awhile. Folks were glad to oblige after what you did for Wills." She started to rise. "I'd better let your mother know you're awake. And Fiona wants to see you too. She and Rachel think the whole thing was their fault."

"Wait." He tried to reach for her hand, but his left arm objected with a blinding flash of pain.

Maggie sat down quickly. Her fingers lightly touched his forehead. "Tucker? What is it?"

"Nothing," he answered through gritted teeth. "I just wanted you to myself for a moment. That's all."

She seemed to relax.

Tucker stared at her in silence. She was so beautiful. She really could be an angel. *No*, he thought, *I don't think angels are allowed to be so stubborn*. Or perhaps she was an angel, with a dash of devilment thrown in. Maggie was minx and magic, shy and seductive, child and woman. She was a thousand things rolled into one. And he loved her.

"You should let me tell Maureen you're awake."

He spoke suddenly, afraid she would slip away this time. "Did I really hear you say you love me?"

Maggie's gray eyes softened to a swirl of silver. "Yes. You heard me."

"And will you marry me, Maggie?"

With a gentle shake of her head, she rose. "I'm going to get Maureen. You're becoming delirious."

She never should have admitted she loved him. In the following days, Tucker brought up marriage time and time again. It grew more difficult by the hour to tell him it was impossible. Nothing she said seemed to convince him.

Finally, she snapped at him in anger that if he didn't stop asking, she would change her mind about staying in Boise for Maureen's wedding. She would go on to Oregon with Susan and her children. That threat, at last, brought the desired result. Tucker fell silent and didn't bring up marriage again.

Surprisingly, Maggie missed his persistent suggestions of wedded bliss. She missed hearing him talking about "we" and "our" and "us." She missed the inference that her future was secure.

And her time with Tucker was growing short. In the afternoon of the twenty-eighth of August, 1867, the Foster train rolled down the bluffs overlooking the Boise River and into the budding territorial capital.

The Branigans were home.

PART II

"Where Thou art—that—is Home."

EMILY DICKENSON

Chapter Thirty-six

Thursday, August 29, 1867
Boise City, Idaho Territory

My dear Aunt Eugenia and dearest Shannon,

We arrived in Boise yesterday, and as much as I loved my native Georgia, I think I am going to feel very much at home here. After crossing a vast desert for days, it was wonderful to see this small town tucked in a valley with a river flowing through it. The oasis of green was a welcome sight.

The wagon train is camped along the Boise River for its second and final night. Tomorrow the others will pull out and continue on to Oregon. It will be difficult to bid them farewell as we have many friends among them.

We have not seen or heard from Keegan yet.

Tucker sent a message by stage to Idaho City, which is north of Boise, to alert him to our arrival. In the meantime, he has found two sections of land where we plan to build our home. When the wagons move out tomorrow, we will journey downriver and begin our new adventure as homesteaders.

I confess I am eager for the day when I awaken in a real bed and can cook breakfast on a stove rather than over an open fire. (Wouldn't your Grandmother O'Toole be surprised to hear me say such a thing!) However, the building may be slow. Tucker suffered a mishap a few weeks ago, but you needn't worry about him. The doctor here says the cracked bone in his ankle is healing quickly and the limp should pass. He is getting around quite well and will be himself soon. I know he is anxious to begin practicing law in Boise as well as to get his family all settled.

I have news which I hate to send to you by letter. I wish you could be with me when I tell you. I have received a proposal of marriage from David Foster, the wagon master, and I have happily accepted. We plan to wed very soon. I hope you will be able to meet him in person before much more time passes. The children have grown quite attached to him, and he is equally fond of them.

I miss you both and had hoped I would find a letter awaiting us so we might know how you are. Is there word of Devlin? Please write to us soon. We send our love.

Your niece and mother,
Maureen Branigan

"I won't ever forget what you done for me, Maggie. Every time I look at my younguns, I'll be thankin' God for you." Susan hugged Maggie tightly, her tears streaking her cheeks.

"I'm going to miss them—and you," Maggie confessed in a whisper. "When I get to Oregon, I'll let you know. I'll find you somehow."

Susan brushed away her tears as she tried to smile. "If you're smart, you won't ever leave Boise. Everythin' you need is here."

Maggie couldn't have replied if she'd tried. The lump in her throat wouldn't have allowed it. Her eyes burned with unshed tears as she watched Susan hugging Maureen and Tucker and the children.

She'd had no idea it would be so difficult to say good-bye to everyone. And she didn't know so many of them would find it hard to bid her farewell either. The hugs, the whispered words of good-bye, the kind wishes for the future continued.

So many. So many friends she hadn't realized she had. So many friends who would soon be gone. Susan and Wills and little Annie. Jake Adams and his seven girls. Ralph Fulkerson and his burly sons. The McCulloughs. Old Mr. Connolly. And Coop.

After all these years together, Coop was going on without David, going back to the farm in Oregon they'd begun together. She knew the decision was hurting both men, although each understood the choices the other was making.

Maggie glanced away from the people gathered around the Branigans and found David talking to the new wagon master, Stan Perkins. She'd heard him telling Tucker last night that Stan Perkins was an experienced man and an old friend. He would see the rest of the Foster train safely through the

Blues and down the Columbia. Maggie thought
again how strange it felt not to be continuing on
with them.

Then her eyes found Tucker. He was leaning on
his cane while he talked to Paul Fulkerson and
Susan Baker. He was grinning, and she thought how
very handsome he looked. At that moment, he
glanced up and met her gaze, and she knew it
wasn't strange at all not to be leaving with the train.

She would be staying with Tucker.

The Branigan wagon stood alone in the abandoned campsite. Maureen held onto David's arm as
the last wagon rolled out of sight.

"Are you sorry not to be going on with them?" she
asked.

"No. Perkins will see them through all right. I
was lucky to have found him here. I hated the
thought of going on without you, even for just a few
weeks."

"I thought perhaps more of them would have
stayed in Boise." Maureen wouldn't have minded
having some of her friends around as they built
their home and rebuilt their lives.

"Boise City never was their destination,
Maureen."

"I know. I just thought . . ."

David's arm slipped around her shoulders and he
squeezed as a chuckle rumbled in his chest. "You're
not going to have time to miss them. Not with a
house and barn to build and children to see to. Not
to mention other important things to worry about."
He turned her in his arms. "Like making you Mrs.
Foster for one."

"You're right. That is something to *worry* about,

Mr. Foster." She smiled. "And it's very, very important to me."

David kissed her soundly—to the accompaniment of children's giggles. When he turned Maureen loose, he cleared his throat and glared at them. "I won't have any more of that, Fiona. You either, Rachel. A man's got a right to kiss his woman now and again without bein' mocked."

The two girls sobered quickly, surprised by his stern tone.

"Because if you don't behave—"he scooped them up, a girl under each arm—"you'll find me doin' the same to you when some young man comes courtin'."

Gales of laughter trailed behind as David carted Fiona and Rachel off toward the wagon.

Tucker walked toward his mother, leading Blue Boy by the reins. He was grinning at the wagon master's antics. "David seems in good spirits." He looked at Maureen. "And so do you. Happy, aren't you?"

It wasn't really a question, but she answered as if it were. "Yes. Very happy."

"Well, we'd better move out too. It'll take us a while to reach our place."

"Our place," Maureen echoed softly. "It sounds wonderful."

"It's not yet, but it will be."

Seated on her swaybacked horse—the same one Tucker had sworn would never make the journey west—Maggie rode beside Tucker. Behind them, David drove the wagon, Maureen at his side, the children watching eagerly from just behind the wagon seat.

They followed the river, enjoying the pleasant breeze that wafted through the poplars and cottonwoods that lined the river's bank. A robin's song, cheerful and bright, burst from the thick branches and was soon returned from the other side of the river. Maggie drew a deep breath. The air was so clean and fresh. She glanced up at the puffy white clouds dotting the blue sky. On their right, the brown foothills rose steadily toward the pine-covered peaks of the majestic mountains beyond. Everything seemed so friendly, as if nature itself were welcoming them.

But it also seemed strange not to be in the midst of many other wagons, strange not to be eating someone else's dust. She felt slightly lost and disoriented and, perhaps, a little frightened. She'd become so used to the routine of the train. What would their days be like now?

Maggie glanced toward Tucker. He was in pain. She could see it in his face. This was the first time he'd been on horseback since the accident, and she knew his ankle had to be throbbing something fierce by now. She was about to suggest that they rest for a moment when she first heard the sound.

"Wait! Branigans!" The faint cry was hardly discernible at first. Then it grew louder. "Wait!"

Tucker reined in and looked behind him. Maggie followed suit.

The rider was sending up a cloud of dust behind the heels of his galloping steed. He was waving his hat with one hand and continued to shout for them to stop. Then he let loose with a terrifying whoop.

Tucker's frown turned to a grin as he dug his heels into Blue Boy's ribs and shot off in the direction they'd just come from. Maggie watched as the two men rode toward each other, sliding their mounts to a halt in unison. The stranger jumped to the ground and hurried toward Tucker who had remained in the saddle. She watched as they clasped hands, saw Tucker slap the other man on the back a few times, heard the shared laughter, then saw the man remount and head toward them, Tucker at his side.

It had to be Keegan.

Maggie nudged her horse back toward the wagon but stopped a short distance away. Maureen had scrambled down from the wagon seat by this time and stood waiting for the two men to catch up with them.

"Aunt Maureen!"

Once again, Keegan vaulted from his horse, this time picking up Maureen and spinning her around. "You're a sight for sore eyes, m'darlin'."

"Put me down, Keegan," she scolded, but her laughter took the sting from the command.

Keegan Branigan, a man in his early thirties, was tall and dark with the same ebony eyes and hair as Neal. While he wasn't as handsome as Tucker, Maggie thought he had one of the nicest smiles she'd ever seen. It started at his mouth and spread all over his face, sending his black eyes dancing.

"I got your message yesterday and come as quick as I could." His voice was oddly attractive—a soft Irish brogue mixed in with a Southern drawl and a dash of Western twang. "You caught me by surprise. I thought sure you'd not be here before next week." He turned toward Tucker. "I mentioned you to Tom Riley, and he's willing to consider you for his firm, Tuck. I think you'll be mighty pleased. And I've told all m'friends that you're comin'."

Then, eyeing Tucker's wrapped ankle, he added, "But it looks as if you'll need a bit of time before you're ready to start to work."

"I'll have to be ready. We have a lot to get finished before winter, and it'll take money for that."

"Well, I'm glad to hear you're ready to go to work. There's a party in a couple of weeks I was hopin' you'd be here for. An important one if you want to meet the right men in this territory. But enough of that." He turned to face the others. "Tell me who we've got here."

One by one, Keegan was introduced to David and the children. Then, as if he'd known all along she was sitting there, observing the proceedings, he turned toward Maggie and walked over to her. "Can this be Shannon?" He eyed her critically. "She's not got the look of a Branigan about her."

"She's not a Branigan," Tucker said as he rode Blue Boy over. "*Yet.*"

A dark brow shot up. "So, and that's the way it is."

"Maggie, this is my cousin, Keegan Branigan. And watch out for him. He's the most Irish of us all, and he's full of blarney. Keegan, meet Maggie Harris."

"You'd better marry her quick, cousin. Once the men of this fair city set eyes on her, there'll be no holdin' them back. Women are scarce enough in the territory, but a single beauty . . ." He whistled through his teeth. "You'll have the wolves at your door."

Tucker laughed. "And you're one of them."

"It might've crossed my mind."

Maggie felt herself blushing. She knew she should set Keegan straight on the matter of marriage between her and Tucker, but it seemed better to ignore it for now. Noting the look of fatigue in Tucker's eyes, she admonished softly, "Perhaps we should rest here a while before going on."

"No, we're almost there. Get your horse, Keegan. I'm about to show the family our new land."

Chapter Thirty-seven

"*C*ome with me." *Holding onto her hand, Tucker* pulled Maggie away from the others. "I want to show you something."

"Don't you think you should sit down and rest for a while?" she suggested again.

For the last hour, Tucker, David, and Keegan had been walking around the acreage near the river, marking out where the house would be, where the barn would be, where the corrals and the crops would be. They'd been discussing cost and the amount of time it would take to get up the first building and where they might buy a few cattle for a reasonable price.

Maggie and Maureen and the children had spent the time unpacking the wagon—hopefully for the very last time. Maggie had felt just a twinge of anger at the way the men ignored them, as if their plans were so grandiose and important that they couldn't be bothered with the business of setting up their camp.

But now, seeing the fatigue in Tucker's eyes, her concern for his health returned. He really had done too much today already.

"Worried about me?" he asked with a teasing grin.

"No!" she snapped, her irritation returning.

"It's nice to have my girl worried about me," he said, as if she hadn't spoken.

"I'm *not* your girl."

The tired look disappeared as his grin increased. "You are, and you know it. You've known it ever since—"

"Don't say it." Her voice was sharp as she tried unsuccessfully to pull her hand free from his. "*That* never happened."

He stopped and drew her close to him, whispering in her ear, "You know it did happen, Maggie. You can't change what's between us."

"I can and I will."

"All right." He laughed aloud. "I give up. I won't say another word about loving you or wanting to marry you or how many children we should have . . ."

Her eyes widened as she looked up into his face. There went that infernal tingling in her stomach again, a feeling that made her feel warm all over.

Then he whispered again, his brown eyes searching her face, intense but gentle. "Mother and David really should have a place to themselves, you know. They'll be newlyweds and will want some privacy. It won't be so bad with the children, but we're adults, you and I. We understand what they're feeling."

When his voice got soft and low like that . . .

He began walking again. His pace was slow but determined. "But you didn't want to hear all this, did you? You wouldn't want me to tell you I'd like to build our house—yours and mine and Rachel's —just the other side of the river. Over there." He pointed toward a stand of tall cottonwoods. "That way, we'll all be close, yet have our own place. Look at that. Lots of tall trees to shade the house and keep it cool in the summer. Plenty of room to spread out, too, as the ranch becomes successful, and we're far enough from town that we don't have to worry about townfolk pushing us out when the capital grows. Cattle is what I want, but we'll have to raise crops too, especially at first. Corn and wheat maybe."

It was crazy, but she was beginning to share his vision. She could almost imagine the tall stalks of corn and fields of wheat and the cattle grazing in the background. She, the city girl, who'd only read about such things in books. It *was* crazy.

"We'll make the house two stories with lots of bedrooms and a nursery and, facing the river, a large airy room for us. We'll paint the house gray. The color of your eyes, Maggie."

For a moment, she could see it all, just as he described it. The large gray house, the two of them sitting on the veranda in the evening, enjoying the cool breeze drifting off the river.

His arm circled her shoulders. "It could be ours, Maggie."

She sighed as reality returned. "No." She felt sad. Terribly sad. "It's your dream, Tucker. Not mine. I'm going to Oregon. I'm going to see Mr. Sanderson and learn the truth about Papa's will. And then maybe I'll go back to Philadelphia, where

I came from. I don't know what it is that I'll do. I just know I'm going to do what *I* decide to do. Not what anyone else decides I should do."

"Why are you so pigheaded?" he demanded.

"Why are you so bossy?" she retorted.

"Lord, you're exasperating." He kissed her.

If she could think straight, she would pull away from him, but there was no time for thought. Tucker's kisses always did that to her. It was hard to remember at the moment why she couldn't allow herself to love him, why she couldn't marry him and live in that gray, two-story house by the river. She would remember later. Much later.

"Well, I'd better be headed back." Keegan rose from the camp stool. "I'll stop by the mill and place an order for lumber. You can work out the details with them when you come to town tomorrow. I'll meet you at Riley's Law Office at two."

Tucker followed him toward his horse. "Keegan, about the lumber . . . It may take me a while . . ."

"I'll not hear another word on it, cousin. I can't have my own kin without a roof over their heads. You'll pay me back as soon as you've got yourself a client or two."

Tucker's pride wanted to refuse the loan for the lumber, but pride wasn't going to put up walls and a roof, and fall and cold weather would be upon them before long. He knew it, and Keegan knew it.

Keegan patted his shoulder. "Corner of Sixth and Main. Two o'clock. Riley is anxious to meet you. He's a respected attorney in these parts. He said he could use a sharp young man. Wouldn't surprise me if you couldn't be a full partner someday." He slipped his boot into the stirrup and swung his right

leg over the saddle. He pulled on the reins, turning
his horse toward town, then came to a halt and
twisted around as he whispered, "Holy Mary and
Joseph, I nearly forgot. I've a letter here from
Georgia. Your mother'll skin me alive." He reached
into his saddlebag and brought out a battered
envelope. "Give it to her and ask her forgiveness,
Tuck. I've not got the courage."

With a chuckle, Tucker took the letter. "See you
tomorrow, Keegan. And thanks."

Maureen clutched the precious letter against her
breast as she moved off toward the river. She knew
she should have read it aloud to everyone, but she'd
been so long without word from her daughter that
she selfishly wanted a moment to savor it alone.

*Mrs. Farrell Branigan, in care of Keegan
Branigan, Idaho City, Idaho Territory.*

Just seeing Shannon's handwriting on the envelope brought a thrill to her heart. Her fingers
trembled as she broke the seal and pulled out the
stationary.

The letter wasn't dated.

Dear Mama,

  *I'm on my way to Idaho! I'm sorry to report
Aunt Eugenia died peacefully a short time after
you left Atlanta. I'm leaving for Independence
tomorrow in hopes of catching up to you, but if
I don't, this letter will reach you soon after you
arrive in Boise.*

  *Devlin came to the funeral, and I tried to
persuade him to come west with me, but as
usual he was being obstinate. The Yankees are
making Atlanta a living hell, and I'm glad to*

*get out of here. I can't imagine why Dev refuses
to leave. One day he'll show up when we least
expect it.*

*I'll see you soon, Mama. Give my love to
Tuck and the little ones.*

> *Your devoted daughter,
> Shannon*

"Is it good news?"

She turned toward David. His blue eyes revealed
his concern.

"Yes. And no." She looked at the short missive
once again. "I'm not sure."

David's arm went around her shoulder. "What
does it say?"

"Aunt Eugenia died shortly after we left Georgia.
I'm not sure exactly when. Shannon's letter isn't
dated. She said she was going to try to reach us
before we left Independence." Her voice fell to a
whisper. "But she didn't reach us, and now I don't
know where she is. She wouldn't have had much
money. We were going to send for her when Tucker
got his feet under him again. She should have
stayed in Atlanta until then. At least there she had a
home. How on earth . . ."

"If she's anything like the rest of the Branigan
family, she's got a good head on her shoulders.
She'll find a way to get here. She may be only a week
or so behind us."

"If only she'd had enough money to take the
stage. David, she might—"

He kissed her cheek. "Don't borrow trouble,
Maureen."

She knew he was right.

"What else did the letter have to say?"

"Devlin went to the funeral. Shannon tried again to convince him to leave, but he wouldn't. Whatever will happen to him? He's still so young, but so filled with hate."

"The Good Book says, 'Train up a child in the way he should go, and when he's old, he'll not depart from it.' I got a feelin' that's how it'll be for your boy, Maureen. He'll find his way. He won't be able to help himself. Not with you for a mother."

Maureen leaned her head against his shoulder. "Thank you, David. I promise not to worry any more. At least, I promise to *try*." They stood silently for some time before she spoke again. "Keegan says it only takes five days for the stage from Boise City to reach San Francisco. Imagine, David. It took us a month to cover the same distance."

"Doesn't matter how long it takes. There's no more travelin' for us. We're home, Maureen. Home to stay."

MAUREEN'S JOURNAL

August 30. We are camped tonight on our new land. Soon we will have a home—one without wheels. It sounds like heaven to me.

One of the first things Tucker did was to transplant a willow sapling from along the river near where the house will be. He christened the land "Green Willows." I cried. He promised on the day we left Twin Willows that we would plant them again, and now we have.

Tucker and David talked long into the night, planning the house which will be David's and mine and the one which will one day be Tucker's (and hopefully Maggie's). But that will take much longer.

We are going into town tomorrow to restock supplies. We cannot plant our first crop until spring. We can only hope the weather will be kind to us.

Chapter Thirty-eight

*T*he city fathers had laid out the plans for Boise City with care—straight streets and square blocks, nestled between the tree-lined river and the rugged foothills. To the north, through the mighty mountains, lay Idaho City with its nuggets of gold. To the south, across the vast desert, lay Silver City with the riches its name suggested.

It wasn't much of a city, to be sure, Tucker thought as he sat beside Maggie in the wagon. Not when compared to Richmond or Atlanta or Charleston. Rutted dirt streets and oddly shaped buildings and no sidewalks to speak of. But it would grow into the plans laid down for it. For some reason, Tucker was convinced of that.

He drove slowly through the streets, acquainting himself and the others with the frontier town with grandiose dreams of looking like the capital city it had become. The Idaho Statesman newspaper was located in a building on Main Street near Sixth. At Eighth and Main stood the enormous new Overland Hotel and not far away was the Idaho Hotel. There was Hill Beachey's Railroad Stage Line and Ben Holladay's Overland Mail and Express Company, joining Boise with cities to the north and east, south and west. The Pioneer Hair Dressing and Bathing Saloon offered warm or cold baths for a dollar and accommodated both ladies and gents. And, of course, there were plenty of saloons of a more traditional nature, offering spirits, not baths. There were meat markets and mercantiles and mills and distilleries and a school and churches and the homes of the city's leading citizens.

Boise was booming.

The Branigan wagon, minus the canvas top, stopped on the west end of town and its passengers spilled out. Maureen immediately linked her arm with David's and told the children to come with them.

"Maggie," she added, "why don't you go with Tucker? He moves much too slowly with that cane of his, and I've a long list of things to get done before we head back." With that, they walked away at a brisk pace, the three children in their wake.

Tucker saw Maggie's mouth open in protest, then clamp shut as her eyes met his. She had to have guessed, of course, that he'd put Maureen up to this, but he was glad she hadn't refused.

"Let's have a look around, shall we?" he said, offering her his left arm.

She hesitated only briefly before slipping her fingers into the crook of his elbow. He wished he weren't handicapped by his ankle and the blasted cane in his right hand. He wanted to walk with Maggie pulled close to his side. He wanted to let all of Boise—the whole world, in fact—know that she was his.

Of course, letting the world know and helping Maggie understand were two entirely different things. He didn't know why she resisted it so hard. He knew she loved him, but she still wasn't able to trust him entirely. Somehow he had to break down that wall she'd built around her heart. It might take some time, but break it down he would.

Buildings were going up everywhere along the streets of Boise, houses and businesses alike. The sounds of hammering filled the air. Tucker set a slow pace as they traversed the dirt streets. Some buildings on Main Street had boardwalks in front. Others didn't. Some were built even with street level. Others were several steps up.

They moved along, looking in shop windows, taking in all the sights and smells of the town, enjoying the bustle and sounds of civilization.

"Wait," Tucker said suddenly, stopping in front of a shop. "Let's go in here."

It was a tiny dress and millinery shop, the interior narrow and deep. As soon as the bell rang overhead, the proprietress appeared from the back of the building. She was a heavy, squat woman with gray hair that resembled a bird's nest. A pair of spectacles perched on a pug nose. She held a needle in one hand and wore a thimble on the thumb of the other.

"Hello. Hello," she chirped at them. "Welcome to Mrs. Moore's. That's me. Do come in."

"How do you do, Mrs. Moore," Tucker said as he bowed formally. "I'm Mr. Branigan and this is Miss Harris. We're new in town. We were just passing by, getting acquainted with your fair city, and I couldn't help noticing your little shop."

"Oh, I'm so glad you did." Her gaze flicked over Maggie. "Well, well. Isn't she a picture of loveliness."

"That's why we've come in. Miss Harris's birthday was a short time ago, and I was unable to find her just the right gift. Do you suppose you might have something for her? Something very special. A dress for an important occasion."

There was a sparkle in the little woman's eyes as she walked a circle around Maggie. "Such skin. My, my. Of course, she's been in the sun too much, but still. Such skin. My, my. And the hair. Beautiful. Oh, yes. I have just the fabric. The palest of blues. With just a touch of silver, I think. Yes, silver. That's what she should have."

"And a hat to match?" Tucker asked.

"Of course. Of course."

Maggie turned wide gray eyes up at him. "Tucker, I really can't—"

"You have to have something special to wear to Mother's wedding." He knew that would stop the argument. He looked at Mrs. Moore again. "When can you begin?"

"Oh, right away. Right away."

"I want the very best, you understand."

"Naturally. Naturally."

Tucker grinned. He wondered if the woman always talked in doubles. "Then I'll leave you two ladies alone. When should I come back for Miss Harris?"

"Give me an hour. Oh, yes. At least an hour. I'll need measurements and . . ." Her voice trailed away as she disappeared into the back of the shop.

"Tucker, really." Maggie was glaring up at him.

He shrugged, then bent down to kiss the tip of her upturned nose. "I couldn't help myself. You wouldn't deny me this little pleasure, would you?"

"You haven't the money for such nonsense. There's nothing wrong with my gray dress."

"I want to do it, Maggie. Don't you know it gives me pleasure?"

A singsong command floated down the dim hallway. "Come along, Miss Harris. Come along."

Tucker tipped his hat toward Maggie. "I'll be back in an hour. Enjoy yourself."

The expression on her face was so funny he had to laugh. It clearly said that an hour with the chirping Mrs. Moore would be anything but enjoyable.

He started whistling the moment the shop door closed behind him. He might as well find Riley's office. It wasn't long before two now. Leaning on his cane, he limped his way down Main Street.

Yes. He was going to like it here.

Maggie hated to admit it, but she *was* starting to enjoy Mrs. Moore. Her enthusiasm was contagious. She seemed to bubble and float her way around the small fitting room in the back of her store, her nonstop chatter filled with lightness and joy. And the bolt of fabric she pulled out was truly beautiful. Maggie didn't think she'd ever seen its equal. An icy blue satin shot through with silver thread.

"My dear, you have perfect shoulders. Has anyone ever told you that you have perfect shoulders? Well, you do. You do. We simply must show them to their advantage. A wedding, did I hear Mr. Branigan say?" She patted Maggie's cheek. "Is that *your* wedding, my dear? Such a handsome groom, too. Oh, yes. Quite handsome."

"No," Maggie answered stiffly. "It's his mother's wedding."

Why was it everyone kept assuming she was going to marry Tucker Branigan? She wasn't. No matter how many people asked her, no matter what Tucker said or did, she wasn't going to marry him.

She wasn't.

She really wasn't.

MAUREEN'S JOURNAL

September 13. *The men rise long before dawn and work on the house until they have to wash and leave for their employment in town, Tucker to his law office and David to Mr. Robie's lumber mill. Upon their return each day, they scarcely take time to eat the meal Maggie and I prepare before they are once again sawing and hammering.*

But their work shows. The house is almost complete. It is far from the red brick house at Twin Willows or the white pillared mansion of Sugar Hill, but I think it will seem a castle when we are living in it.

Each day, they cross the river to Tucker's land to chop down trees for the cabin he intends to build. It will be only one room at first, but it will establish his claim to the land.

Maggie and the children work equally hard. Maggie has cut up the canvas cover from the wagon and has used it to make coats for the children, lining them with cloth from the things they have outgrown. Neal catches fish in the river for our supper. Fiona and Rachel, still inseparable, gather wood for our fires and have collected the smooth river rocks for the chimney.

We are all in good health.

Chapter Thirty-nine

*T*ucker leaned back in his chair and stared at his office ceiling. He knew he should be giving more thought to the papers spread across his desk. After all, this was his first case for Tom Riley's law office. It could make or break him with Riley—and with this town. But he just couldn't tear his thoughts away from Maggie.

Time was growing short. Every day she worked as hard as everyone else, as if it were her home, her land—just as he wanted it to be. Sometimes he thought she was weakening, and then that stubborn tilt of her chin would return and she would start talking about being on her way to Oregon.

He rose from the chair and walked to the window, glancing out at the busy street. He could hear sawing and hammering coming from the lot next door. Another new building going up.

He wished he would hear something from Harry. If they couldn't find Sanderson, how was he to prove that Seth had no right to the Harris girls or their inheritance? Of course, Maggie wasn't a child anymore. She was a woman, and if she would agree to marry him, he could protect her from her uncle. He and Maggie and Rachel could be a family.

But he wasn't really worried about Seth's claims. If Seth had any legal authority, he would have used it years ago. The man would probably never even show up in Boise. He'd probably returned to Philadelphia to salvage what he could before he lost it all.

Tucker was more concerned about Maggie's refusal to trust him. Every once in a while, she allowed him a glimpse of the love she had stored up inside her heart, but then that wall would go up again. How did he break it down for good?

He raked his fingers through his hair as he turned back to his desk.

It wasn't that he didn't understand her desire to know the truth. He'd give almost anything to know what had driven his father to take his life. Oh, Tucker understood the external reasons, but he would never comprehend the complete internal collapse of the man he'd always loved and admired.

Maggie's search was different. He could help her find out what was in her father's will. With time he could probably win the release of her money now held in trust—if it actually existed. But even that wasn't what Maggie was really after.

She's looking for a place to hide, a place where no one can ever hurt her again, he thought as he sank onto his chair.

That was it. Maggie believed that if she didn't

love, if she didn't care, if she didn't trust, no one could hurt her. But that wasn't living. That was just an extended death.

But how did he prove it to her in the short time he'd been given?

Without warning, the door to his office burst open, admitting his cousin. "Time to quit, Tuck. You need a bath and shave before we pick up the ladies."

"Pick up the—" His eyes widened. "The party at Horace Clive's ranch. That's tonight?"

"Don't tell me you forgot the most important social event in the entire territory?" His cousin laughed, a booming sound in Tucker's small office. "Well, lucky for you, I didn't. I presumed on some friends, Chuck and Peg Jones, to let Maggie and Maureen dress at their place. Peg's going to keep an eye on the children too."

Tucker opened his mouth to speak.

"Don't worry," Keegan interrupted. "Maureen sent along your clean suit. Come on. I've a pretty young thing of my own waitin' at the party, and I'm anxious to get to her."

Maggie turned in front of the mirror, her eyes wide and unbelieving. Could that girl possibly be Maggie Harris?

"You look beautiful," Rachel whispered, almost reverently.

Tears clouded her vision, Rachel's words recalling a voice from the past. Her own voice.

"You look beautiful, Mama."

Elizabeth turned from her looking glass, the belled skirt swaying beneath the shimmering satin fabric. "Thank you, darling." She kissed Maggie's forehead.

"Will I ever be pretty like you?"

"Oh, my dear. You'll be ever so much prettier. Look." She drew the little girl to the mirror. "Look at your lovely hair. And those eyes. Maggie, young men will someday spout poetry about your eyes. You know how your father can't deny you a thing when you look at him."

Maggie didn't believe a word of it. Her hair was a riotous, dull brown mop and her eyes were just a plain, ordinary gray. Her mother, on the other hand, had hair the color of gold and eyes just like a summer sky. The baby was going to look like Elizabeth. Sometimes, Maggie was jealous of little Rachel.

"You don't believe me, do you, Maggie?" Elizabeth sank into the voluminous puddle of her skirt as she knelt to hug her daughter. "Trust me, dearest. Someday, you'll find yourself looking into a mirror, and you'll be wearing a beautiful dress, something silvery to match your eyes. And you'll look and discover how pretty you've become."

Maggie still couldn't believe it.

Elizabeth sighed dreamily. "It was on a night like that that I fell in love with your papa."

"Will I ever be pretty like you, Maggie?"

Rachel's question brought Maggie back to the present with a jolt. The familiar words sounded bittersweet in her ears. "You'll be far prettier than I'll ever be, Rachel." And like her mother, she drew her sister toward the mirror. "You'll be the belle of every ball. You look just like Mama. Just like her."

Rachel turned quickly and gave Maggie a tight hug. "I'm so glad we came here, Maggie. I love you."

"I love you, too."

*   *   *

Tonight was the night, Tucker decided. Tonight he was going to get Maggie to agree to marry him. He wasn't sure how, but it was going to happen.

He checked his reflection in the mirror, his fingers rubbing his smooth chin. It still seemed odd not to have a bearded man looking back at him. He'd had his beard since he was seventeen and still couldn't believe he'd rid himself of it so quickly. All it had taken was Maggie to wonder aloud what he would look like without it and off it had come. He knew, without a doubt, why he kept it off. Because, although she'd never said so, Maggie seemed to like him better that way.

Tucker turned and grabbed his hat from a nearby chair and left the dressing room. Keegan was waiting for him in a black carriage outside the bathing saloon.

"You don't hardly use that cane anymore," his cousin commented as he stepped up into the carriage.

"Another week or two and the doctor says I can throw it away. Not soon enough for me."

"From my last look out at your place I'd say it hasn't kept you from doin' much."

Tucker shrugged. "David's having to do more than his share. But we ought to be into the house in a few days. Just a few rooms and bare floors, but it'll be nice for the women to be in a house again."

Keegan stopped the horses in front of a wood frame house on Market Street. It was two stories tall with a wide porch across the front. Young poplars were planted throughout the yard, and a white picket fence surrounded the lot.

"You wait right there," Keegan told him as he passed the leather reins into Tucker's hands. "I'll get David and the ladies."

Keegan hurried up the walk leading to the front porch and disappeared through the open door. Tucker stared at the house, thinking how nice it would be when he could give Maggie such a home.

Maureen appeared first. She was wearing a satin gown the exact same reddish-brown shade as her hair. Her auburn tresses were swept high in a smoothly elegant style. A simple satin ribbon, with a brooch pinned at the center, circled her throat.

He remembered her looking just like this once before. In fact, he'd seen her in the same gown, but it was so long ago it seemed more like a dream. He'd been just a schoolboy. He'd come down the stairs, and there she was, standing by the window, watching for Farrell to return from overseeing the plantation. He half expected to see his father come striding through the doorway.

But it was David Foster who walked out onto the porch to stand beside Maureen.

"Evenin', Tuck." The big man looked a trifle uncomfortable in his suit and top hat.

"David," he replied, hiding his amused smile.

David took Maureen's arm and guided her down the steps and toward the carriage, helping her up into the seat behind Tucker, then sitting down beside her.

"I'm not sure what's keeping Maggie," his mother said as they all gazed at the house.

As if on cue, Maggie stepped through the doorway, pausing on the top step and gazing toward the carriage. The impact of her beauty nearly knocked Tucker off his seat.

Mrs. Moore's silvery-blue, off-the-shoulder creation revealed not only Maggie's long neck but a delightful suggestion of cleavage. Short, puffed sleeves circled her upper arms. The bodice fit snugly over her slender torso, clinging to her softly rounded breasts. The skirt swelled over several crisp petticoats, the fabric draped in a most becoming fashion.

Her mass of golden-brown hair, swept up from her neck, curled around her face and was hidden beneath a perky Marie Stuart bonnet, bedecked with a pale blue feather and a tiny artificial bird. Her gray eyes, more silver tonight than usual, watched him uncertainly, as if she were afraid he wouldn't approve.

Tucker didn't know when Keegan followed her out of the house, but suddenly he was there, taking Maggie's arm. "Your carriage awaits," his cousin told her, loudly enough for the others to hear.

"But it's hardly a carriage fit for a princess," Tucker whispered in her ear as she settled onto the seat beside him.

Tucker's words, her new gown, the fancy black carriage.

Just like in a fairy tale, Maggie thought as Keegan turned the horses east on Market.

Perhaps this was a night for fairy tales and fools. Perhaps this was *her* night.

She was very much aware of Tucker sitting next to her. He looked so terribly handsome in his dark suit, lean but muscular. His face, with its strong, square jaw and those probing brown eyes, revealed such strength of character and intelligence. For tonight, every woman at the party would be jealous of Maggie Harris.

The matched pair of palominos trotted briskly along the country road, quickly leaving Boise behind. Keegan carried on a merry banter, pulling Maureen and David into a three-way conversation.

But Maggie and Tucker sat quietly.

Maggie wouldn't have heard if anyone addressed her anyway. Her thoughts were carrying her far away. First she remembered the night Tucker taught her to dance. She remembered their first kiss. She remembered the second time they'd danced together, and the way he'd whispered that she could trust him. And she remembered the night he'd made love to her beneath the stars.

She felt her face grow warm and was glad no one was looking at her. It seemed scandalous to be thinking such thoughts with Tucker's mother sitting only a few feet away. What would she think of Maggie if she knew?

Thankfully, her time for leaving was growing close. She wasn't sure how much longer she would be able to resist the way Tucker looked at her or the loving things he said, if she were forced to stay. But Maureen and David's wedding was in two days, and Maggie meant to take the next stage after that out of Boise.

Why?

There was a funny little skip in her pulse at the silent question.

Why are you leaving?

Because I must. Because I can't marry him.

Why not? Cook was wrong about your father. He loved you. Why couldn't she be wrong about Tucker? He loves you too.

But . . .

So what if love is for fairy tales and fools? Be foolish, Maggie. You may never have another chance.

Chapter Forty

*T*he Horace Clive ranch house was a monstrous place built of stone and glass. A stairway inside the front entrance led to a ballroom that encompassed the entire second floor. At one end of the room, another story above the ballroom, was a balcony where an orchestra was playing softly. Built-in benches, covered with velvet cushions, provided seating in several small alcoves. The windows were thrown wide to let in the cool evening breeze at the end of a hot September day.

In the first flurry of arrival, Maggie was introduced to so many people it made her head spin. She was glad she had Tucker's arm to hold on to. She felt terribly shy and unsure of herself among so many strangers, all of them elegantly clad, many of the women dripping with diamonds. She'd never expected so much wealth so far from civilization.

Apparently the Wild West wasn't as wild as she'd once thought.

Keegan was the first to whisk her away for a dance. He joked with her, dropping whispered comments and scandalous gossip about different people in the room, until she couldn't help smiling. By the end of the dance, her fears were forgotten.

David waltzed with her next. She felt very tiny and fragile next to him and was reminded of the first time she'd seen him. How frightened she had been when he'd turned toward her that morning in May. Never would she have suspected that he had the most gentle of hearts. She was glad for David and Maureen, glad they had found each other. She knew they would be happy.

There followed dance upon dance in other men's arms. Maggie surprised herself at how well she managed to follow their leads. It was as if she'd been dancing at balls all her life.

"Lovely young woman, your Miss Harris."

Tucker tore his gaze from Maggie. "Yes, she is."

Horace Clive grinned affably. "Not enough eligible young women in these parts yet." He indicated the dancers with a jerk of his bald head. "I'd keep an eye on her, if I were you."

"I intend to." Tucker's tone was a trifle brusque.

"Don't take offense, Mr. Branigan," his host replied with a low chuckle. "I meant it as a compliment."

Tucker relaxed. He knew he was being overly sensitive, mostly because he'd been relegated to the sidelines while every other man in the room was getting to dance with Maggie.

Horace Clive, tall and beanpole thin, was a chatty

fellow in his mid-fifties. His bald head gleamed in the light of the lamps and candelabra. "Keegan tells me you're homesteading west of town."

"Yes. David Foster and I have both claimed our hundred and sixty acres. We just about have David's house finished."

"I remember what it was like when I first arrived. Thank heaven I didn't have my family with me. It was hard enough on me. I admire your mother and Miss Harris for putting up with it all. They must be amazing examples of the fair sex."

Tucker glanced toward the dance floor again. "They are."

Horace settled onto the bench beside him. "And I hear you're practicing law as well? With Tom Riley, I understand. Good man, Tom." He took a sip of punch, then made a face. "Awful stuff, but Mrs. Clive won't have strong spirits in the house." He set the cup on the floor, then turned to face Tucker. "Keegan also tells me you hope to raise cattle on your land. Been lots of talk of the success of cattle operations in Texas. Beef. That's the word from the east. Send us beef. We've fed a lot of the miners around here. No point in shipping good meat back east when the miners in the Basin will pay top dollar. But that'll come to an end. Farsighted men will plan for different times, better ways."

Tucker nodded and made sounds of agreement in appropriate spots as he watched the way a dark-haired man was placing his hand in the small of Maggie's back and guiding her around the floor. Wasn't he holding her just a little too close?

"Did your cousin warn you of the trouble we've had along the road west of the city? Horse thieves and bandits. We think they're holed up in the hills north and west of you. Keep an eye out for them.

They strung up the former sheriff last year for aidin' murderers and horse thieves. Maybe when we finally get ourselves a mayor elected things will get better."

Damn, if that fellow didn't look like he was sniffing Maggie's hair and enjoying her cologne.

"Ah, well. I see Mrs. Clive has some more guests for me to talk to. Pleasure meeting you, Mr. Branigan. Hope you're up to dancing soon. Come see us any time. I'd be glad to show you that bull of mine. You might want to think about breeding your cows with him."

"Thanks. I'll do that," Tucker replied absently, scarcely knowing he did so.

Maggie's dance partner was whispering something in her ear. And she was laughing!

Still puffing from a strenuous reel, Maggie plopped onto a cushion beside Tucker. "It's so warm," she managed to get out as she waved a fan in front of her face.

"I've had enough of this." Tucker grasped her hand and pulled her up from the bench.

He moved surprisingly fast despite the limp as he led her across the ballroom and down the stairs. In a flash, they were out the front door. He kept walking until they were far from the house and cloaked in the darkness of night. Faint music spilled through the open windows to serenade them.

"What's wrong?" Maggie asked breathlessly.

"Too many men were holding you."

With that, he spun her into his arms. Holding her against him, he swayed slightly from side to side.

"I can't dance, so this will have to do," he whispered near her ear.

"Mmmm. I like it."

They remained silent for a long time. Maggie closed her eyes and allowed herself to be lost in the sweetness of the moment.

"What do you want, Maggie?" he whispered.

She pulled back and looked at him, surprised and not knowing how to answer. "Want?"

"To be rich? To be free? To be happy?"

"I don't—"

"I know what I want," he said, his fingers closing around her upper arms. "I want you. I want to love you and protect you and earn your trust and make you happy. I don't want to be your master, Maggie. I want to be your husband."

"I can't marry you, Tucker." Her eyes filled with tears. Why couldn't he believe her? And why didn't *she* believe it anymore?

He drew her close. He pressed her head against his chest. She could hear his heartbeat through his shirt.

Thump *thump*. Thump *thump*.

The sound made her feel special.

Thump *thump*. Thump *thump*.

As if she were wrapped in a cocoon of love.

Thump *thump*.

"Maggie . . ."

She turned her face up to him. She could feel him watching her.

His words were whisper soft. "The greatest freedom is found in loving another. Let yourself love me."

"I do love you." Her reply was broken, as if it were torn from her against her will.

"Love isn't just words, Maggie. It isn't love if you keep it to yourself. You have to give it away."

Heat spread through her veins as she lifted on

tiptoe to meet his waiting lips.

Her hands slid up his arms to weave through his hair, drawing his mouth ever harder against hers. She strained toward him and found herself silently cursing the yards of satin that separated them. She ached to be a part of him, to lie with him, to be consumed by him.

His fingers played lightly across her bare flesh, moving ever closer to her breasts. With a groan of delight and frustration, she let her head fall back. She closed her eyes and reveled in the wild sensations that ran rampant through her body.

He stopped his gentle lovemaking so abruptly she nearly toppled over backwards. She would have if he hadn't caught her, pulling her almost roughly against his chest, snapping her head back up again, forcing her to look at him. "I won't take *no* anymore," he said, low but clear. "I said I wouldn't try to be your master, that I won't tell you what to do. And I won't. So help me I won't. You'll have as much freedom as you want. But *this* is different. You *are* going to marry me."

"Yes, Tucker."

"We could be married day after tomorrow, along with Mother and David."

"Yes, Tucker."

"And no more arguments. Do you underst— Wait. What did you say?"

Maggie smiled, warm and dreamy. "I said yes, Tucker."

As he wrapped her in a tender embrace, she thought how glad she was to have become a believer in fairy tales, how happy she was to become a fool for love.

Chapter Forty-one

With the lumber from Robie's Mill, David and Tucker had built a small, three-room house with a loft for the children's bedroom. The main room of the Foster house would serve as both parlor and dining room, much of the space filled with a table and benches. The kitchen was little more than a side table, where food could be prepared and dishes washed, and a large stone fireplace. David had built an oven into the side of the fireplace for baking. The third room would be the newlyweds' bedroom.

Across and downriver from the Foster homestead, the two men, with Keegan's help, had constructed a log cabin from the cottonwood trees. Tucker and Maggie's first home.

Tucker arose early that morning and rode Blue Boy across the river toward the cabin. He sat on his horse amidst the trees, staring at the crude structure where he would bring his bride later that night.

He'd been so excited when she'd said she would marry him, but now . . .

How could he bring Maggie to such a place? A single room. A simple tick mattress lying on the floor. What was he offering her? Hard work and then more hard work. It might take him years to build that home he'd promised her. Oh, he knew she had what it took to make it—he'd seen what she was made of on the journey west—but was it fair of him to ask it of her? Especially when something better might be waiting for her in Oregon?

Suddenly the door to the cabin opened, and Maggie stepped outside. Her honey-brown hair tumbled and curled in its beautiful disorder around her shoulders. She was wearing one of his mother's old dresses, one she had not yet found time to cut down to fit her. It hung on her delicate frame like a sack, yet she still looked unbelievably pretty in it.

Maggie tossed back her head, turning her face toward the rising sun. "Good morning, sunrise!" she shouted, then picked up the skirt, revealing not only her attractive calves but a pair of bare feet, and raced east along the river's edge.

Bemused, Tucker waited for her to disappear from view before riding up to the cabin. He dismounted and walked slowly toward the cabin door. He hesitated with his hand on the latch, then lifted it and pushed the door open.

It was like walking into a meadow. Throughout the room, buckets and jars held wildflowers in an array of colors. On the wall above the bed was strung a patchwork quilt, and a matching one covered the bed itself. He knew immediately that Maggie had made them, although he didn't know when she'd found the time. Much of the fabric he recognized. Some dresses that Fiona had outgrown. The shirt he'd ruined in his fall down the wall of the Snake River canyon. One of her old worn gowns. And pieces of the blue fabric from the ball gown he'd ordered from Mrs. Moore.

Dear Mrs. Moore, he thought as he ran his callused fingers over the quilt. She must have given most of these scraps to Maggie, even though he still owed her money for the dress and hat she'd made. He should have known it would be more than he could afford. And still the good woman had been generous with Maggie.

Poverty, that's what he was offering Maggie. The morose thought made his shoulders slump—and then he looked around the room again. She had decorated it for their wedding night. She knew what her home would be like, yet she was happy about it.

So help me, he thought, *you won't have to live like this for long. I'll build you that house with the bedrooms and nursery and the veranda. I promise you, Maggie.*

Maggie sat in the loft, her legs dangling over the edge near the ladder. Behind her, Fiona and Rachel was arguing good-naturedly over who would get to sleep closest to the small glass window.

Maggie was relieved that Rachel wanted to stay with Maureen and David until Tucker could add on a room or two to the cabin—and she felt just a little guilty because of it. But she couldn't imagine sharing a room with her sister while Tucker . . .

Her face grew warm. Tonight. Tonight he would make love to her again.

"Look," Fiona said, her face pressed close to the window. "Someone's coming."

"It's Mr. Jessup!" Rachel exclaimed. "Maggie, it's Mr. Jessup."

Maggie pulled back from the edge of the loft and jumped to her feet, hurrying over to the window to peer out above Fiona's and Rachel's heads. Sure enough, it was Harry, dismounting in the yard and followed by a stranger in a black suit and hat.

Harry couldn't have come at a more perfect time. To be there for the wedding. She'd thought they would never see him again. He'd been Tucker's best friend since boyhood, and in their short time together on the wagon train, she'd thought he had become her good friend too. She meant to give him a severe scolding for leaving without saying good-bye—just before she begged him to stay in Idaho.

She whirled away from the window and scrambled down the ladder to the parlor below. She glanced down at the shapeless dress she was wearing, and then at her bare feet. Perhaps she should take a moment to change. After all, she didn't know whom he had brought with him. She didn't want to be an embarrassment to everyone.

The door opened, revealing David.

"Maggie—"

"I know," she interrupted, her voice excited. "Harry's here. I saw him from the window. I was going to put on my shoes and comb my hair."

David moved to one side as the man in the black suit stepped through the doorway.

"Hello, Maggie," he said, smiling uncertainly. "I think I would know you anywhere. You look very much like your mother."

There was more gray in his black hair. The blue of his eyes didn't seem so sharp, nor did he seem as tall.

"Mr. Sanderson?" she whispered.

He nodded.

She felt dizzy and sat down quickly on the bench beside the table. Harry and Maureen and David all entered the house as Marcus Sanderson moved toward her. Maggie's surprised gaze moved from one of them to the next, settling finally on Harry.

"That's why you left? To find Mr. Sanderson?"

"Tuck asked me to."

She shook her head. "He never told me."

"He didn't want you to get your hopes up."

Maggie turned her attention back to her father's old friend. "Please sit down, Mr. Sanderson."

He sat in the rocker across from her.

"May I—may I get you something to drink? I think there's still some coffee."

"I'd like that."

Maureen motioned for Maggie to stay seated. "I'll get it." On her way to the tiny kitchen, she glanced up at Rachel and Fiona, who were observing everything from the loft. "Come down, children. I need some help outside."

Maggie's gaze was still locked onto Sanderson. She had the strangest feeling that she'd been pulled back in time, that her father would appear at any moment and invite his friend to stay for supper or perhaps to go duck hunting or to join them at the lake for a week or two.

She was only vaguely aware of Maureen handing Sanderson his coffee before herding everyone else out of the house and closing the door behind her.

"You really are more like Jeremy, now that I've taken a closer look," he said at last. "Although you're much prettier."

Self-consciously, she touched her tangled mop of hair.

"I didn't know they were dead, Maggie. I would have written. I would have checked up on the two of you."

She shook her head, unable to speak.

"Mr. Jessup told me a little of what happened. You were right to try to come to me. Your father never meant for anything to go to his brother, especially not his precious daughters. He knew what a wastrel and drunkard Seth was. Your uncle must have altered the will somehow, or he never would have gotten away with it."

Tears misted Maggie's eyes. "I knew Papa hadn't meant for us to be with him."

"I remember Seth well enough. A coward, only brave when he was bigger and stronger than someone else, who would cut and run at the first sign of trouble. Everything he ever did failed. Mr. Jessup says Seth has bankrupted everything, but I find that hard to believe."

"It must be true," Maggie answered as she dried her eyes with the handkerchief Marcus Sanderson passed to her. "He turned out all the servants years ago. He got rid of all the horses except two, one for his buggy and one saddle horse. I heard him talking with a man from the mill once, and it sounded very bad." Her chin lifted. "He blamed us because Papa left us some money, and he couldn't get it."

Sanderson revealed a slight grin as he brought the cup of hot coffee toward his mouth. When he set it aside, he leaned forward, his blue eyes staring into hers. "I'm afraid it's not just *some* money, my dear. It's a very large fortune your father put into trust for you."

Maggie shook her head, disbelieving.

"It's true, Maggie. It's no wonder Seth was angry that he couldn't get his hands on it and blamed you for all his troubles. Even he would have had trouble losing such a fortune."

"Uncle Seth said the money in the trust was lost too."

Now Sanderson frowned. "That *is* a possibility. There doesn't seem to have been anyone looking out for your interests since your parents died. I'll have to look into the matter. I'm on my way back to Philadelphia to do just that."

She couldn't help smiling. It sounded so preposterous.

Sanderson rose from his chair. "I want you to come back to Philadelphia with me on today's stagecoach. You and your sister. It could be that we can salvage Harris Mills yet, and there are the legal matters to disentangle. And, of course, there's the trust."

"I can't go back, Mr. Sanderson." Maggie stood before him. "Today's my wedding day."

"You could postpone your wedding. We may need you there to clear things up. We don't know what your uncle might be doing."

Tucker stood with his hands jammed into his pockets. "We'll postpone the wedding until you get back, Maggie," he said, unknowingly mimicking Marcus Sanderson. He couldn't look at her when he said it, so he stared upriver—toward *their* place.

Of course, she had to go back with Sanderson. She was an heiress. What had he to offer that would keep her here? In truth, what had he that would ever bring her back? Once she left, once she stepped into that glittery world of wealth and was introduced into society . . .

"I'm not going with him, Tucker, and we're not going to postpone the wedding."

He turned around.

There was that stubborn lift of her chin, that defiant glitter in her silvery-gray eyes. "I'm staying."

"Be sensible, Maggie. It will be a long time before I can build a decent home, before I can buy you more pretty gowns. We may even go hungry. Is that what you want for yourself? Is that what you want for Rachel? Without you there, Sanderson may not be able to free that trust for you."

"I don't care. I'm not going."

"You're so damned stubborn."

"I love you."

"You're not listening to reason."

"I love you."

He stepped toward her. "You'll probably regret it."

Her arms slipped around his waist. "I love you."

"I give up," he whispered as he buried his face in her hair.

"I knew you would."

Chapter Forty-Two

Once again, Peg and Chuck Jones opened their home to Keegan's family, this time for a double wedding.

In the upstairs bedroom they had used to dress in just two days before, Maggie picked up the bouquet of roses and handed them to Maureen. "You're so very beautiful," she said, blinking back sudden tears. "I hope you'll be happy."

Maureen's dress—faded and turned but beautiful all the same—was a deep forest green. The neckline was modest, the sleeves long. Her auburn hair was caught in a simple chignon and dressed only with two pearl-studded combs. The brightest light came from her eyes, not her jewels.

"I will be," Maureen answered as she glanced once more at her reflection in the mirror. There wasn't so much as a shred of doubt in her voice. "When you share yourself with the man you love, you become a fuller person." She turned toward Maggie. "But you already know that, don't you, Maggie?"

Maggie nodded as happiness flooded through her. She most definitely knew what Maureen was talking about.

"Mother . . . " Fiona peeked around the door.

With a rustle of petticoats, Maureen turned from the mirror. "Come in, Fiona."

The child was wearing a small version of her mother's gown, her pretty auburn tresses clustered in ringlets at the back of her head. She hurried across the bedroom and hugged her mother's waist. "You look so pretty."

Maureen knelt on the floor. "So do you."

"Tucker says to tell you Judge Griffin is here." A mischievous glint entered her green eyes, again just like her mother's. "Mr. Foster is too nervous to sit down. Tucker says he's going to wear a hole in the carpet and for both of you to come quick."

Maureen laughed as she rose gracefully. "Then we'd better not keep them waiting." Her gaze met with Maggie's. "Are you ready, my dear?"

"I'm ready." She picked up her own bouquet of flowers—wildflowers the same blue as her ball gown—and preceded Maureen out of the room.

The two bridegrooms were waiting in front of the parlor fireplace. But Maggie scarcely noticed David. Her attention was instantly captured by the love staring out at her through Tucker's eyes.

His fingers touched her elbow as she reached him, and together they faced Judge Griffin.

"Dearly beloved . . ."

Yes, she was beloved. She knew it without question, without reserve.

". . . promise to honor and obey . . ."

Strange how those words might have frightened her at one time. But when one was cherished, there was no fear in honoring—or even obeying. She had never felt more free in her life than she felt now.

". . . pronounce you man and wife . . ."

Such few words bound a woman to a man for a lifetime.

"You may kiss your bride."

Tucker's dark eyes searched her face, so intense, so loving. She felt herself quiver in his arms as he drew her to him to seal their vows with his lips.

The room erupted in cheers, and suddenly they were surrounded by well-wishers. Rachel hugged and kissed Maggie.

Then Harry grabbed her. "I've been wanting to do this since the day we met but didn't dare because of Tuck." He kissed her full on the mouth before winking at Tucker.

"That's the only one you'll ever get," Tucker grumbled in jest.

Maggie and Maureen exchanged hugs and then she and David and then Neal and then Keegan and then . . .

Maggie gasped and felt the blood rushing from her face as she stared at the open front door. The room grew silent around her. Rachel was standing beside her again, her small hand cocooned within Maggie's.

"It wasn't easy to find you," Seth said gruffly.

Tucker stepped forward. "This is a private home, Harris."

"I came for my nieces."

"My wife isn't going anywhere with you."

Seth's face darkened. "So I was right. You did want her money."

Tucker's fists clenched as Maggie reached out and

took hold of his arm, silencing him before he could respond.

"Just leave," she told her uncle softly. "You haven't a claim on us."

"You're wrong there, Maggie." Seth held out a white piece of paper covered with writing in black ink. "This here says I've got some rights. You may have married this Reb, but I can still take the little baggage back with me where she belongs."

Maggie couldn't seem to breathe.

"I'd like to have a look at that, Harris," Tucker said. He loosened Maggie's fingers from his arm and stepped away from her.

Maggie forced herself to draw some air into her lungs. *Don't let Rachel see you're afraid.*

Tucker took the paper from Seth's outstretched hand. She could feel his body stiffening even from across the room. When he turned around, she knew it wasn't just a bad dream. It was truly happening.

She must have looked about to faint. Keegan moved quickly to her side, placing his hand beneath her elbow. "Who is this man?" he asked.

"My uncle," she answered breathlessly.

"Maggie." Rachel was crying. "I don't want to go with him!"

She knelt beside her sister. "You won't have to, kitten. I won't let him take you anywhere."

With those words, her fear vanished. She didn't care what that sheet of paper said. Uncle Seth wasn't ever going to harm her or Rachel again.

She straightened and walked toward her uncle and Tucker. Her voice was cool and controlled, and only her eyes revealed the storm raging inside. "We all know that paper is worthless, Uncle Seth. How much did you pay to have it drawn up? It wasn't worth it, whatever it was."

"It's legal," he blustered. "Just ask your fancy Reb lawyer."

"Do you know who was here in Boise, Uncle Seth? Marcus Sanderson."

"Sanderson!"

"You remember. My father's attorney. He wasn't dead the way you told me. He's on his way right now to Philadelphia. He says he's going to find out what you've done since Papa died." She was warming to her subject, the anger seeping into her voice, making it louder, stronger. "What *have* you done, Uncle Seth? Enough to put you in prison, perhaps?" She reached out and took the paper from Tucker's hand. "You can't hurt us anymore, and you can't take Rachel away from me." With that, she tore the document into tiny pieces of paper.

Seth made a threatening move, but Tucker's deep voice stopped him. "I suggest you leave while you can, Harris. Once the truth is out, the law is likely to be looking for you."

The veins stood out on Seth's forehead as he stared at Maggie. "The money is gone from the trust, you know. He's married you for nothing. Sanderson will find that out." His gaze darted to Tucker. "I'll get even with the Branigans for messin' in my affairs. Maybe not here, not now—but the Branigans will pay. You remember that. Some day—"

Tucker's jaw clenched as he leaned forward. "Get out," he growled.

Seth Harris turned and hurried down the walk toward his tethered horse.

Silence gripped the parlor for a long time.

Maggie felt a strange feeling wash over her. She'd been afraid of her uncle for so many years, yet he was a coward, just as Sanderson had said. When she'd stood up to him, he'd cut and run in typical Seth Harris fashion. In her moment of courage, she had freed herself from him forever.

Finally, Maggie turned toward Tucker. "He's gone," she said.

And she knew he would never trouble her again.

A single wax candle flickered in the far corner. The heady scent of wildflowers in jars and buckets drifted above them, surrounded them. Tucker braced himself on one elbow as they lay on the bed, Maggie in her new nightgown, Tucker still wearing his trousers and shirt.

Maggie pressed herself closer against him as she slipped her hands beneath his shirt, her fingers splayed across the firm muscles of his chest. It seemed she'd been waiting for this moment for an eternity.

His kiss sent a warmth spiraling through her that no fire could have provided. Her lips parted, emitting a soft moan even as she allowed entry to his gently probing tongue.

When he drew back, she opened her eyes to gaze upon him in the dancing light of the candle.

He smiled knowingly, then leaned over and nibbled at the hollow of her throat. "You know when I first began falling in love with you?" he asked, his lips still touching her flesh.

"No."

"When you waved that knife at me. And you would have used it, too."

She laughed low but didn't deny it. "I think for me it was when that snake slithered over my foot, and you made fun of me."

Braced once more on his elbow, he looked down at her. "I didn't expect you, Maggie." His fingers released the tiny buttons of her nightgown.

She knew just exactly what he meant. "I was always going to be alone." It was hard to breathe when he touched her like that. "Just me and Rachel."

She rose slightly and allowed him to pull the nightgown over her head.

His lips traced the same places his hands had traveled just moments before. Maggie turned languorous eyes upon him as he kissed first one breast and then the other; she rocked gently beneath the caresses of his loving hands. She ached for more, yet was in no rush. They had nowhere to go. They had all night. They had a lifetime.

And she meant to savor each moment even as she savored his body, his touch, his love.

He petted and stroked her in wondrous ways, sending rivers of want crashing through her. And she returned the touch, disrobing him and allowing her eyes to feast upon him in a bold, possessive manner. Finally, when the ache became too great, they lay flush against one another. His body was wonderfully warm and strong and male.

"I love you, Maggie."

"Yes." More plea than reply.

He moved above her, she lifted to him, and together they plunged into a tumultuous storm of loving.

MAUREEN'S JOURNAL

November 15. For the first time in weeks, I take pen in hand to record my thoughts.

We had our first snowstorm yesterday. The land is white as far as the eye can see, and the mountains stand as frosty sentinels, majestic and strong. Keegan tells us the snow rarely stays long in this Boise Valley. In my snug little house, I am willing to let it stay awhile. The children do think it fun. It is so different from Georgia.

I find I have come much farther than two thousand miles to reach the place I am today. From Georgia to Idaho was only the physical change. It is the change in me I see above all—from the pampered Maureen O'Toole of Sugar Hill whose most difficult task was deciding what dress to wear each day, to Maureen Foster of Green Willows who cooks and washes and sweeps and sews from sunup to sundown. There are times when I wish for the ease of my life in Georgia, but they are brief. I am needed here, I am loved, and my life is full. Much fuller than I ever dreamed it could be.

I have found that home is something you take with you in your heart, not a place to live.

EPILOGUE

August 1869

Maggie awakened before dawn. The bedroom was bathed in darkening degrees of shadows. She could hear Tucker's steady breathing beside her and knew that he still slept. She considered sliding closer to him. She never tired of feeling his bare flesh against hers.

But she decided against it. She didn't want to awaken him. He had an important trial starting soon, and his office desk was piled high with papers and briefs. With the success of his law practice and his involvement with territorial government, his days were always long, but even more so in recent months.

Besides, they had been awake late last night, making love and talking until the wee hours of the morning. She smiled. He *definitely* needed more sleep after last night.

Moving carefully, she slipped from beneath the

covers, reaching quickly for her robe on the chair near the bed. She tied the belt around her waist as she padded on bare feet across the bedroom.

In the hallway, she paused near a second bedroom door, but all was quiet there too. She felt awash with contentment, surrounded as she was by the stillness of morning.

She descended the stairs and opened the front door, stepping out onto the wide veranda that bordered three sides of the house. The morning air was crisp and had that fresh scent which only came after the rain. She breathed deeply, her mouth turning up in a smile.

There had been a tremendous thunderstorm last night. For hours the sky had flashed with lightning and the earth had shaken beneath the thunder. But Maggie had no more fear, no more nightmares. The storm had seemed only an extension of their lovemaking, mirroring the flash and roll of their shared passions.

She leaned her hands against the porch rail, allowing her thoughts to drift.

It seemed impossible that it was two years since they first set eyes on this land. Two years. Hard years. Harder even than the wagon journey that had brought them there. Together they had worked the land, growing wheat and corn that first year and again this spring. And Tucker had spent long hours in Riley's law office, building a reputation as a sharp young attorney with a quick mind who was fair with all men, rich or poor. It was his love for the law, his passion for justice that had brought them the measure of success they now enjoyed. While not rich by any means, Tucker had been able to build the house he'd imagined and had described to her that day in August of 1867.

Maggie ran her fingers along the rail and smiled thoughtfully. They had been in this gray, two-story house only a week, and she loved it dearly. But there was a secret part of her that would always hold a fondness for that one-room log cabin.

Maggie's gaze turned upriver, and she imagined the normal happy chaos of the Foster home. Maureen and David were fine examples that love wasn't merely for the young. Only having her other two children with her could have made Maureen more happy than she was today. At least she knew where Shannon was, but Devlin's whereabouts remained a mystery. Maggie hoped her mother-in-law would eventually hear something from him.

Two years, she thought again. Where had it gone?

She'd had a letter from Paul Fulkerson earlier in the week. Paul and his father had opened their smithy in Oregon City, just as they'd planned. But he hadn't been writing for himself. He had written the letter for his fiancée, Susan Baker. It had taken the young man nearly two thousand miles and almost two years in Oregon before he could convince Susan to accept his proposal, but the tone of the letter revealed the happiness the two of them had found. Maggie remembered how Susan had told her she would be wise never to leave Idaho. She was glad she'd followed her friend's advice.

Settling onto the top step of the veranda, Maggie pushed her long, curly hair back from her face, then turned her head toward the mountains in the east. Unconsciously holding her breath, she waited for it to begin.

The sky began to lighten. The thin clouds that remained to float above the mountain peaks were stained with a changing light—first a blinding white, followed by a rich gold, then, almost suddenly, a blood-red rose, and fading, finally, to the most delicate of pinks.

Maggie loved sunrises. Especially after a storm. They were a reminder that something better awaited those who made it through the night.

"You're up early."

She twisted on the step and felt her throat tighten as she looked at him. At them.

Tucker, his dark brown hair tousled, his eyes still glazed with sleep, was holding their tiny son against his bare chest. "Kevin takes after you. He thinks this is a wonderful time of day to be up."

"It is. I hate to miss the sunrise."

Her husband grinned in understanding as he settled onto the step beside her.

Maggie stared at the sky a while longer before saying, "I suppose I should fix some breakfast before you have to go into the office."

"I'm not going. I thought I'd take the day off and spend it with my wife. Harry can handle any clients who come in today. After all, what's the point of taking on a new law partner if he can't run the office alone now and then?"

"What about that important case of yours?"

"I've something even more important right here. I want a day with you, and I'm going to have it."

"And what's the occasion, Mr. Branigan?"

"Do I need an occasion?"

"Yes. I think you do." Maggie knew Tucker took his work seriously. This was very unlike him.

"Well, I awoke this morning and realized it was two years ago today that you first told me you loved me."

"You were bleeding all over," she whispered,

remembering too. "I thought you might even die."

"Is that the only reason you told me?"

"Maybe that day," she admitted, "but I can't help believing I would have told you one day. I think I always knew my place was with you."

Kevin began to fuss, and Maggie opened her arms for him. While Tucker watched with a loving gaze, she loosened her robe and brought the hungry infant to her breast.

"I never get tired of seeing you like this," Tucker said, his voice almost reverent. "No matter what else is happening, you and Kevin bring balance. Peace. Do you know what I mean?"

She smiled. "Yes. I know."

Tucker leaned against the porch railing, turning slightly so he could see mother and child more clearly. He crossed his arms over his chest, a self-satisfied expression on his face.

For a long time the only sound was the suckling noise made by the baby.

"It was nice of Marcus Sanderson and his wife to send a gift for Kevin," Tucker said.

"Mmm hmm." Maggie stroked the dark down that covered Kevin's head.

"His note said he and his wife would be through this way next month and will stop in to see us. I think we should invite them to stay awhile. We've got plenty of room, what with the new house and all, and after all the work he did, straightening out the mess your uncle left behind . . ."

Maggie frowned. She didn't like to be reminded of Seth.

Sanderson had indeed found a mess when he arrive in Philadelphia two years before. The mills had to be closed, the house sold for back taxes. And, for once, Seth had told the complete truth. The money that had been placed in trust for Jeremy's daughters was gone, siphoned off through the years by an embezzling banker—the same man who had told Seth the money would be his if Maggie was married.

But it hadn't mattered to Maggie when Sanderson brought her the news, and it didn't matter to her now. Her dark life with her uncle now seemed more like a nightmare than reality. It was over, behind her. She had Tucker and Rachel and Kevin and a life filled with more joy than she could ever have dreamed possible.

Tucker slid close to her again, placing an arm around her back. "Harry's talking about building his own place downriver. I didn't think he'd ever move out of town. He seemed to like it so much."

"I'm not surprised. Harry's a lot like you. He loves the land. Besides—"she turned her face up toward his—"Harry will want plenty of room to raise his family."

"Raise his—? Harry's not even married."

Maggie laughed softly. "He will be soon. Harry's in love with the new schoolmistress. Haven't you noticed how often he talks about Miss Scott?"

Tucker's arm tightened around her. "No, I guess I hadn't noticed, but I'm glad for him if it's true. I'd like him to be happy. I'd like every man to be as lucky as I am."

Maggie looked up at the morning sun, golden and warm. Birds called from the cottonwood trees along the river. A fish jumped, leaving telltale rings on the water's surface. A bee buzzed above the rose bush at the corner of the house. There were horses in the barn, a fine crop in the fields, a puppy sleeping in Rachel's room—and a house with many bedrooms, just waiting for more little Branigans to fill them.

Then her gaze moved to the baby at her breast, and finally, back to her husband. "I'm the lucky one, Tucker Branigan," she said, and knew that it was true.

For a lucky few, the sunrise never ends.

Author's Note

Dear Reader:

The Oregon Trail is still visible in many places in Idaho (as well as other states), and I've stood more than once looking at the century-old wagon ruts, wondering what it must have been like for the people who made those marks in the earth and on the pages of American history.

Every time I drive along I-84 through the high desert country of Southern Idaho and the Snake River plain, speeding along in my air-conditioned car at 65 mph, I think of the emigrants on those wagon trains who were glad when they put just another 20 miles behind them before sunset. What fortitude and endurance! Can any of us, living in this "instant" generation of computers and fax machines and supersonic jets begin to understand what those people went through to reach their new homeland? If it had been up to me, the West never would have been settled. (I enjoy my creature comforts too much.) Thank goodness my ancestors were made of sturdier stuff.

I enjoyed the research for this project immensely, particularly the excerpts from women's journal's which describe so vividly what they went through as they left behind the familiar past and struggled toward what they hoped would be a brighter future.

PROMISED SUNRISE and the following book in the Branigan series—featuring Shannon Branigan and written by Connie Mason—were conceived as a celebration of the pioneer spirit. Several western states have celebrated their first century of statehood in 1989 and 1990, Idaho among them, and we salute those men and women of yesteryear who made statehood possible.

I loved creating the Branigan clan, and it seemed only natural that I would bring Tucker and Maggie to Boise, Idaho, where they could put down roots along the beautiful Boise River in the shadow of the mountains I love. I hope you enjoyed the journey as well.

All my romantic best,

Robin Lee Hatcher

THE BRANIGAN FAMILY SAGA CONTINUES!

BEYOND THE HORIZON

Connie Mason

Bestselling author of
Bold Land, Bold Love
and *Tempt the Devil*

A Leisure Book

Coming in December 1990

AN EXCERPT FROM . . .

BEYOND THE HORIZON

Connie Mason

Prologue

"Damn Yankee," *Shannon Branigan whispered,*
hating the sight of Harlan Simmons lounging inso-
lently on the elegant veranda as she twisted her
head for one last look at her beloved home and
family. Then she tightened her grip on the buggy
reins and clucked the horse into a quicker trot down
the long lane. Nothing remained for the Branigans
now in Georgia, Shannon thought sadly as she
dashed a tear from the corner of her eye. The old
life was gone: Twin Willows belonged to that
yellow-bellied carpetbagger now; her father was
dead by his own hand, driven to the deed by the
Yankees; and her brother Grady had been slain on
the battlefield, sacrificing his youth for a lost cause.

"Are you all right, dear?"

Shannon turned her head and attempted a smile
at her great aunt seated next to her in the buggy.
Though Shannon had volunteered willingly to

remain behind in Atlanta with Great Aunt Eugenia while the rest of the Branigans left to make a new life in Idaho, separation from her close-knit family was tearing her apart. It all seemed so final.

"I'm fine, Aunt Eugenia, truly."

But was she fine? Vividly she recalled her brother Tucker's parting words.

"We'll write as soon as we reach Boise," Tucker had said.

"Don't worry about me, Tuck," she had answered. "Aunt Eugenia and I are going to be fine. The Yankees haven't beaten the Branigans. They just think they have." But brave words had fooled no one, least of all herself. How long would it be before she could rejoin her family in Idaho?

Shannon wasn't the only family member to remain behind. Seventeen-year-old Devlin had been arguing with Tucker for days about Devlin's refusal to run from the Yankees with his tail tucked between his legs, as he so aptly put it. He insisted on remaining behind to accomplish Lord only knew what. Shannon could sympathize with Dev. Both she and Dev were famous for their tempers and were known as the hotheads of the family.

Though Eugenia's watery blue eyes were dimmed by age, her agile mind grasped and understood perfectly her great-niece's anguish. A tremendous outpouring of love and compassion encompassed this special girl who had given up so much for an old lady unlikely to see the year through.

"You should be going with your family," Aunt Eugenia said in a dry whisper that spoke eloquently of her frailness, her inability to make the monumental journey the other Branigans were undertaking.

"You're my family, too," Shannon reminded her

gently. "I'm here because I want to be, Aunt Eugenia. We'll show those damn Yankees they can't run us out."

Washington, D.C.—April 1867

"The President will see you now, Captain Stryker."

The man who walked through the door to the president's office wore the blue uniform of the Union Army, but that wasn't what set him apart from other young men his age. There was an indescribable power about him, as well as something profoundly mysterious.

"Come in and sit down, Captain Stryker," President Johnson invited. "As you can see, Major Vance is already here."

With a nod and a smile, Blade Stryker acknowledged his commanding officer and friend of many years. Then he directed his undivided attention back to the president. It was the first time he had met President Johnson, and he thought him a rather stern, unprepossessing sort of man.

"I suppose you're wondering why I sent for you," the president began, "but Major Vance assures me you are exactly the man I am looking for."

Blade raised a black eyebrow, slanting Major Vance a quizzical glance.

"I don't know what Major Vance told you, but I hope he mentioned I'm mustering out of the army and returning home."

"Just where is home?"

"Wyoming Territory—mostly," Blade replied somewhat mysteriously.

"Major Vance apprised me of your history, Captain, so there's no need for pretense here."

"I hope you don't think I was betraying a confidence, Blade," Major Vance interjected, "but I knew immediately you were the right man for the job."

"Then you know I am a half-breed, sir," Blade said with quiet dignity, addressing the president.

"I know you are a fine officer and a credit to the army. I am curious, though, as to how and why you joined the war."

"My mother is full-blooded Oglala Sioux, another name for the powerful Dakotas. My father was a French trapper. He fell in love with my mother and married her according to Indian rites. I was raised by the Sioux until my seventeenth year, when Father decided I needed to learn about the white man's world. He sent me east to school.

"When the war between the North and South began, I knew I must fight on the side of freedom for all races. Few knew of my mixed blood, so it was easy to join the Union Army."

"An interesting story, Captain Stryker. May I call you Blade?" Blade nodded. "I am convinced you are just the man I need. Will you listen to what I have to say, son?"

"Of course, sir, but it won't change my mind about leaving the army."

"There has been increasing unrest on the plains," President Johnson explained. "The great Indian tribes are unhappy with the treaty of '57 dividing the plains into territories and giving the Indians boundaries. Not only are the different tribes encroaching upon each other's hunting lands but they are openly warring with whites. They are attacking wagon trains and emigrants traveling the Oregon

Trail, disrupting communications and preventing the railroad from meeting its deadline.

"These atrocities must stop, Blade. People are dying every day, not only whites but Indians. But as long as guns are being smuggled to the Indians, these unprovoked attacks will continue."

"Excuse me, Mr. President, but haven't the Indians been complaining for years about being cheated, of Washington not living up to the treaty agreement? What about dishonest agents who deliberately lie and cheat Indians out of provisions due them?" Blade challenged boldly.

"Blade, we don't know the Indians are being cheated," Major Vance injected in an effort to disarm Blade's criticism.

"I won't deny there are dishonest men out there, but that is not the point. Guns are what I'm talking about," President Johnson continued. "Illegal weapons delivered into the hands of hot-blooded young men of the tribes who use them to raid and kill indiscriminently."

"I don't see how I can be of help," Blade said carefully.

"We think someone at Fort Laramie in Wyoming is arranging for the guns to be brought west by wagon train. Whoever this man is takes delivery, then sells the weapons to renegade Indians."

"You suspect an army man?" Blade asked.

"Not necessarily. It could be one of the townspeople, but all the information we have thus far indicates the involvement of someone directly connected to the army."

"And you want me to find out who that man is," Blade surmised astutely. "I've already turned in my resignation."

"All the better," President Johnson replied.

"We've already lost one man, a special agent sent to Fort Laramie to investigate, who was never heard from again. What I'd like you to do is carry out an investigation as an Indian, someone least likely to be suspect. Go back to your tribe. You're bound to learn who is dealing in guns from the young braves of the tribe. They are the ones to watch. But it is vitally important, Blade, that no one, absolutely no one, knows you are a special agent or connected to the army or office of the president. I've enough trouble on the homefront without answering to charges of concentrating on far-flung frontiers."

"I understand, sir. If I decide to accept, is there some special way I'm to travel to Fort Laramie?"

"Major Vance has made arrangements for you to travel with a wagon train as guide. You'll take them as far as Fort Laramie, where they will pick up a new guide and continue on to Oregon."

"The wagon master is a man named Clive Bailey," said Major Vance. "He runs the trading post at Fort Laramie. We think he is one of those transporting illegal guns across the plains. Your first priority will be to learn if our suspicions are correct. This Bailey could very well be the man we're after.

"I know you are familiar with the territory," Vance continued, "and it would be essential for you to rely on your Indian instincts. The wagon master will be informed you are a half-breed."

"I see," Blade acknowledged stiffly. "A half-breed who is considered barely human; a half-savage whom people fear and despise." He couldn't keep the note of bitterness from creeping into his voice.

"It is the only way, Blade," President Johnson said by way of apology. "Life as you know it will cease to exist if you accept this assignment. Your only contact will be Major Vance, who is being sent to Fort Laramie as second in command under Colonel Greer. Do you have an Indian name?"

"Among the Sioux I am known as Swift Blade."

"When you reach Independence you will become Swift Blade. All your Indian upbringing must be utilized if you are to survive. Forget the ten years you've lived as a white man and rely solely on your Indian instincts. Will you accept the assignment? A reward goes along with the capture of our man."

Blade looked at Vance for guidance. They had been friends for a long time and he respected the major's views. Besides, Blade wasn't a rich man and the reward would come in handy. "You would be doing the country a great service, Blade," Major Vance reminded him.

It was enough.

"I'll do it, sir," Blade replied, answering the president's question.

Chapter One

*G*olden daffodils bloomed on the hillside and the gentle breeze was fragrant with the promise of spring, yet Shannon saw nothing but the fresh mound of earth at her feet where Great Aunt Eugenia had just been laid to rest. Who would have thought a little over a month ago when the rest of the Branigan family left for Idaho that Eugenia would die so abruptly of heart seizure? Though she had been too frail to survive the long overland trip by wagon train to Idaho, Eugenia wasn't in ill health when one considered her great age of eighty-nine.

Not once did Shannon consider herself exceptional for selflessly volunteering to remain behind in Atlanta with Aunt Eugenia instead of joining her family on their trek West. To Shannon it was an act of love, for she cared deeply about the old woman. Sense of family was strong in the Branigan clan and

Shannon had inherited more than her share. Sometime in the future she planned to join the rest of the Branigans in Idaho, traveling by train, for it was only a matter of a year or two before the railroad stretched from coast to coast.

But Eugenia's sudden death had changed everything. There was still a possibility, albeit a slim one, that Tuck, Mama and the little ones hadn't left Independence yet. It was that small chance that had provoked Shannon into selling Aunt Eugenia's house to a despised Yankee and using most of the money to purchase a train ticket to Independence, hoping to catch up to her family before they started West with the wagon train.

"Come on, Shannon. Standing here staring at Aunt Eugenia's grave won't bring her back."

Venturing a watery smile, Shannon turned and followed her brother Devlin from the cemetery. He was right; Aunt Eugenia wouldn't want her to grieve. Thank God Dev was still in Atlanta and had heard about Eugenia's death. He arrived just in time to lend Shannon the support she needed. Dev had a penchant for turning up at the right moment. Hard telling where he'd be a week from now, but at least he was here to help her with the funeral and her travel arrangements.

"Are you certain you won't come with me, Dev?" Shannon asked hopefully. "There is still a good chance we can catch up with the family."

"Positive, Shannon. I've already had it out with Tuck, so don't you try to persuade me when my mind is made up. I wish you all well, but I'm taking charge of my own future."

The funeral had been a large one, for Aunt Eugenia had been well loved in life. But sadly, nothing Shannon could do or say stopped Devlin

from leaving shortly afterwards. He hugged her
fiercely, wished her well, and departed. Her aunt's
passing and Devlin's leaving created a void in
Shannon's heart that nearly defeated her. But Shannon
knew Eugenia's philosophy wouldn't have
allowed for maudlin sentiments. She recalled their
last conversation.

"Once I'm gone, get on with your life, Shannon,"
the astute old woman had advised. "Don't let the
horrors of war and the loss of loved ones stunt you
emotionally. You're an exceptionally strong young
woman with beauty and brains to match. Love will
come one day when you least expect it, and I
suspect you will embrace it with the same courage
and selflessness that made you volunteer to remain
in Atlanta with me."

Those were the last words Eugenia had spoken,
for that night she had suffered a seizure and died.
They were words Shannon would have cause to
remember time and again.

Before Shannon left Atlanta she posted a letter to
her mother in care of her cousin, Keegan Branigan,
who lived in Idaho City and had urged the family to
settle in the West. If she wasn't able to catch up to
her family, the letter would reach them shortly after
their arrival.

Dear Mama,

*I'm on my way to Idaho! I'm sorry to report
Aunt Eugenia died peacefully a short time after
you left Atlanta. I'm leaving for Independence
tomorrow in hopes of catching up to you, but if
I don't, this letter will reach you soon after you
arrive in Boise.*

*Devlin came to the funeral, and I tried to
persuade him to come west with me, but as*

usual he was being obstinate. The Yankees are making Atlanta a living hell, and I'm glad to get out of here. I can't imagine why Dev refuses to leave. One day he'll show up when we least expect it.

I'll see you soon, Mama. Give my love to Tuck and the little ones.

> *Your devoted daughter,*
> *Shannon*

Independence, Missouri—June 1867

"I'm sorry, lady, the Branigan party left Independence over two weeks ago. By now they are well on their way along the Oregon Trail."

Weariness etched deep lines across Shannon's brow and profound disappointment dulled the sparkle of her deep blue eyes. With a toss of her rich chestnut curls, she quelled the urge to vent her famous temper at God for allowing this to happen. Still, it wasn't the end of the world, Shannon thought, squaring her narrow shoulders.

"Two weeks isn't such a long time," she mused aloud. "I haven't enough money left for the stagecoach, but if I join another wagon train I might catch up with my family."

"Beggin' yer pardon, lady," the man said, "but it's gettin' a mite late in the year. Most wagon trains have already begun their journey."

A look of absolute horror crossed Shannon's

lovely features. "You mean I'm stranded in Independence until next spring?"

The man she spoke with owned the outfitting store which, sooner or later, most emigrants found cause to visit while in Independence. He seemed to know everything and everyone.

"Well now," he said, scratching his whiskered chin, "might be yer in luck. There's a wagon train formin' outside town fer latecomers."

"Who do I talk to?" Shannon asked, heartened. Perhaps God hadn't abandoned her after all.

"Have yer man talk to Clive Bailey, he's the train captain and organizer. He owns the trading post at Fort Laramie and is carrying supplies to sell in his store. If you can't find him ask for a man who calls himself Blade."

My man? Shannon thought dully. But before she could give voice to the question teasing the tip of her tongue a deep male voice asked, "Did someone mention my name?"

He stood like a tall shadow in the doorway of the store, with the sun at his back blotting out his features. The breadth of his shoulders touched the jamb on either side and the magnificent expanse of torso and slim hips was supported by legs as sturdy as oaks. Shannon shuddered, feeling oddly threatened as he moved toward her with the rolling gait of a stalking panther, his pelvis pivoting in a manner so blatantly masculine that Shannon felt a dull red crawl up her neck.

"This young woman was askin' 'bout joining yer wagon train, Blade," the storekeeper explained as he turned away to help another customer. "I'll leave you two to make arrangements."

Blade turned the full magnetic power of his penetrating black eyes on the young woman—he judged her to be under twenty—staring at him with unrestrained curiosity. She was a fetching little thing, he reflected, with chestnut hair neither red nor brown but rich and glowing with golden highlights. Her pert nose sported a sprinkling of tawny freckles and her full lower lip was caught between small white teeth. Deep blue eyes, wide and intelligent, sloped upward at their corners. A thrill of anticipation caught Blade by the scruff of his neck and refused to let go as Shannon fearlessly met his gaze, her eyes narrowing when she belatedly perceived what made this man so different from any others she had met.

He was an Indian!

Not only was he a member of a race feared and despised by good people everywhere for their cruelty and heathenish ways, but he wore the tattered jacket of a Union army soldier, thereby adding insult to injury. He looked ruthless, dangerous, and quite capable of violence.

"If you and your husband want to join the wagon train you have little time left in which to outfit a wagon. Clive Bailey is the organizer. He'll advise you if you need help," Blade said, a brash smile hanging on the corner of his mouth. The young woman's reaction when she recognized his heritage amused him.

It was puzzling, Blade thought in a burst of insight, that impeccably turned-out in his army uniform, his hair cut to a respectable length and his face pale from Eastern winters, no one suspected he was Sioux. Yet now, dressed in buckskins, his shoulder-length hair held back by a rawhide headband, his skin burnt a deep bronze, he was unmistakably identified as a half-breed "savage."

"I—have no husband," Shannon stuttered, momentarily stunned by Blade's blatant sexuality.

His eyes were the dark black of night, mysterious and unrelenting, framed by thick, spiky lashes. His brows, finely drawn and faintly slanting, were velvet black. His mouth was wide and sensual, one corner tilted just enough to reveal the sardonic wit that doubtless lay behind his ruggedly handsome features. And there was no denying, Shannon admitted with brutal honesty, that the Indian was handsome. His features spoke eloquently of a bold nature, and those large strong hands suggested a power and strength she could only guess at.

"You're not married?" Blade repeated sharply. "Single women aren't welcome on this wagon train unless they are traveling with family. How old are you Miss—?"

"Branigan. Shannon Branigan. I'm twenty, old enough to take care of myself."

"Hardly old enough to undertake a hazardous journey on your own. It is out of the question, Miss Branigan. Go back home where you belong."

Shannon bristled indignantly. No Indian, no matter how imposing or intimidating, was going to dictate to her. "Perhaps Mr. Bailey will have something to say about it."

"Clive Bailey might be train captain, but I'm wagon master and guide. Without me the wagon train can't leave Independence. I say you're not going. Furthermore," Blade stated, "I know of no other wagon train willing to take on an unattached woman as young and pretty as you. I suggest you find yourself a husband, Miss Branigan, if you want to travel West."

His dark face was stern and unrelenting, but undaunted, Shannon pressed on, forced to resort to the feminine wiles she abhorred. But desperate times called for desperate measures.

"I have no home, Mr.—Blade, that is your name, isn't it?"

Blade nodded warily. "I am known as Swift Blade among the Sioux, but Blade will do."

"My family left two weeks ago for Idaho. I remained in Atlanta to care for an elderly aunt who died unexpectedly and left me all alone in the world." She batted feathery eyelashes, managing to squeeze out a tear from the corners of her eyes.

"So you can see how desperate I am to leave." Her voice assumed a tremulous quality few men could resist. But Shannon had already realized that Blade was not like most men. "If I joined your wagon train, I might be able to catch up with my family."

"Spare me your tears, Miss Branigan," Blade said, unmoved. "A beautiful young woman like you on a wagon train would only cause trouble. Big trouble. My answer is still no. Now if you'll excuse me, I've some last minute purchases to make."

Blade's refusal unleashed Shannon's famous Irish temper and she lashed out viciously at the handsome half-breed whose language sounded far too refined for an Indian, even while his bold, dark features spoke eloquently of his savage ancestry.

"Somehow I doubt you have the final say on this wagon train, Mr.—er, Blade," Shannon observed, her lip curling derisively. "What civilized man would trust his life to a wild Indian? You might speak like a white man, but you are pure savage. What poor soldier did you steal that jacket from? Let's hope he still has his scalp."

Stunned by her scathing insult, Blade stood stiffly aside as Shannon pushed past him and out the door, her skirts swaying in angry motion around her shapely ankles. It was the first time he could remember being rendered absolutely speechless by a female!

"Damn infuriating woman," Blade muttered beneath his breath as he approached the counter to make his purchases. When he passed a woman customer lingering nearby, she deliberately swept her skirt aside, her face a mask of disgust and fear. With Sioux uprisings now threatening the frontier, few if any decent citizens had any truck with savages.

Outwardly, Blade exhibited no reaction to the woman's insult, but inwardly he seethed with impotent rage. How ironic that he was good enough to fight for equality for all men, yet was treated like an outcast for the very reasons that persuaded him to join the war. Having lived as a white man so many years spoiled him; he had grown unaccustomed to being openly shunned and ridiculed. He felt shamed, for he had nearly forgotten his proud heritage and the noble people whose features he bore.

As Blade Stryker, handsome, mysterious army officer, women were drawn to him like bees to honey. He was sought most diligently by some of the loveliest ladies in Washington. But his transformation from army captain Blade Stryker to Sioux half-breed Swift Blade changed him overnight into a loathsome creature unworthy of respect. Even Clive Bailey, who needed his expertise on the trail, treated him with barely concealed contempt.

Blade had been in Independence nearly a month, snooping and secretly searching each wagon train for hidden weapons as they formed outside the city. Thus far he had found nothing incriminating, which was why he had narrowed his sights on the wagon train Clive Bailey had organized. Blade thought Bailey a wily scoundrel. He was damn slick, a dishonest type who probably cared little that providing guns to Indians could result in the loss of countless lives for both whites and Indians. If the man was a gun smuggler, Blade intended to find out. As special agent to the president, he took his duty seriously. No woman, no matter how beautiful, was going to interfere with his assignment. And intuitively Blade knew Miss Shannon Branigan represented more trouble than he needed.

"I'm looking for Clive Bailey."

Clive Bailey peered over his shoulder at the striking, chestnut-haired woman addressing him. She was a looker all right, Clive decided, raking her tantalizing face and form with slow relish.

"I'm Clive Bailey. What can I do for you, miss?"

Shannon had rented a buggy and driven herself outside town to where the wagon train was forming so that she might speak to Clive Bailey personally. Fortunately, the Indian wagon master was nowhere in sight and Shannon visibly relaxed. That man was far too intimidating for her liking. "I'm Shannon Branigan and I understand you are the man to talk to about joining your wagon train."

"Do you and your husband have a wagon, Mrs. Branigan?" Clive asked, disappointed that the little beauty was already spoken for.

"I'm not married," Shannon said, lifting her chin defiantly. "Does it matter?"

"You're going West alone? What about your family?" Clive was dismayed by Shannon's willingness to undertake the hazardous journey alone and unprotected.

"To make a long story short, my family left for Idaho two weeks ago with an earlier wagon train. I want to join them and yours is the last wagon train forming this spring."

"It's more or less an unwritten law that young women travel only in the protection of family or husband. I'm sorry, Miss Branigan, but I don't think—"

"Please, Mr. Bailey, can't you make an exception?" Shannon implored. "Isn't there some family I could travel with? I'd work hard, and I could pay something for my passage West. I just don't have enough money to stay in Independence till spring."

"You are far too young and beautiful to be traveling alone, Miss Branigan, and there are too many unattached males along for me to believe your presence would go unnoticed or unappreciated. But perhaps this one time . . ." he relented, never one to turn down an opportunity when one presented itself. Shannon Branigan looked ripe for the plucking, and he was a man who relished tender, ripe fruit.

The fiery glow in Clive's pale eyes should have alerted Shannon, but she was too excited to notice.

"It's out of the question. Miss Branigan has no place on this wagon train."

Shannon raised startled eyes to meet Blade's determined gaze.

"You've met Miss Branigan?" Clive asked, furious that a half-breed savage had the audacity to address a lady.

He had employed Blade as wagon master and guide because Blade had been highly recommended and Clive needed him. This late in the year most qualified guides had already been hired. It grated on Clive's nerves to see Blade put on airs, as if he were as good as a white man. But at this late date Clive was grateful to find a competent man to lead them to Fort Laramie. Clive had too much at stake to wait around until next year, his cargo too precious for lengthy delays. If Clive hadn't had problems obtaining his goods, he would have left weeks ago.

"We've met," Blade said tersely, favoring Shannon with a brief nod. "And I won't have her disrupting my wagon train."

"You seem to forget you work for me," Clive said bluntly. "I can always find another guide."

Blade's anger simmered as he struggled to keep from boiling out of control. Orders from Washington were to investigate Clive Bailey, and the only way he could do that was by remaining with the outfit. However, he felt obliged to point out the dangers involved in accepting an unattached female. Especially one as lovely as Shannon Branigan. "Who will protect her when every randy buck on the wagon train starts fighting over her?"

"I can take care of myself!" Shannon shot back, angered over the way the two men talked over her but not at her, as if she weren't capable of making her own decisions.

"The hell you can!" Blade blasted, his hot temper erupting. Then realizing how he sounded, he softened his voice. "Look, Miss Branigan, I have nothing against you personally, I just don't want to see you hurt."

"Strange words from a savage," Shannon snorted, tossing her tangle of chestnut curls.

Clive roared with laughter, delighting in Shannon's show of spirit. If the intimidating half-breed wasn't built like a bull and looked tougher than a two-bit steak, he would have put him in his place himself. "The lady is no cream puff, Blade. I think she will manage just fine. I'll see that no harm comes to her." And bed her in the process, he thought.

Blade's full lips tautened, stung by the smug expression on Shannon's face. He didn't like the way things were going one damn bit, but he had little power to change them. The strange light in Bailey's eyes told Blade exactly what plans the man had in mind for the unsuspecting Shannon Branigan. Still, he might be able to salvage something out of this, find a way to thwart Bailey's devious intentions for the young woman. She was too innocent to realize what Bailey intended for her and determined enough to make her way West some other way if she didn't travel with them. If she had to go, at least she would be where he could keep an eye on her, Blade reflected, though why it should matter to him totally escaped him.

"All right, it's your decision," Blade finally agreed.

His decided lack of enthusiasm did little to bolster Shannon's shaky conviction that she was doing the right thing by traveling alone. She wasn't ignorant of the dangers involved, just determined to catch up with her family. Tucker always said she was too stubborn and impulsive for her own good. "But I insist on finding Miss Branigan a place on the wagon train myself," Blade added.

"See to it, Blade," Clive ordered, sending him off with a careless wave of his hand.

Try though she might, Shannon couldn't take her eyes off Blade's loose-limbed gait as he strode off, his spine stiff and proudly defiant. His moccasined feet made silent footsteps on the dusty ground and his taut buttocks, tightly encased in fringed buckskin trousers, moved with sinuous grace. His shoulders beneath the offensive blue jacket were wide and impressive. Then, incredibly, her imagination took her on a forbidden path, for she could almost feel the smooth bronze skin of his torso beneath her fingertips.

Mercifully, Clive Bailey interrupted her dangerous mental journey.

"Miss Branigan—Shannon. May I call you Shannon?" When she nodded, Clive continued smoothly, "A word of caution about the half-breed. He comes highly recommended, but as you just saw he has lost none of his savage ways. It is unwise to trust him. I strongly urge you to steer clear of Swift Blade. Well-bred young ladies don't consort with Indians."

"I appreciate your advice, Mr. Bailey, and I assure you that Blade is not someone I'd care to associate with." Shannon had thought Blade full Indian but felt little comfort in learning he was a half-breed.

"It's just as well, Shannon, and please call me Clive. Everyone else on the wagon train does. It will be a wonderful experience, you'll see," he predicted. Especially for me, he added silently.

Chapter Two

Shannon hung on for dear life as the awkward prairie schooner, pulled by eight lumbering oxen, jerked into motion. Beside her on the unsprung bench sat the very pregnant Callie Johnson and her young husband Howie, who wielded the whip above the oxen's sturdy backs with amazing dexterity for an Ohio farmer.

Shannon was more than happy to be sharing the Johnsons' wagon rather than buying her own and hiring a driver. The cost of purchasing her own equipment was more than double what she paid the Johnsons for her passage. She hated to give Blade credit for the idea, but it was working out well. Callie was grateful for the company and someone with whom to share the chores, for her pregnancy hadn't been an easy one. Howie was also agreeable, concern for his young wife reason enough to share their wagon with a virtual stranger. Another pair of hands was always welcome on so arduous a journey.

From the corner of her eye Shannon saw Blade working his way down the line, speaking with each driver, offering encouragement where needed. Less than a week ago she had been introduced to the Johnsons, each sizing the other up as potential traveling companions. After a few hours spent in their company, Shannon felt right at home with the young couple, impressed by their courage and determination in seeking a new life despite their parents' objections to their marriage.

Callie's parents were wealthy tradesmen, while Howie's were poor dirt farmers. Despite countless obstacles and against all odds, the unlikely couple fell deeply in love, meeting in secret. When Callie became pregnant, they fled Ohio, fearing reprisals. Oregon and a new life beckoned and nearly all their savings were used to purchase a wagon, oxen, and the supplies necessary for the trip. They were married in Independence just a few days ago. Callie's condition was the only drawback to the great adventure they had undertaken.

"Everything all right, Howie?"

Blade's deep voice brought instant awareness and a tenseness to Shannon's body. For an electrifying eternity, black eyes burned deeply into blue ones, and Shannon was aware of nothing but his overwhelming presence. The very arrogance of this half-breed seared her, confused her, scattered her wits.

"Everything's just fine, Blade," Howie grinned with boyish enthusiasm.

"We'll keep to the old emigrant trail along the Blue Ridge Road," Blade informed him, finding it difficult to concentrate on anything but the play of sunlight on Shannon's chestnut curls. "I'll see you at the nooning."

With a curt nod, he rode off on his rangy gray pony. He looked every bit the savage with a battered felt hat covering his shoulder-length black hair. His superbly conditioned body was clad in deerskin trousers, with rows of long fringe along the seams, the same disreputable army jacket he constantly wore, and moccasins on his feet. The long knife attached to his belt looked dangerous and lethal. Once Blade disappeared from sight Shannon slipped back into her mental musings.

Her trip to Independence from Atlanta had been tedious and uneventful. She had taken a train from Atlanta to St. Louis, then traveled by riverboat on the Mississippi River to Independence. Thank heavens she had arrived in time to join Clive Bailey's wagon train, for it was the last of the season. Composed mostly of latecomers and stragglers, the wagon train was small compared to others, which sometimes numbered two hundred wagons. Clive Bailey's outfit consisted of fifty-six wagons and two hundred people, including emigrants and outriders. They were accompanied by a herd of five hundred cattle and other diverse livestock owned by the emigrants.

They left Independence just as the sun broke out of a bank of gray clouds. With slow precision the wagons rolled forward, each taking a previously assigned position in line. At the wagon master's signal, outriders galloped far ahead of the line with a whoop and a holler, working off some of their pent-up impatience. The prairie schooners then lumbered across the Missouri border and into the prairie.

At first the track was narrow, checkered with

sunshine and shadowy woods, until, beyond an intervening belt of bushes, a green oceanlike expanse of prairie stretched to the horizon. For Shannon it was a moment of high excitement as well as one of nostalgia, for never again would her life be the same, never again would she see her beloved Atlanta and Twin Willows. She imagined how Tucker and her mother must have felt when they left on their own journey west.

After an hour or two, both Shannon and Callie joined most of the other women and children who made the going easier by walking beside the swaying, lumbering wagons. Mile upon mile of black-eyed susans grew in abundance amidst the tall prairie grass, and Shannon soon found herself stopping frequently along the way to gather up huge bouquets of the beautiful flowers.

"Don't lag too far behind, Miss Branigan."

Startled, Shannon glanced up to find Blade staring down at her from atop his gray pony, his dark eyes regarding her with penetrating thoroughness. Realizing how she must look with her sweat-soaked dress clinging to her body in a revealing manner—for she had long since shed her petticoats—Shannon gathered the armful of flowers to her bosom, unaware of how wonderfully the yellow flowers complimented the golden tones of her skin.

Shannon didn't realize she had lagged so far behind until Blade rode up to remind her. Callie had gone inside the wagon to nap, and Shannon couldn't resist the urge to stop and pick wildflowers. Belatedly she noted the last of the wagons had left her far behind.

"I—didn't realize," Shannon stammered. "It won't happen again." The last thing she wanted was to draw attention to herself.

"Be certain it doesn't," Blade warned sternly. "We can't afford delay. It is too late in the year to accommodate daydreamers who become lost on the prairie and slow us down."

"I said I was sorry!" Shannon snapped, wondering why Blade was making so large an issue out of a small lapse. "I promise to be more careful."

Then, before Shannon knew what he intended, Blade swooped down and lifted her into the saddle in front of him. "What are you doing?"

"Taking you back to the wagon."

"I can walk."

"Look ahead. At the rate you're going you won't catch them until nightfall. I'm responsible for every person on this wagon train, including you."

Blade's hand was a hot brand against her ribs as he held Shannon firmly against the hardness of his body. The contact was electrifying, and far too stimulating for Shannon's liking. Why should a man like Blade affect her in such a strange manner when dozens of beaux back in Atlanta had failed to move her? She had reached the ripe age of twenty with her heart untouched and her emotions intact, and no savage was going to change that! One day she hoped to meet a man she could love and marry, but only with the approval of her family. Nowhere in her life was there room for a half-breed who wore a Yankee jacket with a confidence and pride that irritated her.

Every place that Shannon touched, Blade burned. The little minx had no idea what she did to him. He was more than a little confused at the power exerted over him by a spoiled Southern belle he'd met mere days ago. From the moment he saw her he knew she was someone special, someone who could mean something to him if he allowed it. It was for that reason that he rebelled against the crazy attraction that sprang to life the moment they came into contact with each other. Shannon Branigan represented a dangerous distraction he could ill afford to indulge. The assignment he had accepted required all his wits about him. The only way he could function properly, Blade decided, was to make Shannon hate him, and from all indications he was succeeding only too well, for the fiery Irish lass couldn't wait to be rid of his annoying company.

Just being a half-breed earned Shannon's contempt, Blade reasoned. Most respectable women steered clear of Indians, though Blade had to admit that some of the females on the wagon train appeared eager to claim his attention. But not Shannon Branigan, which was probably good considering his unaccountable attraction to her. But Lord, she smelled delicious, like the sweet-scented wildflowers she still clutched to her breast. And she felt so soft, so damn soft, causing his hand to tighten almost painfully against her ribs. With a will of its own his thumb separated from his palm and grazed the curved underside of her breast.

The light brushing stroke was so fleeting, Shannon thought she had imagined it. But she didn't have long to dwell on it, for Blade was already lowering her to the ground beside the Johnson wagon.

"See that you don't stray again," he warned. Then he rode off toward the head of the long line of wagons, leaving Shannon flushed and confused.

"My, he's handsome," sighed Callie, an incurable romantic. After her nap she had climbed into the seat beside Howie. Now she descended to join Shannon.

Shannon snorted, an explosive, unladylike sound. "He's a half-breed." Her tone indicated no other explanation was necessary.

"I don't think I've ever seen a more compelling man, red or white. He's so powerful and outrageously virile that just looking at him frightens me." Callie shivered delicately. "It's no wonder he has all the young women on the wagon train agog over him."

"Not me," Shannon denied, blue eyes snapping. "The other girls are welcome to him."

"Nancy Wilson will be glad to hear that," Callie teased. "She was a mite worried when you joined the wagon train. Until you arrived, she was considered the prettiest single girl of the group. I know she hoped to be noticed by Blade."

"I have no desire to compete with Nancy Wilson," sniffed Shannon, recalling the brown-eyed blond beauty who looked to be her own age. She traveled with her parents, three younger siblings, and an older brother. Shannon remembered Todd Wilson vividly, for he spent a great deal of his free time making cow eyes at her.

After the first easy day, the emigrants camped that night beside a creek where water and firewood were plentiful. Blade had made the decision to ford the relatively placid water the next morning. Shannon saw little of Blade. He spent the evening going from wagon to wagon offering advice and words of encouragement. She noted that he ate with the Wilsons, having been invited by Nancy who, Shannon noted with a hint of disgust, hung onto his every word with breathless awe. Instinctively Shannon knew that these very people who depended on him for their lives would shun him like poison once the journey was over and they no longer needed him. She felt certain Blade knew it too.

After supper was cleared away and the dishes washed and stashed in their places, Callie retired inside the wagon while Howie bedded down underneath. Previous arrangements called for Shannon to share the wagon with Callie, but she felt so guilty about separating the young couple that after she had donned her voluminous gown and robe, she sent Howie inside with his wife, insisting she'd rather sleep outside on such a warm night. But Shannon soon found she was too keyed up to sleep. Seeking a place she might be alone, she wandered to the outer perimeter of the camp and sat down on a rock, staring at the star-studded sky.

"It's a lovely night."

"Oh!" Startled, Shannon leaped to her feet, relieved to see Clive Bailey looming beside her instead of the intimidating half-breed. "You frightened me."

"Sorry," Clive mumbled, his tone far from contrite. "How are you getting on with the Johnsons?"

"Just fine. I'm positive it will work out well for all of us."

"Glad to hear it." He paused, choosing his words carefully. "But if for some reason things don't go as they should, I'd be more than happy to offer my own wagon for your use. I refrained from doing so in front of the half-breed, but please keep in mind what I have offered. You are a lovely creature, Shannon Branigan," he added, his voice low and insinuating.

Shannon felt the first prickling of alarm when

Clive sidled closer, replaced by panic when his words and their barely disguised meaning left his lips.

"Mr. Bailey, I'm not certain what you are suggesting, but I have no intention of leaving the Johnsons' wagon—for any reason. Now if you will excuse me, it is time I returned to the wagon."

She turned to leave, but found her way blocked by the hard wall of Clive's chest. Short and stocky, Clive was an immovable force before Shannon's meager strength. "Are you trying to frighten me, Mr. Bailey?"

"The name is Clive and the last thing I want is to frighten you, Shannon. I just want us to be friends —good friends," he hinted. He raised a thick hand and stroked her shoulder in an awkward attempt to smooth her ruffled feathers. Evidently he had gone about this all wrong, he reflected wryly. The girl was as skittish as a young colt and required patience and gentling if he intended to seduce her.

"Then I bid you good-night, Mr.—Clive," Shannon said coolly, shrugging off his offending hand. Before he could stop her she whirled and fled to the safety of the shadows.

Shannon was panting when she reached the line of wagons, not only from being out of breath but from incredible anger. How could she have thought Clive Bailey a nice man? she wondered bleakly. What made him think he could insult her in such a vile manner? She prided herself on her ability to judge character, but this time she'd been wrong. Clive Bailey was a slimy worm and she vowed to steer clear of him in the future.

Just before she reached the Johnson wagon, Shannon felt a hand curl around her waist and froze, preparing to vent her Irish temper at Clive

Bailey, certain he had followed her. She found herself staring into Blade's stormy features. "What do you want?" she spat, suddenly weary of confrontations. Clive Bailey had been more than enough to deal with for one night.

"Stay away from that man," Blade warned, his tone implacable. "You are too young and inexperienced to know what he's after. Set your sights elsewhere."

"If you are referring to Mr. Bailey, I assure you I have no designs on his person."

"Then quit enticing him," Blade advised bluntly.

"Entice him. Entice him!" she repeated, numb with disbelief. "Whyever would I do that?"

"Don't try to deny you lured Bailey out here tonight to meet you. You are even dressed for a midnight tryst," Blade observed dryly.

Shannon sucked her breath in sharply, stunned by Blade's cruel taunts. She didn't deserve his contempt, nor would she stand for it. "You were spying on me! How dare you!" she exploded.

Shannon raised her hand to strike him, but to her dismay found her wrist suspended behind her in a viselike grip as Blade caught her to him, molding her unfettered body to his. He shuddered in suppressed delight when the firm peaks of her breasts stabbed into the muscular wall of his chest. Something inside Blade erupted, and before he knew it he was kissing Shannon, discovering the soft shape of her lips, tasting the sweet essence of her. She gasped in shock, affording him the opportunity to slip his tongue into her open mouth.

Blade's superior strength easily conquered Shannon's valiant struggles as shock rendered her nearly witless. At first Blade meant only to teach Shannon a lesson, to demonstrate what could happen to innocents who became involved with men they couldn't handle or things they didn't understand. But to his everlasting regret, what he accomplished instead was to prove to himself how susceptible he was to the Southern belle's fatal charm.

The kiss went on—and on—driving the breath from Shannon's lungs and turning her legs to jelly. Never had she been kissed in such a manner—or felt so utterly transported by an act she felt certain was meant to degrade.

Perhaps punishment had been Blade's original intent, but it was soon forgotten as the sweetness of Shannon's first timid response warmed his heart. It was that tentative stirring of passion that jolted Blade abruptly to his senses. What in the hell was he doing?

Just as Shannon felt herself on the brink of a great discovery, Blade broke off the kiss, steadying her as he backed away. "Play with fire and you are likely to get burned, Miss Branigan," he said pointedly, his voice deliberately harsh. "Enticing men can lead to trouble, as I've just demonstrated. I could have taken you right here on the ground in sight of all the wagons if I wanted you. Chivalry as you know it doesn't exist on the Western frontier. Keep away from Clive Bailey and the other men sniffing around you. But if you find you have an itch that needs scratching, I'd be more than happy to take care of it." Blade knew he was being deliberately cruel and insensitive, but he felt it necessary to impress upon Shannon the danger she faced on this journey.

That was the last straw! "You—you filthy, savage bastard! You're the one I need to beware of!"

Blade winced, the viciousness of her words scalding him, yet he had asked for it. He had meant to teach her a valuable lesson and succeeded, at the cost of his own pride. He didn't usually treat women with such casual disregard, but his assignment demanded nothing less than total concentration, and the only way he could do that was to make Shannon hate him. It was in Shannon's best interests to think of him as a despicable savage, he told himself sadly. And it was neither the first nor the last time he'd be referred to that way.

**WOMEN WEST
THE PASSIONATE, WILDLY ROMANTIC SAGA
THAT TAKES TWO BOOKS—
AND TWO BESTSELLING AUTHORS—
TO TELL!**

PROMISED SUNRISE by Robin Lee Hatcher (November 1990). Their beautiful plantation destroyed, their lives ruined by the invading Yankee Army, the Branigans leave all that was familiar to them and move west, joining the refugees of war. Their harrowing journey across an untamed continent is the stuff of dreams—and legends. For on the trail, love and danger, passion and romance are constant companions.

BEYOND THE HORIZON by Connie Mason (December 1990). The powerful story continues . . . as beautiful Shannon Branigan, separated from her family, valiantly attempts to find them. Trusting a half-breed scout named Swift Blade to help her, she soon falls helplessly in love and discovers *he* is all the family she ever needed.